CONTRACT

—ON—

TIME

MARCIA A. OSTER

Order this book online at www.trafford.com
or email orders@trafford.com

Most Trafford titles are also available at major online book retailers.

Printed in the United States of America.

ISBN: 978-1-4669-5547-9 (sc)
ISBN: 978-1-4669-5546-2 (e)

Trafford rev. 09/27/2012

www.trafford.com

North America & international
toll-free: 1 888 232 4444 (USA & Canada)
phone: 250 383 6864 ♦ fax: 812 355 4082

CONTENTS

CHAPTER ONE

LIFE WITH FATHER

The sunlight is streaming through my bedroom windows as it has for countless past summers. Lazing in bed, my eyes slowly pan this familiar room. I selected the purple gingham curtains and comforter when I was twelve. That was the spring mother lost her battle with cancer. The porcelain horse figurines stand in groups on the bookshelves, tabletops and dressers where I placed them as I acquired them over the years.

As I have every morning for the past twenty-four years, I swing my legs over the side of the bed and walk through the sitting room portion of my bedroom, through the walk-in closet to my bathroom. On the return trip, I select my clothes for my morning ride. My calico cat, Peepers, has settled comfortably on the sundrenched window seat to bathe. My daily outfit rarely varies. I pick up soft faded blue jeans, a cotton gingham-checked blouse to tie over a purple t-shirt. I pull on my favorite black boots and grab my hat before heading downstairs to the kitchen.

It's just after 6 a.m. when I enter the spacious white with ivy motif kitchen. Cook is preparing the finishing touches on this morning's breakfast at the island worktop. In her early sixties, Cook resembles my childhood imaginary grandmothers with her gray hair tightly pulled back into a bun on the back of her neck under a hair net. Her brown eyes are always soft and tender looking, no matter how stern the rest of her face tries to look. She's pure German, a bit stout, strong as an ox and speaks with a slight accent. I've always called her Cook. I always have to look in father's checkbook for her real name. In fact, while balancing father's checking account, I often find where he's written her paycheck out to 'Cook' Heishman. Since my three older brothers have all moved (been driven) away, father and I eat in the breakfast area of the keeping room most mornings.

Already seated behind his morning paper, my father sips his black coffee and nods in my direction.

With a slight smile he says, "Good morning, Katherine."

I slide into my usual chair, father folds his paper and nods for Marie, the maid, to begin serving. Father's brown hair is speckled with gray at the temples. His light brown eyes are very solemn inside their heavy dark brown lashes this morning. I notice his mouth with its tight narrow upper lip is slightly curled at the left corner indicating his displeasure at something. All I can do is wait. Sooner or later, he'll tell me.

Marie serves the half cantaloupe filled with fresh fruit pieces. Then she brings the hot oatmeal and cinnamon toast that constitutes our Thursday morning breakfast. Here, you can tell what day it is, by the menu. I quietly consume my smaller portions and wait. When father's finished, he nods for Marie to clear.

Father says tersely, "Come to my study," before he rises and strides through the kitchen into the hall. I rise with a long sigh and head up the front stairs. He'll use the circular stairs from his master suite to go directly into his study.

With one calming deep breath, I knock on the closed study door. I hear father say, "Enter," his voice muffled through the heavy wooden door. Clasping the cold hard handle, I slowly open the door. As I pictured in my mind, he's seated behind the massive cherry desk, a nasty cigar burning in the large ashtray by his right hand. He's shed his tweed jacket and propped his brown leather boots on the desktop.

Father says, "Sit," gesturing at the left dark gray leather armchair. I comply, trying to appear at ease and calm. He launches into how he's unhappy with how I'm working the newest stallion. I relax immediately.

I've heard him blow off steam before. He finds something to sound off about at least twice a week. I find it's easier to agree and do whatever he suggests for at least the next few days. My brothers, on the other hand, never figured out this game. I remember the screaming matches that occurred between them. Suddenly I realize he's not speaking anymore.

When father says, "Are you listening to me, Katherine?" I glance up. His eyebrows are knitted together and his mouth definitely looks unhappy.

I explain, "I was just remembering when the boys lived here." Honesty is best with father.

Father sharply says, "Well, they're gone now. Stubborn, pigheaded and unwilling to hear good advice. Are you deciding to follow in their footsteps?" I can't help sighing at his hard tone.

I reply, "No," before falling silent just gazing directly at his eyes.

Father reaches over, picks up and takes a long draw on his cigar and then says, "Go. Get your chores done." Dismissed, I leap from the chair, walk calmly from the room and quietly close the door. Taking the steps two at a time, I snatch my hat from the end of the banister before bolting out the front door and across the porch.

Turning left, I follow the curving driveway until reaching the split leading to the stables. It's almost 7 a.m. and several of the hands are already grooming and working various horses. I return waves to several of the hands and continue inside the main stables. About eight stalls down on the right is the animal father mentioned. Lance's Moon is almost three years old. He's a bay-colored Morgan and already sold to a family in Norfolk for their fourteen-year-old daughter. I've been working to get him used to both a saddle and pulling a carriage. He's about fourteen and a half hands high and very even-tempered.

Our head groomer, Tom, is in the process of trying to get a saddle onto Lance, who is definitely in his stubborn mood today. If I hadn't personally put the first saddle on Lance four months ago, I'd think someone had spooked him about saddles. After 45 grueling minutes, Tom and I manage to get the saddle into place. Lance is a gentle natured horse. I can't for the life of me figure out why he doesn't like wearing the saddle but will gladly pull a carriage in full harness for hours on end.

The saddle in place, I easily swing up onto Lance's back. Lance calmly walks to the paddock, revealing that he likes being ridden. I started riding him bareback about six months ago. This morning, Lance is eager to go through his paces. Once his workout is complete, I turn him over to Joey to cool him down. I walk back to check on Pegalea who's due to foal any day now. A quick peek into her stall shows she's calm and still not ready. At seven years of age, she's had four foals without any problems. I won't disturb her. The rest of the morning is filled with the usual jobs on a stud farm.

Shortly after noon, I'm enjoying a nice hot shower before heading down to the 1 p.m. lunch. I'm hoping that father has settled down and lunch will pass without incident. Lately, he's so tense about everything. He was dating Daisy Swift over the past two years. Something happened last month and Daisy's name has been dropped from all conversations. I'll never hear the whole story. If I run into Daisy in town, maybe—from father—never.

I'm surprised to find the dining room empty. Noticing my quick peek into the kitchen Cook says, "I haven't seen Mr. Dillon since this morning." I raise my eyebrows in surprise. After a rapid trip to the empty master suite, I quickly head upstairs. The door to the study is closed. I lightly tap and when there isn't any response, slowly open the door. At the sight of my father sprawled partially on the desk, I know something's very wrong. I quickly walk around the desk. When I touch his neck, his pulse is rapid and erratic. I grab the phone and dial 911. My repeated attempts to rouse him fail. I'm glad to hear the sirens.

The next eight hours are a nightmare. I use my cell phone to call Devin in Texas. Devin is two years older and my favorite brother. When father and I arrive at the hospital, the emergency room doctor says, "heart attack". I thought mine would stop in my chest. My first thought is 'impossible'. Father is strong as an ox, very active and never been sick a day in his life. Devin's calm voice is a welcome relief from my current nightmare. He'll fly up in his jet. He'll call our brother Dorin in Boston and our oldest brother, Dustin in New York City. I'm glad not to have that chore. Dustin is 8 years older and always been overbearing.

Devin arrives within three hours. I rush into his open arms as he says, "Hey, don't look so worried. Father's tough." Devin's rich baritone voice and dark brown eyes have their usual calming effect. Devin always makes everything all right.

Devin continues with, "You look thinner, has father been on your case again?" while intently studying me.

I shake my head before quickly telling him, "No more than usual." We sit holding hands while waiting to hear from the doctors. After 40 minutes, Devin rises to try and get some answers. He returns with a cup of coffee and a frustrated look. Slowly shaking his head at my questioning facial expression, he sits. After waiting another 90 minutes, a nurse appears and suggests we go down to the cafeteria and have something to eat. She'll page us when the surgery's over.

I select a chef's salad and a bright red apple. Devin has the roast beef dinner and says it's better than what he got in the Marines. Our conversation is bursts of talking and periods of quiet thinking. Devin has a cattle ranch outside of Dallas. One of his neighbors, Frank Dailey was in the Marines with father centuries ago. I talk about the horses. Devin talks about his cattle and various ranch happenings.

Once we're back in the lounge, we again anxiously wait for some news. It's almost 9 p.m. when a doctor strides in still wearing his surgery greens.

When Dr. Trenton says, "Mr. Blackwood?" Devin rises and nods.

Dr. Trenton continues, "Your father is out of surgery. I had to perform a double bypass to correct two badly blocked arteries near his heart. You father's in the recovery room. You'll be able to see him one at a time in about half an hour. Right now he's hooked to a lot of intimidating equipment but he's a very strong man. I suggest you go home, get a good nights rest and return in the morning. We'll call if there's any drastic change in his condition." Dr. Trenton appears to be in his late 50's with brown hair heavily streaked with gray. His hazel eyes are ringed with wrinkles and very tired looking. Tall and very thin, he has a friendly smile. I notice his slender hands as he shakes Devins' before leaving.

Devin says, "Let's go home. Father's out of it and like the doctor said he's strong." taking my arm and gently steering me out through the hospital.

A familiar silver Rolls Royce is sitting outside the front entrance. Maxwell, father's ancient driver, gets out and opens the back door.

I thought Maxie was about 100 years old when I was a child. In my teens, I was shocked to discover he's only ten years older than father. Rapidly approaching 70, Maxie hasn't changed. His prematurely white hair and twinkly blue eyes never change. He always has a friendly smile and wink for me. At only 5'7, I've been taller than him since I was 16. He's slim and always dressed in the dark gray uniform with its polished gold buttons, black boots and cap. Tonight, I get a solemn nod before I climb into the back seat. Devin quickly follows. The ride home is so quiet that I lean against Devin and fall asleep.

The next two weeks while father is in the hospital are very stress filled. He's unhappy with his room, his diet, his doctors, his nurses, his medicine and life in general. Daisy tries to visit and father is totally rude and unbearable towards her. I spend most days in the room with him. He complains about his incision, his pain, his food, my being with him, and my leaving him alone. After two days, Devin leaves. Father is so rude and obnoxious.

Devin says, "I don't need this," packs up and goes home. He calls that evening to apologize for abandoning me.

When I tell Devin, "It's OK. I'm used to him," I'm lying. I really wish Devin would have stayed. I know that's selfish, Devin has his own spread to run.

After father comes home, he really becomes unbearable. Dr. Trenton visits and suggests father go on a two week cruise. My first thought is father'll never go for it. I'm shocked when father abruptly readily agrees. Two months after his heart attack, I watch Maxie drive away from the house-taking father to Richmond to catch his flight to Florida. The entire house sighs in relief once he's gone. I feel guilty because I'm also relieved to have father away from the house. The next two weeks are very pleasant.

I'm surprised by a phone call from Miami on Friday evening. It's father's voice that says, "Katherine. I'm spending two weeks here in lovely Miami. I'll see you when I get home. I'm glad Dr. Trenton suggested a cruise. I think it's put years onto my life." Something about his suddenly staying in Miami makes me vaguely uneasy. I just can't put my finger on why. When father returns Saturday in a hired limo instead of calling for Maxie, I learn why.

I'm in the study writing out checks when Lindy, the upstairs maid dashes in and says, "Miss Katherine, you best hurry downstairs, your daddy has returned with a woman!" Lindy is a full-blooded Jamaican and over 6 feet tall. She's strong-willed and strong-bodied. At 68, she has six children, a dozen grandchildren and no intention of retiring. I'm always amazed at how quietly and quickly she moves for her size. I asked her once why she hasn't any white hairs. She firmly says, "I pull them out and they don't dare grow back."

At the foot of the stairs, I find father introducing his new bride to the household. Father turns and says, "Eleanor, this is my daughter. Katherine, come meet your new mother." I feel like he physically punches me in the stomach. My eyes widen and my mouth drops open. Sensing the beginnings of an asthma attack, I begin fighting the choking feeling. When I look up into his eyes, they have hardened. He's displeased at my response or lack of it, perhaps.

I finally stutter out, "Pleased to meet you." Well, this explains the large quantity of women's apparel purchases on the VISA bill I opened yesterday. Eleanore's dressed to the teeth in obviously new clothes. Her black hair is eloquently coiffured in tightly permed curls that contain very little gray. Her black eyes are narrowed in displeasure and hard looking. There are a multitude of lines around her mouth and eyes—smoker's lines. Her face is long and the skin is leathery in appearance. Her nose is long and sharp and presently slightly flared in what appears to be controlled anger. She's plump and probably diets to try and retain her figure. She's almost as tall as I am but I would venture to guess she's nowhere near as pleasant natured. I attempt a small smile and extend my hand. She takes my hand in a firm grip and weakly smiles back.

Eleanor says, "Hello. Your father has told me a lot about you. We'll have to see about getting you a nice man. A woman your age should be married and having her own family." Her words are honey-coated but her voice is sweetly phony. My father smiles like she's the most precious thing in the world. My heart sinks and dread flows through my entire body. I stand frozen in place while he gives her a tour of her new home. I listen as he says she can make any changes she desires, so this place will be comfortable and home to her.

Once they have moved out of sight, I dash upstairs. In my room, I quickly call Devin and explain what's happened.

Devin immediately says, "If you need a place to live, little sis, you call. My jet will be up to get you in a heartbeat. I don't know how you've stood living with the bastard all this time." It's reassuring to hear his voice.

I tell him, "Thanks." relief clearly evident in my voice.

I'm startled when my bedroom door flies violently open and strikes the wall. My father rages in a loud harsh tone, "I will not tolerate your being rude or unfriendly towards Eleanor." I quickly stand and raise my hands towards him. I quickly tell him, "I'm just surprised. Congratulations." At my words, he visibly relaxes and nods. Quickly turning, he strides from the room.

It only takes me several days to realize that nothing I do will ever please Eleanor. My father, who would never tolerate any change or variety in his daily life, suddenly jumps and bows at her every suggestion. I watch as my mother's portrait is moved from the formal living room to the attic. All new furniture is purchased for several rooms in the house. Several of the servants who have worked here all my life are suddenly gone. Lindy is the first to go.

By the end of the third week, I'm unable to keep anything I eat down. Then, when I think things can't possibly get any worse—Eleanor's children move in. There are only three bedrooms upstairs besides the study and central sitting room. I'm in the double one on the back with its high arched separation.

I come in Wednesday close to noon to shower before heading down to choke on lunch with Father and Eleanor. In my room, I find a woman sitting on my bed reading my journal.

I quickly grab it from her and say, "That's personal." as she rises. She retorts, "Don't get all hot and bothered. It's pretty boring reading. I'm Jaycee Hartman. We'll be sharing a room for awhile." My eyes widen and I step backwards in confusion.

"Why?" I ask.

Jaycee flatly states, "Well, mother says the boys can't sleep together in the same room. I told her I don't mind sleeping with another woman. My tastes run that way anyhow, if you know what I mean." I don't at the time. I'm busy realizing who mother must be and wondering how this woman keeps such a thick layer of make-up on her face without it slipping off. She has the same heavy black hair as Eleanor and the same cold black eyes. I beat a hasty retreat to the bathroom to shower and change to avoid incurring fathers' wrath. My closet is now crammed full of the ugliest clothes I've ever seen. My stuff is pushed together or knocked to the floor in the far corner. I hastily dress. When I step into the bedroom, I notice several large boxes stacked in the sitting room area. I lock my journal, wallet and checkbook in my wall safe before heading downstairs.

In the formal dining room I'm presented with the sight of the Hartman clan. Jaycee has changed into a hot pink colored jumpsuit with a low cut front that reveals her smallish breasts and freckled chest. Eleanor sits at the opposite end of the table from Father. Today she's decked in navy blue skirt set with a cream colored lacy blouse. She gestures with her cigarette hand for me to take the seat beside Jaycee opposite the two male things also seated at the table. Once I'm seated, Eleanor performs the introductions.

Gesturing at the male on her immediate left Eleanor says, "This is my eldest son Harold." He's balding and paunchy looking around his black eyes, with a double chin under his big black mustache and goatee. As Eleanore continues, "This is Dennis, my baby." I allow my eyes to take in the younger one seated near father. This man is a dirty blonde with brown eyes in a rough complexioned pockmarked face. His nose has been broken many times and not well set. He leers at me like his older brother. I feel the need for another shower when I notice a swastika tattoo on Dennis left forearm. Hard, stone cold killer eyes on this one. I give a nod towards each in turn. Father signals and the meal is served.

Later, up in the hayloft in the stables, I ponder my life. I'm uneasy about staying here any longer. I'd be welcome at Devin's but I've always lived here. I guess I've inherited my father's dislike for change. I hate to judge people on their appearance so I'll hang in here awhile. Deep in thought, I lay back for a minute and when I awake, it's dark. I never wear a watch so I have no idea what time it is. Panicky I almost fall from the loft rushing down the ladder. Like a thief, I sneak in the back door. The kitchen clock reveals it's after 8. Dinner is at 7 and attendance is mandatory.

Cook glances up as I enter and slowly shakes her head before she says, "Your father's looking for you, Miss Katherine." Her soft tone is betrayed by the fear in her eyes. I square my shoulders and try to slip past the dining room doorway to go upstairs to dress.

Father abruptly bellows, "KATHERINE!" so he must have caught my movement. I turn towards him and he motions to enter the room.

As I step hesitantly into the room father continues, "You're not dressed for dinner. Where have you been?" His icy tone is filled with displeasure.

I tell him, "I fell asleep in the loft." I'm no liar.

Father orders, "Go to your room. I'll be up shortly." I beat a hasty retreat. In my room, all my stuff has been moved to half the room. My horse figurines now sit in a large cardboard box in the corner. I sit stiffly in the rocker in my sitting room and wait. I hear heavy tread across the central sitting room before my door flies open. Father reaches back and quickly shuts the door before turning to face me.

He begins to rant in a loud sharp tone, "Since I have returned with Eleanor, I have heard and seen nothing good from you. You pick at your food. You're sloppy with your chores and you're rude to Eleanor. I simply cannot tolerate this behavior. Eleanor offers excuses. You shame me." I have never seen this side of him before. I sigh. His hand across my face is totally unexpected and throws my head into the wooden rocker back.

Father grabs my hair and pulls me to my feet. He stiffly says, "Come with me." I walk haltingly after him. Once I'm inside the study, father closes the door and points to stand beside the desk. Expecting a tongue lashing, the pain from the first lash of the switch across my back causes me to scream.

Father sternly orders, "Stand still and take your whipping." I begin to turn but the flailing switch stinging across my arm and chest cause me to immediately turn my back towards him. As the blows continue to fall, I drop to the floor and try to curl into a small ball. I don't know if he continues to hit me after I black out.

When I open my eyes, I'm lying on my back and my blouse and bra are open. Squatting astride me, running his hands all over my breasts is Dennis. In the moonlight, I can see his lurid facial expressions. With a quick painful motion, I bring my knee up between his spread legs and hit pay dirt. He shrieks in pain and grabs his groin with both hands. I bring both legs up and kick him in the chest. My back and arms burning, I roll to my knees and flee on shaky legs to my bathroom. I slam and lock the door to the sounds of Dennis laughter.

In the bathroom, I strip off my bloodied shirt and examine the red and bleeding welts on my back, arms and buttocks. I put suave on and take several aspirin for the pain. Taking a soft fleece nightgown from the closet, I step cautiously into my room. Sprawled across my bed is Jaycee, naked and asleep. I get a blanket from the blanket chest and curl up in the corner of the sitting room farthest from her. Falling asleep is almost impossible but the pain pills must have kicked in because it's daylight when I awaken.

Naked, Jaycee is standing over me frowning as she says, "How come you slept on the floor? You could have pushed me over and got into bed." I'm eye level with her shaved privates and backed into a corner.

Jaycee asks, "Did your daddy beat you bad? We heard your screams. Denny said they turned him on. Do you like boys or girls?" My head is spinning. I wave my arm at her and try to rise.

Mistaking my action for a request for assistance, she reaches over and helps me up. With a slight smile she says, "Boy, those welts look ugly. Want me to put some suave on them?"

I quickly tell her, "No thank you." The clock reads 9 a.m. Closing my eyes causes me to sway.

Jaycee lightly grabs my arm and says, "You better sit down. You don't look so good. Your daddy was in here a few minutes ago. He looked kind of sad. Maybe he's not mad at you today." Somehow, her words don't cheer me. I sit heavily on the bed and watch her walk naked into the bathroom. When I hear the shower start, I dash to the closet for some clothes. I dress as quickly as I'm able, slowed down by the extreme pain from the welts, some of which start bleeding as I move. I'm confused. Although father often beat the boys, he never took the switch to me. I want to call Devin but hate the thought of leaving my horses.

I'm half way to the garage before realizing I'm dressed for town. I shrug and continue inside the garage to unlock my Jeep Grand Cherokee. At the sight of this sleek black machine, my heart lifts a little. I quickly drive by the house and out the gates, turning towards Richmond. At the bank, I grab my purse from the seat beside me. A quick glance inside reveals I grabbed my wallet and checkbook from the safe but I don't remember doing it.

The Vice President, Mr. Winters greets me, "Miss Blackwood. Good morning to you." as I enter. You have to pass his office doorway to get to the teller's area. Feeling uncommunicative, I just nod and smile. Mr. Winters pales once he gets a good look at my face. A glance in the nearby mirror reveals a switch mark across my one cheek and a gray color to my face.

Mr. Winters rushes over and gently escorts me into his office as he asks, "What happened?"

Before I can stop myself, I tell him, "My father beat me." Mr. Winters gasps and falls silent.

After he recovers, he quickly asks, "What are you here for?"

When I say, "I want my money from my accounts transferred to a bank in Texas," Mr. Winters goes really pale.

Mr. Winters calmly says, "Child, this is very irregular and sudden. Perhaps you should speak with your father before acting this hastily." There's concern and panic in his gray eyes. Mr. Winters has always appeared gray. His hair, mustache and suits are usually different shades of gray. Today's white shirt and navy tie don't deter much from the rest of his slender gray appearance.

I sharply say, "Mr. Winters, I'm 24 years old. Please do what I ask without calling my father. His name **is not** on my accounts. I'm not interested in the accounts containing his name. He can have those." I lean forward and stare directly at him.

Mr. Winters quickly asks, "Child, we're talking billions of dollars. What bank? Where in Texas?" panic is now clearly apparent in his voice.

When I state, "Devin's bank in Dallas will do fine. I believe you handled the initial transfer six years ago." Mr. Winters gives a resigned sigh and leans back. I've got him in a corner. Within 45 minutes, I have the receipts and all the necessary documents detailing the transfer to the Dallas National Bank where Devin's money is. I love these new fax machines. I'm sure Dallas National Bank is thrilled with their newest depositor. Mr. Winter's gives me his solemn word he won't call my father.

To reaffirm this, I say, "I don't think you'd want to be responsible for him beating me again." Mr. Winters flinches at my hard words. I'm sorry I said them but don't regret it. After finishing my business at the bank, I return to the Jeep and drive to a nearby park. Once I've parked under a large shade tree, I call Devin on my cell phone.

Devin has caller ID so he says, "Hey, little sis. This can't be good news." I sigh at the sound of his voice and suddenly find myself weeping hysterically. It takes several minutes to get myself under control.

Devin waits patiently before he asks, "What's wrong? Why are you crying?" His voice is sharp but sounds controlled.

Between sobs and gulps of air, I softly tell him, "He beat me last night."

Devin says, "Oh, Katie girl. What do you want me to do?" He's keeping his voice calm and low but I can picture the expression of hatred on his face.

I calmly tell him, "I transferred my money already. I won't leave the horses. Can you send the rig? I'll just bring the most important ones. About six?"

Devin says, "You have more than that. Let me get all four rigs on the road. I want to bring plenty of feed, straw and blankets."

There is a brief silence and Devin asks, "You have three or four stallions?"

"Four." I tell him.

Devin states, "Well, you're not leaving them. Get the breeder books and logs. We'll stud them from here. How many mares are close to foal?"

I say, "None. Both Pegalea and Gray Lady foaled over six weeks ago."

Devin says, "Good. They'll travel well. Now, you go back home and be cool until I get there with the rigs. It should take me about 48 hours. Can you hang in there that long?"

I take a deep breath before saying, "Knowing you're on your way, yes. I'll stick it out." and squeezing my eyes shut.

Devin says, "Good girl. Go home, if he beats you again, head for the nearest motel. I'll find you. I love you, little sis. Take care." He's gone.

The hardest thing I've ever done is drive back home. My father is standing on the front steps as I walk towards the house from the garage. My first instinct is to run to the Jeep and head for Texas but I stiffen my burning back and keep walking. I walk up the steps slowly, waiting for him to make the first move. Looking up, there are tears in his eyes.

Father says, "I'm so sorry Katherine. I don't know what got into me. I swear since this surgery, I'm not the same man. Can you forgive me? Did you see a doctor?" As he reaches towards me, I flinch. It's a reflex motion but father quickly draws his hand back.

I calmly say, "No. I just drove to town to get away for awhile." I'm hoping Mr. Winters is a man of his word.

Father says, "I'm glad you came back. I realize this disruption to your life is rough. Since I'm in love with Eleanor, I failed to realize you might not see things the same way. Can you forgive me?" as he's following me inside and up the front hall stairs.

I tell him, "Yes." without pausing in my climb. When I reach the top and turn, he's standing half way just staring upwards.

I turn away and walk into my room. Once again, more of my stuff is packed away and Jaycees' things are more in evidence. I decide it's time to pack my own things. A short search locates two empty boxes in the attic stairway. I quickly fill them. After silently dragging down two of mothers' sea chests, I fill them with good clothes. I stack the boxes and chests in the back of my closet and cover them with clothes. Quickly changing into my usual top and jean combination, I walk to the stables. There, I immediately corner Tom. Steering him inside the big office, I advise him that Devin's coming for my horses and let him know which ones need separated.

Tom quietly says, "Miss Katherine, I was shocked to hear about your daddy beating you. I'm glad you're going to stay with Mr. Devin. We're afraid for you in that house with those strangers. I don't like the looks of any of that Miss Eleanor's offspring. Don't you worry about a thing, Mr. Devin will pull into the lower paddock with those rigs, I'm sure. We'll have the animals ready to be moved before anyone knows what's happening. You count on me. I love you like you're my own daughter." He suddenly has tears in his eyes and puts his arms around me gently.

Tom whispers softly, "When you're by yourself, you watch your back girl. Benjamin says both them men look at you lustfully when you're not looking." before moving away as Father strides into the main stables. Benjamin is our butler. Benjamin misses nothing that occurs in the house. Every servant who works there is another pair of eyes for Benjamin. It's faintly embarrassing to know that every one who works here knows what father did. It's reassuring to know that they're also watching out for me.

Trying to behave normally, I have Markie saddle my favorite stallion, Fermeau. I named him that because he was born during a bad flash flood.

We almost lost him due to the fast rising water. (Fermeau is Fast Water in French.) I don't relax until we've cleared several fences and Fermeau's running flat out. At six years of age and almost fifteen hands high, he's a magnificent black beast. Bred from an Arabian stud and Andalusian (Spanish) mare, he has the good points of both breeds. His black mane and tail are fine and silky from the Arabian blood. He has their great stamina, grace, intelligence and longevity. From his dam he inherited great presence and his athletic high step. Fermeau loves to run and jump. When he begins to tire, I head back to the stables at a walk.

Tom is waiting to take him after I dismount. He tells me, "Your father and Miss Eleanor have gone to town for the evening." I acknowledge I heard him before trudging to the house. Finding my room deserted, I pack a multitude of items into suitcases. Benjamin quickly responds when I ring.

Appearing in the doorway, Benjamin says, "Yes. What do you need, Miss Katherine?" The sight of his gentle old face always makes me smile. He's only about 5'4" tall but of giant stature in my eyes. I quickly explain about Devin and he nods.

With a gentle bow, Benjamin says, "I'll have these bags stowed in your Jeep without anyone being the wiser." Within seconds, Jerry and Markie are at my door and the cases go into large barrels. I'm sure they'll be carried out the servant's door and to the garage via the hidden path.

Locking the bathroom doors, I enjoy a leisurely bath trying to soothe my welts. Carefully applying suave and a heavy soft sweat suit, I curl up in my window seat and stroke Peepers after she comes slowly out from under the bed. She dislikes everyone but me and hides herself very well. I'm blankly staring out the windows when she suddenly leaps off my lap to slide under the bed.

Seconds later, Jaycee opens the door, enters the room and says, "Oh, you're in here." disrobing as she crosses the room.

She asks provocatively, "Care to shower with me? I could rub something into those nasty welts."

I frown and tell her, "No thanks. I just had a bath. I'm fine." Out of the corner of my eye, I watch her walk naked into the bathroom and leave the door open. I'm not ashamed of my body but I've never paraded immodestly around in front of someone I recently met. While she's in the bathroom, I slip my feet into sandals and walk down to the kitchen. Cook fixes a light omelet and some fresh fruit. I sip ice water and sit quietly at the breakfast table. I'm about half finished with my omelet when Dennis walks in and sits opposite me.

In a falsely cheery voice Dennis says, "Here you are. Want to take a ride on my bike? I watched you ride that big black horse. I'll bet you'd love a big throbbing machine between those pretty tight thighs." reaching over to take my fork and begin eating my omelet. Suddenly, I'm no longer hungry. The thought of climbing on his bike is about as appealing as enduring another beating.

I tell him, "No thanks. My back's bothering me." He nods, trying to appear to be sympathetic. Cook frowns as he eats my food. She slowly shakes her head and returns to preparing supper. I sit for a minute and ponder my options.

I head into the basement and the big walk-in safe to retrieve my inherited pieces of mother's jewelry. There are several athletic duffel bags in one corner. I pick one up, remove the plastic wrap and open the bag. I glance quickly around the basement to see if anyone is lurking nearby before entering the room located behind one of wine racks. I close and secure this door before crossing the room to key in my code to open the safe. We have individual codes. It leaves a computer record of who was in the safe last and when, but I'm only taking what's mine. From the appearance inside the walk-in safe, someone's been inside recently. Things have been moved around and several boxes are open and empty. I quickly locate my boxes and using my own codes, open them. Inside, the contents are undisturbed and quickly removed. I can't wait until tomorrow; I'll place the bag inside my Jeep now. Tom has someone watching the Jeep because of my cases anyway. The first box contains mother's jewelry and some of Grandmother Morgan's pieces. The second box contains old gold and silver coins from Grandfather Morgan and the third, the bearer bonds and a multitude 17th century gold pieces from Grandfather Blackwood.

While removing the old coins, I recall my last summer in Texas at Grandpa Morgan's. I was close to twelve and mother had just died. Grandpa Morgan came for her funeral and he insisted I return with him. Tall, thin and tough as nails, Grandpa Morgan could have walked off the screen of any old western movie. He was always clean-shaven and his reddish brown hair had very little gray. His eyes were hazel and twinkled with merriment—or devilment depending on his mood. He never raised his voice but always commanded the utmost respect from his hands and acquaintances. Devin owns the old Morgan spread now. Grandpa Morgan refused to fly so we rode the train back to Dallas. It was a relaxing two-day trip. Grandpa Morgan and I played cards. He genuinely listened as I told him about mothers last months of life. Those three months in Dallas with Grandpa were the happiest of my life. Grandpa Morgan died the following spring without my ever getting a chance to see him again.

The neighboring ranch belongs to the Dailey's. Frank Dailey took over several summers back when his father, Old Man Dailey, dropped dead on the southern range. Frank has two sons. Kyle is five years younger than I. Blake is seven years older. During that summer, Grandpa Morgan and I often went to visit the Dailey's. Where my father is dark, Frank is blonde-haired with friendly gray eyes. Frank is about three years younger but heavier than father. They were in the Marines together. Kyle always looked up to me. I was seven when he was born. Kyle's mother let me help her tend him. This made me feel very grown up so I became really attached to Kyle. Of course, Blake was already fourteen when Kyle was born. Blake's idea of fun was teasing the living daylights out of me.

That summer, at nineteen, Blake was already thinking and acting like a man. The few times I came into contact with him, he slipped into his old habit of teasing me fiercely. By the summers end, I was head over heart in love with Blake. Kyle was in love with me. Mrs. Dailey (Karen) wasn't feeling very well. She tired very easily and was glad for my help in the kitchen and with watching Kyle. I was thrilled to ride over, often alone, and help her during the afternoons. Mrs. Dailey had beautiful sky blue eyes and light soft reddish-blonde hair. Blake resembles her in coloring more than Kyle.

I was sad when the summer ended and I was forced to return north to school and father. In December just before Christmas, Mrs. Dailey died. Grandpa Morgan called to tell me that she had cancer. Since she never complained, by the time she collapsed and Frank took her to the doctors, she was full of cancer and beyond help. She died two weeks later. Frank was so devastated that he called Father. I remember father flying to Texas for her funeral. When he refused to let me attend, I was heart broke. I wanted to be there for Kyle and at twelve, I was helpless. When Grandpa Morgan died the following spring, I remember screaming at my father that I could have seen Grandpa one last time in December. Father simply got a sad look on his face and walked away.

Sounds in the basement bring me back to the present. I quickly close and replace my boxes before flipping on the camera to scan the basement. I watch Harold help himself to several bottles of expensive wine before heading back upstairs. Once the basement lights are out, I key open the safe door and quickly slip into the dark basement. Rather than risk being seen in the house, I walk through the basement to the back stairs. I key in my security code and the door swings open soundlessly. I climb quietly up the steps and scan the surroundings before walking calmly up the last few steps and across the grounds to the hidden path to the garage.

Tom is standing near the office in the stables. He quickly takes the bag and promises to secure it in the Jeep. With a sigh of relief, I get a blanket before climbing into the hayloft to hide and sleep tonight. About dusk, Markie brings me a bottle of cold water, a light sandwich and some diced fresh fruit from Cook. The hands all know where I hide in the loft. I thank him with a smile. Curled under the blanket, I sleep until Markie wakes me around four a.m.

Markie softly says, "You best get up to the house before the Master misses you." He watches as I sleepily climb down the ladder. I walk back through the stables to check on the foals before heading to the house. A handy excuse—in case I get caught. I quickly slip upstairs to shower and dress.

I'm seated at the breakfast table when I hear Benjamin open the front door to retrieve the morning paper. He nods and winks as he places it on the table by father's place. Even footfalls sound in the hall as Cook sets tea and toast in front of me. She's been making light fare since I've had trouble keeping things down.

Father says, "You're up early this morning. Are your injuries bothering you?" as he slides into his place and unfolds his paper. It amazes me that he refers to the results of my beating as 'injuries' as though I fell or was in an accident. I wonder if what he did consciously bothers him at all.

I tell him, "A little. I'm anxious to work with the foals this morning." He then nods to Marie to serve breakfast after she's done pouring his coffee.

This early, I don't expect anyone else. Eleanor usually appears around 6 on the mornings she goes to Petersburg to open her florist shop. Other mornings, she's out about 9 or 10 after having breakfast served in bed. Harold is a delivery person at the florist shop and usually comes down about 7:30 and leaves without breakfast. I wonder if he drank the bottles of wine himself or plans on selling them for a hefty price in town. I'm glad I won't be around in August when the cellar inventory is done and the shortages are noted. Father will not be pleased. The other two offspring don't ever put in an appearance until after noon.

Once I have eaten what I'm able, I rise and nod for Marie to clear. With a smile and slight nod towards father, I leave the room to head for the stables. Pegalea's foal is a filly and already bonded with me. When she sees me approaching, she tosses her head and gives her shrill little whinny before galloping all out towards me. She nuzzles my hands and then bumps against my hip once I've climbed over the fence. I'm not too worried about her traveling to Texas. Gray Lady's foal is a colt and very nervous and high strung. Gray Lady is a frosted-tip Appaloosa. She's actually white and visiting children always remark that she's not gray in color. I end up explaining that her name is a Registered Breed name and doesn't refer to her color.

When the colt sees me, he bolts for Gray Lady's side. Her glance seems to say, "He takes after his father." I smile and realize he may have to be sedated for part of the trip to keep him from hurting himself. You never know how a horse is going to travel. The colt will only tolerate us around when Gray Lady or Pegalea's filly are near. Tom usually has his hands full with the colt.

I'm anxious for Devin to arrive. My morning passes quickly with stable work and helping with the horses. This morning, Lance gladly takes the saddle. His workout is a breeze. I realize I'll miss him while making a note in the logbook that he's ready to go. Above my writing is Tom's bold writing about how well Lance's responding to the harness and carriage workouts.

When I enter the house at noon, no one appears to be around. Benjamin advises me that father has gone to town with Eleanor and won't be returning until extremely late. I'm glad. This'll give me a chance to make an escape without a battle. I stride into father's study to leave a letter of explanation. I won't leave without telling him where I've gone. Father has always been terrified one of us would be kidnapped. Perhaps that's why he has kept such tight reins. I guess as his youngest, I'm the most vulnerable.

It takes several hours to write out the necessary checks and update everything for father. I leave him extensive notes on his computer and printed to hard copy. After removing my individual checks from his desk, I sit to write the letter of explanation. I'm sure he won't mind my going to stay with Devin. I let him know the horses and relating studbooks I've taken. I place the letter in an envelope and write, MR. DILLON BLACKWOOD on the front before sealing it securely with tape. I don't want anyone else reading it. My tasks completed, taking one last look around the study, I gather up my checkbooks.

I walk through the bathroom, place the checkbooks in the one sea chest and again cover it. Armed with fresh clothes, I step back into the bathroom and securely lock both doors. I take a nice leisurely hot shower and wash my hair. It takes me quite some time to dry my long hair and then braid it down my back. My long dark auburn hair reaches past my waist when it's not braided. I gather up my dirty clothes and place them into a laundry bag. In the closet I remove all the clothes from the floor and off the chests to fill the bag. I drape the bag across the top of the sea chests and step into the bedroom.

A rough hand clamps over my mouth and a strong arm pins both my arms to my sides. Jaycee rises from her seat on my bed. Harold turns from looking out the windows in the sitting room. I struggle, but Dennis's grip is like steel. He moves his hand over my mouth slightly, which blocks my nose. Lack of oxygen causes me to panic and struggle madly. Jaycee harshly orders, "Unblock her nose, fool. You're suffocating her. We want it enjoyable when we play with her." while she's removing her clothes. Harold is opening his pants and walking slowly towards me.

My eyes are wide and my heart is pounding. "Devin!" My mind screams silently. Into my ear, Harold hisses, "Scream and I'll kill whoever comes to your rescue." Once the tape is in place, Dennis grabs my arms. In spite of fierce struggling, they put me onto the bed on my back. After placing my arms at the bedpost, Harold tapes my wrists together and then my arms to the bedpost. I try to kick her but Dennis lunges down, grabs my left leg and brings it upwards twisting it painfully. I scream silently into the tape, tears streaming from my eyes as pain shoots from my hip across my pelvic area. I feel like I'm going to vomit. I fight the nausea because with my mouth taped, I'll choke. I'm screaming into the tape.

Suddenly, Devin's face appears above and beyond Dennis' left shoulder. Tom silently and quickly grabs a surprised Harold. Devin grabs Dennis under his arms and yanks him backwards. Jaycee screams like a banshee and lunges at Devin. He brings his elbow swiftly up and knocks her cold. Devin thrusts a struggling Dennis at Sam and with a quick yank, the tape is removed from my mouth. Someone cuts the tape binding my wrists to the bedpost. Devin pulls me quickly up into his arms, wrapping the comforter securely around me. Tom softly exclaims, "Sweet Jesus." as I weep and shake uncontrollably in Devin's arms.

To Tom Devin coldly says, "I should kill the bastard."

I tell them, "Please, just get me out of here. Devin, take me home. Please." I'm gagging and my body begins jerking and trembling. Wrapping me in the comforter, Devin lifts and carries me into the bathroom. He sits me on the edge of the tub and starts the shower running. The comforter drops to a sodden mess as Devin pulls me to a standing position in the shower. Devin stands behind and steadies me as I scrub myself clean.

Finally, Devin takes the sponge and says, "You're all clean, little sis. Come on; let's get you dried and away from here." He's soaked to the skin but he only grabs a towel for me. As he wraps the towel around from behind, his glance falls onto my back as he hisses, "Bastard!" I hear his teeth grind and then clamp together. He's seen the welts.

Devin says, "Katherine, some of these look infected. Let me put on some suave." Then he strides to the medicine chest to find an antibiotic suave. I'm clutching the towel in front and violently trembling again. Devin gently applies the suave and with paper tape attaches gauge bandages over the inflamed welts.

Marie is waiting in my closet with a soft tee, cotton shirt, clean panties and jeans. Stepping inside as Devin leaves; Marie gasps at the sight of my back and quickly drops her eyes.

Marie says, "I'm sorry, Miss Katherine."

I tell her, "It's all right. I'm going with Devin. Let me write you a check and send you a reference letter. I don't think you'll be safe here after today." Marie nods in agreement at my statement and helps me dress. Marie is probably not much older than me. She started working here about four years ago when her mother became ill and unable to work. I've been sending her mother money secretly ever since. Marie has long black hair and long dark lashes around her black eyes. Her olive complexion and small stature reveal her mother's Spanish blood. In hardly any time at all, my hair's dried and pulled back with a ribbon. I pad barefoot into my bedroom. When a shudder passes through my body, I close my eyes.

Devin touches my shoulder as he says, "Let's get your shoes on. Tell Sam what needs to go." I point to the boxes in the sitting room and say, "There are two of mother's old chests in the closet and two laundry bags of my clothes. In the attic stairway are several other boxes. Mother's portrait is in the attic." Devin nods. I ask Devin, "Is Peepers under the bed?"

Devin looks away before he says, "She's dead. Benjamin found her body in the trash and called the stables. He thought something might be wrong in your room. We came up as fast as we could. Thank God for Benjamin. I was waiting for you to sneak out and meet us." Devin shudders at the thought of what would have happened if he had waited much longer.

"Where . . . ?" I ask.

Devin says. "They're drugged, bound and gagged in the cellar. Tom thought it best to not harm them. The way father is, he's as apt to sic the law on us." I nod and sit at my small desk to write a large check for Marie and one for Tom. I have a feeling that once Harold talks, Tom won't have a job. Sam works for Devin.

I hand the check to Devin but he explains, "Tom's coming with us to drive your Mustang. I'm driving your Jeep. Markie's driven a rig before so he'll drive the one I brought up. Are you ready?" I nod and he pulls me to my feet for a quick hug. My hip and left leg hurt fiercely but I try not to limp.

"What's wrong?" Devin immediately asks.

When I tell him, "I think they hurt my hip on the bed," he sweeps me into his arms and carries me downstairs. All the servants are waiting.

Cook kisses and hugs me saying, "We're going to miss you. I'm not sure I'm going to stay here with that woman and her brood."

Devin tells her, "You come down and cook for me."

While giving Devin a brief hug, Cook says, "I'll ask my Mister how he feels about Texas and call you."

Devin says, "You do that. I'll pay for the move down and get you a nice place." Cook nods and I can see the idea pleases her.

Giving me a big hug, Benjamin says, "I'm gonna retire—starting today. My son's been wanting me to anyway."

I say, "Tell Maxie goodbye for me. OK?" Benjamin nods and his eyes have tears in them.

Devin says, "You'll all get big checks and letters of recommendation. You all know my phone number and address in Texas." Most of the servants nod and walk slowly away after shaking his hand.

It's almost an hour later before the Jeep pulls out onto the road and heads south to meet with the waiting four rigs and my Mustang. Devin carries me to the Jeep after Tom pulls it to the front steps. Cook brings several of my grandmothers' quilts to wrap me in to cushion my ride. She's prepared a large picnic basket of goodies and several thermos containing coffee, tea and lemonade. There's a familiar blue ice chest on the back seat that's full of bottled water. Water's all I can drink without getting sick. Once we're on the road with the four rigs behind us and the Mustang bringing up the rear, I lay my head back and sigh.

Devin reaches over and covers my hand with his saying, "It's over."

I turn my head towards him to softly ask, "Is it?" Devin quickly nods before turning his attention back to the road. All six vehicles are equipped with CB's tuned to the same channel.

CHAPTER TWO

AT GRANDPA MORGANS
WITH DEVIN

Each rig has an intercom system to monitor the sounds of the horses. If there's any kind of ruckus, we'll immediately pull off the road and slowly stop. The first rig contains Gray Lady, Pegalea and their foals. I listen to the sounds of horse movements but nothing panicky. The second rig contains the four older stallions. The third rig has the younger stallions and the fourth contains my six mares. I'm sure Devin has a handler in with the younger stallions, at least. This trip will be long and tiring. We'll probably have to stop every two hours to check the animals—sooner if problems arise. Lady luck seems to be riding with us because the roads are dry and the horses remain quiet.

We actually stop every four hours and let the stallions run their pent up energy off. We're taking I-85 to Atlanta, Georgia and then picking up Rt. 20 to Dallas. There are plenty of nice truck stops and rest areas. We don't have to worry about speed traps; Devin sets the pace at forty-five miles per hour. Like me, he worries a sudden stop might put a horse down and break his leg. Each animal is secured in a special harness and tether, but accidents still happen if you get careless.

Devin says, "There's no hurry, sis. Frank Dailey is watching my spread while I'm here. I told him what father did and Frank was as shocked as me. He agrees Eleanor must be behind building up father's rage. We both know father's always been one to let things build until he can't control himself any longer. Do you want to talk about what was happening when we rescued you?" His eyes are on the road but his heart is tuned to me.

With a light tone and a smile, I tell him, "No. Maybe after some time has passed—maybe never. You got there in time and saved me for my future husband. Devin to the rescue as usual." Inside, other more dangerous thoughts are bouncing around in my head. I have a feeling I'll be having cold sweats and screaming nightmares for a while after today. The movement of the Jeep and the sounds of the horses put me to sleep. I open my eyes as the Jeep slows to pull into a rest area. Once we stop, I stiffly climb out and stretch like everyone else. Then we pair up and check the rigs.

It becomes my job to soothe each animal while the men clean out the stalls and put fresh straw down whenever necessary. Gray Lady's colt is calmly lying beside the filly without any sedation. I'm glad. I don't like the use of drugs, even the herbal or natural ones. This is over thirteen hundred miles of interstate travel. I'm extremely glad when we cross over into Texas just past Shreveport, LA for the last one hundred ninety miles. All the horses are doing well. We're up at 5 a.m. each morning and running them until they're tired before we load them. Tom and Sam have regulated the feed to slow their metabolisms down. The filly jumps, kicks and runs when we lead her out. She really takes to Devin and he ends up handling her exclusively. Fermeau is a real trooper about traveling. We've taken him to several shows for steeple chasing so this is a familiar routine for him.

It starts to rain heavily shortly before Shreveport, slowing us down even more. This makes the trip longer, but safer. By the time we're within two hours of the ranch, the rain stops and the sun comes out. I don't remember the entrance to Miramosa being as beautiful as it is today. Someone has stretched a big Welcome Home banner across the driveway.

Devin chuckles and says, "Kyle. I'll bet." When I sigh and close my eyes, Devin pats my hand. "This will feel like home in no time at all. You'll see." It's almost ten miles back the drive from the main highway. Grandpa Morgan loved his privacy. Devin did some extensive remodeling to modernize the almost two hundred year old ranch home. The charming shutters are painted John Deere Green and the old covered wraparound porch is as inviting as usual.

We drive past the house back to the stables on the left. There's a small army of helpers flowing from the stables and barns to empty the rigs. As they're turned into large paddocks, the stallions race and jump and frolic like young colts. I believe they all realize the journey is over. Devin advises which stalls are for which horse. Each animal's blankets and buckets are placed in their new stall. Bringing familiar bits of home for their new place. After a bit of running and frolicking both foals are busy nursing, which is a very good sign. My stuff is loaded into the big pickup from the rig. Together with the Jeep it's driven up to the house.

We walk into the two-story foyer, with its triple window arrangement and up the L-shaped staircase directly to my new bedroom. "Round to the right, I thought you'd have the largest of the three empty bedrooms. The little bedroom back there is pretty much empty. You can get a desk and set up a sitting room for yourself, if you want." Devin opens the door to a plain white bedroom.

Setting my case down, I tell him, "This is fine."

He empties his hands to come over to put his arms around me. "It'll take some time to feel like home. I want you to buy whatever you want for in here. If you don't like the furniture or the rug, we'll get new." I smile and look down. The rug is a pale gray.

"I know this is much smaller than what you're used to, but the whole house is yours to do with what you want. You can take a nap or shower. When you're rested, come down and see the new sunroom and family room. The kitchen has all the modern conveniences except a cook." He teases. I sense he feels a little awkward.

Keeping my tone light to try and lighten the load on his mind, I say, "Hey, I'm sorry to just dump all this on you. Your home is beautiful and you know how I hate change. It's fine, honestly. I'll probably be swept off my feet by some big Texan and out of here in no time." I'm sure what he saw when he opened my bedroom door keeps playing through his mind. He strides from the room to tell the men bringing my things up to put them in the back bedroom for now. A shower suddenly sounds very good. I feel badly because Devin has a ton of work to do now that he's back.

While I'm unpacking clean clothes, Devin sticks his head in and says, "Hey, little sis, across the hall is the master suite, I have a walk in shower and whirlpool, feel free." He's gone before I can say anything. The idea sounds good after a check in the second bathroom reveals a tub/shower combination.

The master suite has cathedral ceilings and a big walk in closet. I found it looking for the bathroom. Devin has a king size four-posted bed with a dark gray spread and matching drapes. The same gray carpeting runs through the entire upper floor. That's Devin, cheaper by the yard. Inside the master bath, I hesitate between the whirlpool and the walk in shower. The whirlpool wins and I luxuriate in it for over an hour.

It's after twelve then I wander downstairs. He's right about the newly modernized kitchen. I quickly find fixings for lunch and start cooking. I'm thinking I might as well earn my keep. The fresh steaks go under the broiler. I quickly boil noodles and make my butter sauce for over them. There are lots of frozen vegetables in the freezer so I select Devin's favorite, white corn. It's easy to make French Onion soup from the steak juice in the broiler. When Devin troops in at 12:55, lunch is ready.

"Smells like a woman in here!" I hear Frank Dailey's voice and turning quickly dash into his open arms. "My Miss Katie, you surely grew up." I smile. Only Frank has ever called me Katie. He always said Katherine was for old maids. He looks the same, only a bit heavier and some gray hairs have sprouted on his head.

Suddenly slightly embarrassed, I tell him, "Mr. Dailey! You look good."

"Don't you dare call me **_Mr. Dailey_**. It's Frank, same as before." He and Devin quickly wash while I set the food on the dinette table. As I sit, I notice Frank's eyeing the switch mark on my face. He reaches across and gently touches it.

He sadly shakes his head saying, "I can't believe that Dillon struck you, even with the evidence clear in front of my eyes." Then he offers grace. The two men quickly consume every bit of the food and empty two full iced tea pitchers before heading back to work. Frank hugs me saying he's headed home but I'm to come and cook anytime in his kitchen. Devin teases that I'll be too busy cooking here for him unless Cook comes from up north. As he's leaving, Frank winks and crosses his fingers.

I busy myself cleaning the kitchen. Once everything is spotless, I head upstairs to settle into my room. About 4, I slip downstairs and dig out chicken to fry for supper. Devin loves fried chicken, corn bread and creamed potatoes. Judging from the amount of fresh meat and supplies, someone went to the market to be ready for my arrival. In spite of all that's happened, I find myself humming while I'm preparing dinner. I jump when the phone rings but let the answering machine get it.

"Katherine! I know you're there. Pick up the phone. I need to know why you had to sneak away like a thief." It's father and judging from his tone of voice, he's totally enraged. I back away from the phone before running outside to escape the hard sound of his voice. Someone must have seen me burst from the house because Devin comes running from the stables before I've warmed the seat on the swing.

"Katie girl, are you all right?" He takes the stairs two at a time and plops heavily into the swing beside me.

"Yes. Father's leaving a nice message on your machine. Devin, I don't want to talk to him." I find myself sobbing and trembling.

"You don't have to talk to him. I'll handle this. That man has run rough shod over you for years. You've done your time. What's cooking?" He asks as a breeze brings the smell of dinner out through the open window.

"Dinner! Oh, God, I left it!" I dash inside to the sound of Devin's hearty laughter. The phone is silent and the chicken is getting a little crispy on the bottom. I deftly turn the pieces as Devin comes inside.

He says, "Fried chicken. You remembered. Smells like mother's." I nod as he's hugging me. Cook taught me how to make many of mother's old dishes and a few of her own.

By the time Devin returns at 5:30, dinner is as ready as Devin is to eat it. Once everything is again gone, he leans back and sighs. "Guess I'll call father now. Don't sweat it. I'll call him from upstairs. I'll let him know that until you call him, he's to leave you alone." I suddenly jerk my head around towards him. At my wide-eyed look, he appears to read my mind.

He calmly says, "I won't tell him how I found you. You'll have to tell him about that yourself. If Cook's left, with Tom and Benjamin gone, he's going to be busy hiring. I'll let him know he's not welcome here without an invite." At his words, my breathing slows.

My first thought is father wouldn't believe me if I told him what happened. Whenever I told him something unpleasant he always said I had too vivid an imagination. Well, my imagination never prepared me for those three animals. Devin said Jaycee is probably a Lesbian.

I'm still standing stiffly at the sink when Devin returns about 15 minutes later. He chuckles into my hair and says, "Well, imagine father at a loss for words."

I shake my head and he continues, "Evidently it was quite some time before the trio was discovered in the basement, like almost two days. Cook has given notice and will probably call here. He found Benjamin's letter of resignation and then your letter after he'd discovered Tom, Markie and George all gone from the stables. He's fit to be tied. Of course, he said if he didn't have Eleanor he didn't know what he'd do. She's taking right over and getting new servants so his routine isn't too badly interrupted." lightly resting his chin on my shoulder.

"Eleanor knew what they were planning. Jaycee said she was deliberately keeping father in town overnight." I'm not speaking very loud and this is the first time I've spoken at all about that day.

Devin's head comes up sharply and his body stiffens, he says, "Then she's up to something. Katie girl, I need to call Dustin and tell him what's happened. I'm sorry, but he's the estate executor. You know he won't come here and it'll be just as embarrassing to him."

He's holding his breath. I lean my head back against his shoulder and breath in his after shave and male scent. I say, "It's OK, you're my brothers. Tell him, I just want to put it all behind me and go on with my life."

Devin exhales and relaxes before he says, "I'm glad to hear you say that. By the way, father said you left four of your yearlings there. He'll send you a check once they're sold." He moves backwards so I can step from the sink.

I tell him, "They're Fermeau's but the mare's were fathers." Devin nods as we walk through the dinette into the new family room.

Looking around this newly built room, I smile and tell him, "Very nice. This is new and yet totally in sync with the rest of the house. I like the fireplace and all these windows and the lofty ceiling. You've made this a very friendly room." He has firm comfortable leather furniture; low glass topped wood tables, a massive TV and entertainment center, bookcases of movies and a low mat oval carpet in the center of the room. Done in earth tones, the windows have floor to ceiling cream-colored sheers with wooden shutters on the lower half of the windows. I stand and turn examining the features of the room while Devin sits in what is obviously his recliner watching with a broad smile. The circle complete, I walk over and curl up on the end of the couch nearest Devin.

"It's you and yet, I can picture Grandpa Morgan in here too." At my praise, Devin gives me another wide smile before turning on the TV. I jump when the phone rings, but Devin reaches forward to answer it. "Yes, my offer was sincere. You're welcome at Miramosa. No, visit with your grandchildren for a while. I'll have a prefab home setup for you to live in. No, it's no trouble at all. We'll see you when you arrive. Yes, I'll send you a cash voucher for your moving expenses and a map right to my front door. OK, back door. Good bye." He hangs up and turns to give me a big grin.

I ask, "Cook?"

He nods and says, "Her husband is excited at the prospect of retiring to fish in Texas. Tom should enjoy hearing that." At his words, both our faces get soft looking, remembering fishing with Tom when we were younger.

Rising from the couch, I tell Devin, "I'm going to bed. I find I'm rather tired."

With a quick glance my way, "You've had a rough week. Go to bed. You're in a different time zone. 5 a.m. comes an hour earlier here." Devon reaches up to squeeze my hand while I'm passing. I stop to plant a kiss on his forehead.

Devin asks, "How's your back?" I see how soft and loving his brown eyes are.

I tell him, "Healing nicely. The horse suave worked better than the antibiotic cream." chuckling, he releases my hand.

Upstairs, I'm faced with a strange room, strange bed and strange feelings. Tired, I quickly don a cotton gown and crawl between the white sheets. In bed, my eyes drift close. Dennis is in my bed, trying to pin me down. I struggle and scream and scream. The light comes on and reveals a terrified, groggy looking Devin, pistol in hand. I throw my arm over my eyes against the light and gasp for breath. There's the sound of the pistol bouncing on the nightstand.

Devin lifts me into his arms, "It's all right. It's just a bad dream. God, your screams almost ripped my heart from my body. Shhhh, cry, let it out. I'm right here. You're safe." gently rocking me in his arms and stroking my hair until I stop trembling and crying.

"Sorrrry." I stutter out.

Chuckling, Devin says, "Nothing to be sorry about. Bad dreams happen to the best of us. Lay down. I'll get you a little wine and me a little whiskey." Rising, he grabs the pistol as he leaves.

He's back with a small on the rocks glass half full of a dark liquid, "Drink." he says. I do. It's slightly sweet and very smooth. Devin turns out the light and sits beside me until I drop back to sleep.

I open my eyes to sunlight streaming in through the two large windows in this totally strange room. I shudder until I come awake enough to realize I'm at Devin's. For a few minutes I thought I was in a motel due to a horse show, sale, equestrian event or studding. The clock on the bedside stand says 8 and it must be wrong. Quickly finding the necessary clothes, I go downstairs. Devin has made flapjacks, tea for me and coffee for himself and Tom.

Devin teases, "Good morning, sleepy head. I let you sleep in this one time." I flush when I realize he's probably been up for at least 3 hours and had to make his own breakfast.

Tom says, "Don't tease her, Mr. Devin. She's had a rough week."

The men leave the dish work. I gladly clean up the kitchen. Once that's done, I realize no one will make my bed anymore. Back upstairs, to make my own bed and tidy up Devin's. He has a lot of dirty clothes piled in the master suite. I grab a basket and bring them down to the laundry room. Another trip upstairs gets my own clothes that need washed. Before long, I'm hanging wet clothes out back on the lines.

Franks voice cuts through my daydreaming, "Well, that's a sight for sore eyes." as I'm hanging up tea towels on the line.

After removing several clothespins from my mouth, I tell him, "Good morning, Frank."

He dismounts from his horse. While he walks to the nearby trough, he says, "Good morning to you Miss Katie. Looks like you're settling in all right." I gather up the empty basket and walk to the fence to chat a bit. At my smile, he raises his eyebrows.

I tell him, "It feels so early American West. With you watering your horse and the lines full of laundry behind me." he quickly nods.

He teases, "No early American woman ever filled out her jeans like you do." I blush. This is an older pair and a bit tight. I lost some weight due to the past few weeks stress and now my newer jeans are too big.

He drawls, "No disrespect intended, Miss." in his version of an old west accent, sweeping his hat from his head in a slow arc towards me. I laugh and it makes me feel lighter. Frank follows me into the house after tethering his mount to the old post.

Helping himself to coffee, he sits at the table. He slowly asks, "What are you going to do with yourself down here?" sipping the hot strong black coffee.

I shrug, "I don't know. Cook is coming down from up north, so doing Devin's cooking will be eliminated. I don't know if he'll want me handling his books. I can work my own stock and handle my own studding." My voice winds down and I shrug again. Devin strides inside and grabs another cup of coffee.

Devin tosses his hat <u>at</u> the hook saying, "Thought that was your mount out back. Is that border fence still sorely in need of repair?" I pick it up and put it <u>on</u> the hook.

Frank drawls, "Yup. I was up on the knoll and saw Miss Katie hanging laundry. Figured a neighborly visit was in order. Her just arriving from up north and all." Devin looks strangely at Franks sudden western movie type talking.

Then he laughs, "Well, partner, you drop by anytime. The pots usually strong and hot and Miss Katie makes a mean meal when she gets herself out of bed before noon." I know he's going to tease me awhile about that.

Both men rise and head back to work. I sit pondering my new life. Finally, I rummage through the refrigerator and bring out stew fixings. With a smile on my face, I make beef stew and biscuits for lunch for my cowboy brother.

When he saunters in close to noon, his nose perks right up. He says, "Smells powerful good in here, little Missy. Have you rustled up some good grub for your working man?"

Smiling, I lift the lid on the stew, "Yup. Stew and biscuits."

He leans over the pot saying, "Smells mighty good, yessuree, mighty good. Let me just wash up and set myself at the table." Plopping his dirty sweaty hat on my head, he heads to the sink. There isn't any conversation at the lunch table. Tom joins us and the stew seems to evaporate out of the pot. I'm glad I made a double batch of biscuits. Both men manage to eat all but the two I got my hands onto.

I ask, "Devin, what do you want me to do?" as he's rising from the table.

Devon replies, "Whatever you want. Whatever you used to do for dad. My office is in the corner of the sunroom. There's checks need written and supplies need checked against the orders. Some times the stores don't send everything and we run short. Cook whatever you want for dinner. Frank turned down lunch but I'll bet he and Kyle show up for supper. I don't think there's been a woman at the Dailey's since his Mrs. died. Seems to me, Kyle mentioned something about frozen pizza's being delivered by the truck load." I smile at the memory of Kyle always wanting pizza as a meal choice whenever he was asked. Morning, noon or night, pizza was his only request.

Once Devin is gone, I find a nice large beef roast in the freezer. Pot roast is usually a big hit, especially if I make gravy and real mashed potatoes. I peel potatoes after I get the roast seasoned and into the oven. I decide on homemade cinnamon rolls and honey glazed carrots. I bring in the dry wash and put everything away. The kitchen gets a good washing top to bottom. I set the dining room table with the everyday dishes.

When Devin comes inside at 5, the necessary checks have been written and a new list of supplies all made out. Giving a low whistle at the kitchen smells, he says, "Been cooking and cleaning. Smells real good. Frank will be here close to six. Kyle can't wait to see you again." I nod and we both head upstairs to wash and change. I brush my hair out and use several large combs to bring it back away from my face. I'm downstairs before Devin and turn when the back door opens. Frank's entire face lights up and he broadly smiles.

He teases, "Smell that food, Kyle, that's woman cookin'." My hand flies to my throat at my first sight of Kyle.

I say, "Oh, you're a man." Then I could bite my tongue as Devin laughs from behind me. Kyle is tall, and very thin but blonde like his father. He nods and blushes, gray eyes suddenly downcast at my statement.

I apologize, "I'm sorry. That just slipped out. I guess I thought you'd still be 7."

He gives a slow charming smile and says, "No ma'am, just like you, I filled out some." then blushing at his own bold statement. Frank pounds his back.

Frank says, "Let's get to the table before I drown in my own saliva." All three men head for the dining room. I bring in the cinnamon rolls. Kyle jumps to hold my chair. Devin and Frank chuckle and begin filling their plates. I thought they were going to arm wrestle for the last cinnamon roll.

Frank got it. While buttering it, he says, "Still quick."

With a wide grin, Kyle says, "That stuff is going to kill you dad.".

Frank retorts, "I'll go out with a smile. Miss Katie, you can come cook for me anytime you're bored. Right, Kyle?" Kyle nods and as he has through the entire meal, his eyes rest on me. He always was in love with me. I think he's still suffering from it. Kyle insists on helping me with the dishes. Frank and Devin make their escape out to the back porch. I was hoping for some of that massive beef roast for sandwiches for lunch with leftover gravy. The three men left nothing but dirty dishes and grunts of satisfaction.

Kyle and I sit on the big swing on the back porch. Kyle pushes the swing with his long legs. Pushing my hips back, I let my feet dangle. Frank is sitting on the top step, propped against the railing. Devin's in an old wooden armchair. There's a nice air moving. Once it's dark, Frank and Kyle climb into his old green pickup and head home. Devin and I walk inside.

He puts his arm across my shoulders. He teases with a smile, "That was a good dinner. Maybe you should go help Frank when Cook gets here." I raise one eyebrow then head upstairs to bed leaving him to deal with the lights and doors.

I slowly crawl into the still strange bed and drop to sleep. My dreams are of running from an unseen danger. Then I'm grabbed and thrown to the ground. The wind is knocked out of me. I lay listening to the storm rage around me. Totally awake, I realize I've fallen out of bed and there really is a bad storm raging outside. I sit up as Devin appears in the doorway of my room.

"Crawling under the bed?" He teasingly asks.

I tell him, "No, I fell out. Man, your floors are hard." He gives me a hand up and then strides over to close my windows. I get a couple of towels to mop up the rain that already came in. I don't get back to sleep until the storm quiets down. I made sure I set the alarm for 6 a.m. It's very loud. I jump when it comes to life. I'm up and downstairs before Devin, but just barely. I have the coffee brewing. He grabs a cup on his way out and winks before putting on his hat.

My daily routine becomes make breakfast, work the horses, make lunch, tidy the house, and make dinner. I discover that mid morning is a nice time to take a ride on Fermeau. Afternoons are too hot. I find myself riding deliberately towards the Dailey place. No one has mentioned Blake. I seem to be constantly wondering where he is, what he's doing and if he's married. One of my afternoon rides after several rainy days finds me riding towards the fence and watching Frank as he struggles to remove a calf from a muddy creek edge. The calf is in mud up to his shoulders. The cow is tied to Frank's horse to keep her from joining the calf. Frank is thigh deep in the mud struggling with the terrified calf.

I turn and ride far enough back for Fermeau to take the fence. Frank watches while we approach and easily sail over the fence. I grab my rope from the saddle and securely tied one end to the saddle. Fermeau looks at me like I'm crazy but he stands still. I walk to the edge of the mud and toss the other end to Frank.

He shakes his head and chuckles, "It's only mud, you won't dissolve. Get in here and help me. I can't let go of him to put the rope around his body. He's mired too deep to put it around his neck." I sit to remove my boots.

Franks says, "No. Leave them on or you'll loose your footing in here. This is deep." He's right. My first step almost throws me off my feet. It pulls right up into that damaged hip/groin muscle. I grimace.

Frank warns, "Watch yourself. Go slow." While still maintaining a firm grip on the struggling animal. I don't know how long it took us to get the rope around the calf. I struggle from the mud to slowly back Fermeau to help him pull the calf free. Frank laughs once the calf is freed and runs crying to his mother. I look down and see why. Both of us are almost covered completely in mud.

Frank says, "Come on, we'll go to my place and you can clean up. I don't think it's fair since you rescued me to track this mess into your brother's house." Rather than climb into my saddle, I plan on walking. Laughing Frank throws me up onto his horse and swings up behind me. We take a fast hard ride back to his place. I lean back against his firm chest, safe in his arms. I'm remembering when my father used to put me in front of him and ride with me just like this. Frank leaves our horses just outside his laundry room entrance. He struggles out of his boots and everything but his jeans.

He says, "Wait here." before dashing inside. There's a deep sink between his washer and drier. Frank returns within several minutes with a large white man's bathrobe, "Step into the laundry room, strip and put this on. By then, I should be done in the shower and I'll tap on the door." I nod and follow him inside. His muddy clothes are dumped in a pile in front of the sink. Once he's closed the door, I strip and put on the bathrobe. I even have mud in my hair, especially, the end of the braid. The robe is huge but very soft. I hate getting it muddy. There's a tap on the door.

Frank says, "Katie girl?" I open the door. Frank's in an older blue bathrobe.

He says, "Come on. I left the shower running to clean it." We hustle through his entire house back through his bedroom to the large walk in shower. He leaves me at the shower door and ducks back into his bedroom.

Once I'm in the shower I see a blur of the blue robe come into the bathroom only far enough to get clothes from his closet. Above the loud sounds of the shower water he hollers, "I'll leave you clean clothes here until yours are washed.".

I yell back, "OK." to be heard over the sound of the water. The hot water feels good and I'm soon clean. Wrapped in a large white towel, I discover women's clothes lay beside the sink. He must have kept Karen's clothes. A quick peek in the closet reveals all her clothes. He selected blue jeans, a pretty blue blouse and panties and socks. I grab a bathrobe tie to, put through the belt loops, as the jeans are really big.

Frank is in the kitchen making iced tea and putting store bought cookies onto a plate. He asks, "Tea?"

I nod as I ask, "Shall I start the washer?"

He shakes his head saying, "All ready did when I heard the shower stop."

He stops, scanning me from head to toe before he says, "God, you are a tiny one. Karen was small but you're tinier yet." Shrugging, I take the iced tea. He motions towards the sunlight breakfast room. How strange to see that nothing has changed from the way Karen set things up when the house was remodeled. The brightly decorated kitchen with its yellow and white daisy motif and tiles.

Frank and I sit at the wood block colored table with our iced teas and chocolate chip cookies. Frank says, "Thanks for your help today. I wasn't sure how I would get out of that mess. I was afraid to leave the calf and go for help."

Nodding, I tell him with a smile, "That's what neighbors are for." He silently agrees. Sometimes when I look at him, he's looking at me so piercingly. It makes me slightly uncomfortable. Now I figure it's because I'm wearing his wife's clothes.

Rising, I tell him, "Let me get my things into the drier." Before walking quickly to the laundry room as the washer stops.

Frank calmly says, "There's no hurry. I can call Devin and tell him where you are if you think he's worried."

I tease, "He won't worry unless dinner's not ready when he comes in from the stables." Frank gives his loud booming laugh. It startles me but makes me smile. Before long, I'm back in my own clothes and headed for home. It was easy to persuade Frank to let me make something for dinner before I leave. The honey orange chicken pieces, scalloped potatoes and homemade biscuits will probably not go to waste.

For Devin, I make Cooks famous hamburger stroganoff with noodles and creamed peas. It's easy to whip up another batch of the biscuits and have everything ready in plenty of time. Devin comes in, washes up, eats and heads back to the barn. He has a couple of cows due to drop and he's worried about one of them. At 8 I walk down to the barn but nothings happening. Devin tells me to go to bed.

I'm much busier when the prefab house is brought in and set up in the far side yard. Devin had them put it on the old concrete slab where the springhouse used to stand. There's a handy electric hook up, capped water supply and old septic tank hookup. I spend three days scrubbing the inside. There's a lot of plaster dust and road dust to be cleaned off. I line the cupboards with plain white contact paper and hang pretty curtains at the windows. I figure Cook can change what she wants after they settle in. After giving the carpeting a good vacuuming and scrubbing the inside of the new refrigerator, it's all ready.

Cook and her husband Truman, arrive the following day. Cook is thrilled with the little house. Devin sends two men up from the stables to help Truman unload the U-Haul truck they drove here. Truman sold his old car and plans on purchasing one in Texas. Devin says there are several pickups and a couple old sedans they can use. I already have a nice turkey roasting in the oven. Before we went to bed last night, Devin requested the turkey. I saw a fresh one delivered on Friday. I had suspicions it would be Sunday's dinner. The bird was in the oven before we left for church. By the time we got home, it smelled pretty good in the kitchen and immediate vicinity.

Cook and Truman gladly join us for Sunday dinner. Cook makes her famous whipped potatoes and creamy smooth gravy. I made the bread stuffing the same way she taught me. Judging from the looks I get during dinner, I didn't forget a single bit of her lessons. I refuse all offers of help with the dishes. Cook gladly retreats to her new home to unpack and settle in. In the early evening, I take a big pitcher of lemonade and some angel food cake over for a light snack. Truman is glad to see me and for the excuse to take a break.

The next morning, Cook is in the kitchen at 6 preparing a nice breakfast. Several times I think she wants to talk about Virginia but she keeps falling silent. Once breakfast is completed, I take Fermeau for a long ride and end up finding Frank working on some damaged fence line.

I call, "Howdy neighbor!" and his head jerks around and he smiles broadly.

He says, "Hello Katie girl. Whatcha doing out this far?" wiping sweat from his forehead with his sleeve.

I tell him, "Cook arrived and I'm bored. Need a cook at your place?"

Raising his eyebrows, he says, "I'd never refuse the good cooking of a nice looking woman. Like I said before, you're welcome to cook for me anytime. In fact, leave a list of what you need to prepare your best dishes. I'll stock the pantry." I walk Fermeau through a break in the fence and steady the wire as Frank pounds in the nails.

Shaking his head, Frank says, "You head up to the house awhile. This is man's work. Here comes Tim to help me." I watch an old pickup bounce across the field. I swing up onto Fermeau and with the gaze of both men on my back, ride for Franks.

In the kitchen, I find fixings for beef stew and again make homemade stew and biscuits. All Frank's meat is frozen and the small stew pieces cook up easily while I clean and slice the vegetables. I find a brownie mix and make them while the stew simmers on the stovetop. There are lemons and oranges in the pantry so I make orange-lemonade and a pitcher of fresh iced tea. Before Frank arrives for lunch with Kyle, I've mopped the slightly tracked and sticky kitchen and breakfast area floors clean and scrubbed the stovetop.

Frank exclaims, "Good heavens! When I said you could cook for me I didn't mean you had to prepare feasts!" while looking slowly around the kitchen. Kyle elbows past him and grabs a brownie from the plate where I'm piling them after cutting them.

He says, "Hush up dad. I like the sight and smells of Katie in the house here." I get a brief hug before Kyle goes to clean up. Frank just slowly shakes his head and goes to the laundry room sink. I enjoy watching the two of them eat. Frank takes a couple bites and raises his eyes to heaven to smile. Kyle just shovels the food in like he's been starving for a week. He was always a hollow child—now he's a hollow man.

I have a nice chicken thawing in the sink for dinner. I'll stuff it, make the whipped potatoes and corn and leave Frank to finish it. While hunched over lunch, he said he can make gravy and whip potatoes, just doesn't usually make the effort.

Kyle says softly, "That's the honest truth." with a smile. I wave them away from clean up so they head back to the ranch work. It's an endless hard job. Everything is done quickly. I'm able to make the gravy and unstuff the bird before I leave. At home, Cook has prepared her wiener schnitzel dinner. Truman says I missed out on fresh caught fish for lunch.

Devin reiterates, "Flaky as pastry." as Truman smiles. I know that Cook makes a nice seasoning for fish as well as being good at the cooking preparation part.

I'm up in the morning to enjoy Cooks breakfast before riding Fermeau over to Franks to cook and clean. I discover mounds of laundry in both men's rooms. It's a lovely day. I soon have the wash lines cleaned off and filled up. Frank laid two massive steaks out for dinner and a ham slice for lunch. I find canned pineapple, honey and brown sugar for my sauce for the ham slice. Cheese sauce potato slices go into the oven for with the ham. I find crescent rolls in the refrigerator and frozen mixed vegetables. Kyle's only comment is that he would prefer the vegetables on Sunday. Frank laughs and says, no vegetables, no dessert. I made a busy day spice cake with drizzle icing. Kyle eats a small amount of the vegetables and a large piece of the cake.

I make homemade barbecue sauce for on the steaks. Frank says he'll grill them. I get potatoes into aluminum foil for baking on the grill. The market brings fresh sweet corn and various other goodies. I open the husks slightly and butter and salt them. I leave Frank instructions to finish the corn and potatoes on the grill before starting the steaks.

This pretty much becomes my new routine. It's September before I realize that three months have passed and I feel at home at Devins. I'm also quite at home at Franks. After Kyle and Frank consume another large lunch, they head out to round up some strays. I put a large beef roast into the oven and ride Fermeau back home. My new routine is to return in the Jeep. The days will be getting shorter. I don't want to ride home in the dark. This particular afternoon, I'm back in plenty of time to peel and cook the potatoes for the mashed. I've made a tomato vinaigrette salad that Frank has requested I make again. I'm bent over the oven, my butt to the room, removing the large roast.

I hear, "Well, that's a sight I certainly never expected to see in my father's kitchen!" The voice is low, husky, and very masculine. Suddenly I realize it's Blake. With my startled jerk, my right arm comes in contact with the oven side. At my exclamation of pain, he's beside me in an instant. I'm quickly pulled to the sink and cold water is run over the already nasty looking burn. I'm very conscious of his hand holding my arm under the water, the arm encircling my waist, the firm warm chest at my back and his after shave and soap smell. I slowly look up at his face taking in every inch before settling on his beautiful sky blue eyes.

Blake says, "I'm sorry, pretty lady. I had no intention of startling you and causing you to get hurt." He raises my arm to his lips to kiss the burn and raises goose bumps all over my body. I shudder as my nipples peak and fire races through my groin as he continues, "I'm Blake Dailey and you are?" He raises an eyebrow and slowly lowers my arm, not releasing me.

I tell him, "I'm Katherine Blackwood. You don't remember me." I'm mesmerized by his gaze.

He softly says, "Little Katie Blackwood. My, my, my, you have filled out nicely." His glance drops to my tee shirt and when I look down, my face flames. He slowly turns me to face him, studying my face intently. His hand drops to my lower back while the other lifts my chin.

He says, "Little Katie Blackwood. I never would have guessed." Then dropping his arms and swiftly grabbing the potato pot off the burner as it boils over. I turn the burner down and turn back to the still open oven door.

He says, "Let me get that out, it looks heavy." stepping around me and deftly removing the large roast pan with the meat in it. While I drain and whip the potatoes, he diligently stirs the gravy over the heat.

Frank comes in and says, "Well, I see you two have gotten reacquainted. Guess you won't be teasing her so much now, huh son?" as he begins scrubbing at the sink.

Blake huskily says, "Nope. I never expected a woman in the kitchen. In fact, I startled her and she burned herself on the oven. Guess I'll have to take her out to dinner to make up for it."

Franks eyes cloud over briefly with an emotion I don't recognize before he laughs and says, "Hell, she's been working so hard, we'll all take her out to dinner tomorrow night. Right Kyle?" Kyle grunts and he face appears stormy looking. They must have had a hard day on the range. Frank and Kyle must be tired. They are certainly out of sorts over dinner. Blake seems to delight in teasing both of them.

Frank says that Blake has returned home to help around the place. "It's a good thing too, cause I was just thinking about hiring on another man. At today's wages, that's expensive. This way, it saves Blake's inheritance and I can train him to run the place." Frank's jovial tone brings a smile to Blake's face and a dark frown to Kyle's. I realize that Kyle may not be happy with his big brother's return home. If Blake had stayed away permanently, Frank probably would have left the place to Kyle.

With Blake's coloring being so close to Karen's, I often wondered if Frank wasn't partial to him over Kyle. I know sitting at the table and looking into Blake's eyes, there's a lot of his mother in him. Once the meal is completed, Frank insists that the boys do clean up while he and I sit on the porch swing. I try to argue but he insists. Since I've been raised to respect my elders, I comply. I feel slightly uncomfortable on the swing with Frank and as soon as I can, I excuse myself to head for home.

I want to be alone to daydream and think about handsome Blake. Driving home I can't stop thinking about his firm arms and slender artistic hands. My mind recalls every detail about the dark hairs growing on his hands and lower arms and the dark heavy chest hair at the collar of his tee shirt. At 32, his face is matured and has a few more lines than at 19. His chest is fuller and like his arms, more muscular. At home, I almost run the Jeep into the back of the garage with my lack of attention to my surroundings. I walk up to the house, greet Devin and go right upstairs to bed.

Devin's voice comes through my closed bedroom door, "Are you sick?"

I quickly open the door and ask, "No. Why would you ask me that?"

He shrugs, "Well, you were in an awful hurry to get upstairs . . ." letting his voice drop as he looks into my face.

I tell him, "Blake Dailey's back home." and he laughs out loud.

Then he asks, "And you're still in love with him?" I blush and look away, embarrassed that he remembered my teenage confidants with him.

He laughs and pats my shoulder saying, "Well, I'm sure Blake will find you most pleasant to look at. Hell, he might even decide to court you." I give him a wide-eyed look and shut the door in his laughing face. His laughter fades as he goes back downstairs.

The next morning I'm greeted with him singing, "Blake and Katie sitting in a tree K I S S I N G!" Cook gives me a strange look and tries not to smile.

Now I have three hungry men to cook for at Franks so I increase the portions I make. Friday night, all three men take me out to dinner. We end up at a popular steak house that also has a dance floor. I end up dancing with Frank during several slow numbers. Kyle and I two step a little while he shows me the steps. Suddenly, Blake who was buying drinks for this flashy blonde asks me to dance during the next slow number. Frank argues I'm his dance partner for the slow numbers but Blake still pulls me into his arms out on the dance floor.

We move together like one person. Blake slides his hand to my lower back and pulls me tightly against him. He's all male, all right. I smell beer on his breath and believe he's slightly drunk. He grinds his groin against my short black skirt and my entire body throbs and responds. His eyes travel from my face to my neck and on down my body. My lavender colored silk blouse clearly reveals that I like what he's doing. I blush as I look up into his eyes. His other hand slides up under my hair and pulls my head back. I hold my breath praying for him to kiss me. His lips are soft at first and then his tongue pries my lips apart and enters my mouth. I gasp and let my mouth fall open. As his tongue boldly explores my mouth, he pulls me tighter.

I hear, "That's enough boy. You had too much to drink. Katie girl ain't no common bar room floozy." Frank's voice is low but his tone is hard and sharp.

Blake raises his head and grins at his dad saying, "I never thought she was common in any way." Frank grabs Blake's upper arm but Blake shrugs and drops his hands from me. I turn and frown at Frank. I'm confused by his actions and then realize that my father would probably have reacted in the same way.

I softly tell him, "It's OK Frank. Let's go back to our table." When he turns to me, his face softens before he takes my elbow to escort me to the table.

Once I'm seated, I scan the room. Blake's gone. My heart drops and when Frank asks a little later if I'm tired I agree so we can leave. Frank leaves me at Devin's and Kyle hasn't spoken a word to me since I danced with Blake. I know he's jealous.

For the next several days, Blake avoids me. I'm so confused. I had this notion that maybe he was falling in love with me. It's Kyle who finally reveals that Frank and Blake had a massive fight. Blake moved into the cottage at the southern most tip of Frank's property. Kyle wasn't around when they fought so he doesn't know what it was about. The very next morning, I make a nice batch of fried chicken, homemade biscuits and brownies. I load everything into the picnic basket and ride down to the cottage. I'm disappointed to find it deserted. I leave the basket on the porch in front of the door. As I'm walking away, I change my mind and go back and check the door. It's open. I walk inside and leave the basket on the dining room table. I'm surprised that the place is spotless. I expected dirty dishes in the sink or some signs of a male living in residence. Blake must be very tidy. Back on Fermeau, I'm at Franks in plenty of time to fix lunch for them. Today, I don't stay to eat, but leave before they arrive.

I don't feel well the next day. I call and leave a message for Frank on his machine. I'm surprised when Blake appears in my bedroom doorway with the picnic basket filled with red roses saying, "I hear you're not feeling well from your Cook. Perhaps these will cheer you." At the sound of his deep sensual voice, I swing my legs over the bedside and sit up. I can't keep the smile from my face or my eyes from lighting up.

Advances into my room, he says, "There, she looks better already." He suddenly halts and asks, "May I?"

I tell him, "Yes." but I seem to be suddenly out of breath.

Blake says, "You look better already. Tell me. Is it me or the roses?" He sets the basket on the bed beside me.

I tip my face upwards telling him, "Both. I had a sinus headache, but it's gone now." while watching his eyes.

Tipping my chin up with his fingertips he says, "Good." and lowers his face to kiss me. As his lips touch me, a jolt runs throughout my entire body. I jerk and throw my arms around his neck.

He raises his lips from mine, smiles and says, "Oh, you like that?" I silently nod. He calmly continues, "Is it all men or just me?" Suddenly, anger flows through me and I push him back.

I angrily tell him, "I'm no whore!"

As his eyebrows rise he says, "I never said you were, Katie girl. I just wondered if my kisses thrilled you more than other men's kisses." I blush and lower my head.

I state, "I've no other men's kisses to compare them too." but suddenly I flash back to my bedroom all those months ago and the room tips around me. When Blake grabs my arms, I scream into his face and faint. Cook found the smelling salts. She is applying them liberally under my nose while a very pale Blake holds me upright in the bed.

She asks, "Are you all right now?" concern all over her face. I sheepishly nod. I feel the beginnings of a massive blush and know my face is fiery red.

Looking into my eyes, she asks, "Nasty memory suddenly return?" I nod and look away. When I turn back, she's gone.

Blokes voice rumbles from behind me, "You took about ten years off my life, Katie girl. What nasty memory?" I lean my head back against him and tears begin flowing down my face.

I gasp out, "I can't . . ." and then my voice fails me. He wipes the tears from my face with his fingertips.

He slowly asks, "You weren't raped—were you?"

I shake my head, "Almost. Devin . . ." My voice croaks and my throat goes closed. For a brief moment I think I'm having an asthma attack but as I relax, I find I'm able to breath easily enough.

He softly says, "It's OK. I don't need to know unless you want to tell me." I shake my head violently back and forth.

I firmly tell him, "No. I can't tell anyone yet." He stops my head movement with his hands.

He muses, "I guess that's why you're here instead of in Virginia. Is it too late to ask you to have dinner with me?" I've never heard Blake sound unsure. He's usually cocky and teasing.

I quickly tell him, "I'd love to have dinner with you." my eyes downcast and looking at his very masculine taunt blue Jean clad thigh jutting out from my left hip. I realize I must be sitting between his spread legs on the bed. A quick glance to the right reveals his other leg, straight resting near mine. As though he suddenly senses our position in my bed, he pushes me away from him and off the bed.

He asks, "Tonight?" I can only nod. He slides from the bed and strides to the doorway.

He tells me, "I'll be back at 5. Do you have evening clothes?"

I nod and ask, "Like for the theater?"

He softly says, "Like for the symphony." He pauses and continues, "Something long and white?" At his words, I nod again. He gives me one of his slow sensual smiles before disappearing from the doorway. My heart is so light, it could just bust.

I'm over in Devin's shower singing when Cook says from the doorway, "Miss Katherine, should I put your roses in a vase?" I holler yes, please and go back to my singing. Wrapped in a big white towel, I dash into the back bedroom to find the only white colored gown I own. It's long, clingy and has a silvery sheen to the material. The sleeves are long but worn off the shoulders. The deep V accentuates my nice breasts and the built in bra holds them firmly up. The back drops just as sharply and the long skirt flows from my narrow waist across my hips to billow around my long nicely shaped legs.

I work diligently to get my hair up onto my head in the front and then let the ends drop in long ringlets and soft curls down my back. I have several nice silver combs to help hold the hair in place. Cook brings me up a light snack around 3 but I hardly touch it. I'm ready by 4:30. Devin gives a low whistle as I enter the kitchen. Cooks' hand flies to her throat and she beams with pleasure.

Devin teases, "You're not going out with a man wearing that—are you?" Beyond him I catch a glimpse of Blake wearing a black tux and looking so handsome I can hardly breathe.

I tell him, "I certainly am." feeling as though I'm floating towards Blake. Devin follows closely. Blake is devouring me with his eyes. A slow smile twitches around his mouth before he says, "Well, I believe I'll have the most beautiful woman at the symphony on my arm tonight."

Devin comments, "And remember she's my little sister." from behind me.

Blake softly chuckles and says, "Impossible." I hand my wrap to Blake who deftly places it around my shoulders and under my hair. With Devin close on our heels, Blake takes my elbow and escorts me through the mud entry to the side porch and the back driveway. Parked just off the porch is a sleek black Thunderbird.

At his first sight of the beautiful vehicle, Devin exclaims, "Wow, a 70's model."

While opening my door, Blake proudly boasts, "1971, V-8, all original and less than 75,000 miles on her." Inside the black leather seats are soft, supple and very comfortable. Blake helps me settle my dress inside before closing the door. Devin is walking around the car like a child looking at a much-desired toy in a store window.

He shakes Blake's hand and says, "I'll trade you my sister for it."

Blake's says, "Maybe." before sliding behind the wheel and glancing towards me to see my facial reaction to his words. I smile softly and purse my lips. Devin always wanted to trade me for something.

I'm surprised when we drive to a nearby private airstrip and alongside a massive black jet. Blake informs me, "The symphony's in Houston. You don't mind flying, do you?" I shrug and then smile. I'm thinking I'd fly anywhere with you but I can't tell him that. In hardly any time at all, I'm settled in the plane's luxurious interior and the T-bird is loaded in the belly of the jet. Blake settles beside me and the jet taxies for take off. We're in Houston in a heartbeat and back in the T-bird headed for where ever Blake has dinner reservations.

I've never been to Houston. I'm torn between watching the sights outside the window and gazing at Blake as he drives. Blake wins, hands down. He pulls up to Charley's 517 on Louisiana Blvd. in the theater district. A valet parks the car. Blake takes my elbow and escorts me inside. This is a very elegant and cozy restaurant. Judging from the diners already seated, very formal and obviously used for pre-theater dining and socializing. The maitre d' knows Blake by name. We're escorted to what appears to be their best table. The service is very professional and quick. Blake orders roast quail dishes for both and a very expensive wine.

Blake states, "You look beautiful in that gown. I don't recall mentioning that when you floated into the room. Actually, you took my breath away, Katie girl." Somehow he even makes my nickname sound sensual. He checks the wine and gives his approval before the waiter pours. Once we're alone again, he lifts his wine glass towards me.

He says, "To a lovely enchanting evening." We touch glasses before sipping the smooth, dry wine. I nod my approval as we set our glasses down.

Blake seems content to sit and lightly hold my fingers across the tabletop until our dinner is served. The silence is not strained but comfortable. The quail is delicious and since I haven't eaten since breakfast, easily consumed. We pass on dessert.

Blake softly says, "Until later." as he pulls my chair from the table. We collect my wrap and step outside to the waiting T-bird. The Jesse H Jones Hall for Performing Arts is nearby. We're in a very private box in plenty of time for the opening number of the symphony. Blake holds my hand during the entire performance. We're separated only during intermission when I flee to the ladies room briefly. By 10, we're headed back the road to Blake's cottage in the T-bird. I didn't realize where he was headed until the headlights flashed across the front of the cottage.

Before climbing from behind the wheel, Blake turns towards me and softly says, "I'd like to dance with you before taking you home." I float from the car into his arms for a brief kiss and then into the living room area of the cottage. Blake puts a Beethoven CD in and drapes my wrap across the sofa back. I don't know how long the CD played or how many times it played through. I do know the longer it played, the closer we got. Blake suddenly stops dancing to release my hair from its combs and pins. I hear them dropping onto the hardwood floor around us. He fingers are combed through my hair as he lowers his lips to mine and fire flows through my entire body. He groans into my mouth and continues tasting me with his tongue. My own hands are up in his hair, then on his back and then back in his hair. I arch my back and lean my head back as his lips trail across my neck and down onto my shoulders and breast tops.

Before his hands slide to my waist, he says softly, "So easy." and he steps away from me. I look up through partially lowered lashes.

"I," He clears his throat and continues, "need to get you home it's almost 1 a.m. Katherine, I want to make love to you but I swore long ago not to deflower any woman I wasn't married to. Don't be hurt or disappointed, feel special." He plants a kiss on my nose and turns to pick up my wrap. My body is throbbing and my heart is pounding but at his words, I do feel special. It's almost 2 a.m. when he pulls to the side porch where the light is burning. He walks me to the porch and gives me a soft kiss as Devin opens the porch door.

Trying to tease but sounding very upset, he asks, "Should I have a shot gun?".

I openly joke with him saying, "No. I'm still intact big brother. Blake is a gentleman." I touch Blake's face before slipping around Devin and heading through the house to the foyer and stairs. I'm in bed in record time and hear Devin's tread in the hall.

He says, "Little sis?" through the door.

With a smile he can't see I ask, "What?".

He opens the door and sticks his head inside asking in his big brother voice, "How was your first date?" I smile again, safe in the darkness of the room.

I tell him, "Heavenly." He chuckles softly before quietly closing the door. It's almost noon when I rise in the morning. Cook has a florist box in the kitchen.

She says, "Good afternoon, Miss Katherine. These were delivered for you first thing this morning." She's fairly beaming.

She tries to admonish me by saying; "Those headlights sure came up the lane late." but ends up softly smiling as she turns away. I open the box with her watching to reveal a dozen pink baby roses.

She says, "Oh, Miss Katherine, they're precious." setting a vase beside me. I read the card while she places them into the vase.

The card says, "Katie girl, we missed you yesterday. Hope you are feeling better. Frank." My face falls and Cook frowns.

"They're not from your man?" She quickly asks.

I flatly state, "They're from Frank." shrugging I set the vase in the center of the breakfast table. Blake's red roses are in my room. When Devin comes in for lunch, he assumes the roses are from Blake.

I quickly explain, "Frank." Devin gives me a strange look before he begins eating his lunch. I don't eat much lunch so Cook is upset with me. I don't hear from Blake until around 7 when he calls to inquire if he might join Devin and I for church tomorrow morning. I readily agree, my spirits immediately soaring. I'm fussy all evening. I keep going up stairs, selecting a dress for church and then changing my mind.

Sunday morning, I end up putting on the navy and white dress I originally selected. Resembling a two-piece suit with white collar, leather belt and cuffs, the skirt is slit up the back and form fitted. I dig out navy heels and a pair of navy ribbon covered combs for my hair. Blake arrives at 6:15 wearing a navy pin striped suit. Devin gladly climbs into the back seat of the T-bird. Devin is wearing his usual brown suit with cream-colored shirt and rust colored tie. Some of his routine type actions reveal father's blood in him. This makes me smile. Church is over far too soon. When I invite Blake to stay for Sunday dinner, he accepts. Devin is thrilled to have a guy to pal around with. Cook has prepared veal Marcella with creamed potatoes, fresh homemade dinner rolls and green beans almonde'. Everything is delicious. Once dinner is finished, we change into riding clothes and take a nice long ride. Blake selects my Arabian stallion, Sultan to ride. A massive white animal, Blake sets and looks well on him. Devin goes with his own stallion, Justice. Today I select Pegalea because she's so anxious to go. Once we're headed across the north paddock I realize the humor in our horse selections. I'm on a mare and the two men on stallions.

The ride is fast, long and exhilarating. We return walking our mounts and after leaving them in stable hands safe keeping, walk to the house. Devin pours whiskey for himself and Blake. In the kitchen, I get Cooks devils food cake sliced and onto plates. Devin ends up cutting a second slice before Blake and I have finished our first. Blake leaves after he and Devin play several rounds of pool on the table in the basement game room. I wander around while they're playing and generally spoil their shots. Finally, totally frustrated, Blake throws me up onto the table and begins tickling me. I'm not very ticklish but enjoy his hands on my body anyway.

When Devin dryly remarks, "She's not ticklish." Blake is forced to halt his attempts and pull me off the table. I walk Blake to his car and get a nice long kiss before he drives away.

Inside, Devin is sitting starring into another glass of whiskey. He flatly says, "I'm not sure I like the way he touches you. Sometimes his face looks hard and mean when he's looking at you. Like he's playing a game with you or something." I'm startled by his words.

I tell him, "You're wrong." sitting down in the opposite recliner.

He says slowly, "I hope so, little sis. I truly do." before downing the remainder of the amber liquid and setting the empty glass on the table. Picking up the Sunday paper, he begins to read. I wander upstairs to lie down. Sometimes this new Blake also confuses me. I feel as though he's testing me about something. I wish I knew what.

CHAPTER THREE

BLAKE, KATIE GIRL AND DILLON

While I'm having my breakfast, the phone rings. Devin answers and turns to me saying, "It's for you, Frank Dailey." I raise my eyebrows and walk over to take the phone.

I hesitantly say, "Hello." while Devin smirks from the breakfast table.

Frank sounds so concerned when he says, "Katie girl, how are you feeling? I've been worried you might be really ill." that for a minute I feel guilty.

"No, I'm fine. Thank you for the lovely roses. I just had a miserable sinus headache." I quickly tell him.

I can hear his long sigh before he says, "Good. Will you be feeling well enough to come over today?" now sounding unsure.

I quickly tell him, "Certainly. I'm back to normal now." watching Devin shaking his head and grinning as he rolls his eyes upwards.

Frank replies, "We'll see you later than. Good bye." more cheerful sounding before he hangs up. Over the next three weeks, my routine at Franks is the same except I dash out after making dinner to dine with Blake at the cottage. Frank must have assumed I was going home to eat with Devin. This particular Friday, Blake has made a nice oriental stir fry dinner.

We're eating by candlelight. The dining room is situated in the corner of the living room area and totally visible once you step into the living room. As we've been doing for the past week, we're feeding each other. I'm so happy. Although tonight, I find that Blake is better with his chopsticks than I am with my fork.

A gruff man's voice says from the darkness, "What the hell is going on in here? Why aren't the lights on? Who's the woman you're keeping in my cottage?" Blake jumps and pivots to face an enraged Frank who at that moment flips on the overhead track lights.

Frank exclaims, "Sweet Jesus, Katie girl?" Now for several moments Frank is amazed and confused. Then his face darkens in rage as he begins advancing towards Blake.

He growls, "If you've soiled her, so help me, I'll kill you!"

I fly to my feet and scream at Frank, "Don't touch him!" my hands outstretched. At my words, Frank seems to be come madder instead of calmer like I hoped.

He bellows, "So—you're lovers!" I watch as he hunches his shoulders and charges Blake like an enraged bull.

I thought I would witness an all out blood fight. Calmly, Blake steps to the side and brings both hands up locked together. His motion coupled with Frank's already enraged forward movement flips Frank backwards onto the floor in a neat arc. In two seconds, Blake is kneeling on his father's throat while Frank struggles helplessly.

He leans into his father's face saying, "First, I'm in love with Katie. Secondly, you should have enough respect for Katie's morals to realize she'd never just give herself to any man. Third, you're old enough to be her father. You old goat! You should be ashamed of your lecherous feelings towards her virginal young body." Blake's voice is cold, calm and low. After I hear him say he loves me, my heart swells and the rest of his words seem unimportant.

Frank bellows, "Get off me!" as he's gasping for breath.

"Are you going to act like a gentleman?" Blake softly asks.

Frank says, "Yes. Show some respect for your father." Blake quickly leaps backwards and off. I step up and put my arms around him from behind, burying my face in his soft knit shirt.

I whisper, "You love me." and feel his chuckle rumble against my cheek. I don't see Frank rise but I hear the front door slam. Blake sighs and turns to take me into his arms.

He softly asks, "What have I done?" before his lips find mine and I don't really care. He raises his head but our earlier playful dining mood is broken.

"Are you still hungry?" He softly asks.

I tease him, "For food?"

Smiling, he asks, "Shall we take a walk?" I nod because I sense he has adrenaline still surging through his body from his clash with Frank. We grab our denim jackets and slip out the front door. The cottage only has one door and two of the sides don't even have any windows.

Outside, dusk is beginning to settle over the fields. There's an old path that runs towards Devin's place and Blake heads down it. For the first half hour, Blake and I walk silently; hands clasped together across each other's hips. Blake seems to be doing some heavy thinking. I'm still digesting his statement that he loves me. We're headed through a patch of trees. Blake suddenly perks up, halts and pulls me against him.

"Shhhh." He whispers. I lean against him listening to his heartbeat. When I hear movement, I stiffen slightly. Under my ear, Blake's heartbeat remains slow and steady. After a few minutes Blake shifts slightly and puts his hand to my lips. I nod slightly but hear nothing out of the ordinary. It takes me a couple minutes to realize that I don't even hear the sounds of the night. Blake reaches into the back of his jacket and removes something that a shaft of moonlight reveals is a gun. He exerts a slight downward pressure and we slowly crouch low to the ground. I'm literally kneeling between his spread legs, tight to his groin as he squats on his heels. Movement in the bushes to our right reveals sounds of men moving quietly through the woods. They're too quiet to be up to anything good. All sound stops at the edge of the woods.

Someone says low and in a deep masculine voice, "His car's there."

"There's a Jeep on the other side. He's got company. Maybe we should come back." This other man's voice has a definite Bronx accent and sounds comical.

"The boss says to deliver the message by tonight. You want to tell him otherwise?" This is the lower voice again and he sounds unhappy.

"No and I don't want to walk through these damn fields and woods again. Man, something is eating me alive." Mr. Bronx sounds so unhappy and uncomfortable.

The other man says, "Keep your voice down, the man's got ears like a hawk. Remember, he kills first and then asks. That's why he's the best at what he does and why the boss don't want no one else handling this hit." Blake stiffens and then cocks the gun. The noise is loud in the quiet of the night.

Both men say, "Shit."

Blake calmly says, "Move and you're dead."

"We ain't movin. We got a message from the boss." Mr. Bronx sounds more confident now.

Blake growls, "Keep your mouth shut." before I hear his sigh.

He softly asks, "Paper or personal?"

"Personal and very wet." The other man's voice is still low and I notice slightly raspy.

Blake rises and pushing me behind him says, "I'm not alone. I don't want others involved."

Mr. Bronx asks, "You got pussy with you?" and Blake stiffens.

He growls, "I should kill you for that." and both men shuffle around slightly. The moon is out fully now and I clearly see them. They look strange in their city clothes and probably shoes.

"Look, Tigerman, it took us two weeks to locate you. We gotta give you the message and carry your answer back." It's the other man talking again.

Blake angrily states, "Tell the boss I'm retired. End of message. Now leave before I shoot you for trespassing." It doesn't take either man long to disappear back through the woods the way they came. Blake stands and listens long after I no longer hear them.

He leans his face into my hair saying, "I never wanted you to know where I've been or what I've been doing. You can walk away now. I know you'll never tell a soul what you've heard." I shiver as I realize that I may be the first person he's ever offered that option. When I don't answer immediately, he stiffens and steps back.

I say, "No." grabbing the front of his shirt. "I don't care what you were. I love you Blake for what you are. I've always loved you. Tell me what you want me to know or I'll forget what I've heard here." His arms slide around to pull me close and up for a kiss. I let my mouth drop open as I mold myself to him. Suddenly he raises his head.

As he gently pulls me along the path to the cottage, he says, "No. You need to know the whole truth not just the few words you heard here."

After we enter the cottage, he checks the entire place in the dark before pulling me into the master bedroom. I shed my jacket and slip off my boots in the living room. This room is sparsely decorated like the rest of the cottage. There's a queen sized bed, large dresser and two wooden chairs. A large gun cabinet sets in one corner and a large chest along one wall. I watch Blake shed his jacket and lay the gun on the dresser before turning to face me. His face is so open and uncertain looking my heart goes into my throat.

After a deep breath, he says, "I want you to know I never killed a child or anyone who wasn't rotten to the core. That doesn't make it right but I have a very strict code of ethics for a cold-blooded killer. Katie girl, not even my father knows that for the past 10 years I've been a professional hit man for who ever has enough money to meet my price. I'm selective in my jobs and hell, I can't make excuses for what I've done. For, what I am." He turns away. I walk over and around to look up into his face.

I calmly tell him, "I knew and loved the boy. I want to know and love the man. You said you're retired. Men retire from the army all the time. Our armed forces kill for hire and what they believe in." I gasp as he suddenly pulls me into his arms for a kiss. I arch my back and grab his hair with both hands.

He raises his head and asks, "Will you marry me, Katherine?" I shudder as wave after wave of passion sweeps through my body.

I tell him, "Yes." as he bends to again claim my lips.

He says, "Now. Tonight. We'll fly to Vegas. I want to make love to you."

Then he glances down and he says slowly, "My God, I've torn your shirt." shaking his head. "I don't remember doing that." I smile and open my shirt again.

"It's all right. Whatever you want." I softly tell him. He shakes his head again.

Shaking his head, he says, "No. I want you as my wife. It's been so long since I've been with anyone, another couple hours won't matter." Opening a dresser drawer and pulling out a tee shirt he says, "Here. Put this on, I'll call my pilot."

As Blake strides towards the kitchen phone, it begins ringing. I hear his terse answers. He says, "Yes. How did you get this number? Never mind. I told your messengers I'm retired. I don't care how much the woman is willing to pay. I don't kill . . ." There's a long pause as he's obviously listening. Then he says, "I see." It's silent for a long time again. I find myself holding my breath.

Finally, Blake says, "Yes, I know you have good sources. I'm retired—get someone else. That's my final word." When I hear the sound of him replacing the receiver, I step into the kitchen.

Seeing me, he states, "I'm feeling sort of old fashioned. Would you mind going up to Virginia first so I can officially ask your father for your hand?" I frown at the thought of going back. Then my body trembles with a sudden onslaught of bad memories.

He gathers me into his arms saying, "Hey, I'll be there. Trust me when I say I'll kill anyone who touches or hurts you." His words aren't spoken lightly. I also think there's something he's not telling me. But, I believe in fate.

Finally, I say, "All right. You never met him—did you?"

He asks, "Your father?" and I nod.

Blake says, "At my mothers funeral, remember, he's a good friend to my dad. I recall him being a bit stiff and old fashioned in his actions and spoken thoughts." I pull him closer and lift my face to look into his eyes.

I start out hesitantly, "Maybe I better tell you what happened so you'll be better prepared for Father, Eleanor and her brood." He gives a slight nod at my words. Then it sort of all tumbles out in a rush of words leaving me crying and enclosed in his firm embrace. He remains strangely silent for quite some time, digesting the information.

He says, "No one should have to go through that in their father's home or any place. Those are the kind of people I eliminated." I hug him.

I tell him, "Well, I need to pack for our trip."

Blake says, "Let me get a few things ready. Then I'll drive you over to pack your bag. I want to talk to Devin before we leave. He's a good man.

I want to do the honorable thing for once." He pulls a large black suitcase from the shelf in the walk in closet of his bedroom. I smile as I notice all his clothes hung neatly and evenly spaced in the large closet.

I tell him, "Lots of room for my stuff."

He says, "I'll bet you don't have much stuff. I picture the pantry getting more items for the meals you'll prepare than this big old closet. There's a second bedroom and bathroom upstairs." He volunteers.

I ask, "For your son?" He gasps and turns quickly to face me. I watch the idea sink in and his face soften.

He says, "My son. Yes, we'll have a son and a daughter and anything your heart desires. Eventually, I'll build a bigger house. This will be our honeymoon cottage and love nest." He slips into the bathroom and gathers his shaving stuff. Realizing he has dreams like I do, I pick up a black knit shirt and inhale his scent.

Seeing my action, he says, "They're clean."

I tell him, "I know. They have your scent."

He closes and picks up the suitcase saying, "Yes, you leave your scent all over my furniture after you've been here. It's maddening." I reach over, pick up the gun and hold it out. He raises an eyebrow before he takes it. Setting the case down, he brings out a slimmer black leather case and places it beside the larger case. The pistol goes into the small of his back.

I tell him, "It doesn't bother me." In my mind, I'm wondering if he'll kill Dennis or Jaycee because of what I told him. I'm also wondering if I secretly want him to do just that. We walk out to the car.

He says, "Let's take your Jeep." I hand him the keys.

He softly says, "Just like that."

With a smile, I tell him, "Yup."

The ride to Devin's is short and silent. I have butterflies in my stomach. When we arrive, Blake pulls me into his arms for a kiss as the back porch light comes on.

Devin asks, "You're home early, little sis. Hello Blake. Problems?" as we walk with our arms around each other up the porch steps.

Blake says, "None whatsoever, unless you make one." with his old teasing tone. Devin's eyebrows go up. He steps back from the door to gesture to come inside.

I ask Blake, "Should I pack?"

He says, "Yes. Devin or should I say, Mr . . . . Blackwood, I need to talk to you." At Blake's words, Devin's face lights up and he says, "All right!" before grabbing Blake's arm and pumping away.

I duck past and head upstairs. I grab a large suitcase and begin packing. On impulse, I pack for Vegas as well. Earlier I watched Blake place his tux in a garment bag and into the larger case. I'll have to purchase a white dress. For a few moments, I'm upset because I forgot mothers wedding gown. Then I realize we're going there first. Blake appears behind me and lifts the closed case from the bed.

He asks, "Do you have a white dress?"

I tell him, "My mother's is in the attic at home. I'd like to wear it if it fits. It belongs to me and was our great grandmothers. It's very simple and beautiful." I tip my head and wait for his response.

With a smile he says, "I can't wait to see you in it.". Devin appears in the doorway to grab me and give me a tight hug.

Devin says, "Congrats little sis. You were right. A big Texan has already taken you away from me. Lucky for me, Cook's here."

Blake says, "I'll take this to the Jeep to give you two a couple minutes alone." Devin says, "Thanks man."

I start with, "Before you say anything, I told him what happened in Virginia and I'm not pregnant." Devin loudly laughs and hugs me again.

Devon says, "Read my mind, little sis. I knew you had the hots for him. He must be one hellova man to resist your little pointy charms." I look down and blush.

I exclaim, "Oh God, I forgot I had this on." I'm still wearing Blake's shirt.

Devin says, "Well, I was curious when you arrived in a man's tee shirt." With a slow smile, he continues, "I'll bet that would make a nice impression on Father."

I shake my head and tell him, "We're checking into a hotel. I refuse to sleep under that roof. Blake wants me only as his wife so I'd be alone and defenseless. Secretly, I don't want to see my old room.—Ever again!" My voice ends up being quite shrill.

Nodding in agreement, Devin says, "Get changed, I'll keep old Blake company. Be happy little sis, you've earned it." He's gone. I dig out a nice blouse, bra and jacket. While slipping into dressier shoes, I decide on nicer slacks but end up with an entire new outfit. I dash into the back bedroom to get great grandmothers ring on its delicate chain. My mother and her mother wore it around their necks when they wed. I want to keep with tradition. Both men rise as I step into the family room.

With a smile and slight bow Blake says, "Whoa, it was worth the wait."

Devin grins and says, "Did you get the ring?" I nod and turn to show Blake.

I explain, "This was my great grandmothers. I'm supposed to wear it around my neck when I marry my true love." Blake reaches out to touch it.

While examining it, he says, "Beautiful. Just like you are." Devin shakes his hand and kisses me before we walk out to the car.

Bending at Blake's window Devin asks, "Should I call Frank?"

In a slightly flat tone Blake replies, "No. We'll let it be a surprise." This raises Devin's eyebrow but he remains silent. He waves as we back into the turn around and head out the driveway. Watching the road Blake says, "My pilot should be at the air field by the time we arrive. You need gas, any preferences?"

I shake my head saying, "What ever you want—I'm easy."

Chuckling, he says, "I always thought that especially the way you mold yourself to me when I kiss you."

I smugly tell him, "I like your kisses." This makes him laugh. I also like his laugh. He's far too serious most of the time but now I know why. The pilot is gassed and ready for take off. My Jeep is loaded inside and we're settled in the lounge area.

When we're airborne, I turn and say, "Can we please stay at a hotel? I can't bear the thought of going upstairs." He nods and smiles.

Blake quickly agrees with, "Of course. I hadn't planned on staying at your fathers. Devin told me the layout of the place and how few bedrooms there are. We'll have connecting suites so I can keep you safe." He brings my hand to his lips and glances up across my knuckles. I relax and sigh.

Blake continues, "I asked Devin not to call your father. I don't like to be expected anywhere. It's an old habit but one which has kept me alive."

With relief, I say, "That's good. He'd tell Eleanor and heaven knows what she'd plan to do to us."

With a smile at my words, he says, "No one will do anything if it's within my power to stop. I intend to be fully armed and alert while we're there. I'm warning you ahead of time so you won't be upset by my detached attitude." He slides his arm around behind.

I lean back and with a smile say, "Thank you. I understand." I lean close to whisper, "Tigerman."

His mouth drops open, Blake gasps and says, "You shouldn't call me that. I like it from your lips but that was my code name."

Shocked at my stupidity, I say, "I'm sorry. I should have realized that. God, I hope my careless remarks won't get you hurt or killed . . ." My face is taunt and pale.

He touches me lightly saying, "Don't go there. You don't have a reason to worry. As long as we treat each remark as a chance coincidence, so will everyone else. Hiding in plain sight has always worked. You should have seen some of my disguises." He softly smiles before he whispers, "Perhaps, I'll don one for you sometime." Now there's that teasing mischievous tone and facial expression I'm so familiar and in love with. I touch his lips and he quickly kisses me.

We're in Virginia far too soon. I feel more comfortable realizing my Jeep has Texas plates and with Blake driving, is less recognizable. I'm surprised at the Jefferson Hotel to see the Jeep now has different Texas plates. I glance up at Blake.

"I'll explain." He says. We're rapidly checked in and left in our second floor suite. This is an old elegant five star diamond rated hotel.

Once our suite door is closed, Blake turns and says, "I have my own Texas plates and phony registration for your Jeep. It's amazing what you can do with a good computer and printer." He's watching my expressions.

With a soft smile, I tell him, "Obviously."

When I glance around the large room, I'm surprised at only one king sized bed. "Sofa opens into a bed." He says with a slow sensual smile.

Shaking my head, I tell him, "We sleep together, then I'll feel safer."

He comes over to take me into his arms and says, "You will not be safe in my bed." I throw my head back and arch my hips against him saying, "Good! Because I can't wait to start my role as Mrs. Blake Dailey." He reaches down to cup my buttocks and pull me up against his throbbing groin.

Blake teases, "We could practice . . . but only after I've spoken with your father." I sigh as he releases me. The man has unbelievable control over his body. He does these deep breathing exercises and stretches while I'm hanging up things.

Removing white sweats from his case, he says, "It's after 1 a.m. We should go to bed, darling."

When I tell him, "I'm going to pack our things together before we leave." He shrugs. When I turn back, he's naked and pulling the sweat pants up over his very male body parts.

I strip completely and heart pounding in my chest, walk naked to the suitcase. He grabs and tosses me on the bed, throwing my nightgown on top almost simultaneously. The man is quick.

He teases, "Cover up, woman or tomorrow you'll limp into your father's house and he won't have any trouble realizing what we've been doing." Then he walks to the other side of the bed and slides inside. I slip into the gown and the bed. He pulls me into the center and his arms. After planting soft kisses on my face and shoulder, he reaches back and turns out the lights.

I slept very soundly. When I wake in the morning, I lay with my eyes closed for a few minutes. I feel the soft texture of his well-washed sweat top under my cheek. My right hand is up under the top and curled in what feels like a very thick coarse mat of chest hair. My right leg is across his right thigh and my knee is pressed into his groin. I take a deep breath of his masculine scent as his chest rumbles with laughter under my ear.

He tells me, "I know you're awake, open those pretty brown eyes and remove your virgin knee."

I quickly comply and ask, "Am I hurting you?"

He dryly replies, "Ardently. I wanted to reverse our positions but also wanted to enjoy watching you sleep. You have this little smile on the corners of your mouth and your eyelashes and lids flutter like crazy sometimes." He rolls to his side and then sits up. I get up and rush around the bed to touch his face.

Rearing his head back from my touch, he asks, "What are you doing?".

I tell him, "I've never seen you before you shave. I wanted to touch your beard." He looks at me like I'm crazy and chuckles before going into the bathroom. I start to follow then stop as he lifts the seat and turning smiles.

Mischievously, he asks. "Want to watch?" I blush and his eyes widen before he says, "A blusher. I'm going to have a blushing bride." My hand goes to my throat and I turn away just before I hear the water sounds. I guess he really had to go. He's shaving when I look in the bathroom again.

I tell him, "I have to go." He shrugs and gestures at the now down lid. I chew my lower lip before taking a deep breath, entering the bathroom and lifting my gown, sit and go. I jump at his loud laugh.

He asks, "Another first?" I feel another blush creep up my neck to my face before I nod. I let my head drop and my hair falls like a wall beside my face. When I glance over, I'm alone. By the time I wash up, he's practically dressed. A glance at the clock says it's after 10.

While clipping a holster to his belt, he says, "I've ordered a light breakfast from room service." He removes an ugly black 9 mm pistol from the slender leather case and inserts the clip before placing it in the holster. I watch as he removes a black cylinder that I suddenly realize is a silencer and places it in his jacket pocket.

I volunteer, "I could put that in my purse." He smiles but shakes his head. I say, "Spare clip?" and he smiles widely.

Blake calmly says, "I don't plan on using all 11 shots but thanks anyway. Even counting your father, it's only 5 people."

I realize he's joking so I say, "Well, they have servants. Since many of the old ones left, I don't know how many. At least 6 or 8, you'll run short."

He comes close to divulge, "I have a spare 9 mm. You could put it in your purse and be my back up." I think he's surprised at my answer.

I tell him, "OK." He shrugs and removes the second gun from the case and inserts the clip.

Then he asks. "Can you handle a gun?"

I proudly tell him, "Yes. Father insisted that I learn to handle a pistol, rifle, sword and knife just like the boys. He was pleased that I wasn't timid towards weapons and I am actually a crack shot. I even went so far as to become proficient in bow and crossbow."

When Blake says, "You would do anything to increase his admiration of you?" He deftly hit the nail on the head.

I admit, "Yes. I think I was trying to show him I was as good as any male."

Cupping my chin he asks, "How'd you make out?".

Sadly I tell him, "No penis—no equality." Several old hurts float to the surface. Blake's face scoops down and kisses my sadness away.

After raising his head, he asks, "Did I chase those bad old hurts away?"

Slightly breathless I answer, "Yes." Room service knocks. Blake takes the tray at the door and tips the man.

Turning to face me he says, "If at all possible, never let them inside the room. You compromise your safely." I nod and add that to my list of things to remember to keep us both alive. I have a feeling I will be learning a lot of things from this man and not all of them pleasant. Our breakfast is fresh fruit, toast, tea and flaky croissants. We sit for a while. I tell him father's habits from when I lived with him. Blake says we'll try and arrive just after lunch. Everyone should be mellow from eating.

I watch the clock with dread. Finally at 1:45, Blake rises and taking my hand pulls me from the chair saying, "Time to face your father. Actually, you should draw some comfort from the knowledge that I'm terrified of asking for your hand. I'm not sure he'll remember me." I shake my head and touch his face.

I tell him, "He'll remember Frank Dailey's oldest son. He'll be pleased that I've selected a first-born Irishman's son. Trust me." In hardly any time at all, we're formally dressed and in the Jeep heading south through Petersburg.

Blake almost drives past the driveway. He says, "You'll have to direct me."

And with a start I tell him, "Turn left, at the two white posts." He applies the brakes very firmly and smiles.

I quickly tell him, "Sorry." He pulls around the driveway loop and stops at the front door. Taking a deep breath, he climbs from the Jeep and comes around for my door.

Taking my hand, he says, "Come on, princess." While gently tugging me from the Jeep. With a firm arm under my elbow, we walk up the seven steps to the porch and across to the red front door. Blake boldly punches the doorbell.

The door is opened by a mean looking man about mid 50's who coldly asks, "What do you want?"

When Blake says, "This is Katherine Blackwood. We would like to see her father, Dillon Blackwood." Blake's voice is ice filled and his face is hard set. I realize he knows this man and visa versa. The man shuts the door in our faces. I gasp and my eyes widen in shock. That is totally against southern hospitality. We should have at least been asked into the foyer. I can hear muffled voices through the door and obviously Blake is able to understand whatever they're saying. I watch a multitude of emotions flow across his face before it becomes passive and the door opens to reveal an old man—my father! I sway against Blake who slides his arm around my waist.

Suddenly his face lights up and reaching towards me, he says, "Katherine! You've returned home to me!" I step back away from him.

I harshly tell him, "Never!"

Blake reaches his hand towards my father and says, "Mr. Blackwood, Blake Dailey. May we come in?" At the sound of Blake's voice, my father turns slowly to look at him. I realize that he didn't even notice Blake before he spoke.

Father says, "Of course, please forgive this old man's lack of manners. I apologize for my manservant leaving you on the front porch. That simply wasn't done in my time." My God, he's talking like he's 90 years old. As I study his face, he appears 90 years old.

As we follow him into the formal living room on the right, he asks, "You're Franks' boy?" I get quite a jolt at the sight of this totally redone room. It's still a pleasant room but with all the heavy antique furniture, definitely formal. Father gestures at a Chippendale piece which must have cost a mint. Blake and I sit. Father slowly sits in the armchair opposite to study first me, then Blake.

After a few moments, he says, "How is Frank? Not ill, I trust." There's concern in his eyes and sadness when he looks my way.

Blake answers, "No, sir. My father is in the best of health. The reason for our visit is to ask for Katherine's hand in marriage." My father's face goes white and then he looks strangely calm.

Father rises, saying, "Yes. If you would please accompany me to my study upstairs, we can speak in private." Without a backward glance or giving Blake the opportunity to answer, he strides from the room. Blake leans towards me and opens my purse. He reaches inside, engages the slide and puts my hand on the pistol.

In a whisper, he tells me, "Stay right here. Let no one take you anywhere else. Do not be afraid or ashamed to pull the pistol from your purse. Let no one get close to you. This settee is against the wall and there is only one door. Watch it. Stay put." He kisses my forehead and strides after father.

"She's fine. Don't dilly dally boy." Fathers' voice drifts back. I grip the pistol and watch the door. Before too long, Eleanor glides in and sits in the chair father just vacated.

Gazing down her nose at me, haughtily she says, "So what do we owe the honor of this visit? Did you run out of money? Do you expect to move back home?" I turn slightly to watch the doorway and her.

I calmly tell her, "I have plenty of money and need nothing from here except my mother's wedding dress from the attic. I will never move back here."

She smiles slyly and leans forward to ask, "Pregnant?"

Leaning towards her, I sharply tell her, "No, I'm still a virgin. No thanks to your bastard son trying to rape me." I'm as surprised as she by the venom in my voice.

She straightens and haughtily says, "I cleaned out the attic months ago, all your precious mother's stuff was sold or destroyed." She's pleased at the tears that form in my eyes before I blink them away.

Quickly recovering I tell her, "Well, then I shall have a new one of my very own." I watch as Jaycee and Harold walk into the room. Jaycee leers and licks her lips as Harold strides through the room to the far window. As he passes behind his mother, he grabs his groin luridly. I tighten my grip on the pistol and lean back. I don't think I'll have any problems shooting any of them.

I sigh with relief as I hear Blake's raised voice from the hall as he says, "Katherine has been left alone far too long. Our conversing is done." Blake stops at the doorway, steps inside and immediately to the left.

He says in a tight voice, "Rise and walk towards me." I do.

Harold must have moved because Blake's eyes shift behind me to tell him, "Stay by the window buddy." With two large steps I'm near enough to Blake to remove the pistol and turn.

Harold puts his hands up and steps back saying, "Oh, mother, she has a nasty gun." I hear fathers gasp from the doorway before I watch him step into the room.

From behind me, Blake growls, "Don't touch her.".

My father harshly says, "I'm her father. You, sir are not half the man your father is."

Blake pulls me back against him saying, "Move into the room sir." My father quickly complies. Blake continues, "We're leaving and with or without your precious blessing, I'm marrying her. At least with me, she'll never have to fear being beaten or physically abused in way or manner. As for her dowry, I'll send you a quarter of a million dollars. For the way you beat her, I should send you to jail."

Blake turns and draws his gun quickly saying, "Step where I can see you or I'll kill you through the wall, Weasel." I keep my back to Blakes' and point the gun at Harold when he takes a step my way.

Blake says, "Put your gun down." I hear the sharp sound of the gun on the woodwork. Blake continues, "Good. Now kick it into the dining room over there. Good. You still take directions well. Walk in here and stand over there next to your master."

When he enters my line of vision, the man absolutely emanates hatred as he says, "You're dead, Tigerman. You don't got it any more. This pussy is going to be your death warrant. I never heard you warning anyone before."

The sound of the pistol is loud and a hole appears in the man's forehead as Eleanor screams. Father rushes to her side. Blake grabs me around the waist and strides towards the door. Dennis rushes forward into the foyer until Blake levels his gun at him. A quick shot to the knee puts Dennis on the floor. Eleanor's screams follow us all the way down the front steps. I run around the front of the Jeep and crawl across the driver's side. Blake chuckles but follows closely. He has the Jeep in gear and headed down the driveway before I'm buckled.

He's on the cell phone to the pilot as we head north to Richmond. With a frown, he says, "Damn, I should have put our stuff in the Jeep. That was stupid." I realize he can't leave the black leather case.

"I'll pack, you check out." I tell him. At the hotel, Blake strides across the lobby towards the front desk. I take the key and head for our suite. I'm packed and quickly double checking as the porter arrives for our bags.

In the lobby, I'm greeted with the sight of Blake in handcuffs standing beside a State trooper. I scream and run towards him but the trooper catches me before I reach him.

He roughly growls at my ear, "He's under arrest for murder."

I frantically try to explain, "The man had a gun! He threatened us. Blake was protecting me." The trooper is stern looking and retains his steel grip on my arm.

The trooper says, "Mr. Blackwood called and said this man went wild and started shooting people in his home. Your step brother was shot and the butler was killed." I look at Blake.

Blake's tone is calm but firm as he says, "Just be quiet, Katie girl. I have people who'll handle things. I'm entitled to a phone call. Sir, please allow my fiancée to stay here at the hotel until I'm released."

The trooper shakes his head saying, "She's an accomplice. I have a female officer coming to arrest and escort her to jail." I sway slightly at his words and then stiffen my back and lower lip.

I ask him, "Does my father know this?"

The trooper continues, "Your father is not an officer of the law. Your step mother mentioned you pulled a weapon from your purse." Then he abruptly grabs my purse and quickly removes the pistol saying, "This one matches her description." For an instant, pure hatred flows over Blake's face before he forces his calm one back.

As two troopers escort him out, Blake says, "Make your one call to Devin Blackwood in Dallas, Texas."

I watch as a large black female police officer in the familiar blue uniform strides into the lobby. I'm taken outside by the State trooper and then checked for additional weapons by the female. I stiffen and try to block the recurring images of Jaycees hands. My hands are cuffed behind me, like Blake's and I'm put the in patrol car. The ride to the station is quick. Inside, I search for any sight of Blake but the officer seems to rush me through the booking procedures. I've all ready been read my rights. Here, I'm finger printed, photographed and booked before being allowed my one phone call. They take my purse, belt and jewelry.

Devin answers on the first ring. He quickly asks, "Katie girl, are you OK?"

I tell him, "Yes. I've been arrested and so has Blake. Father and Eleanor are behind this. Please. Help us." I'm softly crying in spite of trying very hard not to.

Trying to reassure me Devin says, "It's being taken care of. I've been making calls since the man at the hotel called. Blake has a contact in the hotel. Don't worry. Blake seems to have some powerful friends. I've been told to sit tight." He sounds like he's nailed to the wall. There's a lot of pain as well as frustration in his voice.

"Then I'll be all right." I tell him calmly, "Blake loves me and he promised to keep me safe."

As she hangs up the phone, the officer says, "Time's up." She roughly grabs my arm. I find myself alone in a holding cell. About 30 minutes later, another female officer comes and escorts me to an interrogation room where I'm told that my lawyer is waiting.

The man in the room says, "Miss Blackwood, please have a seat." I do and he continues, "Now, tell me exactly what happened from the moment you and Mr. Dailey entered your father's property." He sits across from me and starts a small recorder. I frown but tell him exactly what happened. I give him facts, nothing else. He's thin, dressed in a tan suit and has a tough looking face. His accent reveals he's not a Virginia native. I don't trust him. His dirty blonde hair is combed across his bald spot and he needs a shave. I gather the over powering aftershave is to hide the booze smell.

He suddenly prompts, "Mr. Dailey gave you the pistol for your purse." I frown and at my refusing to answer he harshly says, "Miss Blackwood, I'm your attorney. You need to be straight forward with me."

I tell him, "I'm not saying anything that might incriminate Blake." I clamp my mouth shut and clasp my hands still in their handcuffs tightly on the table in front of me.

Picking up the recorder, the man says, "I'm trying to see if I can get you out on bail. I'll be right back." Then he leaves. I'm very uneasy. Before he returns, a male and female officer arrive and motion to come with them.

I tell them, "My lawyer said he'd be right back."

The woman yanks me up from the chair saying, "There's been an unforeseen problem. We're transferring you to the state correctional facility until your hearing." This seems like an unheard of procedure but I'm alone and defenseless. I'm worried about Blake. The female officer is very rough with her handling of me. Finally I try and go alone with her peacefully. She still practically jerks my arm from its shoulder socket. At the unmarked police car, once the back door is opened, she slams my head into the roof of the car and I black out.

I don't know how long I'm unconscious. My vision takes a few minutes to clear. I'm now cuffed on my back on a metal cot. A folded blanket placed underneath does little to soften the metal springs and pieces of the bed frame. My right arm is cuffed to the top of the bed. My ankles are taped together. I sigh in relief when I realize that eliminates rape. I'm in a small metal shed, judging from the rippled pattern punctuating the walls. There are various metal shovels, chains, and tools hanging and standing near the walls. It's not a very large shed. There's one window and sunlight is streaming in swimming with particles of dust.

I lay still, listening but there are only bird and running water sounds. I'm afraid to yell in case the closest person is my captor. Time drifts slowly past, I judge the passing hours by the changing of the sunlight. Finally, the sun goes down and it begins to rain. It's October and I'm cold. The temperature in the metal shed rapidly drops as the night progresses and the rain gets harder and continues. By working myself around, I'm able to get the tape from my ankles and sit up. Feeling slowly around, my hand encounters a cylinder which a brief examination reveals is a flashlight. Engaging the switch, I'm glad it lights. Beside me, on a small table is a plastic bottle of water, a box of tissues, a package of peanut butter crackers and a urinal.

I'm upset and scared but tell myself Blake will find me. At the foot of the bed is another blanket which I gladly pull up over myself. I take a drink of the water and from the taste, realize it has something in it. I'm so thirsty that I drink anyway. When the calm feeling starts I realize the water will make me sleep. When I open my eyes, it's dark and still raining heavily. The noise of the rain on the metal roof is almost maddening in its constant ear deafening pounding. When I can't take anymore, I drink more of the water and sleep.

Someone was here while I slept because they emptied the urinal and brought a tin containing two sandwiches. They're peanut butter and jelly and slightly soggy but good. It's still raining and very damp in this shed. I notice that a second heavier blanket has been left. I wish I wore a watch so I'd have some idea of the time. With the rain, it's so dark I can't tell if it's day or night. After a while, I'm forced to drink more of the water which puts me to sleep again. I've always had a very sensitive reaction to any kind of medication so I'm sure I'm sleeping for fairly long periods of time. When I wake this time, it's quiet and no longer raining. The bad news is, when I put my feet over the side of the bed, there's almost a foot of water in the shed. I quickly pull my feet back onto the cot and scream in terror.

After screaming a couple of times, I simply sit and cry. I get the flashlight and try to see if the water is rising rapidly. It doesn't appear to be but with all the rain, if I'm in a low area . . . that thought makes me tremble in fear. Reaching up for a hair pin, I realize someone has cut my hair off at my shoulders. This starts me crying again.

I tell myself out loud, "It'll grow back silly girl." Now I'm mad because I was going to try and use the pin to open the cuffs like they do on TV and in the movies. A brief search reveals that there aren't any pins in the bed around or under me. Trying to calmly think of another alternative, I scream when the door to the shed slushes open.

"Ssshhh . . ." The low voice is immediately recognizable. I clamp my hand over my mouth to keep from calling Blake's name. He moves quickly to the cot and has the cuff open with a little pick from his belt in an instant.

He whispers, "Shoes?"

I softly tell him, "Yes."

Tugging gently on my arm, he says, "Come." I stand into the cold and now higher water.

At the door, he says, "Watch." I realize the ground drops sharply downward. He guides my hand to his belt and begins walking away. I grab tight and struggle to keep my footing. We wade through the icy cold water almost to my breasts before beginning to climb.

As we begin to ascend, Blake grabs my arm to keep me from falling. Once we're out of the water, we walk along a sharply upsweeping narrow path. Blake is almost invisible in his black outfit and mask. He stops at a heavy rope and opening a black bag removes a black jumpsuit.

He says, "Strip. Put this on." I quickly comply with his help. The jumpsuit is fleece lined, a little large and warm. He slips sneakers on my feet and places me into a harness.

Into my hair, he asks, "Climber?" I shake my head.

He says, "OK. We'll go together." I watch him slip into the gear hanging low on the rope. Turning me to face him, he clips us together saying, "Legs around my waist, hold on tight." As he lifts me, I comply and sigh. He plants a soft kiss on my forehead. I feel his muscles tense under my hands as he begins the ascent.

The climb seems to take forever and his breathing finally gets ragged towards the top. He stops and hangs briefly, calming his breathing. He whispers, "Quiet." I give him a hug in response.

He says, "Wait." Then he unhooks and struggles over the crest first. I turn to the cliff face and as he pulls, walk up to try to help.

Releasing my harness, he says, "Good girl." He quickly gathers everything into the bag which is hanging on the end of the rope. Slinging the bag over his shoulder and taking my arm, we walk silently through some trees along a rough path. He opens the door to my Jeep. I realize the interior light is out. He softly closes the door and sprints to the driver seat.

I'm more terrified as he drives along without headlights than I have been all evening. I stifle a scream at a movement sound from the back but Blake squeezes my thigh. I look over and he's smiling. I'm surprised again when the dirt road takes us onto a gravel road and then Rt460. Blake turns east towards Petersburg. He relaxes and pulls on the headlights.

"Are you all right?" He asks.

"Yes. I knew you'd come for me." As I speak there are frantic movements and noises from the back. Blake pulls to the side of the road.

Blake says, "Let's get him into the back seat." Then he opens the hatch and lifts a blanket. Underneath, the moonlight reveals my father bound and gagged. Blake deftly removes the tape. My father chokes and inhales to speak.

While he is cutting the ropes binding my fathers' wrists and helping him to set up Blake says in a low voice, "Keep your mouth shut old man. This is your fault. Did you really think someone was holding Katie for ransom?"

Blake hands him some bottled water saying, "Drink this." My father quickly drinks and looks my way.

He asks me, "You weren't harmed?" I shake my head because I don't trust myself to speak. My face feels tight with anger.

Father continues while watching Blake, "They called and wanted 3 million dollars. Or was that a trick to get you out of jail?"

Blake grinds his teeth and takes a calming breath before responding to fathers' cold words with, "No. I was already free by then. My people had me released shortly before Katie's disappearance was discovered. When I heard she was missing, my first impulse was to hunt you down and kill you with my bare hands. You stupid old fool! She would have drowned if I hadn't gotten her out of that quarry when I did. If I hadn't stopped you, you'd be dead now. That was all a setup to kill you. Get in the back seat." Blake quickly flips the back seat open and gestures at father. I watch my very pale and old father climb stiffly into the back seat before Blake slams the door. He quickly pulls me into his arms and kisses me.

Blake starts, "I'm so sorry that my carelessness put you through all this." I touch his lips to silence him.

I whisper, "No. We'll just be three times as cautious in the future. I love you." He guides me into the front seat. We're soon headed east again. No one speaks for the longest time.

Blake finally says, "Tell me everything that happened from the moment we were separated." It takes me a while, but I carefully recount every thing I said, saw and endured. Blake listens, hands clenched on the steering wheel. A couple of times, I thought he would snap the wheel right off the column. When I'm finished, he reaches across to squeeze my hand.

He glances to the back and says, "I killed a college to save your hide, old man. You owe me a big one—no several big ones. You get yourself a good body guard when you get home, 'cause somebody wants you dead." I gasp at Blake's words. My father only makes a sound of disbelief.

My father coldly says, "If you killed, it was for your own satisfaction. You're so hot for my daughter you can't stand the thought of anyone else touching or having her." Now some of my old father's steel is returning to his voice. His ordeal is over and his confidence is rapidly returning.

Blake's hard words are spoken through partially clamped teeth. "I'm in love with your daughter. If it were lust, I would have taken her body weeks ago. She's going to be my wife, not a sperm receptacle." My father gasps.

Father says, "Katherine, I will not allow you to associate with this killer. I'll speak with Frank and Devin. This relationship will not end in any union." We're at the turn off for father's place. Once he's on the driveway, Blake stops and turns to father.

Blake roughly tells Father, "Get out."

Father quickly fires back, "Not without my daughter. Why don't you come to the house and face your own father! He knows you for what you really are now!" Father says and Blake narrows his eyes.

Blake calmly says, "If this is a trap, you die first." putting the Jeep back in gear before slowly continuing on up the driveway.

My father retorts, "Yes, killing is your forte." before falling silent. The front of the house is a blaze of lights. Devin's big white pickup sits framed in the lights at the foot of the stairs. As the Jeep stops, the front door opens. Frank, Kyle and Devin step quickly outside into the lights. Devin is down the stairs first to pull my door open and haul me into his arms.

He says, "Thank God you're all right."

Blake says, "I kept my part of the bargain." Frank strides around the front of the Jeep as Blake climbs out. For an instant, I thought he would throw his arms around him, glad he was alive. I'm as shocked as Blake when Frank halls his fist back and hits Blake in the face as hard as he can. Caught unawares, Blake goes quickly down. I scream and try to run to him.

Devin's arms tighten and he says, "No. He's a cold-blooded killer. His father owed that to him." I scream into Devins' face before he clutches me to his chest.

Frank rages, "All those years, I thought you were doing something respectable." Blake holding his hand to his mouth, climbs to his feet as Frank continues, "Now, you come here to kill my best friend. You bastard! You're no son of mine! My son died ten years ago. Get your things off my property and get out of my sight." Kyle stands trembling at the foot of the stairs. He's obviously torn between his love for his father and his feelings for his older brother.

Kyle finally manages to choke out, "Jesus, Blake." I can barely hear his words although we're standing close to him. I turn back and now Blake's standing, fists protectively raised.

Blake says, "I didn't come here to kill Dillon. I came here to save his worthless hide. You saw the evidence of the beating he gave Katherine!" Frank takes another swing at Blake who easily dances back out of reach.

Blake turns and says, "Go with Devin."

When Devin won't release me in spite of my fierce struggling, I bring my knee up into his groin. Surprised, Devin releases me to grab himself in pain. I violently push father backwards when he tries to prevent me from running around to Blake's arms.

Blake pulls me back from his father's grasp and whispers. "Be ready."

Franks hands are on my arms. Devin is coming up behind Blake.

"Go." I tell Blake as I throw myself backwards against a surprised Frank. Blake slips quickly into the Jeep and drives out the driveway.

My father says, "Come inside." and tell him, "No. Devin, take me back to Texas."

Devin slowly shakes his head saying, "First, we need to talk to you. There are things about Blake you need to know." A newly born instinct tells me to act shocked and go timidly home with Devin and then wait for Blake. I allow Devin to lead me into the house.

Seated in the living room, father tells a very enraged Eleanor leave us alone to talk and shuts the door in her face. He strides to the same armchair and sits. Devin pulls me down onto the settee beside him. Kyle stands in the far corner, his face unreadable. Frank sits heavily into the other armchair and nods at father.

Father says, "First off, you were kidnapped and held for ransom. I received a call from Frank after Kyle met one of Blake's old business associates. The man wanted to know if Blake took a very profitable hit which he had turned down. Evidently this man was asked to kill Dillon Blackwood in Virginia. Kyle recognized my name and immediately told his father. Thank goodness, they called Devin. From this, we assumed since Blake hustled you up here that he planned on killing me. The kidnappers sent me a package containing your hair. Then they called and said I'd be bringing the money to a place they would designate within 48 hours. Secondly, Blake easily got himself released from jail. Then he boldly slipped into my home to threaten me and then strike a bargain for your safe return. Once the kidnappers called, he would rescue you while I made the drop. In exchange I was to have the charges dropped against him and you. I pulled some strings to get the charges dropped. When I went to leave the money, he grabbed me and threw me into the Jeep. I thought he was going to kill you. Katherine, the man is paid to kill innocent people. He safely brought you back so I'll keep my part of the bargain and let him escape." Father sighs and leans back against the chair looking over at Frank.

Frank says, "Dillon, you don't worry about a thing. Devin and I will keep Katherine safe in Texas. She will refuse to stay here with you. Katherine, you'll be safe with us. I won't let that killer anywhere near you." as he leans towards me. I smile weakly. I have such a miserable headache. I ache for Blake's arms around me.

Turning to my brother, I say, "Devin, please, take me home. I'm so dirty, tired and heart sick." I lean back against him.

Devin says, "Of course, little sis. I'm so sorry Blake isn't what he seemed. A good man will come along and rescue you. Frank, let's get her to the Jet and home. Father, please be careful." Devin stands and shakes his hand. My insides are churning. Both of my fists are tightly clenched. I let father hug me before we walk out to the truck. Devin drives. Frank and Kyle sit silently in the back seat. I lean my head back and refuse to look at or speak to anyone. It's almost morning by the time we pull up in front Devin's main door. I dash from the truck, inside and upstairs. I don't hear Franks truck leave.

I'm in the shower when Devin opens the bathroom door and asks, "Katherine, are you all right?"

I sharply tell him, "I'm fine. I'm going to bed. Please, just leave me alone to sort things out." I hear the door close and cry into my hands. I take several aspirin and crawl into bed. After 10 hours of sleep, I'm refreshed. However, I'm very disheartened by the sight of my butchered hair. Setting my lips firmly and getting a grip on my emotions, I quickly pack my duffel bag with jeans, practical tops and shoes. I pack nothing but the bare necessities. I insert all my cash and great grandmothers ring. Devin quickly strides from the stables as I walk from the house towards the old garage to get the Mustang.

He says, "Good morning. Where are you off to?" I'm enraged at his condescending tone.

I tell him, "To town. My purse and things were taken so I haven't any money. I need to report my cards stolen." He shakes his head.

He says, "I have your stuff. The police returned it to father. I'll get it." He turns me back towards the house.

I tiredly ask him, "Am I a prisoner?"

He frowns gazing down into my face. "No. Why would you ask that? Do you believe I would take father's side? More importantly, do you think I would ruin your chance at true love? Katie, I've seen how you look at Blake. You knew about his past—didn't you?" I hesitate, looking intently into his face. Is this a trap—a ploy?

I decide against lying and tell him, "Yes. I knew. I love him. So, what happens now?" There is only love and genuine caring in Devin's dark brown eyes.

Devin says, "You're a big girl. You make your own decisions. I still remember what your back looked like and what those beasts were planning on doing in your own bedroom. I'm not sure why Frank reacted so violently towards Blake. Something must have happened between them before you left . . ."

He stops talking and again stares intently into my face before he asks, "Something you're fully aware of, I take it?" I nod.

I explain, "Frank and Blake fought earlier that evening. It was over me. Frank's in love with me." I look up and watch the realization dawn on Devin's face.

Devin says, "Yes, that would explain a lot of his facial expressions and actions around you. Jealousy is a vicious monster and a tough emotion to control. I wonder how father would feel knowing that his best friend is lusting after his daughter?" He's deep in thought. Inside the house Devin strides through to the sunroom. Laying in plain view on his desk is a familiar manila envelope. As he picks it up, I shudder. His eyes sadden and he opens it and removes my things.

He says, "Here . . ." holding my things out for me to take and then dropping the empty envelope into the trashcan. I drop everything to run into his arms.

I tell him, "I'm sorry I hurt you." He chuckles.

He says softly into my hair, "It didn't hurt that badly. I knew you wanted to run to him but didn't want father to see me let you." He bends and retrieves everything from the floor as I stand mutely over him.

Devin says, "When you and Blake run, promise to take your cell phone and let me call you. If that's not possible, just call and say you're happy and OK." He hugs me saying, "Tell Blake I still think the world of him." I nod and hug him.

"He'll keep you safe. That's one thing I know for sure." Devin releases me and strides back towards the stables.

I head for the Mustang and town. I cash several large checks at three different bank locations and secure the cash in the duffel bag back at the house. After lunch, I ride Fermeau over to the cottage. It's deserted. I walk through the inside and all evidence of Blake is gone. Inside the closet, lying on my torn blouse is a single red rose. I pick both up and head back to Devin's. He will come. I know it as surely as if he had carved it on one of the walls.

For the next couple of days, I rest and pack and repack my bag. The next morning the phone rings. It's Frank.

He says, "Hey, Katie girl, how about taking pity on two single men and cooking us a good meal? Kyle has been so down in the mouth. I'm afraid he's going to make himself sick." I realize that this would have been quite a blow to Kyle. Suddenly I feel badly because of how selfish I have been lately.

I cheerfully ask, "Sure. What would you like?"

When he answers, "Anything you make and your face at the table, if you can manage both." Frank sounds more cheerful.

I tell him, "OK." Once he's hung up, I think I'll ride over. I can use that as an excuse not to stay too long. It's now early November. I grab a heavy jacket and leave a note for Devin. Fermeau is ready to run. We have a good ride across both properties. Frank comes out of his larger barn as I ride up.

He immediately says, "Good to see you, Katie girl."

Sliding down from Fermeau I tell him, "Please don't call me that. It's Blake's name for me." Frank looks abashed and nods in silent agreement.

He says, "Sorry. I guess you want to forget him." I just purse my lips and turn away. He lightly touches my arm and says, "I hope you can get Kyle to eat. He's off his feed and miserable." I nod.

"I'll do my best." is my reply.

In the kitchen are fresh pieces of meat cut like country style boneless ribs. I guess barbecue ribs are on the menu. I get them going before starting the thinner steaks for sandwiches. I fry green peppers, onions and garlic. The steaks go into the pan briefly and get topped with cheese on the large hoagie rolls. I make a large tossed salad and have everything ready as the men troop inside. Kyle's face brightens before he rushes to hug me.

He quickly asks, "Are you OK?"

I tell him, "I'm fine. Frank says you're not eating." He nods and looks into my face.

Kyle says, "It smells good in here." His stomach growls loudly.

Frank laughs saying, "She's working her magic already. Let's get washed up, boy." They clean up while I set the food on the table. Kyle eats a good portion of his hoagie but nowhere near as much as he would have three weeks ago. Frank's right, he looks like he's making himself sick. I'm saddened. Hurting Kyle was the last thing Blake intended. I wonder why Blake took up killing.

I make up my mind to ask him after we're married awhile. The men head back to work. I clean up the kitchen. I find a lot of laundry to wash and hang out while the ribs cook in the oven. When I bend over the open oven door to remove the heavy rib pan, I'm hit with such a wave of loneliness and aching for Blake that I'm crying without realizing it. I sit the pan on the hot mat. I'm startled when a tear hits my arm. I reach up and my face is wet. Using a nearby dish towel, I dry my face and close the oven door. "Soon." I quietly tell myself.

I have the clean clothes inside and away and the noodles all cooked and seasoned when Frank and Kyle come in for dinner. Kyle seems to eat more of the ribs and looks a little heartier. Once dinner is over, Kyle escapes to his room. Frank helps with the dishes.

Frank asks, "Thanks. He seems much better. Think I could impose on you for the next couple of days?" I nod while drying my hands.

I tell him, "I'm going to head home before it gets much darker." Frank walks with me and waits as a hand saddles Fermeau. I wave as I ride towards home. A glance back at the house reveals Kyle silhouetted in his bedroom window, watching. Over the next three days, I fix every one of Kyle's favorite dishes. By the weeks end, he's back eating like he used to. Friday, Frank insists that Kyle go into town with some of the boys like he used to. This leaves Frank and I alone for dinner. I'm very uneasy.

Frank says, "Katherine, there's something been on my mind. You'll probably think me an old fool but." then, drawing several deep breathes before continuing, "I'm in love with you. Will you marry me? I swear I'll make you happy. I'll wait to touch you until you say you're ready." He softly finishes. His eyes are full of love and hope. I shake my head.

I reply, "I can't marry you Frank. I'm in love with Blake." Rage fills his face before he turns away, his fists clenched at his sides.

When he says, "How can you love a man who kills people for money?" his tone is loud and hard.

I quickly retort, "How can you love a woman younger than your son?"

Frank says, "My son is Kyle. I have no other. Answer my question, Katherine." He turns back to my face.

I harshly reply, "It's always been Blake. It will only be BLAKE." He reaches to touch me. I hastily scramble back away.

Frank begins to plead, "Please, Katherine, I'll make you happy. You'll lack for nothing. I can give you children." I raise my hands towards him, palms facing him.

I raise my hands palms facing toward him to say angrily, "No. Just like my father, you don't hear my words. You don't hear my heart." He steps towards me. I turn and flee out the door. I hear his heavy footsteps close behind me. At my whistle, Fermeau leaps the fence and gallops towards me. Grabbing a handful of his silky mane, I'm up and onto his bare back in one smooth motion. He quickly cuts back towards home as I let him run full out. My last sight is of Frank, bent over trying to catch his breath at the first fence we went over.

During the next week, I refuse all of Franks calls. I tell Devin of his proposal and what he said. Devin sadly shakes his head and agrees I'm safer away from Frank until he calms down. I anxiously await Blake's arrival. I've started sleeping in newly purchased sweat suits. My bags and I are ready to go.

CHAPTER FOUR

BLAKE, VEGAS, AND MANILA, UTAH

I knew Blake would come in the middle of the night. He's unaware of Devin's feelings towards our being together. I sense he's in my room before he reaches out to softly touch me. I lift my left hand reaching out towards him. He chuckles and whips the covers off. Leaning close, he whispers, "Are you ready?"

Quickly getting to my feet, I tell him, "I'm past ready." Lifting my sweatshirt, I place his nearest hand on my breast.

He groans and then says, "No, we have to get out. Where's your bag?" His hand remains firmly cupped around a now tightened nipple and breast.

I softly tell him, "It's in the closet. I have to tell Devin goodbye. He wants us to be together."

He replies, "No. It might be a trap. I'm sorry. I can't trust anyone until you're mine. You can call him." I smile although in this semi dark room, he can't see it. The male hand is gone. I slip into my canvas shoes and pick up my jacket from the chair. I grab my purse and follow Blake downstairs and outside where two horses are tethered. Blake slings my duffel bag over his head and once I'm seated on the large gelding, swings up onto the stallion. He comes up beside me and caresses my face before spurring his mount forward. The gelding has little trouble keeping up with the stallion. Within 20 minutes, we stop part ways across at a private field where a large chopper is waiting. A man standing in front of a horse trailer takes our mounts and Blake's cash. No words are spoken and I follow Blake to the chopper.

Once I'm buckled and Blake's settled he makes an up motion with his thumb and the pilot nods. Within another 15 minutes we're at a private airfield and walking up shaky stairs into Blake's jet. Not a word is spoken until we're airborne.

Leaning towards me Blake says, "You're a pretty special young lady." And then he claims my lips.

Once my lips are free, I ask, "Why?"

Touching my hair and shaking his head he answers, "Any other woman would have had at least one question." I glance away.

Embarrassed, I tell him, "It looks pretty bad. I had a girl at a salon in Dallas trim it a little. She asked if I got mad at my hair. I told her someone did this to it."

He turns my face back to face him telling me, "The hair will grow back. I missed you so badly every second of every day and night. Were you all right?" I nod and turn to look into his eyes. I slowly recount again everything that happened during our separation.

When I'm finished, he smiles and says, "We're on our way to Vegas to get married. This is a short flight. We'll be in Vegas and married within four hours." He kisses my hand before I settle back into my seat.

Within minutes, the jet begins to drop before we touch down at the airport. A large black limo is waiting. Our bags are placed in its trunk. Blake and I climb inside. We are at the Stratosphere Hotel and Casino before my seat is warm beneath me. In spite of it being almost Thanksgiving, Vegas is warm and pleasant. Our spacious suite has a mini bar and wall safe. I watch Blake place his slender black case on the low table in the sitting area.

Blake says, "Now, we buy you a wedding dress." We change into jeans and comfortable tops and head to a nearby shopping mall. Within an hour I have found a beautiful short white evening dress. Blake waits patiently, the dress in its garment bag slung over his arm as my hair is washed, trimmed and placed in small curls carefully on the top of my head. Back at our suite, Blake showers first and shaves while I shower. He quickly dresses in his black tux and then helps me with my dress, small veil and grandmothers' ring.

He steps back and smiles broadly saying, "You're a beautiful bride. I'll have a photographer take pictures for Devin." He runs his hands down my bare shoulders and arms to clasp my hands. He glances at a nearby clock. "We have 10 minutes to get down to the chapel. This is the last chance for you to change your mind." I shake my head and he laughs. Taking my hand in his, we walk down to the front desk where a bouquet of white roses and carnations is waiting. Then we go over to the observation tower and our assigned wedding chapel. We sign the necessary papers and with the two witness's provided by the chapel are quickly joined as man and wife. Blake slowly lifts my veil and kisses my lips. The ready photographer takes several pictures. Blake and I head back to our suite.

Once I'm carried over the threshold, he sets me down and pulls me into his arms. My bouquet slips from my fingers to the floor at our feet. His lips and hands begin doing wicked things to my body. Everywhere he touches and strokes, little fires of passion start.

He huskily whispers, "Undress me." I gladly comply. His jacket, ascot, vest and shirt go to the floor. I open his belt and he steps from his shoes as I remove mine. My dress is strapless and very fitted. Once the zipper is opened, it slides from my breasts to the floor. I'm wearing tiny lace panties and grandmothers ring on its delicate chain, nothing else. With one smooth motion, he lifts me into his arms and places me on the bed. We become truly husband and wife.

While we are laying side by side, ask him "Remember the time in the barn when you slid your hands up under my tee shirt and then gasped and leapt off?"

He's silent, thinking a minute before he says, "Yes. That was the day I realized your breasts were budding and I shouldn't be sitting astride your slender hips anymore." He smiles and brings my teasing hands to his lips for a kiss.

I reply, "Well, that was the day I started wondering about that hard object you kept in your jeans that moved around some." He throws his head back and laughs. He rolls from the bed and goes into the bathroom. I hear the whirlpool start before he returns.

With a romantic sweeping bow he says, "My Lady, your bath awaits. A nice hot bath will soak some of the soreness out of those muscles. I'm sorry to say, but we're not staying. Too many people know we planned to wed. Therefore, this is the first place they'll descend upon. Once you're bathed and dressed, we're leaving for a safe place." I nod and kiss him before sliding into the warm swirling water. I smile and then he signals it's time to dry and dress. We nibble briefly on fresh fruit, warm bread rolls, pieces of cheese and meats before gathering our things. I hardly have the suitcase closed when the porter arrives for our bags. Blake has us quickly checked out. We're back in a limo and airborne again.

Once the jet levels off, I ask, "Where are we going?"

With a sweet smile Blake says, "Manila, Utah. It's up near Wyoming and close to the Colorado corner. It's not exactly a tourist trap. There's a lot of nothing up there. I plan to enjoy you for years." Then he gives a diabolical laugh, twirls an imaginary mustache tip and cups my breast. The teasing look on his face brings a slow smile to mine. The old Blake, my favorite one, the one I hoped that I had married four short hours ago. My lack of sleep catches up with me. Blake wakes me after we've landed. My Jeep is already unloaded from the jet. It now has a large metal carrier on top and a good sized trailer behind.

I slide into the front seat and before I drop back to sleep he says, "Supplies." He places a soft pillow between me and the window before covering me with a blanket. The ride doesn't seem very long. We're in a cabin in some mountain forest above a pretty lake. Once he carries me across the threshold, I notice Blake looks tired. Although he protests my helping him unload, he's not hard to convince otherwise. Inside the large spacious cabin are a multitude of cardboard boxes and surprisingly nice furniture. There are pretty curtains at the windows hiding the wooden shutters. I'm surprised to notice the layout is the same as the Dailey cottage. Noticing my glances: Blake chuckles.

He explains, "I sold copies of the plans to my friend and he built this place using them. I wanted them modified. Upstairs are two bedrooms, another bath and the attic."

The living room sports a massive fireplace but it's only a single story to the ceiling. This makes it warmer and cozier. We carry everything inside as a rosy colored dusk begins to fall. Blake finds sheets for the queen sized bed. I locate towels, perishables for the refrigerator and blankets. By the time Blake returns to make a fire, I have the bed made and water going for hot cocoa. The fire in the fireplace gives off limited heat. Blake goes to the basement and starts the furnace. Within an hour, the chill is off the place and we're nestled together in the firm bed, asleep.

At 4 a.m., our growling stomachs wake us. Blake stretches and climbs from the bed. Then he scoops me up and carries me to the bathroom. He pulls me into his arms and gently kisses me.

While he's pulling my nightgown over my head and turning me towards the tub, he says, "Get into the tub and soak. I drew you a nice bath. I'll make breakfast and then give you a nice massage." The water is hot and it does soak a lot of my aches away. I walk into the bedroom wearing a large dark green towel and find my clothes laid out on the bed. I smile and quickly dress. Blake is just flipping the omelets as I step near to give him a nice hug.

While deftly flipping the omelets onto warmed plates he asks, "Feeling better?"

Reaching for a plate, I say, "Yes. Those look and smell good."

Holding my chair while I slide onto it, he teases, "Sit. This morning, I wait on you. We'll continue your wife lessons another day." When he pulls out his chair, there's no soft cushion like on mine.

As he pours hot water over my tea bag I tell him, "Thank you.".

"Not a problem. So, in typical male fashion, I want to know. How was I?" He sips his tea after adding sugar.

When I tell him, "Best I've ever had." He grins almost shyly taking my hand in his so I tease him with, "Of course, you are the only one I've ever had . . . so . . ."

He nibbles my fingers and flashes those beautiful sky blue eyes across the table. "So . . . I'll be the only one you'll ever have, Mrs. Dailey." He finishes.

I softly tell him, "I hope so." Then, we delve into the delicious omelets. We wash dishes together and several times find ourselves in each others arms just nestled together.

Blake says, "Thursday is Thanksgiving." I realize I have no idea what day it is.

He says, "It's Monday, darling." While helping me slip into a nice fur lined white leather hooded jacket. He pokes through the boxes until he finds the jacket, boots and snowsuit he purchased. He puts on a black suede jacket. We sit and put on the hiking boots. He even has a silk scarf for across my mouth and nose if the wind picks up. My first view off the front porch is breath-taking.

Extending my arms in a slow arch, I exclaim, "Oh, Blake, this is heavenly."

While slipping his arm around my waist, he says, "Close enough, especially with you here." We walk for several hours through the surrounding woods and eventually down to the lake. We stand under the shelter of some trees and watch the ducks and geese on the lake.

He asks, "Does all this isolation bother you?" I lean against him, safe in his arms.

I reply, "No. I like the quiet and the solitude and you." He chuckles.

While we're walking back up to the cabin he jokes, "Well, I've worked up an appetite. Let's call for a pizza."

Inside, I smell something already cooking. He puts my jacket on the hook beside his. Then we sit on the deacons' bench to remove our boots. There are his and her matching soled leather moccasins for inside. The oven contains a large beef roast and various well cooked vegetables. It only takes me a few minutes to whip up homemade biscuits for the now empty oven. While Blake slices the meat, I make gravy. After we both eat a hearty lunch and wash the dishes, we slip into coats and sit on the porch in the two high backed wooden rocking chairs. The swing is at the opposite corner and we quickly discovered, directly in the path of the north wind that's now blowing. Higher on the mountains and under some of the trees are patches of old snow. As we sit and rock, Blake holds his arms up and I move over into his lap.

While I'm safely wrapped in his arms, he says, "It's going to snow soon." I nod in agreement. It smells like it. "We have three months supplies and there's a nearby town with an old fashioned country store for perishable staples." I sigh at his words and turn to receive his kiss.

I tell him, "Good, then we'll be safe and happy here." He holds me tightly until we begin to get cold and are forced back inside. Blake brings up plenty of wood for the box on the back and front porches. He has turned the furnace off and started the two wood stoves going. There's one in the sitting area of our bedroom and one in the central corner of the living room. That stove is massive and makes the room toasty warm when Blake gets it going. We have roast beef sandwiches and fresh fruit salad for dinner. Curled together on the couch, I sigh against Blake.

He asks, "Comfy?".

"Yes. I want this time to never end." I tell him.

"It doesn't have to." He quickly says. "We can live here for months or years or the rest of our lives. I can secretly purchase this cabin from my friend and we never have to leave." I smile at that thought. At dusk, Blake closes the wooden shutters and secures the place before lighting a lamp. We have electric. Blake explains that because the opposite side of the lake has expensive retreat cabins belonging to wealthy recluses, the electric company put lines through this property. The upstairs back bedroom is set up like a little sitting room and has a large screen TV in one corner.

Blake brags, "We even have cable TV." turning the set to the weather channel. The picture is clear and he's right, a massive front is bringing a lot of snow to the west and headed our way.

We make it an early night. I get a nice massage from my husband before we nestle together in the bed to sleep. We wake in the morning to a winter wonderland. Blake was up several times throughout the night to feed the wood stoves. The place is warm and blanketed by almost four feet of snow.

Gesturing at the outside, Blake tells me, "It started around midnight." as I prepare bacon, sunny side eggs, tea, toast and oatmeal for our breakfast. He brings in more wood to the box inside and stamps his feet. His cheeks are rosy red and there are snow flakes in his hair and eye lashes. I kiss them away. He laughs and begins kissing in a more serious mode.

I tell him, "Breakfast is ready."

He sighs sadly and says, "Then I shall have my dessert later." After breakfast is consumed and cleaned up, we tackle the assortment of boxes cluttering the living room.

I discover my husband has purchased a lot of clothes for me. There are heavy flannel and cotton night gowns and sexy lacy negligees. I like the soft flannel shirts and sweat sets also. A couple of the boxes he carries upstairs after his initial glance inside.

He says, "For another time." I shrug and continue unloading my assigned box. Several boxes contain candles, wicks and kerosene lamps, sanitary products for me (my favorite brand and preferred type), perfumes, medicines and things we might need to survive alone for many, many weeks. All the empty boxes are carried to the attic. I put medical supplies together and marked the outside of the box. Blake asked me to do an inventory of our supplies. He wants it on the computer and a printed list for us to keep track of what we have.

He calmly states, "Trips to town should not be wasted or too frequent.". I find a box with needlepoint crafts inside. There are dresser scarves to embroider, as well as pillow cases and table clothes, napkins and a baby quilt. I discover a king sized comforter to candlewick and one box contains pieces of material to make a quilt with.

Blake returns from a trip upstairs and finds me in the middle of the craft supplies. He says, "Those were some of my mothers' things she never got a chance to make. She remarked to save them for you after she found out she was dying. I often wondered if she knew we'd end up married. I'll have you know I was often teased about beauty being right under my nose and my needing glasses. At the time, I couldn't imagine what she was rattling on about. At her insistence, I packed them all up and put them in metal barrels in a storage unit in Dallas. They've been there all these years, waiting for you to return." I find myself crying and Blake pulls me into his arms.

Blake consoles me, saying, "She was so special. I know she would have hated me killing for a living but loved me for marrying you. You were the daughter she never had. Did you know she had eight miscarriages during her marriage to my dad and everyone was a girl?" I shook my head, crying in earnest now.

Blake says, "Hush. I didn't want you to cry harder." His lips find mine and his hands pull me against him. He carries me into the bedroom and we remove each others clothes. I'm so eager for everything to be right this time, but he's cautious and again makes me slow down.

Blake says, "Easy. We have all the time in the world to enjoy each other." It's quite some time before we rise and shower together upstairs. The bathroom upstairs has a walk in shower. We dress and watch the weather channel before heading downstairs to finish sorting through the boxes in the living room. We only have about a dozen left and Blake calls a halt.

He says, "Tomorrow's another day." He brings up a fresh turkey from the basement and puts it into the refrigerator. It's Tuesday. I have a roast chicken in the oven for dinner. We have hot roast beef sandwiches and the left over vegetables for lunch. Feeling brave, we venture outside and start to make a snowman. The wind picks up again and drives us back into the warm cabin.

Blake says, "Man, that's fierce." While struggling to close the cabin door against the wind. After dinner, we try to watch some TV but the reception is poor. Blake decides on an early night. The whistling of the wind makes me eager for the warm bed and Blake's body. Wednesday passes quickly. I finish with the boxes and do some laundry. Blake carries the empty boxes upstairs and makes a hurried trip down to the woodpile to replenish our supply. The large wood pile is under the back section of the porch which wraps 3/4's of the way around the cabin but is still a cold venture in the icy wind. I have hot cocoa ready for him as he comes inside.

Shrugging from his coat he says, "The wind is really drifting the snow. I piled some boards to try and keep the walkway under the porch from closing completely." I hang it on the hook. He sits and removes his boots and I hand him his moccasins.

I say, "Hot cocoa?"

"Well I'm getting hot and you can call me cocoa if you want to." Rising, he pulls me into his arms for a long kiss.

He says, "You are addicting." as we sit curled together on the couch sipping our cocoa. The rest of the afternoon is spent playing cards and then consuming delicious roast chicken, yams and cheese cauliflower. After the dishes, we dance to a soft piano CD until I insist we go to bed.

I tell him, "I have homemade stuffing to make and put in that massive young turkey you brought up. It's going to take hours to cook." He easily is led to bed. He quickly falls to sleep while I massage his back.

I'm up at 4 and making my stuffing. Blake shuffles out, wiping the sleep from his eyes saying, "Something smells good already." Then he puts a clean fork into the stuffing bowl. I've just poured the cooked celery, onion, garlic and butter seasoned mixture over the bread pieces and tossed them.

After a mouth full, he says, "Oh God, this is good." placing his forehead against the middle of my upper back to steal another fork full. He holds the bird open and I stuff to my hearts content. The inners are boiling in a pan and I already have a dishpan half full of dirty utensils. A couple of quick stitches and the bird goes into the roasting pan and the oven. It's about 5:30 according to Blake's watch. I slide my hands through his sleep mussed hair and he kisses me long and deep. We dance back into the bedroom for a long sensual bout of lovemaking. Blake makes me breakfast in bed.

He says, "The storm has gotten worse. I didn't think that possible. Not even the Jeep will be getting out of here." At my panicked expression, he laughs.

He explains, "Not to worry, we have phones to call for help and all terrain snow vehicles under the cabin. Of course, if you're tired of me already . . ." I roll on top of him and sit astride his hips. He's very ticklish and defenseless in this position. We dress and work together to peel the potatoes to cook to mash. The bird comes out of the oven, totally cooked, brown and splitting open. Blake removes the stuffing mostly to the bowl (a lot finds it's way directly into Blake without ever touching the bowl.) while I make gravy. The corn and homemade cinnamon rolls get placed on the formally set table. Blake carves the bird and I carry everything to the table. Blake offers the blessing while our hands are joined across the table. The meal is delicious but I can't take my eyes from Blake. He looks so handsome, so relaxed, so totally happy.

He asks, "What are you looking at me like that for woman? I'm stuffed and totally unable to give you what you're eyes are making me want to give you." I shake my head softly and reach across to take his hand.

When I ask, "Are you happy here with me?" his eyebrows raise.

He says, "Katie girl, I have never been happier in my entire life. I thought I'd never have happiness when mother died. Like you, my world came crashing down around me. I put a hard shell around my heart and packed my emotions deep inside. I left home and entered the navy seals program. I didn't like the regimentation but found I had a natural talent for the weapons and eventually, the killing. Every person I've killed over the past ten years has been the cancer that killed my mother. Suddenly I realized I was killing myself a little each time. I headed back to the ranch and dad. I never expected your tight little butt sticking up from the oven that day. You looked so familiar but I couldn't place you." Suddenly he stops and looks away.

He says, "My mouth just ran off, didn't it?" I shake my head again.

I tell him, "I wondered what started you killing for money. Thank you."

He rises from the table and begins cleaning. He keeps glancing at me and smiling. I believe I've just stepped inside that hard shell. The other side of the coin is have I weakened him with my love enough to put his very life in danger? While I'm washing the dishes, our power goes off.

"Oh, oh." Blake softly says. "I wondered how long the storm would let us have lights." He quickly lights a candle and then several kerosene lights.

I huskily say, "Romantic." I get pursed lips and his eyes rolled heavenward in response. He lights a fire and I slide the pumpkin pie into the oven of our gas stove.

He's stretched out on the floor in front of the raging fire when I enter the room. He pats the floor beside him. I quickly snuggle down and against him. He leans back on one elbow, holding me against his chest. Before too long, we're flat on the floor, fast asleep. The chill settling in the room wakes Blake.

He says, "Damn." While leaping up to feed the wood stove which is almost out. He tends the one in the bedroom and then comes back with the comforter from the bed. We snuggle together on the couch as the wood stove begins reheating the room. The pie is done and cooling on the counter when we hear the first rumbling noises.

Blake says, "Avalanche." and I shiver. "We're not in any danger." He reassures me.

Blake goes to the basement to tend the generator while I get the pie cut and the cool whip on top. We have our pumpkin pie and are again nestled on the couch when Blake's cell phone begins buzzing. He rises and goes into the bedroom to answer.

I can hear him talking. "Hello. No, we're fine. Thanks old buddy. I knew I could depend on you. No, she's all woman . . . but purrs like a kitten." Blake laughs several times and continues, "No, but I may want to exercise that purchase option." Another laugh as he's listening to the caller speak, "I'll never get tired of her. She's the most beautiful little creature and cooks like a chef. Forget it. She can't see anyone but me. Yeah, for once I am. Happy Holidays." He strides into the room and holds the phone towards me saying, "Just say hello and that you love me." I raise an eyebrow but take the phone and repeat what he said. There's a low husky chuckle on the line.

A man's deep voice says, "You tell him he's one lucky son of a bitch. Sorry ma'am." I hand the phone back and repeat what the man said.

"Yeah, don't I just know it." Blake ends the call and lays the phone down. He tells me, "Our host. Sorry I couldn't introduce you but with cell phones you never know whose ears have picked your conversation out of the air." I nod and store that bit of information for permanent lesson.

We had so much turkey that the pie becomes our supper. Blake double checks the stoves and secures the doors and windows and we go to bed. For the next six days, the snow keeps us safely sheltered from the world. Blake hears the plows and makes sure we stay out of sight. The electric is back on. Blake extinguishes the stoves to stop the tell tale smoke before the sun fully rises. The furnace doesn't keep the place as toasty as the stoves but Blake's' heavy knit black sweater works for me. We stand at the one front window behind the closed wooden shutters and watch the plows go past between us and the lake.

Blake says, "They're opening up the little dirt road for the recluses. I don't think any one's back there but you never know. They keep to themselves and we'll do the same."

The next day, Blake's bored and splits about a cord of wood. I watch from the back porch, sheltered from the intermittent wind, nervous about the ax. He's tired, slightly sore and responds nicely to my full body massage. He spends most of the afternoon sleeping like a baby on the bed. I wake him at 7 for soup and sandwiches. He stretches and sets the tray aside.

Pulling me onto the bed he says, "I'll have my dessert first, I believe." As he begins tasting and working my body to a fever pitch of passion. The soup has to be reheated but the sandwiches are fine. Once he's eaten and I've finished the dishes, he's asleep again when I return.

Over the next two weeks, Blake often picks a day and disappears for most of it. I'm working on a Christmas present for him. Being alone for these brief periods of time are nice. I find myself extremely glad to see him return. He always seems to be glad to return to my open arms. He's checking out the neighborhood, I'm sure. Of course, when he returns with a large deer carcass I realize he may have been doing a little hunting also. After dressing and carving up his kill, he digs out a dehydrator and we make jerky. I begin experimenting with my seasonings and get a delicious marinade concocted.

Blake wants to go to town the next day. Our eggs are low and our fresh cheeses, fruits and vegetables are all gone. We take a nice two hour drive into Manila. Blake throws several plastic crates into the back of the Jeep. The storekeeper is glad to fill them with our food purchases.

Before we go into the actual town limits, Blake turns and says, "You're my wife, Mrs. Blake O'Malley." Then he reaches down and pulling a small yellow envelope from under his seat says, "Put your own ID in here and take these." Inside are driver's license, health insurance cards, credit cards, social security card and even a library card for Mrs. Katherine O'Malley of Harrisburg, Pennsylvania. I smile as I remove all my own cards to the envelope.

I tell him, "Pleased to meet you Mr. O'Malley." as the Jeep stops in front of the Manila Mercantile. I see the proprietors name is Tim O'Leary.

Mr. O'Leary obviously knows Mr. O'Malley. He bellows across the store and rushes forward to pump Blake's hand.

He loudly says, "Blake, you son of a gun! Always good to see an old cash paying customer come to town. Guess you had a little snow up your way?" Blake nods and turns to gesture at me.

He says, "Tim, this is Katherine my wife."

Mr. O'Leary turns faded blue eyes to me and a smile spreads over his face before he hollers, "Mrs. O'Leary! Get your large person out here. Blake's got himself a pretty young bride!" I immediately hear heavy footfalls. Mrs. O'Leary is a massive woman. I'm quickly enfolded in two large arms and closely examined by cheerful hazel eyes. Where Mr. O'Leary's hair is a faded brown in a crown around his head, this woman's brown and gray hair is permed out around her head about a foot.

She teases, "Oh, Ms. Peterson is going to be heart broke. She's had quite a thing for Blake for almost 10 years. It brightens her entire day when a letter comes general delivery for Blake." Mr. O'Leary bellows in laughter and grabs Blake's hand.

Mr. O'Leary says, "Well, I'm assuming you two came for supplies. Business ain't been good since Vernal got a Wal-Mart. Maybe I shouldn't have told you that because you'll desert me too." Blake removes our list and hands it to Mr. O'Leary.

He says, "Nonsense. I would never get the kind of service and friendly personal welcome at a chain store." Mr. O'Leary swells right up. Once they're in the other half of the store, Mrs. O'Leary pulls me into the store next door.

She explains, "This is my ladies shop." I glance around at all kinds of women's apparel and necessities. She says, "I also own the Five and Dime Store next door. Do you need Christmas purchases for your man?" I nod and she drags me through the ladies shop into the Five and Dime after relieving me of my coat. We walk through the connecting storerooms and never set foot outside in the icy wind.

In the course of our conversation, I'm told to call her May. She wants to know if we've been married long. Blake was here in the spring and didn't mention a lady friend. I tell her, "We've known each other since our teens." She nods and I begin purchasing Christmas items and wrapping paper. In the back are several nice flannel shirts and an assortment of men's underwear. Heavy socks, new jeans and black sneakers soon join my purchase pile. It's almost four hours before Blake and I are loaded and back in the Jeep. He put the purchases in the carrier on the top.

We stop at Sam's Diner for lunch. This old metal diner is painted hot pink on the outside and has the usual ripped plastic booths seats and metal type tables. The food is delicious. I have a cheeseburger, fries and thick chocolate shake. Blake gets a fresh trout dinner. Then he steals most of my fries and half my shake. Blake runs into a liqueur store while I duck into a drugstore for several purchases of my own. A certain monthly thing has not put in an appearance since before my wedding so I purchase a home pregnancy test. Our last stop before heading home is the general post office where I get to meet Ms. Peterson.

Blake introduces me with a flourish to a woman who must be 90 years old. Definitely a tall, thin, spinster lady. She's very proper and slightly abashed at the attention that Blake showers charmingly on her.

She takes my hand warmly and says, "Congratulations. I've always liked the name Katherine. With a K?" I nod.

She says, "Good. That was my grandmothers name. My older sister's named Catherine with a C. She turned out to be a wild one." She slowly and sadly shakes her head. Blake picks up his general delivery mail and we say goodbye to Manila.

He exclaims, "Shoot." slowing the Jeep and pulling to the road side.

I quickly ask, "What?"

He turns to face me and says, "Well, we should have stopped at the drug store and got a couple of those baby tests. You haven't, well, you know, since we got married." I smile and touch his face.

When I tell him, "I already picked up one." His laugh is as sudden as the Jeeps movement back onto the highway.

He says, "Great minds think alike." He reaches across to slide his hand up under my jacket.

He softly asks, "Think there's a baby in there?"

I tell him, "I doubt it. I usually get off my cycle with any drastic changes. Trust me when I say with what's been going on, I'm off my cycle." He smiles.

He says, "That's OK. We have plenty of time to make a baby. I'd just rather you're due in the summer when the roads are better." A warm feeling spreads through me at his caring words. It takes almost two hours to get home and it's snowing again. Blake unloads while I whip up supper. I use left over chicken and make a creamy cheesy casserole. Blake always loves my homemade biscuits and often requests them when I figure he's tired of them.

We're both tired from our long day and retire shortly after supper. The next couple of days are spent wrapping gifts and preparing for Christmas. The large envelope in Blake's mail contains several letters from Devin and Kyle. Kyle left his with Devin to forward. I let Blake read Kyle's letter.

November

Dear Katherine,

I really miss you since dad drove you away. I wish he could have left things well enough alone. It was nice having a woman cook and look after us. I'm sure you have run away with Blake but that's OK. Tell him that I still love him. I thought a lot about what was said. It's

really nobodies business what Blake does for a living. I hope the two of you are living somewhere and making love and loving each other.

Please write me and let me know you're OK. I'd really like to know if you have any baby's and what names you give them. Be happy. I won't tell dad anything. He's been really angry lately. Sometimes his face gets really red and he gasps for breath. You know dad, he won't go to the doctors. Devin said you just disappeared in the middle of the night. Blake will take good care of you.

Have a Happy Thanksgiving and Merry Christmas. Love Kyle Dailey.

Blake smiles as he reads and tears have formed in his eyes by the time he's finished. Devin has letters for Blake and I. Mine reads.

Little sis,

I just received the wedding pictures today. I was briefly worried when you didn't say goodbye but I realize Blake couldn't trust us. You look so grown up, happy, beautiful and definitely in love.

I know where ever you are, you'll get this eventually. If there's an emergency, I'll dial your cell phone. I know they're traceable and Blake would be upset if I just called to say I love you.

I missed having you around at Thanksgiving. Cook and Truman were devastated by your leaving without saying goodbye. I explained and now they understand. I didn't say about Blake's past only that our parents were against your union.

I'm sure you're making love like crazy and cooking good meals for your new husband. If you need me, you know where to find me. Love Devin.

Blake hands me his note to read. I have to smile. So to the point for Devin when he's writing another man. It's a relief to know Devin knows I'm safe. I also hope I can write him letters periodically. I miss having contact with him.

Blake,

Thanks for sending the pictures. I want my sister to be happy. That's your new job now. 24 hours a day, seven days a week. Go easy on her at first, she'll be new to the love game. Welcome to my family. You're always welcome at my place even if it's just for an hour. Be safe, be careful and know I'll be your friend and brother. Katie will tell you I'm trustworthy. Time will prove it. Thanks for sending this address for correspondence. Please forward a letter if Katie girl writes me. Love you both. Devin.

No mention of father or Frank. I'm sure Frank called my father once he found out I was gone. Devin couldn't hide my disappearance forever. Blake goes through the rest of the mail and burns most of it. He sets aside several large cash drafts and three packets of cash that are bundles of $1,000 bills. He looks over and tosses the cash into my lap.

He says, "You can have those. It's not blood money. I wired your father a million dollars for a dowry. I thought you'd like to know, he kept it." sounding sadly disheartened at my fathers actions. I realize it's not what he would have done. Blake is obviously more of a man than my father. I thought father would have thrown the money back in Blake's face after refusing permission for our wedding. Perhaps, since I've disappeared he knows we've gone against his desires and figures he's owed the money. This line of thinking makes me very mad. I feel like a brood mare that's been sold to breed. I glance up and he's studying me intently.

He asks, "Whatever are you thinking? Honestly all these emotions have flashed across your face." I rise and let the money fall to the floor.

I softly tell him, "Make love to me." He rises to pull me into his arms and surround me with his love.

I finally get a chance to open the home pregnancy test and the results are negative. I have still not had my monthly but after a long discussion with Blake we decide to see a doctor in the spring. Devin and Kyle's birthday's are in April. I'm wondering if Blake plans to visit then. Two days before Christmas, Blake returns with a nice scotch pine. He brings down one of the large boxes from the attic that contains old ornaments.

He says, "These were my mothers. They were divided between Kyle and I. Some of these are from my first tree." For some strange reason, knowing that brings on a flood of tears. Alarmed, Blake rushes to take me into his arms.

He asks, "What's wrong?" I shrug and gag trying to tell him nothing's wrong. He makes me sit beside him on the couch until I calm down.

He holds me in his arms and says, "You realized that yours are probably all gone?" I nod and sigh against him. He rises and goes up to the attic again and returns with two small square wrapped gifts.

He says, "Well, I shouldn't let you open these early, but I'm getting so easy living with you." Then he hands them to me. As I suspected, they're glass ornaments. The first is *Our First Christmas Together* on a crystal teardrop with our names and wedding date delicately inscribed in script on the face. The second is *For my wife at Christmas* and has a beautiful hand painting of a horse and buggy coming out of a covered bridge in a snow scene.

I exclaim, "Oh, Blake! They're both beautiful." He collects all the kisses I want to give him. We end up making love on the couch, the heavy pine scent in the air around us. We spend the remainder of the day, decorating the tree. Blake has a string of white twinkling lights for on it. He purchased tinsel and garland and a beautiful porcelain angel for the top. When we're done, it's a work of art. We originally planned to use popcorn strings, but Blake ate the popcorn faster than I could string it.

Christmas morning is a clear crisp day and fresh snow fell during the night. Since the roads are clear, we drive to Manila and attend the small church off the square. Mr. and Mrs. O'Leary are pleased to have us sit with them. After the service, Blake begs off on their invitation to dinner and spending the afternoon.

"We haven't opened our gifts and have a long drive home." He explains. May nods and hugs me before we leave.

It's almost 1 when we arrive back. The roast ducks are done to perfection. We have our dinner and then settle in the living room near the tree. I brought my gifts out in the middle of the night and Blake had already done the same. I received a nice pearl necklace, several bottles of perfume, writing paper, two sexy negligees from Victoria's secret, various pretty blouses and practical nightgowns and flannel shirts. My favorite gift was the small 35 mm camera, about 100 rolls of film and a leather camera case.

I tell him, "Oh, I've always wanted one of these." Blake smiles and says, "Well, you have remarked several times about wanting to take a picture of things. Just don't make me the center subject of every one, OK?" I nod and he helps me install the film and batteries and takes several shots of the tree.

We play outside for a while and take several more shots. Blake says he has a friend who'll develop the pictures and mail them back. The day after Christmas we get another massive snowstorm and our electric goes off. We don't get our power back until New Years Eve. We spend the week making love and cooking for each other. Blake does the cooking on New Years Day because I'm not feeling very well. In the back of both of our minds, we're thinking baby.

Blake says, "Maybe we screwed the test up. I'm going to town as soon as the roads are open and get several different kinds. In fact, I'm going to call and see if Tim knows of a doctor you can see. If there's a baby, you should be taking special vitamins."

On January 3rd, our baby hopes are destroyed. I have such cramps and bleeding that Blake thinks I've miscarried. I shake my head saying, "No, this is normal when I've missed several months due to stress. My body saves the misery up for one big hit." He waits on me hand and foot. I have such pain I'm nauseous and can't keep anything down. He rubs my legs when the cramps hit and strokes my belly during severe cramps. Finally, on January 7th, I'm done.

I explain, "See. Four days and goes away."

He shakes his head saying, "You should still see a doctor." I smile and kiss his nearby nose.

I tell him, "It's a woman thing. Honestly, with a miscarriage there would have been afterbirth. Watching mares have problems and miscarry, I've got a pretty good idea what to look for." He begins shaking his head again. It's several days before I can convince him it's OK to make love to me. By then, I'm so horny I could jump his bones. When I tell him that, he gets very aroused and easily led to the bedroom. When I remark about missing the pine smell from the tree, Blake begins bringing in fresh pine every couple of days. We get a large bucket and soak it. When I pour boiling water over it, the scent fills the house. By the end of January, we've got cabin fever and are slightly bored. Blake's trip to town turns into a major shopping spree. We end up with a variety of jigsaw puzzles but even they don't dispel our boredom.

Blake says, "There isn't enough work." I have to agree. I'm used to working the horses and the breedings. Blake misses the ranch work.

On Groundhog Day, Blake remarks, "I hope the little varmint saw spring around the corner." I've been uneasy all week but keeping it to myself. By February, Blake seems edgy and is constantly checking the neighboring woods for signs of intruders.

When my phone begins ringing in the middle of the night, Blake sits up in bed and says, "Bad news." He turns on the light and picks up the phone. He holds it towards me but I shake my head.

He says, "Hello." Then he mouths Devin. I rise up to my knees and Blake pulls me against him.

He says, "When? Will Dustin keep him there until we arrive? No, the roads are clear. We'll head out in the morning. I'll have to contact my pilot and get the jet in here. Tell him two days at the max, weather permitting. No, she's fine. No, it's OK, we were bored with each other anyway." He laughs and ends the call.

He says, "Kyle ran away looking for us. Evidently after he got your letter from Devin, something happened at the ranch. He's in New York City. For some reason he thinks Dustin knows where we are. Luckily Dustin called Devin immediately. Devin says Dustin will keep him safe. Well, I guess the honeymoon is over." He lays the phone down and pulls my gown over my head.

I tell him, "Well, it's been a nice long one." while he begins laying me onto my back and covering me with kisses and his body. Once he's satisfied his passionate desires, he grabs the cell phone and calls his pilot. We sleep for about four hours and then rise and quickly pack. We load the perishables into the Jeep. Blake secures the cabin. We're on the road by 9 and within three hours at the airfield. I don't like New York City but I keep my opinion to myself.

During the flight, I'm thinking about my oldest brother, Dustin. At 33, he's a CEO of his own Financing Corporation in New York City. He's been married to Laura for almost 8 years and has a son, Noah. Dustin is not quite as tall as Devin and is fairly stout. His dark brown hair is thinning on top and his dark brown eyes are usually critical in their glances. My early memories are mostly impressions of how overbearing he was towards me.

The last time I saw Laura was two years ago when they came down for a weeks visit at Fathers. They brought Noah who was four years old. Father just adored him. Laura has her own Photography Studio in NYC and at that time was just opening her own Gallery. She's an ash blonde, extremely thin and her gray eyes give you the impression she's snobbish, which she is. I stayed pretty much away from her because at that time, she smoked like a chimney. I'm sure since she's had to quit, her disposition hasn't improved any. Last year, they discovered Noah has severe allergies to smoke and dust. Since Laura and Dustin both dote on Noah, she immediately quit smoking. I'm looking forward to seeing Noah, who's six now and in the first grade.

Blake brings me back to the present with a tap on my nose. He asks, "Where were you?"

I turn to face him explaining, "Just thinking about Dustin and his family. It's been two years since I've seen him. He's not my favorite brother." Blake laughs out loud at my words, which surprises me.

I raise my eyebrows and he explains, "Devin mentioned something about Dustin being a little hard to take. I took it as a warning." I nod in agreement. It's almost 3 and we're circling the Kennedy airport waiting for permission to land. Finally, we hear the landing gear drop into place. Blake tugs at my seat belt and we hold hands during the landing.

CHAPTER FIVE

THE CRIME IN NEW YORK CITY

Of course, customs has to search the Jeep. I like watching the drug dogs, they really know their stuff. After a clean bill from customs, Blake is headed to Dustin's Manhattan penthouse. Dustin left our names at the garage so they have a parking pass all ready. The attendant pages Dustin. Kyle and Dustin step from the elevator as Blake shuts off the Jeep engine.

I'm as surprised as Blake at Kyle throwing his arms around Blake.

He says, "Thank God you're both all right. Katherine, it was so good to get your letter." As he's throwing his arms around me. Blake introduces himself to Dustin. I turn to face him and get a real shock. He must have lost 100 pounds. I watch his smile as he reads my face.

Spreading his arms after shaking hands with Blake, he asks, "Well, little sister, how do I look?"

I smile and step forward to give him a quick hug. I hastily tell him, "You look good. Blake is my husband."

Turning to key in his code for the doors to the elevator to open, he replies, "I know, Katherine. Devin and of course, Kyle told me all about your flight into nowhere land. I'm sure Blake will offer a good explanation once we're upstairs." We step in and ride silently up. Kyle has my left hand, Blake, my right. Dustin's penthouse is rather grand. You step from the elevator into a short hall that leads directly to the front door. Dustin left the door standing open and we walk into the foyer and step down into the living room.

The living room has a sunken wet bar in the corner which overlooks the pool. I remember my visit several years ago when I was amazed by the curved window wall that overlooks the pool and spa. The living room is still all done in icy white colors with little flashes of red accents. His taste in art hasn't changed. I'm sure many of the ugly pieces are from Laura's gallery.

Dustin gestures for us to sit and walks around behind the bar. Looking at Blake he asks, Can I get you something?"

Blake says, "Scotch rocks." as we take a seat on the love seat. Kyle perches in a nearby armchair starring from me to Blake and back. I notice how he looks almost haggard. Dustin returns with Blake's drink and one for himself.

Blake takes a sip and nods at Dustin, "Smooth." is his only comment.

Clearing his throat, Dustin asks, "Now, who wants to tell me what's going on?" Dustin looks from me to Blake. Blake glances my way and I nod for him to go ahead. Dustin responds better to another man. Except for Laura, he considers most women second-class idiots whose main use on earth is for breeding purposes. Blake explains that we fell in love and wanted to get married. Since our parents were dead set against the union, we left to make our own life together.

He tells Dustin, "We're both legal aged adults." Dustin sits with his usual highhanded expression. He obviously knows something he didn't expect us to tell him.

After a brief silence, Dustin asks, "And when your money runs out, will you go back to killing people to earn more or just live off my sisters money?" Blake's hand tightens on his glass. Kyle gasps at Dustin's statement.

Enraged, I shout, "You son of a bitch!" The words just slip out of my mouth on their own. Now all three men are looking at me. I put my hand to my mouth to keep any other statements inside.

Leaning slightly forward and giving me his old cold look, Dustin says, "Well, that's a new mannerism. I suppose you learned that from your new husband?" Funny, it doesn't scare me anymore.

Setting his drink down on the coffee table and starting to rise, Blake says, "I don't intend to run out of money. You'll be happy to know that your Uncle Sam was more than happy to hire me many, many times over the period of my prior employment. I've retired with an annual pension larger than you make in ten years at your little firm."

Dustin gives his quirkly little smile and calmly says, "Just stay seated. I have a few things I want to discuss. I was wondering the kind of man my sister married. Devin said I'd find you one hell of a man. For once, he was right. I happen to agree that you didn't take the hit on Father. However, someone has. Were you able to discover who?" Dustin leans back and crosses one ankle over his knee.

Staring directly at Dustin, Blake says, I took out the first one. I did my best to find out the source, but to no avail. I've put the word out that whoever takes the hit will answer to me. I don't know if that will keep your father alive or not. I'm well known and respected among my peers but there are a lot of new young upstarts who respect no one and fear nothing." Blake has relaxed back. I'm watching Kyle's face as his brother talks. There's a lot of pride and respect for his brother. I'm glad. Dustin starts to speak as Blake's cell phone rings.

Blake holds up his hand. "Excuse me." It's a queer ring. I don't like the expression on his face.

He says, "Yeah." and then silence as he just listens. "You're sure?" His face darkens and he turns away from me. "Thanks. I owe you one." He ends the call.

He turns to Kyle to ask him, "Why are you here?" Kyle leans forward.

Kyle says, "Dad got a hold of Katherine's last letter. Man, he went ballistic. He started screaming and ranting and raving all kinds of horrible things. I went upstairs, packed a bag and drove to the airport. I knew from Devin that Katherine had a brother in NYC and Boston. I figured you two came here to get lost in the big city." Kyle falls silent looking at Blake.

When Blake asks, "And that's the only reason you ran?" Kyle quickly nods. Blake's mouth is pursed and his forehead is creased in a heavy frown.

Blake says, "That was a very interesting call from an associate of mine. It seems an old boss of mine has placed an open contract on me. Coming here has definitely put my life and everyone around me in danger. I need to pay this man a visit and find out his problem. Dustin can you keep Kyle and Katherine safe or should I contact someone else?"

Dustin actually looks angered at Blake's insinuation of ineptitude when he says, "I can damn well take care of my sister. You go do whatever you need to do. This place is a fortress. No one can get up here without my permission. I have the highest security system available." Blake rises silencing him with his hand gesture.

Blake quietly says, "Good. However, I should warn you that if anything happens to Katherine, your wife will suffer the same fate." Dustin flies to his feet but Blake has his pistol under his chin within seconds. Dustin raises his hands and steps back.

Dustin boldly states, "Don't threaten my family under my roof!"

Blake says, "Don't let anything happen to my brother and my wife." backing towards the door.

With a smirk, Dustin says, "You can't get out unless I code you out." Blake turns at the panel, uses a knife to remove the panel and cuts one wire, the door opens soundlessly.

In a dry tone, Blake says, "I'd get this fixed right away, if I were you." and he's gone. Dustin is left standing with his mouth open and fists clenched at his side.

He quietly says, "You, Miss Katherine deserve that bastard."

Low and slow Kyle says, "Don't call my brother a bastard." His tone is hard. A lot of passion flows beneath his surface just like in his older brother.

I firmly say, "If you're going to yell and fight, I'm leaving."

Both men turn my way and Dustin says, "Don't do anything rash. Remember, if whoever's out to kill Blake gets you, they get him." that superior tone I hate, is back in his voice and stance. Cocky bastard comes to the tip of my tongue but I bite down to keep it there.

Dustin calls the security people downstairs and they send a man up to fix his panel. The guy is here in about five minutes. He shows his pass to Dustin and then takes a look at the box.

The man says, "Very professional job. Did you piss someone off Mr. Blackwood?" I'm glad the man's back is turned and he can't see Dustin's face. And an ugly looking mug it is right now. Kyle comes over and sits beside me. Dustin goes into his office to make some calls. Out of the corner of my eye, I see the gun barrel just before the cold steel touches Kyle's neck and he stiffens.

The man leans over and whispers, "One sound and it's your last. Both of you—get to your feet and come with me." I rise and watch as Kyle slowly does the same. We walk silently into the elevator and the man hits the down button. He keeps the gun pressed against Kyle's neck. When the door opens in the garage, another man grabs me. We're escorted to a very large black car with black windows.

A male voice from the dark interior says, "So, this is the woman who captured Blake Dailey's heart and soul. Please, get in and have a seat." The man is very elderly and obviously very powerful. Kyle is taken to a second car and put in the back seat.

Following my nervous gaze the man says, "They won't hurt him. You have my word." I climb into the back seat. The first man has shed his coveralls to reveal a very expensive looking navy suit.

He says, "Easy as pie, Sir. It was just like you said. Once we got Blake out of the way with the call." The elderly man raises his hand for silence. The ride is not very long and the silence is cold enough to make me shiver. I steel myself against showing any weakness. I still have my purse and the pistol inside. We drive calmly through the streets of New York and into another underground garage. Once the car stops, two men come over and open the door. The elderly man gestures for me to climb out.

"Take her purse." He tells the seated man in the car. For a split second, I debate about going for his pistol so visible as his jacket falls open. A cold gun barrel is pressed to my cheek by one of the men outside the car.

He growls, "Don't even think about it lady." I look up into a pockmarked hard face with dead black eyes. I surrender my purse. Mr. Dead face grabs my arm and pulls me the rest of the way out of the car.

The elderly man says, "Easy, Thomas, don't hurt the lady. You don't want *Tigerman* cutting your balls off and feeding them to you—do you?" Thomas actually blanches so Blake must be one cold son of a bitch. I'm gently escorted into the elevator. We ride up to another penthouse. I'm nervous because Kyle isn't with us.

Sensing my unease, the elderly man says, "The young man will be brought over directly. First, you will have to be thoroughly checked for weapons. I'm not sure how well trained Blake has made you." The room we step into is large and well lit from all the sunlight streaming in through the multitude of large windows. The furniture is all leather and dark colors. There are vases of fresh flowers sitting everywhere and their fragrance fills the room. I'm escorted up a curving staircase to the second level and a very feminine looking bedroom. Thomas pushes me into the room and the elderly gentleman follows.

His voice is quiet, his tone commanding as he says, "Close the door from the outside Thomas. Now, if you would please stand over there. Then I want you to remove all your clothes." The elderly man points to the center of the room. I turn to face him and cross my arms defensively across my chest.

I say, "I don't have any other weapons. There was a pistol in my purse and you have that. Who are you?" I'm fighting for control over myself.

He replies with a slight bow, "Excuse my lack of manners. I'm Aldo Faggini." I'm studying him. In spite of his soft-spoken tone, I detect a cruel heart. His hair is white and full, his eyes are hazel and at the moment, enjoying looking at me. His nose is long and thin and pointed like his chin. He's very slender and taller than my first impression in the car.

He gestures impatiently saying, "Please, don't make me call two of my associates in to undress you. You have my word that no sexual assaults will be made on your person. Once you have removed all your clothes, you may wrap yourself in that robe." I turn my head and see a pale blue silken robe at the foot of the bed.

When he says, "Mrs. Dailey, please, feel free to turn your back but I must insist you disrobe. Now! If you please." His tone has gotten considerably harsher. He is loosing his patience.

I raise my chin and begin removing my clothes. I refuse to turn my back. It's very hard to unclasp the front of my bra, but I do and then slide my panties from my hips. I keep my eyes on his face. He's enjoying this little charade. I step sideways and pick up the robe and throw it around myself. A few quick steps puts the bed between us. He chuckles.

Turning slightly towards the door, he says, "Thomas, you may remove the ladies clothes now." The door opens and Mr. Dead face leers while he gathers my things from the floor. Mr. Faggini bows and leaves. Only then do I allow myself the luxury of collapsing onto the floor beside the bed and crying into my hands.

The door on the left leads to a small bathroom. I wash my face and hands and put a cold cloth to my eyes. Calmer, I return to the bedroom to sit in the armchair in the far corner of the room. I don't know how many hours I sat there before I fell asleep. I do know I'm terribly worried about Kyle. I immediately sense Blake in the room before I even open my eyes. The room is dark. I raise my hand to touch his before he covers my mouth. He pulls me up into his arms. I cling to him silently. He releases me to slip out of a backpack and pull out a black sweat suit. He points and I nod. It takes me only seconds to put the suit on and shed the robe. He pulls sneakers from the pack and I quickly pull them onto my feet. He puts his arm around my waist and steers me to the door. He lifts my hand and makes a rapping gesture. I nod that I understand.

I rap on the door and call out, "Hello? Is anyone out there?"

There are movement sounds and then a man's muffled voice, "Step back from the door." I do and hear the door being unlocked. The door swings inward and once it's open far enough, Blake shoots the man in the head. The silencer makes a little pop noise and the man drops.

"*Very good.*" We hear Mr. Faggini's voice from somewhere near. "He was always a careless man. Unfortunately, another of my associates has a gun pointed at your brother's head. So, if you and your wife would be so kind as to join us downstairs." We hear the sound of him moving away. Blake slips in front and we walk down the curved staircase to the living room. On the longer couch, sits Kyle a man standing behind him with a gun to his head.

Mr. Faggini has taken a seat in what appears to be a throne sized chair. He gestures for us to sit on the small couch near him saying, "Please, Blake, for old times sake. Sit, we'll talk business and then work something out that will be agreeable to all parties concerned. Just like old times." Blake walks the last few steps down into the room and we take the offered seat. Mr. Faggini must have known Blake would only sit in a seat with its back against a wall.

Mr. Faggini continues, "It wasn't easy finding out your real identity. You will be pleased to know that several men endured hours of torture and refused to give you up. Eventually, I found a mutual acquaintance that was allergic to pain." Mr. Faggini looks pleased.

Blake simply asks, "So why the contract?" His gun is casually leveled at Mr. Faggini.

Mr. Faggini says, "Please, lower your weapon. I have need of your services. I was very saddened to learn of your early retirement. I have never come across another man of your morals, integrity and high level of expertise. The simple fact is; I need you to do one last job." The words are spoken in a matter of fact way. It's like he's discussing a dinner menu or family gathering.

Blake reiterates, "I'm retired. Get someone else."

Mr. Faggini immediately shakes his head saying, "No. Only you can do this job. Think of it as a favor. A favor for your wife and brothers lives. A rather large bonus for a job well done, don't you think?" I'm fighting the tears. I have never seen such a cruel hard man. Blake hasn't lowered his weapon. He appears outwardly calm but remains silent. I realize that this upsets Mr. Faggini more than any spoken words. As the seconds stretch into minutes, Mr. Faggini begins to sweat and squirm. Kyle is frozen and the man still has his gun against Kyle's head.

Mr. Faggini's voice is harsh and his lips are now pulled back into almost a snarl as he says, "I'm waiting for your answer, Tigerman." Blake remains silent.

Mr. Faggini leans forward saying, "Perhaps you think you're holding an ace. I have two bargaining chips, one can quickly be eliminated with a simple nod."

Blake slowly says, "You'll need both chips to leave this bargaining table. You think you know me, you definitely know my work. You don't know how close you are to death right now. No body rushes me. A hasty hit man is a dead man. I haven't heard any good reason to come out of retirement." Blake's lips are curled slightly but his body remains in a calm posture. I have my hands tightly clasped in my lap. Kyle has closed his eyes. There is more to this game between these two men than what I'm currently hearing.

Mr. Faggini raises his hands slowly, palms towards us. He says, "All right. How about the man who eliminated Pike?" Blake's sharply in drawn breath brings a slow smile to Mr. Faggini's face.

He boldly continues, "That's right. I found out who took out Pike. Now, do we bargain?"

After a long silence, Blake stiffly says, "We bargain."

Mr. Faggini nods and continues, "I figured you'd want to be the one. It was Ciro Macario, the Columbian. Now, I want you to eliminate Macario. He's been taking over my turf. I want him taken out." The rage and hatred on his face clearly shows his feelings towards this Columbian.

Blake flatly says, "And in return?"

Mr. Faggini smiles like a snake ready to strike as he says, "In return, you get your lovely wife and young brother back. Also, as a special favor, I call off the contract. However, I want the Columbian dead within 72 hours." Mr. Faggini is laying down the playing rules.

Blake is calm again, when he says, "I don't like rush jobs. I need to plan."

Mr. Faggini shakes his head saying, "I have all the information you'll need. My men have been watching and filming the Columbian for the past three months." Mr. Faggini leans forward to continue with, "Ever since he took my granddaughter and turned her into his private whore." My breath freezes in my chest. I see the hurt in his face before he covers it with hatred.

Before rising and striding from the room he says, "You bring me his testicles. I give you Miss Katherine and Master Kyle." I gather the bargaining is over.

To Kyle the thug says, "Get up." Kyle quickly glances towards Blake. Blake nods slightly and Kyle rises. The man keeps Kyle between himself and Blake's gun. I put my hand on Blake's thigh.

I ask him, "Will you be OK?" He chuckles.

Blake says, "Will I be OK? You're worried about me? You're a princess. I have to take this hit. Faggini won't harm you. He'll also release you if the hit goes badly. Don't worry. I remember his granddaughter. She was his whole world. Unfortunately, he spoiled her rotten and she got rather head strong in her teens. She's about Kyle's age. If the Columbian has her, well, I'm surprised he didn't ask me to take her out also." He sounds sad about this young girl's fate. Two men come into the room.

One of them says, "We have the film and information you need. Tigerman, you're on the clock. You have 71 hours and 42 minutes to kill the Columbian."

The thug returns without Kyle he says, "Time to go back to your room *sweety.*" Blake points his gun at the man who steps back, hands raised.

Blake tells him, "Mrs. Dailey to you. Don't forget. Don't force me to give you a lesson in manners." The man nods and doesn't touch me. The door closes silently behind me. Some one already removed the dead man and cleaned up the blood in the hall. A few minutes later, a tray is brought with a light supper of fruit and cheeses. Something must have been drugged because I got really dizzy after eating. When I open my eyes, it's morning. Someone removed my shoes and covered me during the night. I slip from the bed into the bathroom and then put back on my shoes. At 8 the door opens and the man gestures to come out into the hall. I precede him downstairs into the formal dining room.

Gesturing at the seat on his left, Mr. Faggini says, "Sit. Please. I don't intend to keep you locked in a room all day." Kyle is already seated on his right. At his nod, a maid begins serving plates of breakfast. My plate contains an omelet, bacon, toast and fresh fruit. Kyle's plate is identical to mine only the portions are larger. Mr. Faggini has toast and a cup of black coffee.

Gesturing towards the plate I ask boldly, "Is this also drugged?" Mr. Faggini laughs and shakes his head.

He says, "No. I wanted the both of you asleep last night to prevent Tigerman from slipping inside my security again. The man is like a beam of light from a laser, impossible to keep out. Eat, you look pale this morning or is there a little one growing in that lovely flat belly of yours?" I blush at his words and quickly shake my head. When I look up, his eyes tell me he remembers every inch of what he saw yesterday. I realize only his fear or some sort of respect of Blake keeps him from taking me.

To no one in particular, he states, "She blushes, how refreshing. I also admire your bravery yesterday. You would have gone for the gun, no?" He raises one eyebrow.

In complete honesty, I answer, "Yes. If I was given half a chance." I pick up my fork and once I taste the food find I'm rather hungry. Kyle begins eating in earnest only after I do. He's silent. I sense he's feeling helpless and inadequate due to being unable to protect or rescue me. I'm hoping he doesn't try anything foolish. After we're finished eating, Mr. Faggini has us join him in the music room. He sits at a large baby grand piano and plays several classical music pieces.

He asks, "Do you play?" I nod but refuse to play for him. He just smiles softly. Then we're forced to return to our respective rooms until the evening meal.

The mid day meal is a tray of fruit and Italian bread. I enjoy the cup of hot tea with lemon and honey. There are no drugs. A maid comes into my room with a lovely lavender colored evening dress and the necessary accessories.

Bowing before she leaves, she states, "Please, Mr. Faggini requests you dress for dinner." I gather it's not an open suggestion but a stern request. I'm ready when the guard knocks on my door. Again, I'm taken to the formal dining room. Kyle is seated in his same seat and wearing a tux. Mr. Faggini is also wearing a tux and rises to pull my chair out.

Being very careful not to touch me but starring intently while taking his seat he says, "As I imagined, you are breath taking in that creation." I glance over and Kyle is also starring.

Mr. Faggini asks, "Is she not the most beautiful creature you've ever seen, young Dailey?" Kyle nods. The gown is strapless and backless and held in place by my breasts and a firm built in bra. The waist is tight and fitted and the skirt has a slit from thigh to the hem that falls just above my knees. Like Mr. Faggini, I gasp when Blake appears beside me.

Pulling out the chair and sitting without waiting for an answer Blake asks, "Do you mind if I join you?" His hand caresses my bareback. I lean towards him for a lingering kiss. I sense he's establishing his territory.

Blake turns to Mr. Faggini and says, "What a lovely dress you've provided for my wife. I had no idea the dinner was formal or I would have dressed." Mr. Faggini raises his glass in a silent toast and smiles at Blake's words. Another setting is immediately brought and we dine in silence. After dinner, Mr. Faggini insists we retire to the front parlor. He puts on a classical piece on the stereo and sits.

Like some old Baron or Lord, Mr. Faggini says, "Dance with your wife. Then you may take her upstairs for the night. I would not deny young lovers their passions." Kyle has the first dance and then its Blake's turn. After a few dances, Kyle is escorted back to his room. Blake nods to Mr. Faggini and we go upstairs. I'm surprised at the passion he displays once the door is closed.

He grabs the front of the dress and rips it from me saying, "I don't want you wearing this again for anyone." Then he pulls me gently into his arms. His kiss is hard and deep. I feel myself eagerly responding. My mind keeps screaming that this might be our last time together. He picks me up and throws me onto the bed and then playfully jumps over top of me. We wrestle on the bed until our body's demand we give in to our passions. When I awake in the morning, he's gone. I have the sweats back on and only his scent on the other pillow tells me it wasn't a dream. For the next three days, there is no word or sight of Blake. By the third day I'm unable to eat or even leave my room. Kyle comes to visit in the afternoon. He sits on the bed and holds me.

He says softly, "I'm worried about him too." I sigh and lean against him. I have to trust Blake to survive. Kyle leans back against the head of the bed. I sleep in his arms.

"Hey, little brother, what are you doing sleeping with my wife?" I jump at Blake's teasing tone and throw myself into his arms.

Kyle says, "Thank God." Standing and sliding from the bed.

Blake states simply, "It's over." We walk down the stairs. Mr. Faggini is sitting in the front parlor with an ice pack to his face.

He removes it and nods towards me saying, "A small price to pay for the visions I'm still having of your lovely wife, Tigerman." Blake growls as we continue through the room and into the elevator. Blake throws the unconscious man whose body was holding the doors open out into the room with Mr. Faggini. Mr. Faggini has returned the ice pack to his face. It appears Blake broke his nose. Down in the garage, the familiar Jeep is waiting. We pass several men who are simply unconscious in various positions. I don't want to look close enough to see if they are dead. Some things are better left unknown.

Blake is silent as we weave our way out of Manhattan towards Kennedy Airport and our jet. When we pass a sign indicating a right turn to the airport, I turn and look at him. Blake says, "We're driving to Syracuse. I never do the expected."

Kyle leans forward from the back seat to ask, "Did you kill that man—the Columbian?"

Blake answers, "Yes. I also gave Dustin a little scare for his carelessness with my wife. I had several friends throw pigs blood all over her gallery and photo studio late at night. The people I had watching said she urinated all over herself when she walked in and discovered the mess. Evidently Dustin mentioned my threats of retribution once you and Kyle were abducted. I would never harm a woman and innocent child." Blake is watching the road and the rearview mirror.

I tell him, "That must have taken Dustin down off his high horse for a few hours. I know you would never harm innocent people." I lean my head back and go to sleep. I'm awake instantly when the Jeep stops.

Blake's voice says from the darkened interior, "It's OK, we're going to sleep here tonight." It's really dark. There's a lot of snow blowing so I can't see any sign. Blake comes around and gets my door. We're at the Homewood Suites in Liverpool, NY according to the signs in the lobby. Blake gets a two-bedroom suite and refuses the porters help. Blake tips him anyway so the porter goes away happy.

In the suite, Kyle goes into his room and closes the door. Blake and I head into our bedroom. We have a nice hot shower and then dress for bed. Blake orders room service. The three of us sit and eat in the lounge area. Blake starts a fire in the fireplace before room service delivers our dinner. Kyle is strangely silent until after we've eaten. Blake is watching him.

Finally, once the trays are reloaded and placed outside the door Blake turns to Kyle and asks, "What's bothering you?"

Kyle sits heavily into the nearest sofa and sighs before he says, "I don't want to go back home. Can't we go back to where you were and live?" I close my eyes at the expression on his young face. Blake sits across from him and pulls me over into his lap.

He tells Kyle, "That's not possible. You know dad isn't in the best of health. I noticed as soon as I returned home that he's too heavy and headed for a heart attack or worse. The ranch is too much for him. Having you disappear and never return will kill him. Think of all the extra work he has now that you're gone. He won't eat right and he definitely won't accept help from Devin." I hear how much Blake loves his father in the tone of his voice. Kyle nods in silent agreement.

Blake reassures him saying, "You go back. He'll be so happy you've returned, nothing else will matter."

Kyle sighs and says, "Yeah, something will matter. You're the favorite son. In spite of what he's screamed in anger, he still loves you. His pride won't let him admit how happy he was when you returned or how devastated he was when his rage sent you away. You come back with me. Let him see how much in love you and Katherine are. Please." Kyle's tone is pleading. Blake runs his hands up and down my arms as Kyle talks. It has always been hard for Blake to refuse Kyle anything. They share a special love between them that brothers are sometimes lucky enough to have.

Blake says, "I don't think that would be a good thing. I'll give it a try, but I think you're going to discover he doesn't want me there. Especially covering Katherine, it's hard for you to picture but he does want her for himself." Kyle shakes his head and frowns at Blake's words. He doesn't want to let himself believe that his father has sexual feelings towards me.

Kyle says, "I'm sure you're wrong. I was really in love with Katherine but I'm happy you're married to her. She loves you and you're happy. Now I love her like a big sister." Then he blushes and looks away. I smile because that must have been hard for him to say with me sitting here. Blake sighs and shifts his hips under me.

Blake says, "I hope you're right. Kyle, I'm going to take my lovely wife to bed now. She's tired and you look tired. If the weather clears, we'll be headed south after breakfast. Get a good nights rest." Kyle nods and stands when we do. I get a nice kiss on my cheek from Kyle and then we walk to the bedroom. I glance back and Kyle is standing staring into the flames. Inside the bedroom, Blake strips and gets ready for bed. I slip into a heavy flannel gown and crawl into bed beside him. He holds me in his arms until I fall asleep.

I'm alone in the bed in the morning. I discover Blake shaving in the shower. I strip and join him. My attempts at arousing him are unsuccessful. He says, "Kyle." While kissing me and wrapping me in a towel. We quickly dress and repack. Kyle is sitting in the parlor area, his suitcase by the door.

Rising he says, "Good morning."

Blake tells him. "The snow has stopped." Blake goes into the bedroom to make a call and is smiling when he returns.

Blake says, "Faggini canceled the contract. All the players have been notified and we can go home." Kyle nods and picks up his suitcase. I know Blake won't let his guard down for days, possibly even weeks or months. I fear someone out there might not have gotten the word.

Blake tells me, "Wipe the worry from your face. The contract money has been withdrawn. No one will work for free . . . not against me, anyhow."

Kyle ventures, "Friends in high places?" There's surprise on Blake's face before he silently nods. We check out and take the Jeep north in I-81 towards the airport.

Kyle asks, "Can we eat?" Blake chuckles.

Taking the next exit when the road sign says has a Denny's restaurant, he says, "Still a growing boy, I forget. You always were the hollow one." They're 24 hour breakfast places. We park and walk inside. It's busy even though it's mid morning on a weekday. The food smells make my stomach growl and Blake chuckles.

He asks, "Are you also hungry mother?" and I nod.

We get seated at a circular corner booth and quickly place our order. The massive breakfasts are soon gone. Kyle finishes what's left on my plate. I think Blake pegged him right, he's hollow.

They banter over the tab before Kyle says, "OK. You win. You can pay, big brother." Blake chuckles. Kyle is tight with his cash. I recall he always was. While I'm leaving the tip, Blake slides from the booth to walk towards the register.

I stop to zip my jacket and Kyle says, "Come on poky, keep the line moving." Without thinking, I gesture for him to go ahead. He teasingly does and then grabs my coat to pull me along after him.

I glance up as a man bumps into Blake at the register causing him to drop his keys. When Blake bends to pick up his keys, the man gruffly says, "Sorry." Beyond Blake a second man is pulling a pistol from inside his coat.

I scream, "Gun!" Blake drops and rolls. Kyle jumps in front as the man fires. The force of the bullets impact throws Kyle backwards into me. We fall back onto the floor. Blake fires once and the fleeing man goes through the glass doors into the parking lot. Kyle is jerking and making horrible gurgling noises. Blake rolls to his feet and turns to face us, his gun already back in its holster.

Rushing to our side, he says, "Oh God!" He pulls Kyle up into his arms. There's blood everywhere. There are the sounds of footfalls and people screaming while fleeing the restaurant. I sit up and throw my arms around Kyle in Blake's arms. He's jerking and blood is coming from his mouth.

Before his head falls forward, he quietly tells Blake, "I saved her for you."

Blake screams, "No! Don't you die, damn you Kyle! Don't you die on me!" The tears are streaming down his face. Suddenly I realize Kyle has died.

I start chanting, "No, no, no, no, no, no." and I can't stop. Blake finally puts his hand over my mouth to silence me. We sit in the pool of Kyle's blood and listen to the sounds of the approaching sirens. I reach inside to remove Blake's gun.

He puts his hand over mine saying, "I have a permit to carry in the United States. It's OK."

"This guys dead. Police! No body move!" At the officers loud words I glance around. Blake and I are the only occupants of the place. The two officers approach, their guns leveled at us.

As the officer holsters his gun, Blake says, "The man killed my brother. I think he was trying to rob the place. He was at the register behind me. Kyle moved and the bastard shot him."

The officer gestures towards the doors as he asks, "Who shot him?"

Blake calmly says, "I did. I have a pistol in a holster under my jacket and a permit in my wallet. Just reach in and take the gun." The young officer removes the gun while a second and then third officer cover us.

A waitress comes out from the kitchen and begins babbling, "I saw the whole thing. That dead man outside just pulled his gun and shot this poor boy. I think he was going to rob us. He was at the register. If it weren't for this guy, he might have opened fire on everybody. Oh God, mister, I'm real sorry about your brother. I was your waitress." She's crying. I vaguely remember her waiting on us and flirting with Kyle. One of the officers pulls her into the kitchen area. The place is full of cops. The officer with Blake's gun apologies and asks to see his permit.

As Blake gets his wallet out and hands the permit to the officer who says, "I'm real sorry about your brother Mr. Dailey. Is this lady your wife?" Blake nods and reaches over to caress my face. He doesn't realize that Kyle's blood is on his hand. I flinch before reaching up to grab his hand and kiss it.

Since I'm covered with blood, the officer asks, "Is she hurt?"

"No. I'm not hurt. This isn't my blood." I choke and fall silent. The coroner has a hard time getting Kyle's body away from Blake. I finally gasp Blakes hands and pull them free.

I tell him, "Let go, he's gone. Come on, *sweetheart*, let this man do his job." He looks up and his wide blue eyes are full of shock, innocence, hurt and disbelief. I stand and reach out my hands to him. He releases Kyle and watches as the coroners lift his body into a black body bag. Blake turns away and I pull him up into my arms.

We ride in a police car to the nearby police station for questioning. Blake wants to know when they'll release the body. Probably tomorrow, he's told. After several long grueling hours of talking with the police, filling out and signing our statements, we're taken back to the Jeep. We drive to the Best Western at Hancock Airport and get a room. Blake throws our bags on the bed. I strip and walk into the shower. I have blood everywhere. Blake soon joins me in the shower. He seems to want me to hold him. Once we're dry and in clean clothes, he sits staring into space at the end of the bed.

Blake suddenly says, "He was aiming right at you." I'm curled in an armchair looking at the room service menu.

I wasn't really listening so I ask, "What?"

Blake says, "The shooter. He was aiming at you. Someone put a contract on you." I shake my head.

I ask him, "Why would someone want me dead? You're the only person who would gain financially." I lower the menu onto the table.

He slowly says, "I'm the one person who would hurt the most." Then shaking his head, he continues to himself, "No, this has something to do with the contract on your father. Something is still going on about that. I'm thinking Eleanor or her crew is behind the contract. I just can't tie them directly." He brings a familiar slender black case over and opens it on the table. I sit and watch as he meticulously cleans his guns, one right after the other. I remain silent. He's obviously deep in thought. When his stomach growls, he looks up and slowly smiles.

He asks, "Anything good on that menu?" I shake my head. He closes and locks the case. We don our ski jackets and head out to the Jeep. Our other coats are covered with Kyle's blood. Blake brings the case along.

We end up at Peter's Market in North Syracuse. They have a nice deli selection behind the meat department with a selection of hot foods. We end up with deli style sandwiches; hot vegetable soup, slices of pizza and various desert items. Back at the hotel, there's a message from the police. They recommend several area funeral homes for a casket for taking Kyle home. Blake calls Krueger Funeral Home in Mattydale and they agree to handle matters. They'll pick up the body from the corner upon release and then prepare Kyle for shipment. Blake selects a casket from whatever they offered over the phone. After we have eaten, we drive to Mattydale and pay for everything. It doesn't take very long and everyone is really nice. It was on the 6 o'clock news and the funeral director expresses deep sympathy at Blake's loss. I don't pay much attention to anything. I can't believe that Kyle is dead. The inside of the funeral parlor is very new and modern but still smells like death. Back at the hotel, I vomit my dinner. Blake comes into the bathroom to pull me into his arms. I don't think he's fully aware of what he's doing.

He flops into a ball in the bed beside me. I pull the covers up over us and curl myself against his back. He takes my hands and kisses them several times before falling into a restless dream filled sleep. He's up at 5 a.m. pacing in the room. When I switch on the light, he's already dressed and shaved.

He asks. "Did I wake you?"

I tell him, "It's OK. I was done sleeping. Do you need to talk or should I turn the light out?"

He says, "No to both questions. I'm trying to put the pieces together in my mind. There are so many that don't fit. I called the police station. They released the body at 4 a.m. Krueger's has him. I'll call them after 6. I already talked to the pilot. He's ready to go within ten minutes of my next call. You should eat. After last night, you're empty." He sits beside me to pull me up into his arms for several nice kisses.

I hug him and then slip past him and into the bathroom. He has clothes laid out when I return. Room service brings a nice breakfast tray and like a vulture, I fall into the fruit, pastries, omelet and hot tea. Blake just picks.

Over the rim of my tea cup, I ask, "What's on your mind?"

Blake says, "Dad. I don't know if I should call him."

I shake my head saying, "No. You don't know how he'll react. He shouldn't be alone."

Blake says, "I knew you'd say that." Once we've eaten, Blake loads the car and we check out. Over at Krueger's I'm all right until they take us to see Kyle before closing the casket. Luckily there's a bathroom nearby. I was able to make the waste can just inside the door. Blake follows me right inside and then brings a cup of cool water to rinse my mouth.

I quickly tell him. "Sorry."

He hugs me saying, "It's OK sweetheart. I never expected to see him in a casket either." The funeral director asks if I need to sit upon our return. I shake my head. I sit in the Jeep while the casket is loaded into the hearse for the trip to the Jet. It seems like hardly any time at all and we're touching down at the Addison Municipal Airport in Dallas. Blake already called Devin from the air. Krueger made all the arrangements with a local funeral home to pick up the casket. Devin is waiting when we disembark.

As he puts his arms around me, he speaks to Blake. "Man, if I had ever imagined he would get hurt, I'd have kept him here, somehow." Devin's voice is trembling. Blake takes his offered hand.

He tells Devin, "Not your fault. He took a bullet meant for Katherine." Devin gasps and holds me at arms length to look into my face.

He asks, "Why?" and I shrug.

Blake says, "I haven't figured that out yet. I thought perhaps you'd give it some thought from your point of view. Know anyone who'd want to kill your sister except for Eleanor?"

Devin grinds his teeth before he says, "No. I'm coming with you to your dad's. I was over to see him yesterday and he's not good. He's a total wreck since Kyle left. Blake, this may kill him." Devin warns. I turn in time to see Blake glance away. The hour drive to the ranch is over too soon. We have to wait for the hearse for Kyle. Blake wants him taken home so the driver follows us to the ranch.

At the ranch, Devin wants to go inside first but Blake says no. Blake strides across the porch and directly into the breakfast area. I'm close behind him. Devin is practically walking on my heels. Blake comes to a sudden stop at the sight of his father slouched in a recliner in the family room. I'm shocked at the pigsty appearance of the inside of the house. Frank raises his head off his chest and looks at Blake.

Frank says, "So, you've come home. Did you bring your brother back?" Frank tries to rise and slumps back into the chair. Blake walks hesitantly over to look down on his father. He squats on his heels and reaches to touch Franks arm.

Blake says, "I brought Kyle home. Dad, he's dead. He took a bullet meant for Katherine." I'm standing behind Blake and watching Franks face.

He raises his eyes and says, "You look beautiful. I guess married life agrees with you." Then it's like Blake's words sink in. His face gets all red and his mouth pulls back into a snarl as he tips his face to look at Blake.

Frank screams, "YOU! First you steal my woman and then you get your brother killed! You have some nerve coming back here. I threw you out. I'd have welcomed you back but not now. You've killed everything that meant anything to me!" He starts to rise and then whatever he's saying becomes garbled mumbles. He clutches at his face and throat. Blake grabs him and puts him onto the floor.

Blake yells, "Call 911." but Devin is already at the phone. Blake opens Frank's shirt and I get a pillow for under his head.

Devin says, "Possible stroke or heart attack. Send the air rescue." It's a long 20 minutes until air rescue arrives. They give him that new medicine after determining he's had a stroke. Blake drives the Jeep. Devin stays to have the funeral men put the casket in the living room. I suggested there. That room is untouched by clutter. At the hospital, it's a long wait until the doctors come out.

The Doctor says, "Mr. Dailey?" Blake rises and walks towards the doctor who continues, "Your father has had a massive stroke. We have him on a respirator and we're going to watch him closely over the next 24 hours. You should go home. We'll call you if there's any change. There's nothing you can do for him here." Blake nods and we walk silently outside to the Jeep. During the entire wait, Blake said not one word. He slips his arm around me and then helps me into the Jeep. Back at the ranch, as I step out of the Jeep, everything goes black. I open my eyes in Blake's old bedroom upstairs. Blake is sitting on the bed beside me. Devin is standing tense and pale at the foot.

Blake sternly says, "You should warn me." But, there's only worry in his face.

Devin says, "Little sis, you just took five more years off my life. When I saw Blake with your lifeless body in his arms, I thought the worse. What made you faint?" Devin is gripping the end of the bed.

Blake says, "Lack of food probably. I don't imagine dad has much of anything here."

Devin says, "I'll call and have Cook bring our dinner over. She's probably frantic anyway." Suddenly anxious to escape, Devin turns and strides from the room.

Blake says, "I remembered how you've been vomiting everything you've eaten the minute your eyes rolled up into your head. Let's get you ready for bed before Cook gets here with dinner." He's good at getting me ready for bed. I get a nice back rub before Cook's a tap at the door.

Blake says, "Yes." Cook pushes the door open and strides into the room. She has a very concerned look.

Cook says, "I'm happy to see you Miss Katherine but you don't look good. This fried chicken dinner should straighten you right out. If not, I'm going right back and make homemade chicken soup and fresh scones." She sets the tray across my lap and glances at Blake.

She tells him, "I have a big basket downstairs for you and Mr. Devin. You don't look good either. I'm sorry about Mr. Kyle. He was a sweet boy." She has tears in her eyes and turns and quickly strides from the room. I didn't get a chance to say anything. Blake is stealing my drumstick. There are fresh potato dumplings and sweet carrots.

Blake wanders downstairs and returns with a huge plate full of food. He has a beer and sits in a chair beside me. What I don't eat, he finishes. The tray is empty when Blake removes it. Now that I have eaten, I feel stronger. I slip into a robe and quickly head downstairs. I find Blake gathering trash in the family room. I realize he needs something to keep himself occupied. I quickly pitch in. It takes us almost two hours to get the trash gathered, dirty dishes washed and away and the laundry partially done. We make sure the living room is spotless. Kyle's death will be in the papers tomorrow. People are sure to come to call.

I finally say, "Blake, it's after midnight. You need to get some rest. I'm sure the ranch is in just as deplorable a condition." He nods at my words and remains downstairs only long enough to turn out the lights. Once he climbs into bed, he wants my arms around him. He sleeps nestled against me. At 5 a.m. he's awake and climbing from the bed. I quickly follow. While he showers and shaves, I head down to start tea and some breakfast. At 6 a.m. Devin knocks on the back door. Blake motions for him to enter. He already has a mug of coffee.

Devin says, "Morning. I thought you could use some help. Frank refused my offers of assistance. From the looks of this place, his hands have gotten rather slack." Devin sits and grabs a piece of bacon and a homemade biscuit.

Pushing his plate away, Blake says, "Thanks. I dread seeing what needs done."

Blake sadly shakes his head and says, "I can't believe my little brother is lying in a casket in the next room." Devin glances quickly towards the living room. They rise together and head outside.

Blake says, "I have my cell phone." before he kisses me.

I tell him, "I'll call as soon as the hospital does." Then I begin clearing the table. I get the dishes washed and food out for lunch. The phone begins ringing but all the calls are neighbors wanting to talk to Frank about Kyle. I spend the morning explaining that he's had a stroke and is in the hospital. Many want to know where the body is and when they can come by. Most I tell I'll have to ask Blake because of wanting to see Frank as soon as he's able to have visitors. The hospital finally calls at 1. Frank is out of the critical care unit and in the intensive care unit. He's pretty well drugged but we could come by after 6 this evening. I quickly call Blake and relay the message.

Blake says, "OK. We'll do the viewing thing tomorrow afternoon and the funeral the following day. Dad won't be up in time regardless. Plan on an early dinner, say 4 or a late lunch at 2 so we can go up and sit with dad. I love you." He sounds so tired.

I tell him, "I love you too." and the line's quiet. He's in at 2 for lunch. I have a large beef roast and all the fixings.

Blake says, "Sure smells good in here." He comes over and I get a stinky kiss.

I tell him, "Whew. You have been working!" He laughs.

Blake says, "I certainly have. The place is in need of a lot of work. Devin brought four guys over. We've almost got the barns and stables livable. Two of the horses had to be put down. That Sam is a good man." I nod in agreement. Blake quickly showers in his father's bathroom and comes out in a familiar white robe. I feel tears sting my eyes at the sight of Franks robe.

Blake says, "I know, sweetheart, I know. Devin says he wanted to write and tell us about the place but Kyle said no. Now, he wishes he hadn't listened. Kyle must have been doing the work of three guys and almost killing himself." He stops suddenly and sits heavily at the table and lays his head into his hands. I put my arms around him. There are no words I can say to ease the pain in his heart.

I tell him, "Eat. Let's go see how your dad is doing." I get a kiss on my palms and then I'm released to take my seat. Blake dresses while I do the dishes. I already put nicer slacks and blouse on before dinner. Blake comes down in a somber looking navy blue suit. We wave at Sam who's busily working in the front lawn. Blake is silent during our drive to Dallas. We park and walk hand in hand into the hospital and the elevator. Frank is asleep and hooked up to a multitude of monitors and IV's. Blake paces in the room while I sit and hold Franks hand. I talk to him some but it's hard to find things to say. I realize I should call my father and tell him about Frank's stroke.

After an hour, Blake wants to leave. He is distressed at the sight of his father laying so still in a hospital bed. On the drive home I mention calling my father.

Blake says, "You should. I forget he and dad are best friends. If dad dies and your father has to hear then, well . . ." He suddenly stops talking and seems deep in thought. At the house, we sit with Kyle's body for awhile after I call my father. He is very upset that we didn't call sooner. He did, however seem madder at Devin for not calling than me. That seems unusual. He's calling Devin to make arrangements for his flight down. I relay the conversation to Blake but he seems so distant. I end up sitting silently, just watching him. He's staring intently at Kyle although his body posture appears relaxed. Finally, I can't tolerate the silence.

I tell him, "I'm going to bed." Blake nods at my words but doesn't turn or speak. I rise and head quickly upstairs. I slide into a flannel gown and get into bed. After a while, I hear Blake's footsteps on the stairs.

From outside the door, he whispers, "Katie girl?".

When I answer, "Yes?" He opens the door in about three strides he's across the room.

He throws the covers back saying, "I'm taking you downstairs." and scoops me from the bed. I put my arms around his neck and hold on as he strides down the hall and stairs and then back to his father's bedroom. The first thing I notice are the candles burning all around the room. I remember his mother's passion for candles. He has placed white lacy sheets on the bed and thrown the covers wide open. He lays me in the bed and begins kissing me.

He says, "I have to have you here . . . in his bed. You're mine. You love me . . . right?" His slowly spoken words are a mere whisper. I smell beer on his breath.

I tell him, "I love you. There's never been anyone in my heart but you Blake. Please, don't hurt me again." His hands are tender but his needs are urgent. He's gentle but insistent with his touch and kisses. I feel strange being in Frank's bed. I'm definitely confused by Blake's need to make love in his parent's bed.

He gazes down into my face for the longest time before he says, "You do love me. I know that in my heart. Why do I have these damnable doubts in my mind? I had my life all planned out. In Utah, everything was so simple. I couldn't be satisfied just being there with you." He begins planting kisses all over my face and neck. Finally, we sleep until Devin's pounding on the back door wakes Blake with a start at 7 a.m. He jumps from the bed, naked and briefly disoriented. He pulls open the night stand drawer and removes a Colt 45 revolver.

As he begins to stride naked from the room, I holler, "Clothes! Blake." He returns to grab the white bathrobe from the nearby armchair. The pounding has resumed before he can get across the hall in front of the living room and through the kitchen to the back door. I hear Blake laugh and then Devin's distressed voice. I hastily put on my night gown and dash through the house to the two men. Devin blushes at my appearance.

Devin says, "Sorry. I was at surprised the lack of activity, my imagination ran away." I wave before walking back through the family room and up the back stairs. By the time I return, Blake has breakfast started. Devin has a fresh cup of coffee to sip on.

We hardly have the house in order before neighbors begin showing up with casseroles and sympathy. Blake knows all these people and introduces me. Of course, none of them knew we had wed but most are pleased. My father arrives at 10 from the airport. He refuses Devin's offer to meet him.

Devin explains, "Father told me he prefers the solitude of a limo to the uncomfortable silence of my vehicle." Devin shrugs but I know the statement was probably harshly said. We are all surprised at the sight of Eleanor on his arm. Although Blake gets a frosty look, she mostly acts sweet for the guests in the house. From the way her eyes scan the rooms, she's probably thinking she should have held out for Frank. This is a much grander house and grounds than Father's.

Many of the neighbor women treat me as the hostess. I guess since Blake is the only remaining heir, that's as it should be. It feels strange knowing Frank asked me to marry him and assume this very position. After four long exhausting hours, the last guest has finally been shown out. My father and Eleanor left without saying good bye. I ask Blake where they were.

He replies, "They left about an hour ago. Your father looked rather tired. You were in the kitchen. I said I'd tell you." I nod. He walks to stand next to the casket, hands gripping the side of the opening. He says, "Tomorrow, little brother we put you in the ground never to see your beloved face again. I never thought we'd have only 19 short years or I'd have found the strength to stay here." I stand silently beside him. I wondered why he left home. He glances quickly towards me.

He confides, "You never knew dad asked me to go live somewhere else . . . did you?" I shake my head.

Blake continues, "I think with him it's always been a territorial thing. I wonder if he was attracted to you while mother was sick. You were always here, helping with the house and Kyle. I was young and totally naive to grown men's glances. I never had sexual thoughts about you. My memories are of how much fun it was to tease you until your delightful Irish temper kicked in. Your eyes would flash and your cheeks would get these little red areas, right here." He caresses my face with his thumbs and then leans down to kiss me.

Then he continues, "Maybe subconsciously I saw something in the way he watched you. I can't explain my actions over these past few days. Since I've brought you here I seem to want to possess you. I have such a need to know you're totally mine." He touches my lips to silence me.

Blake softly says, "I know you love me. I'm sorry for what Faggini put you through. My contact in the house said he made you strip while he watched. He's a voyeur, always liked to look. I'm constantly amazed by your love for me. Even knowing what I've done, watching me kill a man, you just keep opening your arms and heart. If anything ever happens to you, I'll go crazy." He stops and glances down at Kyle.

After a long silence, Blake tells me, "The hospital has made arrangements for dad to be brought to the funeral in an ambulance and wheel chair. I spoke with them earlier this afternoon. He's responding very well to the medicine and has been insisting on attending his son's funeral. His left side is badly affected and his speech is practically unintelligible. He's going to need a lot of help and therapy. I told them we'd take care of him here. Will you do that? Care for my father? I'll do the bathing if necessary. The doctors think he'll do so much better at home." Blake stops and stares into my eyes. I tip my head and widen my eyes.

I ask in amazement, "Why would I not take care of your father? About the bathing, we'll see how he feels. I don't want to make him uncomfortable or upset." I smile and he lowers his head to kiss me. His arms tighten and pull me up against him fully. With a swift sweeping motion, I'm in his arms and carried upstairs. His love making is slow, sensual and tender. This is the Blake I love.

The following morning, Blake tells me his father is insisting Kyle be laid to rest beside his mother in the little cemetery at a nearby church. Evidently Frank is making the hospital staff's life hell. They have him on a bland diet and lots of different medications. He has very high blood pressure and they want him to lose at least 100 pounds. The funeral home is here at 8 for Kyle's body. Blake follows the casket out to the hearse and stands in the cold wind watching as the hearse drives away. I finally make him come inside.

I tell him, "You'll make yourself sick. Please, come inside." He nods at my words and after several gentle tugs, allows me to pull him inside. Then he goes and sits in the living room staring at where the casket had been resting. There are still several floral arrangements flanking the empty spot where the casket stood.

An hour later, I have to make him come upstairs to get dressed for the 1 p.m. funeral. I lay out his black suit and tie and clean underwear.

I tell him, "Blake, come on, let's shower and get dressed." He responds to my words like a small child to his mother. It takes me almost an hour to get him bathed and dressed. I have to tell him to do everything a half a dozen times and then help him. The funeral home sent a black limo. I'm glad. I didn't want him driving and wasn't sure if he would let me.

Frank is already at the funeral home when we arrive. He's got a male attendant and a female nurse with him. He's strapped into a wheelchair alongside the casket. He struggles to talk but I can't understand his words. The nurse explains he's glad to see me and can't believe Kyle is dead. I nod. Evidently she has been listening to him long enough to understand the slurred words. It's an effort for Frank to talk so mostly he nods at people. Everyone is concerned and understanding of his condition. He shakes Blake's hand. His face is distorted on the left side. My father is shocked at his first sight of Frank but recovers quickly.

Once Father arrives, Frank seems to draw strength from him. The funeral service is over quickly. Blake is distant and silent. I expected him to be. I know some of what's going through his mind. Between his father's condition and his brother's death, it's a bitter pill to swallow as my mother used to say. It's an ordeal getting Frank to the graveside but one that is expertly accomplished by the hospital and ambulance staff. At the graveside, it's bitter cold. There's a north wind that feels like it's blowing directly from the Arctic Circle. I huddle in my chair trying to use Blake's body as a windbreak.

Several of Blake's friends appear at the gravesite after the service is over and the dirt is thrown onto the casket. I tossed a red rose. I couldn't bear to throw dirt onto Kyle. Blake stays behind after everyone else has left. The women's league of the church is hosting a covered dish affair and everyone walked there. The men just materialize around us. I realize they're probably also for-hire killers. Blake motions for me to walk to the church but I shake my head. He shrugs the turns and speaks low and briefly to the men. I don't look at them and don't pay any attention to what's said. I just stand starring into the open grave and shivering. Blake tugs on my arm and when I look up, we're alone. We walk to the church and fill plates with food. It's good and once I take the first bite, I discover I'm hungry and I eat. Blake pushes the food around on his plate and sits starring into space.

Father and Eleanor are constantly near Frank and leave when he does. Blake sits silently and nods at people who offer their sympathy and then take their leave. Blake and I are the last to leave. Our limo is sitting out front at the foot of the church steps. The wind is still blowing. Blake walks past the limo and over to the now covered graveside. I consider getting into the limo out of the wind over following Blake. Another glance at Blake reveals that he's not looking back but striding purposefully towards the grave. I shrug and once the driver has the door opened, climb into the limo.

The man crouching inside off towards the front of the limo springs at me the moment the driver closes the door. He's on me in seconds and puts something over my face as I struggle everything goes black. The nausea hits me before I open my eyes. I blink several times to try and clear my vision. I'm on the back seat of the limo and we're moving. My hands are cuffed to something over my head and I'm covered with a warm blanket. Through the glass divider I see the outlines of the two men as headlights pass us. Someone placed a pillow under my head and along my side.

I yell, "Hey!" The passenger man turns and says, "She's awake, pull over." I feel the car slow and then stop. The passenger gets out and opens the back door and climbs in.

I tell him, "I'm going to be sick." He grabs a nearby ice bucket and discovers I wasn't kidding. He wipes my mouth and gives me some water from the bar to rinse with.

He tells me, "We aren't going to hurt you. We got a job to do and you're going to help us make a lot of money." He appears to be in his mid twenties but muscular. His eyes are light gray and his hair is dark blonde and very naturally curly.

He watches me examining his face and says, "You can call me Mac, Mrs. Dailey. I'm going to take good care of you until we get the OK to let you go." He has a wide smile and a full mouth of white teeth. Judging from the deep lines around his mouth, he smiles a lot.

He looks sad when he tells me, "I can't take the cuffs off, we been told exactly what to do during transport. Do you have to go to the bathroom while we're stopped?" I widen my eyes and glance around. It's dark outside.

I tell him. "Yes." He takes a key and unlocks the cuffs only long enough to cuff me to him.

He says, "I won't look." while turning his face away. He helps me climb from the car. My body is stiff and my arms are asleep from being over my head. When I get out into the wind, I really have to go. We stumble down the embankment into the nearby woods. Luckily, I done this before but not cuffed to a man I just met. I dig several tissues from my coat pocket and then we walk back up to the limo. He again cuffs me securely to the metal ring and fixes the pillows and blankets. The motion of the car soon puts me back to sleep.

The smell of food wakes me and my stomach growls. Mac is climbing into the back. He has breakfast sandwiches, orange juice and coffee. He removes one cuff so I have a hand to eat with. He's even nice enough to rub my arm until the sensation returns and the pins and needles stop.

He says, "We'll stop in a little while and you can go to the bathroom." I nod my understanding and eat as the car begins moving again. We're headed north on Route 20. I would venture we'll soon be picking up Route 85. This has something to do with Eleanor and my father. I'm probably the bait to get father killed. Well, I have supreme confidence in Blake and his abilities so I'll just wait for him to rescue me. Unless, of course, these guys happen to get careless. I remember clearly what happens to guys who get careless!

The driver gets off an exit to a small town and stops at a local gas station. Mac gets the key to the ladies room and again cuffs me to him. It's not easy to go to the bathroom with him standing beside me. It's a small cubicle without a window so he removes the cuff and steps outside.

He warns, "Please. No funny stuff." and I nod. There is a muffled conversation as the driver talks to him and then Mac taps on the door. I unlock it.

He hands in a plastic bag saying, "Put these on." I take the bag and discover a pair of jeans, tee, flannel shirt and clean underwear. There are even canvas shoes and white socks which will keep my feet warmer than these heels and hose. I quickly change, wash up and unlock the door. Mac blocks my exit until we are cuffed together again. He smiles and nods at my docile actions. He steps inside to make sure I haven't left any messages before we climb into the nearby limo.

The drive keeps to the speed limit. We stop only long enough for gas, toilet breaks and food. Shortly before daybreak we're pulling behind a row of old homes that have been converted into little shops in Petersburg. This would be Eleanor's florist shop on the front. The limo stops only long enough for Mac to hustle me from the back across the deck and inside the building. Eleanor is waiting inside and opens the door immediately. She gives me such a look of hatred that I shudder. Mac gives me a reassuring squeeze.

She says with a gesture, "Upstairs, the middle room is ready." Mac takes me quickly through the house and up the stairs into a nice sized bedroom. This must have been Jaycee's room. In the corner on the left is a single bed. Mac immediately cuffs me to a length of chain secured to the old fashion radiator beside it. I sit on the bed. Mac walks across the room to sit facing me in an old stuffed chair. Eleanor shuts and locks the door from the outside. I hear a bolt slide into place and Mac smiles reassuringly. He gestures towards his left.

He says, "Bathroom." I nod. The chain is only about six feet long but allows me some freedom. Not enough to reach the double windows behind Mac or the bathroom.

Our breakfast is brought up through the bathroom. Evidently the bedroom door is going to remain bolted shut. I'm sure the windows are bolted shut also. I didn't get much of a chance to look around downstairs. There was a front room set up like a little florist shop with samples displays. The back area of the house was set up to assemble the arrangements. I caught glimpses of long tables cluttered with ribbons, wires and silk flower assortments. Mac takes the breakfast tray and frowns at the selection under the towel. There is cold cereal in those little boxes and a small container of milk and two of orange juice. We have plastic spoons to eat with and the boxes have to be opened to convert to the bowls. Once glance at the food and I'm gagging. Mac goes into the bathroom and returns with a basin.

He asks, "You been sick in the morning for long?" while I wipe my mouth. I shake my head.

He asks, "Are you pregnant?" I can only shrug. He smiles sort of knowingly.

He says, "I have six older sisters. When two of them were still in high school they started getting sick in the mornings like you. Tessa, she let mom and dad talk her into having an abortion. Nina, she had her baby. Toby is about six now and the apple of his grandfather's eye."

Mac stops and looks away before continuing, "Tessa killed herself a couple years ago. The abortion did something to her insides and she couldn't have any more babies. She just couldn't stand to be around Nina and Toby." He sadly shakes his head and brings me some water to rinse my mouth.

He firmly tells me, "I'll never make a baby and then cut out on the girl." He sits starring at his feet.

Before he looks up, he says, "Do you think Blake will kill me for us grabbing you?" Suddenly I'm reminded of Kyle.

I promise him, "I won't let him. If you take good care of me and don't let anyone hurt me, I'll protect you." He nods.

I hesitantly say, "I'd like a little tea to settle my stomach." He rises and goes downstairs. He returns in about six minutes with a steaming cup of tea.

He hands it to me saying, "I put sugar in it." I sip and smile. The tea helps. After several more trips downstairs for water and a small card table, we play cards to pass the time. I don't think anyone else is here. When I lay down to sleep, I hear Mac playing solitaire on the table. Dinner is some kind of greasy flat hamburgers and cold fries. I had eaten some of the dry cereal in the middle of the afternoon with some crackers Mac found downstairs.

After returning from a foraging expedition, he remarks, "Not much food down there." I gag at the sight of this food and Mac shrugs.

He sadly tells me, "Sorry. This is what the guy brought. I'll ask him for some fruit but I doubt he'll bring it." He's young and hungry. I gladly let him eat my burger. He finds some more crackers in the kitchen and makes another cup of tea.

Handing me the steaming cup, he says, "Sugar's all gone now." I sigh. I'd give him money but don't have my purse. I also doubt he'd be allowed to leave me alone.

I suggest, "Maybe there's some honey or brown sugar downstairs." He shrugs but smiles like he'll check the next trip.

When I want to go to the bathroom, I discover there's another length of chain in there. Mac transfers me from one to the other. At least I have privacy. At night, Mac goes through the bathroom to the front bedroom to sleep. There are two single beds in there. The following days' breakfast is a loaf of bread and a jar of peanut butter. Poor Mac, he does not care for peanut butter. I suggest French toast or a fried egg sandwich. Mac goes down and finds eggs. He returns with two fried egg sandwiches. They're pretty good. We pass the day playing cards. Mac talks about his parents a little. Evidently he's from a farm in the mid west somewhere. Being the only son, he got tired of working from sun up to sun down and finally split. He was in Miami for a while and then worked his way north. I'm surprised to learn he's older than me. He just looks so young. I think he's surprised when there isn't any dinner brought. I guess the bread is to last for a couple of days.

About 9, he cuffs us together and then takes me downstairs. I get to search the kitchen for something to cook. I find a can of chili on the pantry shelf and several hot-dogs in the freezer. We dine on chili dogs. There was a lemonade mix in one drawer which made a pitcher that was rather good mixed with the orange juice in the refrigerator.

Mac says, "You're a good cook." He eats four of the five hot dogs. Several times I call him Kyle instead of Mac. He asks if that was the boy who was buried. I nod and burst into tears. He gets very distressed and hustles me back upstairs. He goes down and cleans up the kitchen. I'm asleep before he returns. I awake with Jaycee leering down at me. I scream. Mac appears in the doorway of the bathroom.

He asks, "Hey! Who are you?" She turns slowly and looks at him.

She says, "This is my old room. Why don't you go back to your room and let Katherine and I get reacquainted? She really likes me. No matter how much she denies it. Right sweet thing?" I shake my head and slide up into the far corner of the bed.

Mac firmly says, "I'm taking care of her. I think you should leave." Mac comes to stand behind her.

She quickly turns and grabs his groin saying, "Oh, my you have quite a hand full there. Are you a back door kind of guy? My older brother introduced me to the fun of back door games." My skin crawls. Mac frowns and doesn't know what she means.

She gives this horse laugh and glances back to say, "I'll bet he doesn't even know what the front door is for. What do you think? I'll bet that pretty husband of yours didn't waste much time getting in your front door." Mac blushes as he realizes what she's talking about. He removes her hand and takes a grip on her arm.

He tells her, "Leave. Right now! Nobody touches Mrs. Dailey while I'm watching out for her." He walks her through the bathroom and the other bedroom.

When he returns, Mac tells me, "I put a chair under the doorknob. I don't like people sneaking past me when I'm asleep. I'm real sorry she scared you like that." I smile because judging from his tone; he's really embarrassed right now.

I tell him, "It's OK. You need to expect the unexpected." I sound like Blake and that makes me cry.

Now Mac is really flustered and unsure. "What's wrong? Why are you crying?" He quickly asks.

The bolt slides on the bedroom door while I'm talking, "I want to go home to my husband. I'm worried about Blake. I don't want to be here." Mac turns to face the door as the tumblers on the locks begin clicking. The door comes slowly open. I recognize the silencer and gun barrel moving the door. I sigh and Mac frowns. Blake slips quickly into the room and closes the door, his gun leveled at Mac. Mac raises his hands.

He quietly says, "I don't have a gun."

Blake says, "Toss the key to the cuffs onto the bed real slow." Mac nods and digs the key ring out with two fingers. I pick the keys up off the bed and unlock the cuffs.

While sliding off the bed, I quickly tell Blake, "Don't hurt him. He's kept me safe."

Blake angrily says, "He's part of the group who grabbed you."

I'm watching his face while I'm speaking, "I gave him my word you wouldn't harm him."

In an ice cold tone, he flatly says, "I didn't."

"I think I'm pregnant." That statement brings his attention fully on me.

He gives in and says, "OK. We leave him cuffed to the bed for the cops." I shake my head no.

"Let him go. Better yet, let him drive us to safety. That will leave you free to ride shotgun." Blake smiles at my words and then looks at Mac.

He asks, "Are you a good driver?"

Mac shrugs as he answers, "I guess so. I've never had an accident." Blake sighs. There is a lot of steel in his voice when Blake says, "You go first, the cars' out back. Anything goes wrong, you die first." This is the cold side of Blake. The killing animal side—the scary side. Blake keeps me between Mac and himself. His gun arm around me, a clear sight on Mac's back. At the foot of the stairs, Mac turns left and stops abruptly.

In a cold voice, Blake tells him, "Keep moving, she's soon dead." Mac moves hesitantly forward.

Blake softly tells me, "You might want to stare at his back, sweetheart." I wish I had. Sitting leaning against the wall and cuffed to the radiator on the right side is Jaycee. Her legs are spread and she's bleeding heavily from somewhere. She has gray duct tape over her mouth and her eyes are wide with terror.

Turning back to Blake, Mac hesitantly asks, "What did you do to her?"

Blake shrugs and explains in a matter of fact voice, "I gave her a good 18 inches of the shotgun she pointed at my face. Devin told me how she stood watching while her brothers got ready to rape my wife. I thought she should find out what rape feels like." Mac shudders at Blake's cold calm words and then continues walking towards the back door. Jaycee kicks out at me.

Blake angrily asks her, "Do you want a couple more inches?" She makes some kind of noise behind the tape but I'm not looking at her anymore. Blake moves me on with a thrust of his hips against my bottom.

Blake says softly, "She'll soon bleed to death; we have to get out of here."

There's another man in a long black duster and black cowboy style hat over by a sleek looking black racing machine. He nods at Blake and motions at the car.

Blake tells him, "Got us a new driver, Mac get in behind the wheel." Blake opens the back door. I slide inside and over. The man gets in beside Mac and slips the keys into the ignition.

He speaks in a very raspy voice, "Follow my directions and you'll do all right kid." When Mac turns the key, the engine just purrs to life.

The man tells Mac, "Take it slow. Don't call any attention to us." A silent Mac nods that he understands. Shifting into first gear, we head out the back alley to the main street. Turning right, we head south. Leaning forward, Blake slips the gun into the back of his jeans under his jacket. Then Blake sits back and lets his breath out in a long sigh.

I turn and look at him; the picture of Jaycee sitting in the pool of blood is still fresh on my mind. I reach my hands towards Blake and he pulls me over against his chest.

He softly asks, "Are you really carrying my child?" I shrug.

I tell him, "I've been sick in the mornings. Mac says his older sisters who were pregnant acted the same way. I haven't had my period this month. Maybe I messed up that test I did in Utah." I lean my head against his chest.

Blake says, "These last few days have been hell. I asked myself over and over again where my head was that I left home without a gun. I don't remember getting dressed or even going upstairs to dress. I reached inside my coat for my gun and had nothing. I stood and screamed at the limo as it carried you away. I had to have the preacher give me a ride home. Devin was waiting at the house. Someone left a message on his answering machine. He was to have me find Tigerman. There was a little matter that Tigerman needed to clean up. The matter was the hit on your father. Devin says your father wanted to stay here and spend some time with Frank while he recuperated but Eleanor insisted she needed to get home. They flew out that night. I was watching when your Mac here walked you into the back of the shop. I saw Eleanor open the door. I had someone watching the place. Once I knew you were safe, I was free to concentrate on the job at hand.

I'll spare you most of the gory details. It was easy to find out who took the hit once I saw who brought your breakfast that first morning." The man in the front seat chuckles softly.

Blake glances towards him before continuing, "Well, those two were always into something over their heads. DynoMike and his halfwit brother, Bulletbrain usually took the wet jobs no one else wanted. They got top pay that way. I've always wondered how long their luck would hold. Last night, their luck ran out all over the ground. Dyno's style was usually sloppy looking accidents. Your father was going to have a boating accident." I frown and look back at Blake.

I tell Blake, "That's ridiculous. Father doesn't own a boat. Besides, he detests being in any small craft on the water." Blake chuckles.

He says, "Eleanor didn't know that. She purchased a rather nice yacht for him. She actually got him out in it several times before you called about Frank. The plan was to get him out on the boat. Then there would be a terrible accident, probably involving an explosion. DynoMike got his name that way. To cut a long story short, the contract on your father is permanently canceled. Eleanor was planning on becoming a very wealthy widow. She recently discovered that the bulk of his fortune was well— actually your fortune. Imagine her surprise at discovering that when she drove you off, the fortune went with you. She was behind the hit that cost Kyle his life. She discovered an old will of your mothers stating the money would revert to Dillon in the event of your death. Of course, your mother never expected you to be married at 12 years of age. Eleanor and your father each took out healthy 10 million dollar life insurance policies on each other right after they got married. She decided the insurance money would have to suffice." He pulls a water bottle from a familiar backpack to take a drink. I grab the bottle and take a long drink myself.

Blake says, "I guess your father will live nicely on the 20 million from her policy. Since she was killed its double indemnity. However, his mind seems to be a bit befuddled. Katie girl, he's currently in a hospital in a catatonic state. They don't think he'll stay that way permanently. He couldn't seem to handle the information that the woman he fell in love with made arrangements to have him killed for money. His mind shut down. I swear, I didn't kill her in front of him. In fact, I didn't even kill her." He falls silent and looks down at me.

With a slight shrug, I say, "You're here, you're safe. Since my father beat me, I have had very mixed emotions about him. The shock of everything that's happened because of him has dulled my love towards him. It really doesn't seem to matter right now about him. I'm so happy you're safe." I nestle back against him and he puts his arms around me.

He sounds so tired when he says, "I swear I'm done with killing."

I reassure him, "I know. You've been forced to do some unpleasant things. Now we concentrate on having a child and getting your dad back on his feet. We have plenty to keep us occupied." His left hand slides down inside my sweat pants to caress my belly lightly.

He whispers, "A child."

The gravely voiced man says from the front seat, "Hey, introduce me to your special lady, ex-Tigerman."

Blake says, "Christian Soldyer, this is Katherine Dailey, my beloved wife. Katie girl, this is my good friend Christian." Christian turns and winks at me over the seat back.

He tells me with a broad smile, "You must be a very special lady to have captured this guy's heart so completely. I've never seen Blake in such a state as when he called for help to get you back. He also says you're a good cook so I'm coming back to find out." He has hazel eyes with dark heavy eyelashes. Now that his hat is off, I can see he's thinning a little on top. His dirty colored blonde hair is extremely straight and unruly. He has a rather large nose but a very sensual mouth. Although I wouldn't call him handsome, he has that certain animal magnetism like Charles Bronson, the actor. After we're on the road about two hours, Christian has Mac take an exit and gives him directions to a nice diner. My bladder is eternally grateful. I'm out of the car and up the steps into the diner before Blake has the door completely open. His laughter follows me as I step inside. When I return from the rest room, Blake is at the table alone.

He says, "Don't look worried, there was a line in the men's room. Actually, Christian is talking to Mac, getting a bit of his background, so to speak. Nothing painful or violent." Then he smiles and hands me a menu. I'm ravenous. I order cheese sticks, the half fried chicken dinner, large order of fries, chocolate shake and Caesar salad. The waitress raises her eyebrows.

Blake tells her, "Baby." She gives me the nicest smile. She has gray hair and is fairly plump. I guess she's late fifties or early sixties. She's a tall woman and from the way she moves, has been doing this for a long time. Christian and Mac return in time to order once Blake is through. He goes with the T-bone steak with Lobster tail side, fries and salad with French. He gets a beer. Christian says he'll have the same. Mac goes with a large burger, fries and a shake. Christian's raspy voice is very arousing to listen to and seems also to affect our waitress. We get the fastest service.

Christian says, "Mac and I will share the driving. I'm taking the next shift. I saw a Walmart just beyond the diner; we'll get pillows and blankets for Katherine. Mac's on your payroll now." Once he's finished talking, he grins at Blake Mac looks sheepish and I realize he probably has little or no money. I share my cheese sticks when they arrive. Luckily the waitress brought a triple order of them. Blake has two beers during dinner. I stick to bottled water. We are four extremely stuffed people at the meals end. I'm actually glad to walk around in the Walmart. Christian left the waitress a hundred dollar tip.

In the Walmart, I select a change of clothes and underwear. We purchase several nice blankets and firm pillows. There is a multitude of bottled water purchased. I discover there's a cooler in the trunk when Christian stops and gets ice to put into it. The cart Mac pushed seems to get a lot of junk food and snacks. I picked up several puzzle type books and sunglasses. Blake chases me in the parking lot. I let him catch me several times. While Christian gets ice, Mac pumps gas and I use the ladies room. Blake is right out side the door when I step out in my clean clothes. He hustles me right back inside.

He says, "You locked the door in my face, woman." He is busy tugging my new sweats off my hips.

I try to tell him, "Blake, the guys." but, he's too busy kissing me to hear. My bra is now unhooked.

Blake says, "I hate those things on you. They're taking a walk and checking the engine and watching the door." The bra is in the trash and my top is around my neck. There's a little cabinet containing the sink. He doesn't dilly dally and I don't seem to have the least bit of trouble keeping pace with him. I clean up at the sink and Blake uses the toilet. My face is flushed and I look totally kissed. I reach for the bra and he shakes his head.

I sternly tell him, "Well, don't make me run, they'll drop like a cow's udder." He laughs and opens the door. Mac is asleep in the front seat. Christian is leaning against the front fender. He opens the back door with a sweeping gesture and winks at me. I can't stop the blush that creeps up my face and is made that much brighter by Christian's chuckles as I'm climbing into the back seat. Blake and I sleep nestled in one corner as Christian drives down the highway.

I'm really glad to see the turn off to our driveway. I have done two long car trips within a seven day period. My back is killing me. Blake digs out the spare key and unlocks the back door. The house looks pretty much as we left it. I walk right through to the back stairs and upstairs into a hot shower. My own familiar clothes feel pretty damn good all over my body. Blake has made a pot of coffee, two cups of tea, oatmeal and a pile of toast by the time I return. He pulls out my chair for me to slide into it. Christian and Mac both rise as I enter the room.

Blake says, "I called Devin and told him everything is all right. He's calling your two brothers to see who wants to take care of your father. Devin says Dustin has power of attorney. I told him we'd work something out if they didn't want to be bothered with him. We could bring him down here with dad." Blake sips his tea and looks very tired around the eyes.

I reach across to squeeze his hand and tell him, "We'll take things one day at a time." I get up and pour myself a large glass of orange juice. All three men are smiling as I take my seat again. Within a week, Mac has replaced Kyle. Blake expresses repeatedly what good a worker he is and that he never complains or needs told twice to do something. Mac is thrilled at the money he's making. Christian isn't a stranger to hard work either. I have three hungry men around the table for lunch and dinner. Mornings have not been very good for me. I know it's unappealing to have the cook vomiting in another room while you're eating.

Frank is making good progress and the hospital is making plans for him to come home. Blake spoke with Frank before he got a hospital bed with all the hanging junk for Frank to be able to get in and out of the bed. There will be a PT coming Monday, Wednesday and Fridays to work with Frank. Blake purchased the little talking computer board. Frank uses it when he really wants to get something across.

CHAPTER SIX

FRANK AND THE FALL

Shortly after Dustin put father into a sanitarium, Frank came home from the hospital. The master suite is now set up like a small apartment. The queen-sized bed has been replaced with an electric hospital one. The rug is removed and everything is rearranged to accommodate his electric wheelchair. We move his favorite recliner and the big screen TV into his sitting room with a love seat for Blake and I to sit on. The necessary bars are installed in the bathroom. His walk-in shower is modified to allow him to use the manual wheelchair to get to the bench for his showers. Everything the hospital suggests to make Franks recovery and life easier, Blake immediately purchases. I spend several hours with the dietitian learning what to prepare and how.

Frank came home 40 pounds thinner and much weaker than when he left six weeks ago. Blake is torn between telling his dad about Dillon and who was responsible for Kyle's death and letting the old wound start to heal. He decides to remain silent for now. Blake goes to sign the necessary papers for his dads release from the hospital. I stay home to prepare lunch and get the last minute things done. Christian hovers around me whenever Blake is away. I gather he's a backup bodyguard. It doesn't bother me. I like the secure feeling. Blake and I actually get to take an early morning ride together. Probably our last if my Wednesday doctors visit gives us the news we expect.

Christian spots the wheelchair van in the drive and says, "The old man is back." I smile. He always refers to Frank as the old man. I've heard him call his own father that, but not disrespectfully. I open the front doors as the attendants are working the lift to lower the wheelchair to the edge of the porch. Frank waves with his right hand and smiles weakly. We've been visiting him about two evenings during the week and on Sunday afternoons. I pretend to sneak him something naughty to eat but usually its things the dietitian says he can have periodically if they're specially prepared. I bend to kiss him before he wheels himself inside.

He learned to operate the electric wheelchair easily and runs it full speed whenever possible. Blake helps the one attendant bring in the rest of Franks things. Frank has gone back to his bedroom. The attendant gives him the pager/buzzer and his speech board.

He immediately types in, "Got to pee." Blake grins and hands him a urinal. The attendant precedes me from the bedroom. I walk him back through to the front doors and watch as they leave. Christian is close behind as usual.

I make a roast chicken for dinner. Most of the gravies and heavy sauces Frank prefers are not on his diet plan. I have a feeling he's planning on going off the diet now that he's home. Blake says no way. If he balks, it's back to the hospital until the entire 100 pounds are gone. I'm in the kitchen making the garlic toast when I hear the chair.

"Hungry. What's to eat?" comes from the board. Blake removed the serving bar from the island to make the main isle wider.

Gesturing at the space that held the missing bar, Frank asks, "What's here?"

Blake explains, "I took it off until you're out of the chair dad. The isle was too narrow for your electric chair." Frank nods at Blake's words.

Pointing to Christian, Frank asks, "You live here now?".

With a smile, Christian tells him, "No sir. I sleep in the bunk house with the new kid, Mac." Frank nods. Blake introduces them. Frank buzzes past and out to the dining room table.

Gliding up to the end of the table where we removed the armed chair, he says, "Let's eat."

He tells Blake, "Get beer." Blake shakes his head.

Blake reminds his father, "You can have one beer in the evening only every other day, dad. Today we'll have wine." Frank nods but grunts his displeasure. I have a pasta salad with a vinigarete dressing for with the chicken. Frank frowns but discovers it's delicious once he tries it. He's not happy with his pureed prepared portions on his plate.

Looking at Blake he asks, "You try neuter me?"

Blake answers, "No dad. We have to follow the hospitals diet plan. We're all going to be eating the same until you're back on your feet." Frank nods and then smiles over at me.

He says "Glad to eat, when I see you." then gives me an *almost* wink. He's pretty tired after dinner. Blake takes him back and into bed. Christian helps with the dishes. I prepared a plate for Mac. Wes thought perhaps Frank should meet the new people individually. Mac gladly comes up and retrieves his dinner after I call. He sits in the breakfast area and quietly eats.

Blake comes out shaking his head saying, "He's going to be a battle every step of the way. Katie girl, he's having some memory problems. He sometimes doesn't remember Kyle is dead. He has a definite block about our marriage. He seems to think Dillon lives on the ranch next door not Devin. He just asked why we didn't have Dillon over for dinner today. The doctors said to just gently remind him of the facts or change the subject if possible. I'm not sure what to tell him about Kyle. I don't want to get him enraged again." Blake and I sit in the living room where we can hear Frank's call or page. I'm happy to nestle in his arms against his chest. He keeps slipping his hands inside my slacks to caress my belly. The phone rings and its Devin. Blake hands it to me.

Devin's frustrated voice comes clearly thru the line, "Little sis, I thought I'd update you on father. Doran just called. He and Dustin are fighting over the handling of father's affairs. It seems Dustin wants to sell the estate and make other living arrangements for father if he is ever released from the sanitarium. Doran thinks it's wrong to sell father's home out from under him. I feel the same way. Do you have any feelings or any opinions you want to voice?" He falls silent, waiting. I relay what he said to Blake.

Blake shrugs and takes the phone to tell Devin, "Hey, that sounds like a pretty shitty thing to do to a guy. If it were my dad, I'd say no way. He may need the familiar surroundings to fully recover."

I can hear Devin's excited and aggravated tone before Blake says, "I think Katherine feels the way I do, yes, she's nodding. Well, if Dustin has the power of attorney, our hands are tied. We can try to contest his actions but my honest opinion is a judge will side with the POA." Devin must be talking up a storm and Blake's listening for quite a while.

Then he says, "Well, we're behind you. In fact, Frank seems to think Dillon lives at your place. No, we brought him home today. Maybe tomorrow evening, he's really tired today. Yeah. Thanks." Blake ends the call and lays the phone down.

Suddenly I ask him, "The cabin in Utah, is that Christians?" Blake's low laugh rumbles in his chest.

He answers, "Yeah. When did you figure that out?" I shrug.

I tell him, "A little while ago. I realized his gravely voice matched the man on the phone."

Blake hugs me saying, "Well, remind me not to try and put anything over on you, Katie girl." Frank bellows and we both dash into his bedroom. He's very distressed because he messed the bed. He wants me to leave and Blake to clean him up.

Blake says, "Dad, we're married, remember? I'd like Katie to help me with taking care of you. She doesn't mind." Frank gets so agitated that finally, Blake nods and I leave. I place a laundry basket outside the doors. Blake drops the soiled sheets into it. I take the sheets out and run them through the washer twice before I dry them. We expected this. The hospital mentioned he might have trouble with his bowels or remembering he can't wait too long to call for help.

Blake says, "That's the biggest baby I hope I ever have to clean up." We are again sitting on the couch in the living room. It's a few minutes before Frank bellows again and we walk back into the bedroom. He wants up and not to be alone. We get him into his wheelchair and then over into his recliner. Blake and I sit while he watches a basketball game on the TV. The next week is so trying I could scream.

I almost forgot my doctors' appointment on Wednesday. Blake comes in at 2 and says, "Aren't you going to your appointment?" I dash upstairs to clean up and dress. He drives. We're both sitting anxiously in the doctor's office when she comes inside and sits.

She smiles and says, "Well, you're going to be parents. You're only about 8 weeks along, but there's definitely an embryo growing inside you. I have a packet for first time parents and special diet for you, Mrs. Dailey. Your iron is low and I'm putting you on special vitamins. There's a list of things you should not do, like heavy lifting, horseback riding, climbing and various other exertions. I would put your due date at about mid to late October. Congratulations." She rises and shakes Blake's hand. We walk silently out to the Jeep. Blake puts the bag of stuff into the back seat. He holds my door and then comes around and climbs behind the wheel. He sits quietly just staring out through the windshield before turning to grin at me.

Mischievously he asks, "Well, *Mrs. Mother to be Dailey* are you happy?" Then he reaches over to caress my face.

I tell him, "I'm thrilled and slightly in shock. Let's get home. Your dad will be expecting his dinner at 6."

Blake sighs and starts the engine as he says, "I never expected in my worse nightmares that he would be the royal pain in the bitching ass he's been for the past two days. Honestly, I don't know where you get your patience from." He backs from the parking spot and heads towards the ranch.

With a smile, I tell him, "My mother." He chuckles. Frank is bellowing as we are walking inside.

Christian comes out to inform us, "He's been hollering for you since you left. He's extremely mad that you would both leave at the same time and leave him defenseless. The PT is in with him now—getting nothing accomplished; I might add." Blake pats Christian on the shoulder and strides back through the house. There is a serious shouting match going on.

Finally Blake strides out and say, "I've had enough of him right now. You tend him. Don't tell him about the child." I get a quick kiss and he's grabbing his jacket. I find a royal mess in the bedroom. Feeling very much like a mother, I light into Frank with full force. He actually shrinks in size and becomes meek. He has thrown everything all around the room, including his lunch tray. I start cleaning up the mess, tight lipped and silent. When the room is again in order, I turn and look at him.

He types into the board. "Sorry." I nod and give him a slight smile.

Dinner is not a big hit. He refuses to come to the dinner table if Blake is eating there.

Blake says, "He can eat in his damn room then. I've worked like a slave all day. I'm eating at the table." Frank slams the tray down after I have left the room but he doesn't throw it against the wall. He does, however, eventually eat it. My roast beef is rather hard to resist even pureed. Since he has trouble swallowing, his food has to be pureed like baby food.

Thursday and Friday are worse than the days before. Finally, on Saturday, Mac comes in to help. Frank takes to him right off. However, after about four hours he begins calling him Kyle. Mac is in playing cards with Frank.

Mac comes to the kitchen where I'm preparing dinner and says, "He keeps calling me Kyle and says he doesn't like my hair cut like this. Isn't Kyle his son who just died? Should I correct him?"

I shake my head no. "Just let him realize on his own that you're not Kyle. Perhaps this will make things a little easier for him or at least Blake." Mac nods and takes iced tea in for the two of them. Sunday morning, Mac plays cards with Frank. Blake and I slip out and go to church. I want to thank God for the baby growing inside me.

Over the next three months, Franks makes wonderful progress with his therapy. His speech is rapidly coming back. Some days, he fights with the therapist about the physical and speaking exercises but mostly he digs in and fights to accomplish what they want done.

I'm putting laundry away in Frank's room and he suddenly says, "Hey, Katie girl, I really like having you stay here to care for me. It brings back memories of your helping Karen when she was so sick. You were always such a grown up little girl. I liked watching you tend Kyle. I knew in my heart in the hospital that if you came here and started taking care of me, you'd fall in love with me. When I get back on my feet, what do you say to the two of us getting married?" I straighten and turn to look at him. His words were pretty good if not somewhat haltingly spoken. The last statement is very clear and very well spoken. He's holding his hand out towards me and looking almost pleadingly. I walk slowly to the edge of the bed and take his hand in mine.

I softly tell him, "Frank, I'm already married to Blake. He asked me to take care of you. I've always loved you like a friend or a big brother." He jerks his hand from mine and glares at me.

He shrieks, "That's a lie! You are NOT married to Blake. No woman would marry a cold-blooded killer. Why would you tell me a story like that? My mind isn't gone. I've watched your face while you tend me. I know love when I see it in a woman's face." I'm watching his face as he struggles to make each word clear.

When he pauses, I tell him, "Everything I've done for you has been out of my love for Blake. Frank, he loves you so much. He's doing the work of three men keeping this place going. He even overlooks your harsh words and cold treatment. I know he has dreams of you playing with your grandson." I put my hand to my mouth in horror. The room is deathly quiet while Frank studies me intently. His glance drops to my breasts and then my slightly round baby stomach. I'm frozen, scarcely able to breath.

In an icy cold hard voice, Frank's lip curls slightly as he tells me, "So, you let him at you. Just like a mare in season you couldn't wait for me to be able to cover you. Any old stud who was near by. You let him thrust into you and pump his damnable killer seed into you. Well, little missy, I hope the child DIES within you! Nothing good will come from bad seed. You'll see." He turns his face away. I dash from the room in tears. Several hours later, Blake finds me curled on our bed, asleep. The dinner isn't cooked. My eyes are red and swollen from crying.

Gently pulling me into his arms, Blake asks, "Hey, what's wrong? Is it the child? Are you sick?" He smells good. I realize he's already showered and changed for dinner. I look up and the tears start again. Suddenly, I'm sobbing and clinging to him.

Frightened now, Blake asks, "My God, Katie girl, tell me what's wrong?" I take a couple of deep breaths and haltingly recount what happened in Frank's room. He remains quiet and sits holding me as I sob against him once I've finished. He begins planting kisses on my head and face.

He says, "I have to get you out of this house. Having you tend him was a mistake. The man is not right in his mind. I've never known him to wish ill on a woman or an unborn child. What is the matter with him?" Blake falls silent.

Christian speaks from the doorway. "Maybe you should have the doctors check his medicine. Some medicines can cause behavioral changes. I'm sorry. I heard Katherine sobbing and came upstairs. By the time I realized you were in here, I already heard too much." Christian averts his face.

Blake immediately says, "No. It's OK. That's a good suggestion. I'm too close to the problem to think clearly. It rips me apart to have that man turn a cold shoulder to me. I will not have him hurting Katie."

Christian says, "I'm going to start dinner. I'm a fairly good cook, you know." Then he pulls the door closed. I hear his footsteps on the front stairs. Blake lays me gently back on to the bed and begins making love to me. I welcome the touching, the security of the holding and his closeness.

Curled together afterwards, Blake says, "Perhaps we should move to the cottage to live. You could come up here and tend him for 8 or so hours. I just realized you don't get any break. I escape outside to the ranch work." I shake my head and put my fingertips to his lips.

I tell him, "It's OK. Mac comes in and plays cards with him. You realize he thinks Mac is Kyle?" Blake nods at my words. There are still a lot of worry lines around his mouth. I plant little kisses on them.

There's a tap at the door. "Anyone hungry in there?" It's Christian. Blake throws the covers over me and strides naked to the door. He takes the tray and after a low whistle, Christian makes a hasty retreat. We discover fried chicken, home fries and a tossed salad on the tray.

When I see the selection, I exclaim, "I hope this is not what he's feeding Frank."

Blake chuckles and says with a smile, "I don't think this one time will kill him. However, I'm sure he boiled Franks dinner. Thank God I don't have to listen to him bitch about it. This is good—almost as good as yours." Blake is eating like a starving man. After a couple bites, I give him a run for his money. Blake puts on a robe and takes the tray downstairs. He returns with fresh warm brownies and vanilla ice cream.

Blake explains, "Cook sent these over for you. Since I caught Mac and Christian with them, they had to share." Blake laughs. I find room for the dessert also. I lay back on the bed and Blake rubs my little tummy and smiles. He gets the baby book and looks under 20 weeks. He has been fascinated with the embryo pictures.

He murmurs, "Second trimester . . . just look at our little guy. Man, I got such a hard on during your sonogram. Did you see that little technician pale?" I smile and nod.

Blake says, "She glanced at my lap. It was just as embarrassing as when I was a teenager. I had no control. The longer I looked, the longer I got." I laugh and check under the covers.

I say, "He's sleeping." and he laughs.

Blake teases, He's exhausted. He worked all day and then he had to pleasure you. Poor guy is plumb tuckered out." He's tracing circles on my stomach.

I say, "Or something." Blake is planting kisses on my stomach. Later Blake insists that I dress for bed and call it an early night. We both sleep soundly. Frank is paging and screaming for me at 4 a.m. I climb from the bed and grab a robe. He's messed all over the bed. Blake and I clean him up. I start the laundry. By then, it's almost 5:30. I start breakfast. Blake goes up and gets ready to start his workday. It's strange the way that Frank acts as though yesterday didn't happen.

I make homemade soup for lunch and big roast beef sandwiches on homemade bread for the men. Mac has been having his lunch with Frank in the bedroom. Then they play cards for an hour. Frank usually naps after this until supper. I know the medicine makes him sleepy and keeps him calmer. Dinner is homemade beef stew and biscuits. This is another big hit all around. Christian joins Mac and Frank for a card game or two. Blake and I go outside and take a nice long walk together. It's a very pleasant May evening. We end up back on the porch swing and are soon joined by Christian.

He tells us, "Old man's having the time of his life playing cards with Mac. All evening, he called him Mac until just a little while ago. When he gets tired, Mac becomes Kyle." Christian sits on the top porch step and leans against the banister post.

In a lazy voice, he says, "It's real peaceful here. Maybe I'll stay on permanent. Your wife is a really good cook. I can spoil your son so badly." Christian is almost talking to himself.

Blake pushes the swing while he says, "You're welcome here as long as you want. We both preferred the country silence over the city noises. Too many people make me uncomfortable, always have. Katie girl makes me mellow." Christian glances back and one side of his mouth curls in a slight smile.

Mac joins us saying, "He's sleeping. I got him to take his evening pills." Blake says, "Thanks." and Mac heads down the steps. We decide to turn in. The next day is a miserable rainy day. We're awakened at 3 a.m. by a severe thunderstorm. The weather channel says there are flash flood warnings out.

Blake groans and tiredly says, "Great, that means we have to move the stock to higher ground. Why didn't they predict this yesterday?" He climbs wearily from the bed. He's been trying to hire a couple more hands but not having much luck. By 5 a.m., he's had breakfast and left with Mac and Christian. I get Franks' breakfast ready. He's obviously spoiling for a fight. Nothing is right. It's too hot, too cold, too hard, too dry, too damp in his room, too dark, the light is too bright. At 11, Blake calls and says they won't be in for lunch. It's a muddy mess already and they're rescuing the stock.

Friday is bed sheet day. I finally get away from Frank long enough to go upstairs and strip our bed. As I'm picking up the dirty linens, I hear Frank screaming and pushing on his buzzer. In my haste to get down the stairs, I step on part of the sheets that I'm dragging. My feet get tangled and before I know it, I'm tumbling down the entire flight of stairs. I try and relax but my first thought is for the child.

I don't know how long I lay unconscious. Probably not very long, because Frank is still screaming and hitting the buzzer. I roll over and try to get to my feet and pain flies into my back and abdomen. I curl into a small ball as wave after wave of painful spasms cut through my body. When I finally get my breath and glance down, my shorts are soaked with blood. I have to get to a phone and call Blake. Unable to stand, I crawl and half slide through the foyer and back the hall to Frank's room. At his first sight of me on the floor at his doorway, he lunges up in the bed and falls silent.

"Phone." I tell him, teeth clenched as the spasms of pain rack my body again. My movements have made things worse. When I look up again, he's flopped back onto the bed moaning. I don't know what's wrong with him. I crawl the rest of the way to the phone laying on the table beside him. I reach up and grab the cordless and quickly dial Blake.

He says, "Yeah." and he sounds wet and busy.

I tell him, "Blake! I fell down the stairs—I'm loosing the baby!"

He hollers, "Sweet Jesus!" then I hear his footsteps pounding on the wet ground and him hollering at the guys, "Katie fell. She's miscarrying. Hold on sweetheart, I'm coming." He says and the truck door slams.

I tell him, "OK." and lay down on the floor as wave after wave of pain again assaults me.

Frank bellows, "Katherine! I need to go to the bathroom!" I jump and moan.

I tell him, "Frank, I'm loosing the baby. Blake's on his way. I can't help you right now." I hear the mattress rustle and then his voice sounds closer.

He asks me, "What are you doing laying on the floor in all that red paint?" I realize he doesn't comprehend what's happening. I don't know how long it takes Blake to get back to the house. It seems like days. Frank lays in the bed and curses my not coming to help him. Then he goes to the bathroom in the bed.

He hollers, "I'm laying in shit in here!" again and again.

From the center of the house, Blake screams, "Katie!" He easily follows my trail of blood. I hear the chopper blades as he throws his jacket over me. I'm shivering and when I look up, Christian has brought a towel from the bathroom to put between my legs. There's blood everywhere. I scream as a wave of the worst pain I've ever felt knifes through me. I draw my legs up. Christian grabs my legs to straighten them and quickly pulls off my shorts and panties. Blake gasps but then realizes I'm delivering the baby.

Christian calmly says, "It's OK, push Katherine. Your body is passing the child."

Blake yells, "Back here!" At the sound of the EMT's coming into the house. I hear their footsteps and when the next wave hits, I push. Something tears from my body and I fall back into Blake's arms.

A strange woman's voice says, "Let me get that." I realize one of the EMT's is a woman. Christian stands and begins tending Frank. Frank complains that I left him all alone and he had to mess in the bed. Christian is very calm and efficient. Blake looks up at his father like he's crazy.

Blake asks, "Doesn't he know she's laying down here bleeding to death?"

It's a few minutes before Christian calmly answers, "No. I don't think he can or wants to comprehend what's going on. Leave it be for now. Take care of Katherine."

The EMT's begin asking Blake questions about blood type and allergies. Blake gives all the right answers. I get an IV in my arm and they start giving me blood and a coagulant. Blake lifts me onto the stretcher and kisses my forehead. When they carry me out through the hall I get a glimpse of my blood on the floor.

The male EMT warns, "Slippery here." Blake has the back end of my stretcher. The woman is walking beside with the equipment. The chopper ride isn't very long but we get blown around a lot. I don't care for the dropping and sensation of being moved around in the air. In the emergency room, the doctor wants to see what I delivered. Blake explains about the fall, when it happened and how far along I was. Then I'm going to sleep and the voices get farther away and stop completely.

When I open my eyes, a very haggard and tired looking Blake is sitting holding my hand. I tell him, "I'm sorry." He shakes his head.

He quickly says, "It's not your fault."

I'm crying softly while chastising myself, "I tripped over the bed sheets. I was in too much of a hurry. Why didn't I toss them over the gallery banister like I always do?"

Blake tries to console me, "Katie girl, it was an accident. Don't blame yourself. The doctor fixed you up just fine. You'll have more children later. We're young. My God, as long as I have you, children are not important!" I nod at his words but my heart is still very heavy with grief.

I tell him, "I feel so empty." He nods and raises my hand to his lips.

He lightly says, "I'll fill you up again in a couple of months. You just lay there and concentrate on getting stronger." My eyes drift shut. I'm in a nice private room. Blake is asleep in the chair beside my bed. He has on different clothes but he's unshaven and weary looking.

From the foot of the bed, Devin says, "How are you feeling, little sis?" Blake jumps and sits up straight.

Devin tells him, "Sorry, I didn't see you behind the curtain."

"It's OK. I've been asleep for quite some time." Blake stands and stretches.

I tell Devin. "I feel numb." He has a bouquet of flowers.

With his arm stretched out towards me, he shyly says, "These are for you." I smile.

I tell him, "You haven't brought me flowers since I was 13 years old." He laughs at that memory. One of my favorite horses died and I was devastated. He made father take him to town to buy me flowers to cheer me up.

I tell him, "Thanks." before turning to tell Blake, "You should go home and get a good rest." He shakes his head as I'm speaking.

He says, "No. I'm not leaving you. Besides, I can't stand dad's constant screaming for you. He finally pushed me too far. In a fit of anger, I told him he got his wish, the child is dead. Man, I felt bad afterwards. He got real white and quiet before he turned his face away." Blake draws a deep breath and continues, "Then he said, 'I never really wished Katie harm.' He hasn't said a word since." Blake comes over to the bedside and takes my hand.

I try to soothe him by saying, "It's OK. I know you lose your temper with him sometimes and right now, he's really hard to take." I squeeze his hand.

From the doorway, Christian says, "Blake, go home. I'll watch over Miss Katherine. Devin is going to drive you home for a few hours. Mac is with your dad. If you get sick, who'll take care of Katherine when she comes home?" Blake nods at Christians' no nonsense tone. I get a long kiss before he allows Devin to hustle him out.

As he settles into the chair Blake just vacated. I tell Christian, "Thank you."

Saying, "No problem. I'd rather look at you over Frank any day." He gives a husky chuckle and takes my hand. I go back to sleep.

The two weeks I spend on my back in the hospital are nothing compared to the two weeks of hell that went on at the ranch. Devin finally lets it slip that Frank is absolutely beside himself over what he said before I fell and lost the baby. He keeps chanting he wished his own grandson to death. Devin says Blake has the patience of a saint. It sounds like all three of them have their hands full. Mac is left to tend Frank because most days Frank still thinks he's Kyle. Frank would do anything for Kyle. I'm happy to hear the doctor say I can go home.

What a surprise I get at the house! The living room is now a bedroom. Blake set up the queen-sized bed from his parent's room in the living room for me. There are even four sets of folding privacy screens across the arched hall entrance. Blake carries me from the Jeep into the house. He doesn't set me down until we reach the bed. Then he gently removes my slippers, robe and settles me back on the multitude of pillows. Frank began bellowing from the moment Blake stepped into the foyer.

Blake says, "Just a minute dad, I need to get her settled. Christian, can you help him get up?" Christian strides from the room with a large smirk on his face.

I can hear Frank quite plainly, "Well, I need to see her. I'm the one who couldn't go visit her in the hospital, you know." Frank is huffing and griping the entire way. He stops just inside the living room and says, "Oh God, Blake, she looks like death. Did they release her too soon?" Blake turns and gives his father a very dirty look.

Blake's tone reveals his total frustration, "Dad, I told you not to say that around her. I warned you that she isn't in the best of health yet. Good Lord, the woman almost bled to death. Give her a break, will you?"

Frank's face crumbles. He sobs, "It's my fault. Katie girl, I'm so sorry I said those things that made you fall." He brings his right hand to his face.

I quietly tell him, "Frank, it was an accident—nothing more. I was in a hurry and got careless and I fell. Blake doesn't blame me for the death of his son. I don't blame you. Please, let's not talk about this any more. I want to forget the whole thing. I want to get back on my feet and have Blake make another baby in me." I fall silent, fearful of Frank's reaction.

I'm pleasantly surprised when Frank says, "I want you both to be happy. I've been a foolish old man. I've had a lot of time to think about my actions. I drove Kyle to his death. I've tried repeatedly to drive Blake away. No, let me finish." He pauses to gather his thoughts and silences Blake who was about to speak. "I should have been thrilled that you chose my son to love. I should have gotten down on my knees and thanked God for all you did for me, Karen and Kyle. I'm not going to guarantee I won't back slide into my old habits but I'm going to try my best to help you two be happy. If it's not too late . . ." He stops and looks from Blake to me. I notice Christian has silently disappeared.

With tears in his eyes, Blake softly says, "It's not too late. Dad, we're family. Katie and I, well, we want to help you get back on your feet."

Frank asks, "Will you leave me then?"

Blake reassures him, "No. I've come home to stay. Once you're back on your feet, Katie and I will build a place of our own, here on the ranch if that's agreeable." Blake sits on the edge of the bed and kisses my hand.

Frank offers, "I'll live in the cottage and you two have this house." but Blake is shaking his head.

Blake's tone is firm when he says, "No. This is your place. You built this for mom. When our little ones come along, you'll be glad for this place for a refuge. Katie and I will probably build a ranch style home. I'm not thrilled with her around stairs." Frank nods and smiles. I lay back and sigh. I close my eyes for just a minute and it's dark when I open them again. Blake is curled beside me. For a few minutes I don't know where I am and my sudden start wakes Blake.

He whispers, "What's wrong?"

I softly whisper, "Nothing. This is just a strange room."

He turns to face me asking, "Do you need anything?" I touch his face.

I tell him, "No. Just your love."

Touching my stomach lightly, he asks, "You have that Katie girl. Doe it hurt you when I move around in the bed?"

I tell him, "No. It wasn't even that rough coming home today." We're laying just holding hands.

Frank hollers, "What's all the whispering about? Is something wrong?" Blake chuckles.

He says, "No dad. We're just talking a little. Katie's fine. Go back to sleep."

Frank gruffly says, "I can't I have to pee." Blake immediately rolls over and gets out of bed.

He tells his father, "I'm coming, hold your water." I laugh at that. Blake throws on a robe as he rounds the end of the bed. The light goes on in Frank's bedroom and I hear Frank say, "Geez, did you have to turn the light on?" Blake laughs.

Blake's tone is teasing when he says, "Yes, dad, I need to see what you're doing. I don't want to have to change the bed sheets. Here's the urinal. It's even empty. If you would turn the light on, you could find it." I hear Frank's harrumph and it makes me smile. Blake returns shortly after the light goes back out. I'm not sleepy and I want to get up. I'm sitting on the edge of the bed when he comes into the room.

Coming to stand between my spread legs, he asks, "Must you go too?"

I admit, "Well, now that you mention it . . . I want out of this bed." Blake scoops me into his arms and carries me into the powder room across the hall. I notice he closed the doors to Frank's room. I get soft kisses on the top of my head and then shoulders.

Blake says, "I don't know how I'm going to stand going four months without touching you."

I say, "Let's sit on the swing." He sighs at my words. He slips on a shirt and grabs a pistol. He's still nervous I notice. We walk slowly to the swing. I end up sitting in his lap. I forgot how hard the wooden slats on the swing are on a tender bottom. I guess I went to sleep. I'm back in the bed and its morning. I smell breakfast cooking. I also hear Frank giving someone a hard time about something. At the beginnings of a faint burning smell, I realize Blake's in with Frank and no one's minding the breakfast. It's not easy to move fast but I rescue most of the French toast from the griddle. Several pieces are too well done and go into the sink.

Warm male arms slide around me, "Thanks. He hollers at the darndest times." I get a few kisses in my hair and he takes over the cooking. I hobble back for a bathrobe and find my nicely cushioned seat at the table. Christian comes in as I'm settling into the chair.

Sniffing the air, he says, "Oh, oh, maybe I'm too late for breakfast. Has the fire department been called?" I really like his low gravely voice.

Blake tells him, "No. Luckily the women's auxiliary squad was nearby." sitting a cup of steaming tea in front of me and the platter of bacon on the table. Mac comes in to take Frank's tray back.

Christian remarks, "That boy has perfect timing." Blake smiles and sits. It's Wednesday. Blake says that today is Frank's female PT for speech and exercises. I understand Frank really likes this Terry person.

Terry arrives at 9 and Christian brings her over to introduce me, "Mrs. Dailey, this is Terry Shunt, Franks PT for this morning." She comes over and extends her hand to me in a very professional manner.

She says, "Good morning. You have my sympathies about the child. I'm here Monday and Friday afternoons and from 9 to 1 on Wednesdays.

If you need anything, let me know." Her words are pleasant; her face is unreadable. I can almost hear Blake warning me against saying too much or getting to close to her. I don't know why. I would put her age at late thirties, early forties. She has black hair and brown eyes. She has a round face and well-rounded hips and bottom. I would put her height at about 5'2". Perhaps it's just her professional attitude that puts me off.

I say, "Thank you." When I pause for breath, she turns and leaves. Christian shrugs and sits in the corner arm chair. This corner gives him a full view of both entrances and the French doors onto the patio. Blake put the head of the bed up against the fireplace. It looks strange but is the best place. Frank certainly does a lot of laughing and teasing while she's here. Her voice is low and her laugh is unusual.

Christian is a very good cook. I learn that Blake will do breakfast and Christian is lunch detail. They are going to alternate with Cook for supper meals. I try to tell Christian that I can cook supper. From the expression on his face you would think I was explaining about putting a new roof on the house in my spare time.

With a stern face and wide grin Christian explains, "You are to rest in bed for the next two weeks at least. I have my orders." On Thursday, Frank is quite a handful for Christian. There is a big conference outside somewhere between Blake and Christian while Mac is playing cards with Frank. Thursday afternoon, Frank is in visiting with me for about 45 minutes. This visit seems to make him more agitated.

Christian whispers after he has him settled back in his bed, "It upsets him to see you like this. Deep down, he still blames himself. Try not to let his words upset you." He smiles softly and I get the distinct impression that he has probably said those exact words to Blake over the past few weeks. Especially the last statement, I'm sure.

Friday morning, after breakfast, Blake calmly announces, "I'm putting an ad in the paper for a housekeeper who can cook. It will especially help while you're laid up and dad will eventually need a housekeeper." He's watching my face for my reactions as he speaks.

I shrug and tell him, "I know I'm not physically able to help at all right now. I'll feel better knowing you and Christian are not killing yourselves trying to do my work on top of the ranch work." He visibly relaxes as I'm speaking. I glance past him and Terry is standing in the archway.

She says, "Excuse me. I couldn't help overhearing you say you were looking for a housekeeper. I'd be willing to take the position under certain conditions." Blake stands at Terry's words and turns to face her.

Blake asks, "Can you leave Frank alone for a few minutes while we discuss this?" Terry nods and ducks back to Frank's room. Blake turns and asks, "Can you let me handle this or will you feel slighted?"

I tell him, "Blake, some days, breathing is an effort. You do whatever you need to do to make your life easier." He leans over and kisses me as Terry coughs from the archway.

Terry explains, "He's got a few exercises to practice while we speak. He heard my offer and says his vote is yes." Blake nods and gestures towards the breakfast area. She precedes him through the family room and they sit at the table and talk. I have every intention of listening intently. However, sometimes when I blink, I sleep. The end result is I miss the entire conversation. I'm awakened by cooking smells and notice Christian sitting in the usual corner chair, reading one of his chess magazines. He's quite a chess player.

With his slow smile, he says, "You look quite rested from your nap." A glance at the clock reveals my nap was over three hours long.

I ask, "Who's cooking?"

Christian leans forward to whisper, "Your new housekeeper. Blake hired Terry. He'll fill you in over lunch. It's safe to say that Frank is extremely happy over this." Christian leans back as Blake comes into the room.

Leaning over for a kiss, Blake says, "You look good, is that you I smell?" The corner chair is already vacant.

I jokingly tell him, "I think it's probably lunch." Blake nods and perches on the bedside.

Blake says, "I hired her. Her only condition was that she gets room and board for herself and her teenage daughter. She wants $100 a day for the four days she doesn't do PT with Frank. On those days, we just pay her the $160 PT fee as usual and she does the housekeeping at no charge. She wants every other Sunday off if that doesn't cause any problems. I think that sounds reasonable. Once you get back on your feet, maybe she can have Sunday's off." He's playing with my fingers while he speaks and glancing up into my face.

I tell him, "That sounds like a good arrangement. She and her daughter can use the two bedrooms that share a bath. That keeps the one bedroom separate for guests or us after I'm able do stairs." Blake nods. With two strangers living here, sleeping in this living room will be a little awkward.

A thought occurs and I say, "Of course, we could move over to the cottage?" Blake shakes his head.

He says, "No, that's a bit too remote. I like having Christian over in the bunkhouse for backup. Sorry, darling, I'm still nervous after all that's happened." I nod and smile.

I tell him, "It was just a suggestion . . . not a request." and get a nice kiss as Terry announces, "Lunch is ready. Will you be dining in here?" I look over at her and shake my head.

My reply is, "No. I need to get out of this bed and get my strength back." Blake smiles his approval and helps me to the bathroom and then the table. Lunch is a vegetable stir fry dish with steak hoagies for the men folk. Terry prepared a nice chef's salad for herself, Frank and I. I steal a couple bites of Blake's hoagie. Terry goes back and eats with Frank so Mac can have a hoagie. She did put several thin slices of the steak between slices of wheat toast for Frank. She's a dietitian and watching Franks diet also. After a rest after lunch, I walk back through to Frank's room. Terry suggests some exercises to build my strength back. Frank and I exercise together. He gets a big charge out of that.

Dinner is roasted fish. Since we're allowed butter cream sauce over our pieces, it's tolerable. Terry again dines with Frank. Her teenage daughter, Heather shows up at 4. Christian drew his gun at the sight of the red mustang convertible coming up the drive at full speed. He and I were walking around the outside of the house for my afternoon exercise. Once he realizes a young girl is driving, he holsters his weapon but still steps in front of me. She comes to a dust-raising stop in front of us.

She asks, "Does Frank Dailey live back this driveway?" I peak around Christian.

In his cautious tone, Christian answers, "Yeah. And you are?"

The girl giggles. "I'm Heather. Is my mom, Terry here?" Yes, I see the resemblance to her mother. This girl is slender with her hair long and loose. She has on a cut off white tee shirt and her small breasts are clearly visible to due a lack of bra. Christian motions towards the house.

He says, "She's around back. Go in through any door and holler for her." Christian won't leave me to escort her inside.

She drives off in a wave of dust after remarking. "You sure have a big gun on you, mister." You should see the one on my husband, floats through my mind as I hug Christian from the back.

I tell him, "You should go up to the house. Let's head back."

He immediately asks, "Are you tired? Should I carry you?" Now he sounds like Blake.

I answer, "No. I'm supposed to be building my strength back up." We walk slowly back to the house. Christian carries me up the half dozen steps at the patio edge. Safely deposited on the deck, I glance over and see Heather sitting in the one lounge chair.

She says, "Mom's busy. She said to wait out here. Is that OK?" Christian chuckles while I'm walking over to sit opposite her.

I tell her, "Sure. It's really nice out here this time of day." Christian lounges on the deck rail where it joins the house.

Slipping off her sandals and stretching her legs out fully, Heather asks, "That your husband or body guard?"

With a teasing tone, I tell her, "Body guard."

"I heard you lost your baby. That must have made you very sad. I hope you get another one." She's starring at Christian and talking to me. It's a little disconcerting.

I tell her, "It did. I'm sure Blake and I will have children." She turns her green eyes back.

She says, "I'm on the pill. No way do I want to listen to my mom bitch if I get pregnant." I glance over and Christian is softly smiling although his face is partially turned away.

She seems to warm up towards me when I tell her, "That's responsible."

She quickly asks, "How old are you?"

I tell her, "I'll be 25 in July."

When she says, "It's July now." I blush.

I explain, "Oh, I lost a couple weeks while I was in the hospital." She nods knowingly at my words.

In a somber tone, she says, "I had my appendix out last summer, it ruined most of August for me. By the time I felt good, it was time to go back to school."

I smile and she continues, "My birthday was yesterday." She looks over at Christian to ask, "How old is he?" I shrug.

I tell her in all honesty, "I have no idea. Probably mid 30's or so. Blake is going to be 33 I think." Whilt I am speaking, the subject of my discussion rides up to the edge of the deck and dismounts. He removes his hat and strides up onto the patio.

He asks Christian, "Company?"

Christians short reply, "Daughter." Blake nods and flops into the closest lounge chair.

Examining her closely, he says, "I'm Blake Dailey. You must be Heather?"

She boldly says, "Yeah. You're a good looking guy. I may decide I like blue eyed guys after all." Blake laughs out loud and crosses his ankle across his knee. Christian nods at Blake before he walks the horse to the stables.

"Mom says you're gonna let us live here. Do I get my own room?" She's talking to Blake now. I'm forgotten.

Blake answers, "Yes. You'll have to share a bathroom. I'm going to have you stay in my baby brother's old room. He's dead." Blake glances away, that last statement may have been harder than he anticipated.

Heather asks, "Can I ride the horses?"

Blake turns back to ask her, "Have you ridden before?" She quickly nods so he continues, "I'll select a mount for you and tell the stable hands to get him ready anytime you want to ride. As long as you're not abusive, the animal will be yours to use anytime."

Heather nods a little sheepishly and then smiles. She tells Blake, "Thanks. I've been riding since I was about seven. My dad taught me. He's dead. I'd like a jumper. I enjoy doing fences and stuff." She stuffs her feet back into her sandals as Terry appears at the back door.

She says, "Dinners ready." She disappears after motioning to Heather. Blake helps me up and inside before he goes to clean up.

I pass most of my fish off onto Christian. He just grins and eats it. He promises not to tell. Heather dines with us and grins mischievously before giving him half her fish.

She says, "I don't like fish either but my mom's this big healthy food freak." Christian also eats her fish. Blake tries to slip part of his onto my plate. Once dinner is done, Heather begins clearing without a word being said.

Blake smiles and as he pulls my chair out says, "I believe I'll tell the cook that fish is for Fridays during Lent for you and I." I smile and give him a soft kiss. I'm rather tired from being up so much, so I'm put into bed for a couple of hours. Blake and I spend a couple evening hours on the swing. Heather has gone back to their apartment to pack. She and Terry are moving in Saturday. Terry is giving up her apartment at the end of the month and storing her things. I thought that's strange but Blake seems to think it's logical.

Terry asks if they would empty the front room for her stuff. She'd like her own things around her. Blake, Christian, Devin, Mac and Pete spend the better part of Friday morning emptying the room. Terry gives it a thorough cleaning and then tries to con them into moving her stuff on Saturday. Blake declines and explains they have too much ranch work. Devin volunteers several of his hands and then Blake gives her two of his (out of guilt, I think).

Saturday is a very interesting day. Christian is, of course, taking care of Frank and watching out for me. I manage to get lunch ready. Blake comes in for lunch and is under the distinct impression that the move is completed.

Christian laughs and says, "They're still packing up her things. From what I heard from Mac, they're going to be most of the day and maybe half of the night. Terry is cleaning the apartment instead of packing. She's cleaning everything before she moves it." Blake rolls his eyes at that statement. I know he's behind in the ranch work from yesterday and now being three guys short . . . he's not happy. He does try and put on a good face. He doesn't want me to feel weak and useless.

I have Christian help with a pair of massive beef roasts. I figure the movers will be starving when they arrive. The trucks finally arrive at 9 p.m. I don't think Terry wanted the guys to eat before they moved her in.

Mac comes in saying, "I'm starving. What smells good?" Christian laughs before he goes to set the table. I have a roasting pan full of mashed potatoes, two large roasts and three roasting pans full of corn on the cob. I must have made a bucket of gravy and six loaves of homemade bread. There aren't any lack of hands to carry the food outside to the picnic tables and eat. Blake went to town and got three kegs of beer.

It's safe to say, I didn't have to fret with leftovers—just dirty dishes. All of Terry's things are carried inside and her bed is set up by 11:30. She tries to get the guys to rearrange her room. Blake finally lays down the law. He says they unload and then they're done. Blake, Christian, Mac and Devin set up her room. It's after 1 a.m. when Blake drops into bed beside me. I start to rub his shoulders and back but he's already asleep. It's a very tired man who climbs from the bed at 6 a.m. He usually gets up at 5 but I turned the alarm off.

When he sees the time, he says, "Damn!"

I tell him, "Relax, lover man. I turned it off. You needed more than four hours sleep as hard as you work." He sighs at my words.

His reply is, "I know, but sweetheart, my hands got up just as early this morning." He quickly goes through to his father's bath to shower and then dress. With Heather and Terry here, he won't be dressing in the living room. I struggle from the bed to make tea and breakfast. Christian walks in as I'm getting ready to set things on the table. I gladly sit and let him finish. Blake comes out.

Sitting on his chair and sugaring his tea, Blake says, "Sweetheart, you should have just poured cold cereal into a bowl." I smile.

Christian shakes his head saying, "Don't complain. She makes the best damn oatmeal this side of the Mississippi." I get a kiss on my forehead before he sits. Mac drags in and grabs Frank's tray. Terry puts in an appearance after 10. Heather isn't up before noon. I already have Sunday dinner started. Terry goes to tend Frank. Christian goes to help Blake. I finally told Christian to leave me a gun and go. He smiles, gets me a nice little automatic pistol and leaves. Heather immediately dashes to the stables to see her horse.

My honey orange chicken is a big hit with everyone except Terry. She seems to think it's not good for Frank. I made the macaroni salad with light Mayo for Frank and she's still not happy. He, however, is thrilled with my cooking. Blake and I get to take a nice walk after dinner. Heather talks about her horse through dinner. Terry heads upstairs to straighten her room immediately after picking at her dinner. Heather is off school until September when she starts her senior year.

When Blake rises at 5 a.m. on Monday, Heather is sitting at the kitchen table having a cup of coffee. He comes quickly back into the bedroom where I'm struggling to dress.

He says, "Geez, remind me to zip before I leave the room." Then he comes to stand in front of me. He has his zipper jammed into his briefs. It takes several long interesting minutes to get it free and up in place. He was zipping as he stepped into the kitchen to start the teakettle and made eye contact with Heather at the table.

He teases in a whisper, "Call me when she's gone." then he heads back to shave while I start the breakfast.

Over the next three weeks, I have less and less to do during the day. Terry begins reorganizing the kitchen to her liking and gets irate whenever anyone doesn't put things back where she now keeps them. This is hardest for Blake who has lived here most of his life and things have been kept where his mother had them. My doctor visit does not get us good news. My weight has dropped again and my blood work all comes back bad. She wants me on a special high calorie diet that, of course, is the exact opposite of Franks. Blake buys me candy, and lots of ice cream. Cook makes me special sugary delights. I discover that if I don't consume it when first handed to me, it disappears.

Frank is out of the bed most of the day and zipping around in his wheelchair. He repeatedly asks Blake when he's putting the house back the way it was. Obviously he doesn't like the bedroom furniture in the living room. Finally, I tell Blake to take it back down. I'm able to do the stairs and I'll be careful. This statement brings a tight line to his mouth and a stiffening of his back. He does, however, have the furniture and our things moved. Then, Frank has a big fit when he finds out I'll be going up and down stairs. Blake gets so angry; he jumps up from the table and walks outside. I quickly follow but I'm unable to catch him.

With a gentle tug on my arm, Christian says, "Let him walk it off." I don't go back inside until he's a good distance from the house.

I seat myself at the table and glare at Frank. I sternly tell him, "You are definitely one of the most selfish and uncaring men I have lived with since I left my father's house."

Frank looks over totally wide-eyed to ask, "What are you talking about?" Terry starts to speak. I quickly give her a hard glance and she closes her mouth for once.

I tell him, "Blake works all day to run this place. He has done everything you wanted to make your life as comfortable as possible. Could you for once appreciate something he's done? Just once, thank him instead of bitching about one thing or another? Would that kill you?" Frank shakes his head and looks away.

He finally says, "I don't like you angry with me, Katie."

I retort with, "And I don't like you hurting Blake day after day after day. Every time you hurt him, you hurt me twice. Think about that the next time you want to say or do something hurtful. Or, maybe you just don't care." I rise and toss my napkin to the table. I suddenly don't have any appetite anymore.

Frank says, "This is my house." I pivot to look at him.

With an agitated nod, I tell him, "Yes. Thank you for reminding me." I grab my coat from the hook and my purse from the counter top. Christian is hot on my heels.

Once we're outside he whispers, "Where are you going?" I walk across the deck and dial Blake's cell phone.

He answers after several rings. "What?" He sounds upset.

I plead through the phone, "Blake. It's Katie. Meet me at the garage, please?" He's there when Christian and I walk up. Christian stops a ways back from where Blake is leaning up against the Jeep. I walk over and put my arms around him.

I plead with him, "Can we please go back to Utah? I'm so tired of your father and Terry and not having any time alone with you. Forgive me for being selfish, but I can't stand the way he hurts you anymore." Blake pulls me into his arms and kisses me.

He says, "Whatever you want. I realized as I was walking that we were wasting our lives here. He's getting stronger and becoming his old self again. Pete can take your horses back to Devin's. Christian can run this place for dad. We'll go away for a couple weeks or so. I want to look into purchasing a ranch that's for sale near here." He pauses to bury his face in my neck.

I suggest, "New game plan. Why don't we move into the cottage while you look into purchasing this ranch? That way, you can help work the ranch but still have time for me?" I get a hug as I am talking.

He softly asks, "That way you can get back on your feet sooner—right?"

I tell him, "Yes. I know you'd worry about your dad if we were out in Utah." He nods and escorts me around to open the Jeep door.

Blake asks Christian, "Sneak into the house and pack us an overnight bag, will you?" Christian disappears like smoke on the wind. Blake meets Christian on the front porch and they converse briefly. Blake brings our bags and we head down the driveway.

We pass through several little towns until Blake spots a little motel he seems to like and he pulls into the parking lot.

He says, "Wait here." I reach into my purse to touch the little pistol from Christian. He returns with the key to our cottage and drives to the end of the row. Number 11.

I tell him, "Two ones together. I like that." and he smiles. He grabs our bags and then insists on carrying me across the threshold. There's no room service but a nearby pizza parlor is glad to deliver a large cheese pizza and six-pack of bottled beer. The room is well worn but clean and comfortable. The bed is queen-sized and the bathroom sports a whirlpool tub and separate shower.

After splitting a beer (I had several sips) and delving into the pizza, we get naked and into the tub. The water swirling around feels delightful. Blake's hands on my body feel delightful too. He just keeps caressing and caressing and then kissing me. After a nice shower and back rub, we have a little more beer and pizza. The beer puts me out like a light. My last sight is of Blake sitting in the one chair by the round table with his feet propped in the other chair, sipping his long necked bottle of beer.

There's a warm butt pressed into the middle of my back. I reach back and briefly check it out before climbing from the nice warm bed and going to my usual a.m. seat. Blake is stretched out on his back when I return and climb back into bed.

He tells me, "I'm not going to work today." I smile and cuddle up close, rubbing little gentle circles on his chest with my fingertips. He continues with, "I am, however, going to use the bathroom." Busily kissing my fingertips before he deftly flips the covers open to walk naked to the bathroom. He certainly did have to go. I am always amazed at the man's bladder capacity. It sounds like a gallon of water at least before he returns to climb back into the warm bed.

Nestling up against me, he says, "Oh, you kept my spot warm." We kiss and just lay together for quite a while. Blake begins moving his legs around. I sense he's getting restless even before his stomach growls.

He says, "I believe I can smell that cold pizza calling me." He rises and walks over to the box containing the remainder of our dinner. I smile as my naked husband sits in the one chair and eats two cold pieces of pizza and drinks most of a bottle of water.

When he asks, "Want some?" I shake my head and wrinkle my nose. The clock says it's almost 9 a.m. I have a feeling Blake called the house while I was in the shower. I let him shower first and he laid out my clothes and packed the car. Of course, we only brought one fresh set. We stop at a diner and have a nice breakfast. We're back at the ranch by noon. Frank is yelling for me as we walk in the back door. He's in the family room.

Taking a seat in the nearby armchair, I calmly tell him, "Hello." Blake heads towards the stables via the front door.

Frank says, "I guess I drove you and Blake away yesterday." His speech seems to be improving by the day.

I simply tell him, "Yes." He senses I'm still a little angry.

He says, "They moved your stuff out yesterday, are you saying goodbye?" He looks so sad and upset and old it's hard to keep my anger alive.

I simply tell him, "No, Frank we've moved to the cottage. Blake and I need time alone. We are newlyweds, you know." He nods at my words and relief spreads across his face.

Frank says, "I thought maybe you two would just drop out of sight again. Terry says my medicine made me say and do nasty things after I came home. I know since they switched a couple of them, I feel better. You know, I've always had this thing against Blake once he turned into a man. Now, with him running my spread and me being in this wheelchair . . . well, it's tough, you know?" I nod and wait for him to finish. "But I don't want the two of you running off. He's all I got left. I know he's a good boy. He's a hard worker and an honest man. I'm happy to hear you're just down in the cottage and not gone. OK?" I nod and he leans back, exhausted from all the talking. He hasn't really used his board in weeks. He really works and concentrates to speak clearly.

Blake doesn't come in for lunch since we had such a late breakfast. I get Christian to drive me to town for groceries after lunch. I want to get the cottage in order. Actually, it looks like someone has already done a lot of work. The place is clean. There are clean sheets on the bed and several vases of flowers in the kitchen and living room area. Once the groceries are all put away and I have supper going, Christian bows and leaves. After he's gone about 15 minutes, I get scared and get the pistol out and put it in the small of my back. I realize this is the first I've been alone in a long time.

I have the table set and dinner already as Blake walks in the front door. I'm wearing a sexy nightgown set and have candles lit everywhere. When he sees me, he says, "Hello, beautiful fairy princess! Can you tell my wife I'm home?" Blake tosses his hat on the hook and sheds his jacket and holster. I bring him a goblet of white wine as he sits and sheds his boots. He takes the wine and then claims my lips.

I huskily tell him, "You're very over dressed, Sir Knight."

He replies, "You are a seductive temptress but I shall resist you, fair maiden. Your wizard doctor says two more months and you, sweet thing, will have to wait. However, whatever you have made for dinner, I will feast upon." I pinch his butt and go get dinner on the table. No wanting to be too cruel, I quickly slip on a tee shirt and Jean shorts in place of the nightie.

Blake teases, "Hello, Katie girl, I'm so hungry I had this wonderful hallucination of you as a fairy princess. Guess I better lay off the wine until I eat something." He holds my chair and we dine on my BBQ beef ribs, buttered seasoned noodles and tossed salad. Blake finishes every morsel and then helps with the dishes although I try to make him sit down. The day catches up with him as we sit on the couch after the dishes are done. I pull a very tired man back and get him ready for bed. He's dead to the world before I get on my cotton gown and into bed beside him.

Over the next two weeks, I establish a routine of coming up and having lunch with Frank after we do our morning exercises. I then return to the cottage to rest and start Blake's dinner. Christian is my escort for these trips. He shows up with a horse and we ride leisurely to Franks place. On rainy days, I get to ride in the truck.

On this particular Monday, Blake shows to escort me to his dads. He's early and luckily, I'm ready to go. He has the Jeep and is strangely silent during our ride.

I ask, "Something bothering you?"

He says, "Later." Then he glances quickly away. I know he's true to his word, so I'll wait. He swings me out of the Jeep and I get a nice kiss. We stroll up across the patio and in through an open French door. I walk back towards Frank's bedroom. Blake follows along planning on saying hello to his dad. What I saw when we rounded the open doors and stepped into Franks room will stay with me for a very long time. I don't know how long I stand frozen in shock with my mouth hanging open before Blake turns me into his chest.

Frank is on his back on his bed. Terry is leaning over his groin performing a very unusual sex act with her mouth. Frank's eyes are closed, so are Terry's. Even after Blake turns me, I still hear Frank's sounds of pleasure. Blake backs quietly from the room and sweeps me into his arms. He strides through to the back patio and we sit on the swing with me in his lap.

Blake says, "Katie girl, I'm sorry you had to see that. Obviously dad is getting his money's worth with Terry's physical therapy." I look up at him and grimace. He begins laughing.

When Blake says, "Not to worry, my preferences do *NOT* lean in that particular direction." I laugh. Then we snuggle together until Terry finds us about 30 minutes later.

She says, "I thought I heard someone on the swing." Blake makes a kind of coughing choking noise before he sets me on my feet.

Blake answers, "Yes. Katie is here to exercise with dad—if you two are finished with your private workout." Terry at least has the decency to flush a little.

She asks, "Have you been here long?"

Blake asks, "About 30 minutes too long. You really should close the doors' to the bedroom. Where's Heather?" She knows full well what he's insinuating.

Terry says, "She's in her room." Blake stiffens before he gently takes my arm.

He says, "In fact, tell dad Katie's not feeling well enough to exercise this morning. You can say her teeth are bothering her." Blake turns me and we walk back to the Jeep. Back at the cottage, I'm surprised when Blake follows me inside. I sit on the couch and after a few minutes of pacing, Blake joins me.

Blake finally begins speaking, "I've been getting various stories from the hands about Miss Heather. Christian confirmed the other day that she attempted to seduce him. Evidently she rode out to where he was working fence with his lunch and removed all her clothes to serve it. He told her to get those little raisins out of the sun before they dry up any more." Blake pauses when I suddenly burst into laughter.

I struggle to tell him, "I'm sorry, that really put a vivid cartoon picture in my mind. Go on."

He continues, "I also wanted to let you know that she's made advances towards me. Her mother has given her free rein with her own body. She offered it to me while you're unable to accommodate me." I raise my eyebrows at his words but remain silent. He caresses my face and smiles.

Then he continues, "Today, however, I believe was the last straw. Yesterday I caught Heather and Mac in a very compromising sex act. When I told Mac she's jail bait, he lost all firm interest. She became very enraged at the lost of her lovers services. Evidently she told Mac she was 19 not 17. He thought she had graduated from high school. What a mess that could have caused! Anyhow, I believe that you better stay away from the house. Especially, after what we witnessed today; I imagine that particular physical therapy is what has mellowed him out this past couple of weeks. I need to talk to him about closing the door or calling you and telling you not to come. Sweetheart, I don't want you having to witness things like that. Are you OK?" He's so worried about me. I smile and nod, then burst into laughter. I'm sure it was probably hysterical or just a release for me. He holds me until I've calmed down and then wipes the tears from my face.

I reassure Blake, "I'm fine. Honestly, the entire incident struck me as funny. Perhaps, now with Terry, he'll forget his feelings for me and things will settle down." I reach over and stroke his lap but he leaps from the couch like I spilled hot tea in his lap.

Blake tensely says, "Don't! I'm sorry, but he's my dad and that act is one that is particularly repulsive to me." He has his back towards me. I stand and slip my arms around him from behind.

I tell him, "Sorry; that was callous. I was checking to see if anything was settling up." He turns at my words and kisses me.

Blake says, "I need to get back to work. Why don't you head over to Devin's and visit with Cook? In fact, why don't I drop you off and pick you up?" From the tone of his voice, to relieve his mind, I better agree.

I tell him with a smile, "That would be nice. Let me grab a sweater." He's quiet in the Jeep over to Devin's. Cook is thrilled to see me and invites us to dinner. Blake quickly accepts. It's late when we finally get back to the cottage and the light is blinking on the answering machine. I duck into the bedroom to get ready for bed. Blake listens to the machine. I can hear Frank's angry tone through the closed bedroom door. I come back out wearing my nightgown. Blake kills the machine volume and glances over at me.

He explains, "Dad's a little mad at us." I shrug and dance over to pull him into my arms.

I tell him, "So what. He'll get over it or we'll go away." We dance back to the bedroom and go to bed. It's awhile before Blake settles down and his breathing becomes regular. We need to get that new ranch purchased and get away from here.

The next morning, Frank calls and wants me to come up and exercise with him. Christian escorts me up and back after lunch. Blake comes in at 3 and says he's made a final offer on the property south of Franks and Devin's. We should know by Monday if it's ours. He takes me over to see the property and it's really not bad looking. The out buildings are all in perfectly good shape. Obviously, the extra money went into the stables, barns and garages over repairing the house; which is livable but a mess. The one nice feature is the new master bedroom suite built onto the back of the house with a nice modern bathroom. Evidently when the parents got too old to handle the stairs, they added this room. The place is terribly dirty and full of trash. The children must have taken what they wanted from the place and left all the broken, dirty and junk items. Blake tells me he'll hire someone to thoroughly clean the place and haul the trash away. I'm to forget any notions of attempting to do it myself. He shakes his index finger and I gently bite him. I have the feeling that Frank will not be thrilled with our new news.

CHAPTER SEVEN

HOMESTEADING WITH BLAKE

J ust like Blake anticipated, the family accepted his generous offer for their parents' ranch. Monday afternoon, we meet with their lawyers and Thursday, we have closing on the ranch. Friday, Blake and I sit at Frank's dinner table. Blake tells his dad that he bought the Newman place so we would be neighbors. I thought his father would rise to his feet and drop dead.

Frank shrieks, "WHAT THE HELL FOR? ISN'T MY COTTAGE GOOD ENOUGH FOR YOU? You're just doing this for spite." Frank throws his napkin on the table.

Terry quickly says, "Now, Frank calm yourself. Your son is a grown man. It's time he moved to his own spread. For once, listen to him instead of screaming over his first statement." I'm as surprised at her words as Blake is by the effect they have on his dad. Frank calms right down, smiles at her and calmly nods.

In a total change of face, Frank says, "You're right, as usual. Congratulations son. At least we'll be neighbors." He places his napkin back into his lap and resumes eating. He's on solid foods again and his weight is continuing to drop on schedule. He actually looks good. Blake was in the process of rising from the table, but he stops and sits once Frank calms down. The discussion revolves around pit falls to watch for and things to take care of. Frank seems to delight in giving Blake advice he really doesn't need but accepts with a smile. I'm so proud of my husband. After dinner, Blake begs off on Frank's invitation to sit and chat for awhile. Back at the cottage, Blake has several lists started of things he wants to accomplish as soon as possible.

While he sits at the dining table, writing furiously, I ask, "Your dad looks really good. Don't you think?" He glances my way.

He says, "Yes. I thought he'd have another stroke at the table, though. Maybe they need to reassess his meds again. He's not as calm as he used to be." I shrug and begin massaging his neck and shoulders.

"You're tense, Tigerman." I whisper in his ear. He growls and leans back for a nice long kiss. I continue to massage his neck and shoulders until he's relaxed. Then I massage his temples. I watch his eyelids get heavy.

Rising he says, "Maybe we should call it an early night." Turning to face me, he pulls me into his arms.

"Maybe we should." I agree. He locks up and soon joins me in the bed. We curl together and sleep.

Like I anticipated, he's up with the sun. He has so much on his mind about this new place. He makes me anxious to move in and I know it's unlivable right now. During the morning, while I thought Blake was out working the ranch, he was actually out purchasing house plan books. He returns for lunch with about 20 books. We spend the entire afternoon looking through and selecting possibilities. I'm glad dinner was roast chicken. I had already made the stuffing and stuffed the bird before Blake arrived for lunch. After dinner, we finish tearing the possibilities out of the books and Blake removes the unwanted books. Our pile of possibilities is overwhelming. We vote to go to bed and start fresh after church.

We attend the sunrise service and stop at a nearby diner for breakfast. Back home, we change into comfortable clothes and sit in the living room. Any floor plan with more than one negative is immediately rejected. I leave him alone only long enough to get the beef roast into the oven with its peeled vegetables around surrounding it. Christian shows up about the time the roast is done and joins us for dinner. We appreciate his sharp eye during our afternoon session. By evening, we have only about two dozen floor plans left. I have to force Blake to retire to bed at 11.

I finally ask, "You planning on sleeping until noon?" He glances over and actually reads the clock.

He says, "Good heavens!" Then he jumps to his feet. He's in bed in record time.

Getting back out of the bed at 5 a.m. is a little rougher. I make him breakfast and tea while he showers and shaves. It's a very tired looking man who sits at my table.

I warn him, "You look very tired. Be extra careful today." When Christian shows with Blake's horse I ask him to keep his eye on Blake. He nods and winks. I'm still relieved to see them return at noontime for lunch. I have homemade soup and large toasted sandwiches. I have dirty dishes when they ride off. Blake looks better. He's back at 4 and once he's cleaned up, back at the plans. I realize his urgency is because he wants the ground breaking started in September—which is in about four days. By the time we go to bed, there are only three choices remaining. Blake wants to show them to Christian tomorrow for his input. I agree with him.

Tuesday at lunch I get to see the final decision. At my smile of approval, Blake squeezes my hand and starts eating. They're gone in record time and he took the plan # and information along. I'll bet he makes a few calls from the range today. After dinner, we ride over and decide where the new home will be built. Blake says we're getting a new well no matter where the new home goes. We decide on a pretty knoll about 10 acres from the original homestead. Blake says Christian will rent the old place once we move into the new one. I believe they have talked about this a lot between themselves. I'm glad that Blake has a man friend to talk things over with. I don't think Frank does that well. He still talks down to Blake like he's a teenager or inexperienced young man.

Wednesday at 6, the architects show up with the initial blue prints for Blake's approval. They need to know where the home is going and to select the contractor. After they leave to go over to the homestead as we have begun calling our new place, Christian sits on the couch and reads his newest chess magazine. I have mending and he smiles every time he glances my way.

The days just fly past. By the following Friday, ground is broken for the basement. Blake waded through all the permits and materials purchases. The surveyors are here for two days. The well crew came Thursday and the well is dug without any problems. Most days, Blake can hardly work the ranch for wanting to ride over to his own place. Christian hires three new hands. Blake begins disappearing for long periods of time. Christian and I smile at each other; we know where he's going because we came across him on one of our rides to visit the new place. Heather has gone back to school and all the men on the ranch have sighed in relief. Of course, she immediately gets a new boyfriend who turns out to be a sophomore at college. Blake says if her mother doesn't care; why should he? I know that her loose behavior bothers him.

The second week in October, I'm hanging out wash and Blake rides up full tilt and leaps from the horse almost before the animal has stopped. I know something's wrong from his expression. I drop the sheet back into the basket and run to him.

As he buries his face in my neck, I ask, "What's wrong?". He's trembling. After a few minutes I realize its pure rage.

Blake says, "Dad sold all the stock. Christian and I just finishing branding the last few stray calves and all these trucks show up. The man had signed bills of sale. Christian went to the house and when he returned, he said they're good. Evidently, dad is up to something. He told Christian it was none of his business what he does with his property." Blake stops and draws several calming breaths.

He says, "He's right. Why should we care? I've only been breaking my back since he had his stroke getting his spread up and running." Stopping; he tightens his arms around me.

He hugs me when I suggest, "Well, then, let's get over onto our homestead. We'll just have the horses to deal with over the winter and we can get good stock in the spring."

Blake says, "Maybe by spring, we'll have some good stock of our own growing in you?" He kisses me and I arch myself against him.

"No. Two more weeks, princess. I'm not taking any chances on hurting you. I can wait and so . . ." Pausing to tap my nose lightly, "can you." Mac rides up and gathers Blake's mount.

Tipping his hat to me, Mac asks, "Christian wants to know what you want done with the horses'?"

With that hurt back in his voice, Blake says, "He might as well round up Katie's herd and move them over to the homestead. We'll hire the men to help get the homestead livable. The bunkhouse may need some work over there too. Tell Christian to get a list of supplies and we'll head to town. You, sweetheart, might as well start packing. I have a feeling my meeting with dad is not going to be a pleasant one. I'm really hurt that he sold the stock without at least asking or letting me know." It tears at my heart.

I tell him, "I want to go with you." He shakes his head but I grab his nose.

I say "I'm not asking, I'm telling." He laughs and pinches my butt cheeks. In my sternest voice, I say, "Ouch. That hurts buster." I say in my sternest voice. He laughs again and swings me around in circles.

He says, "Still the little spit fire—aren't you, Katie girl?" before kissing me and setting me down. I have help with the laundry.

Lunch is a quiet affair. Christian arrives and does most of the talking about what he's accomplished. The horses are moved and settled in. A shipment of hay and straw is being delivered tomorrow. Frank had a big fit when he saw Pete loading hay and straw onto the truck. Christian said Blake bought it and without stock, Frank doesn't need it. Christian took enough for two days. Blake nods. The men have left for town to get the necessary supplies and order what they'll need to do repairs. Most of them are glad to come and work for Blake. His last statement is that we have a four o'clock appointment to meet with Frank. Blake actually grimaces. He's never needed an appointment before.

I'm glad I answered the phone at 2:30. It's Terry. "Katherine, Frank wants you and Blake to dress for dinner at 5 after the meeting. Please wear something like your Sunday dress. Thanks." She's gone before I get a chance to say anything. I go into the bathroom and open the shower door to relay the message to Blake.

He says, "That sounds rather ominous." flipping some of the water my way. I shut the shower door and then nod in agreement. I dig out my navy blue dress and a nice navy suit for Blake.

Arriving wrapped in a nice towel, he says, "Good choice." I quickly remove the towel and dry his back. We dress in silence and are at Franks by

3:49. Terry opens the front door and escorts us back to the family room. Frank is sitting in a nice suit in the one recliner.

Gesturing for us to sit on the couch across from him, Frank comments, "You two look good together." Terry offers refreshments, but Blake declines.

Frank watches Blake as he says, "Well, son, you need to offer me congratulations. Terry has consented to marry me. I'm sorry I sold the stock without mentioning it, but I've been a very busy man lately." There are several long minutes of silence as we wait for Blake's reply.

Blake tells his father, "Yes, Katie and I had an opportunity one afternoon to see how busy you've been with Terry. Dad, I don't think you should rush into marriage. You haven't known her that long and . . ." Frank holds up his hand for silence. Blake respectfully stops speaking.

Frank says sternly, "I'm not asking for your approval or opinion. We're getting married. The preacher will be here at 4:30. If you and Katie won't stand up for us, well, that's your decision. Just like the two of you running off and getting married behind my back, there's nothing you can do about this wedding, SON." Frank put a lot of emphasis on the last statement and word. Blake's body is tense but he remains silent for a long time again.

Enraged, Blake says, "Well, since you didn't ask for my opinion, I won't tell you I think she's after your money. As for Katie and I standing for you, well, I'm sorry, we're busy this evening. I want to be off your property before sunset. You call me when you come to your senses or when your money runs out." Blake stands and pulls me to my feet. I feel like I'm watching a TV or theater production.

Blake's parting words are, "Congratulations dad, I hope I'm wrong and that she'll make you as happy as mom did." Frank gasps at Blake's last statement. Terry doesn't even bother to show us out. I happen to think Blake's very right on target about her. As we're climbing into the Jeep, several neighbors are pulling up out front.

Closing my door Blake says, "Looks like he won't have any trouble finding replacements for us."

Climbing behind the wheel, he turns to face me saying, "Kind of a shame to waste a good dress up. Pretty lady, would you like to go to town for dinner and some dancing?" He gives that slow smile I love. I put my fingertip against my lips and tip my head to ponder.

I coyly say, "Well, I'm not busy and my husband will be packing tonight, so sure, handsome. Let's go dancing." He growls and starts the engine. As he makes the loop to head back to the driveway I notice Frank sitting in the open doorway in his chair. His face is in shadow but I'm sure he regrets his words already.

We stop at a local steak house to have a relaxing dinner of steak, wine and the salad bar. They have a dance floor on the other half of the restaurant so we two step and get into a couple of line dances before Blake whispers he wants to go home. I nod. We have packing to do. Blake stops at the bunkhouse and finds several hands with time on their hands. For a C note they'll gladly help us move our stuff to the homestead. I'm glad we don't have much stuff. Although Blake hired a cleaning crew, the place is still pretty run down in spite of being clean. As we're packing, I discover a lot of the things at the cottage actually belong to Blake. There are already several piles of boxes in the main front room at the homestead. Two large barrels in the kitchen contain English bone china and French lead crystal that Blake purchased new for our new home. We elect to use the everyday dishes from the cottage until we officially move into our new home.

I put clean sheets on the king-sized bed in the master bedroom. It's not bad in here. The carpet cleaned nicely like the expensive indoor/outdoor stuff usually does. There are air fresheners and we open the windows for a nice September breeze. Once we drop into the bed, I'm half asleep. Blake is restless. I hear him walk to the kitchen and then open a beer. He returns and sits in the chair by the open window and drinks. I'm not aware of when he climbed into the bed with me but his butt is against my back when I wake up. I'm disoriented and almost wet on the floor until I open the door to the bathroom. As I'm sitting, Blake comes in.

As he's patiently waiting his turn, I tell him, "We have to leave the bathroom door open. I almost dashed into the closet."

Blake says, "Well, the old two-holer outhouse is just out back and there's two old bathrooms upstairs, for dire emergencies." I shake my head at his words.

I tell him, "I'd never make either one as bad as I have to go first thing." I wash my face and hands. After breakfast, we head to town to purchase a few staples and items of furniture. The main room is empty and we'll need somewhere to sit in the evenings besides the old porch swing. We find a nice sofa and two love seats with firm cushions and wooden arms. Blake calls. Christian and Mac bring the big truck so we can take them today. The store would deliver Wednesday. I knew Blake would never wait. By the time Christian arrives, we have end tables, a coffee table and large screen TV.

The washer and dryer will be delivered on Tuesday and installed in the little utility room. Blake finds several rolls of linoleum that easily fit on the truck. One phone call and two of the hands are ripping up the old curled stuff in the kitchen within the hour. Blake gets a call back that they're going to need plywood. The old floor is pretty rotten in spots. Like every project we start at the old place (as Blake refers lovingly to it) a two hour job turns into a two-day ordeal. We stop at a carpet mart. I find a lovely area rug for the living room. Back at the home we realize we should have purchased table and chairs for the kitchen. Blake and I head back to town while the men use the new plywood to repair the entire kitchen floor.

This trip nets a beautiful dining room set, china hutch, sideboard and eight spoon backed Chippendale style furniture that will be delivered on Friday. We find a nice butcher-block style kitchen table and eight old fashioned spindle backed chairs for the kitchen. We also acquire a new microwave oven, stand, toaster, blender, mixer, set of sharp knifes in their own wood block and a multitude of cooking utensils. Blake decides to install a center chef's island after the new floor is down.

Christian has selected his bedroom upstairs on the right at the top of the stairs. Mac wants the back corner room. I discover on my journey upstairs that there is a small study style room on the opposite back corner. All the rugs in the house were removed and destroyed when the place was cleaned. The cleaning people did a fantastic job cleaning and waxing the hardwood floors. You can almost see yourself in them. I decide area rugs are a necessity. The study will become a small TV room for the guys. It's at the top of the back stairs and easily accessible to the kitchen without entering any of the rest of the house. I measure for drapes and rugs and decide painting will be necessary before I go any further. Downstairs, Blake is agreeable to everything. Like I was worried he wouldn't be.

Mac gladly takes me for a supper run. We return with two kegs of beer for our workers, fried chicken and all the fixings. I got two huge buckets of Buds BBQ'd ribs. We stopped for a supply of paper plates and cups. After dinner I have bones, dirty paper plates and cups that all go into several large garbage bags. Exhausted, we call it an early night. Sunday we're at the sunrise service and a stop at an early opening Hardware City Store gets us the necessary paint and tools.

Blake stops at the bunkhouse and asks if any of the guys want to earn some money painting. I'm shocked at the 100% response. They eagerly trek to the house and paint the living room and dining room before 3. After my roast turkey dinner is consumed, they go upstairs and paint the two bedrooms and study. Of course, 15 guys can get a lot done. Blake is now putting drop ceilings in upstairs. He was up in the attic and I guess the roof is leaking. He and Christian are up there almost two hours measuring and noting materials needed. Of course it rains Monday and we get a real good idea of where the roof is leaking and how badly. I don't like the guys on the wet roof spreading plastic sheets. However, my trip to the dripping attic does prove they are sorely needed in certain spots.

Tuesday, the washer and dryer are delivered an installed on top of the newly laid floor and in the now cream colored utility room. The kitchen and utility room were painted this medium green color. Mac discovers that if you sand the layers of paint off the kitchen wooden cabinet faces, the wood underneath is a white pine and very pretty. The new countertop is that butcher-block style and matches the table top and chair seats. There is a little powder room off the family room that gets a new toilet and sink/vanity. They removed the old linoleum, discovered the floor was totally rotten and the seal on the old rusty toilet was shot. It was easier to paint the room without the toilet and sink in it anyway. Mac did a fantastic job on the cupboards and with the new countertop. Blake worked diligently at installing my new center chef's island. It has a lot of nice drawers and one of those new corning cook tops.

By the end of September, we are happily settled in our little temporary love nest. In my heart, I think Blake was hoping his father would call. We drove over to the house after church the following Sunday. Heather said they were on their honeymoon.

There are three fireplaces on the first floor. The one in the family room must have gotten the majority of use. Blake has professionals come and clean all the chimneys. The one in the kitchen had several bird nests in the top. The living room one was clean but someone blocked the top of it. Our new roof looks really nice and Blake put insulation in the attic and laid a nice floor overtop. The upright freezer went into the utility room beside the deep sink and filled up easily. We're buying our meat from a local butcher shop by the half steer. Devin gets the other half and we both get a good deal.

Thursday night, Blake thinks he hears loud music. He and Christian look for campers or squatters on the grounds around the homestead. Blake calls Devin on Friday and invites him to dinner. Devin requests my honey orange chicken. Devin is our first dinner guest the first Sunday of October. It is the first chance he has to come over to see our place.

After church, I get busy in my kitchen. I'm humming away and warm firm hands cup my breasts. I get little nibbles on the back of my neck and shoulder. Busily nibbling my ear, Blake says, "You sound very happy today, little lady. Are you happy here?"

I tell him, "I'm very happy whenever I'm where you are. But, I do love this home of our own. This is the first place we have lived that belongs to us." I turn to plant little kisses on his face and mouth.

He says with a soft smile, "I never thought about this place that way, but you're right. I've been so excited about the new house that . . . don't play with that, your brother will be here within 20 minutes or so. Katie girl, you're being bad." He sweeps me into his arms and carries me into the family room. When Devin walks into the back foyer, Blake is in the process of giving me a spanking across his lap.

At this sight, Devin asks, "Hey, is my little sis being bad?"

Without hesitating, Blake keeps spanking and says, "Yes. So, I'm adjusting her attitude. And, I must admit, seen from this angle, it is a very nice attitude." After flipping me onto the floor at his feet, I try pulling my skirt back down to my knees. Devin just laughs and parks himself on the love seat.

Looking around he says, "Boy, you can tell you've been working in here. I smelled the paint before the chicken."

Blake teases, "Would you like the grand tour while the cook gets back to work?"

Devin says, "Sure. I used to visit the Newman's periodically, especially during the winter. They were forever running low on supplies. They really let this place go down hill. I like the new flooring." They walk out while I'm getting up off the floor somewhat ungracefully. Since Devin is early and dinner needs to cook, they talk themselves into a nice ride. Devin is shocked when he and Blake ride over to Franks for a visit. I don't think they intended to end up there. I didn't want to leave the cooking pots. Christian and I visit in the living room while they're gone.

He jumps up at the sound of the pounding hooves and dashes through the back hall to the back door. I'm hot on his heels. Blake jumps from Ranger as Devin reins in Howdyboy. They're laughing. They must have been racing. Christian lets his breath out and walks onto the back porch. I shake my head and follow.

Blake says, "You should see dad's place. The yards are littered with trash, beer cans and sporty cars. Heather has a party going on full blast. We walked into the family room and practically stepped on two teenagers going at each other full blast. The young punk never even missed a stroke as the girl screamed and tried to cover herself. We were told to wait our turn." Blake shakes his head and flops onto the wide wooden bench up against the kitchen windows. I climb into the swing.

Sitting on the top step, Devin says, "Man; the inside looks and smells worse than the outside. It looks like it's been one long party since the adults left on their two month cruise. There has to be over a hundred empty pizza boxes stacked in the living room. Things are busted and the curtains are torn out of the walls in spots. Frank is going to have another stroke when he gets home. We looked for Heather but she didn't appear to be home right now. One guy said she probably took the credit card for a pizza run."

Devin is shaking his head as I'm walking to the kitchen. My timer is going off. Blake is stony and silent. It must hurt to see his mothers home in such disarray and under massive destruction. It reminds me of what Eleanor did to my mother's lovely things.

Before too long, we're seated around the formal dining room. Blake offers grace. Christian and Mac are dressed in their Sunday best. Blake even placed lighted candles on the table. We have a nice wine. Once everything is carried to the kitchen for cleaning, I seem to be alone. I don't mind. The newly installed dishwasher is a workhorse. I load it and sneak upstairs for a nice hot bath. The only bathtubs are upstairs. Once that's done, I slip into a lounger and make myself comfortable in the living room. I'm making a crib quilt right now. I did all the embroidery on each square and have the two crib pillows already done. There's a long stitch picture that goes with the set but Blake needs to make my stretcher bars for the canvas before I can start that. It's all teddy bears and choo-choo trains. Now that I don't have the horse work to do, I have discovered the pleasure of needlepoint crafts once my housework is done. My four months are up. I'm ready to take on Blake and start another baby.

I should have known the four of them would take a posse over and end the party at Franks. When Blake finally returns at 10, he's pretty stressed out and tired.

From the back porch he calls, "Hello?"

From the living room I call, "In here."

Walking in and flopping into the one armchair, Blake says, "Well, that's the end of that for a couple of days at least. Miss Heather is not happy. I called the sheriff and we broke up the party." With a weary smile he continues, "A couple of the guys at the party didn't want to go home. Sheriff also found drugs and pot. Miss Heather is on two weeks probation to clean up the house and get her little wild ass to school during the weekdays."

Blake says, "Even Sheriff Ron is shocked at his first glimpse of the grounds and house. His oldest son went to school and was friends with Kyle. He even remembered old man Morgan. That got a laugh from Devin. I haven't thought of your grandfather in years either." He pauses and shifts his hips in the chair. I put my needle into the work and set my hoop down. I walk over and kneel across his lap.

Blake says, "Thinking about Old Man Morgan made me remember his little spit fire granddaughter." His hands slide up under my tee in the back and pull me towards him. Little pecks become deep long wet kisses. When he leans forward to stand; he wraps my legs around his waist. I'm carried into the bedroom and undressed for bed. The next morning, I'm stiff and sore. Blake is very concerned. I have to keep reassuring him that I'm fine just out of practice. He promises to rectify that over the next several months. Between the new home, the homestead and trying to keep his father's place half decent, Blake is a very busy man. The honeymooners return just before Thanksgiving. Frank is walking with a cane now and has totally regained his speech and most of his body movements. We get a royal surprise during our Sunday dinner when the front door bell chimes.

As he's starting to rise, Christian says, "Hello?" Blake stays him with his hand and strides over to the foyer to get the door. Christian still rises to put himself in a backup position. Old habits die hard, I guess. I smile and start to pass more of the mashed potatoes to Mac. I'm startled at the sound of Franks voice and almost drop the bowl.

Frank's tone is light and teasing when he says; "Well, invite me in son. Smells like Katie girl is up to her old cooking tricks. Any chance your father and step mother can get an invite?" He sounds happy. I rise and head to the kitchen for two more place settings. Mac follows bringing his setting to the kitchen.

I whisper, "You can stay."

He shakes his head saying, "I got work. Everything was delicious." I get a kiss on my forehead before he's out the back door in a flash. When I return with the place settings, Frank is standing looking around. Terry has taken a seat at the table.

Frank says, "What a change in this place! Katie girl, you look radiant. Will I soon have a grand child?" Shaking my head I set the plates down to give him a hug.

I tell him, "No. I'm in love. Sit, there's plenty and it's getting cold." Blake fills their wine glasses and I notice Christian's place is empty. The conversation is lax while they load up their plates and eat. Frank looks the best I have seen him in years.

He proudly tells Blake, "I've lost 130 pounds!"

With a smile Blake says, "That's great dad. Married life agrees with you. I'm happy for you." Frank nods and starts eating. Terry takes smaller portions but she eats what she takes. I'm glad I made the large tossed salad. She prefers them. Frank eats the last four of my homemade biscuits although Terry frowns. Once he's finished, he leans back and looks directly at Blake. For a moment, I'm thinking, uh oh, here it comes.

With a smile, Frank says, "Son, I appreciate the good care you took of my place while I was away. Thank you." We rise from the table. Frank shakes Blake's hand before they retire to the living room. Frank wants to see the first floor. Terry helps me in the kitchen.

After the men have moved beyond hearing range, she hisses, "I understand Heather got a bit wild while we were gone but was it necessary to call the cops?"

Surprised at her tone, I look up to say, "That was Blake's decision. I heard about it after the fact." I shrug before telling her, "What your daughter does with her life is no concern of mine." I'm being truthful. I still don't care for the look she gives me.

She warns, "Good. You'll do well to keep your nose out of my business."

Stiffening, I lean towards her to hiss back, "You'll stay healthier if you don't threaten me." For a moment, she's surprised and then I get her slow snake like smile. By the time Frank and Blake return, we're finished with the clean up and sitting in the living room. I'm quilting. Terry is chatting about their lovely cruise. They stay for two hours. We hear all about the cruise. It's a relief when they finally leave. Christian appears at the foot of the stairs. He leans towards me in the doorway before Blake returns from walking his father to their car to tell me, "I heard her in the kitchen. I'll be watching you very closely for a couple of weeks." I get a gentle squeeze as Blake comes up the two steps and up onto the front porch.

Blake teases, "Don't be squeezing my wife." Christian punches his arm as Blake enters the house.

While they jostle their way back through the house to the family room, Christian teases, "Why not? She's just so squeezeably soft." I grab my needlework and join them. The TV comes on and we have a football game in progress. We got a satellite dish installed Thursday. Our reception is poor. We briefly visit the weather channel and then several sports channels before Blake finds a chess match for Christian. Blake and Christian have a game going almost all the time. I got in trouble Wednesday, I bumped the table with the vacuum and all the pieces fell over.

Blake and I are invited to Devin's for Thanksgiving. Blake wants to go so I accepted. I'm making the full dinner here for Christian and Mac. I worked most of Wednesday to prepare a massive turkey feast for the hands. I have lots of volunteers to load the truck and safely deliver the food to the bunkhouse. I'm surprised when all the dishes are returned sparkling clean. We're up in plenty of time to get my meal started before we leave. Blake is in the stuffing up to his elbows while I'm stuffing the bird. He can't stop eating it.

I tease, "You'll spoil your supper." He just shakes his head and grabs another spoonful. I'm bringing my mother's famous jello mold salad and the homemade pumpkin and banana breads. Cook is very insistent that we just bring our appetites.

I'm wearing a shimmery dark green dress with a full skirt and low V neck—bodice. Blake can't seem to keep his hands off. He buries his nose in my cleavage and squeezes my bottom while I'm trying to put in my earrings.

I ask, "Do you want to stay home?".

Chuckling into my cleavage he says, "Yes and no. Are you about ready?" A quick check and I find he's not ready to stay home so we leave. Christian will finish my dinner. I highly doubt they'll consume every bit of the massive quantity of food I've prepared.

I get the shock of my life at Devin's. We walk in and sitting in the living room is Father. I gasp and stop so suddenly that Blake almost knocks me down until he can get his own forward motion stopped. He grabs me around the waist and then catches sight of my father. Devin rises and comes over.

Devin whispers, "I hope you don't mind. The sanitarium released father on Tuesday. I flew up and got him. Dustin sold his home, so the poor man has nowhere familiar to go. I know he spent a lot of time here. He seems quite content but I'll warn you, he's mostly not here."

Bringing me around to face Father Devin says, "Father, Katherine has come to visit."

Father face breaks into a wide smile as he says, "Katherine, how grown up you are! Who is this handsome man?" looking beyond me at Blake.

I explain, "Father, this is Frank Dailey's son, Blake. We're married." Father looks at Blake and offers his hand.

Father says, "Good to see you again. You'll have to forgive me. I've forgotten your wedding. I have forgotten a lot of things lately. It's a shame about Morgan. He was a good man. Sit; tell me all about your married life. How long have you been married?" Blake and I sit across from Father. Blake tells him that we have been married less than two years. Devin brings over our wedding picture for Father to look at.

Looking up at me. He remarks, "You should have worn your mothers dress." I'm struck speechless.

To cover my shock, Devin lies. "It was ruined when the attic roof leaked, Father." Father smiles as though he remembers.

Leaning forward, he says, "What a strikingly handsome couple you make. I'm so glad my Katherine has wed Frank's boy. Am I going to have grandchildren in the near future?"

I tell him, "Father, I took a nasty fall at Franks and had a miscarriage about four months ago. We're going to try for another child in about six months. It looks like you'll have to wait at least a year." His face registers shock and then he solemnly nods.

Sounding faintly jealous when he says, "Don't push yourselves. You've plenty of time for children. Once my boys came along, I basically lost your mother's attention to her babies."

Blake smiles and says, "I plan to keep Katie's attention for many years to come." Cook comes to the door to announce dinner. Devin and Blake get Father into a wheel chair and push him into the dining room.

Looking up from the chair, he explains, "I'm not good on my feet right now." It's a little sad to see such a proud man reduced to this. The conversation over dinner is about our new place. Father seems anxious to see the homestead and eventually our new home.

He remarks, "It looks like I'll be relying on Devin's charity since your brother sold my home while I was in the hospital. I guess Dustin figured I'd just curl up and die. Well, I may make some changes in my will and he'll be sorry." He resumes eating. I watch Devin's eyebrows go up at the statement. Blake just smiles and keeps eating. Cook fusses over Father and he eats up the attention.

He says to her, "I hope you made your famous mincemeat and raisin pie." She nods and winks. I remember that was always his favorite. Blake tries some but it's too sweet for his palate. He sticks to my pumpkin bread with fresh whipped butter and then Cook's homemade cream cheese.

After dinner, we retire to the family room. Father enjoys watching any type of horse show or racing. Devin finds a steeple chasing event. Father is glued to the action. Blake puts his arm around me and I lean back against him. Devin winks at us. After the show goes off, Father is visibly tired. Blake says we're going back home now. Father just nods. They have made the sunroom into father's bedroom. At the Jeep, Devin remarks he may have to add an additional bathroom if Father's visit becomes permanent. Blake shakes his hand and we head home. I'm rather tired, mostly from stress I think. I wasn't sure if Father would erupt or not anytime during our visit. Devin was watching closely too. I think he was worried Father might recall he didn't want Blake and I married.

In our bedroom, Blake says, "I was worried your father might get his memory back when he saw me. I'm not so sure his brain isn't scrambled worse than the doctors have theorized." I hang up his jacket and put his stickpin away. He unzips my dress and we dress for bed. I'm so tired that Blake finally gives up his attempts to excite me and pulls me into his arms to sleep.

Friday is basically a lazy day. Frank calls about 3 to talk to Blake. Blake relays the conversation. Evidently Devin called and invited the newlyweds over to visit father. Frank is badly shaken by the sight of his old friend. Devin warned them but you don't realize the severity until you're looking at him.

Blake has pretty much given the hands the weekend off. They have to tend the horses in the morning and at night. Blake and I ride down to the new house. We have a nice picnic until the air begins blowing then we head for home. Sam takes the horses and we walk briskly to the house. While I'm cleaning up the picnic stuff, Blake is busily eating whatever he can get his hands onto. Christian comes running down the back stairs.

Running for the back door as he passes, he hollers, "Stables are on fire!". Blake drops the food from his hand to run after him. I finish putting the food in my hands into the refrigerator before I grab our jackets and follow him.

My first sight of the stables as I round the corner of the garage is horrifying. The building is almost fully ablaze. I scream in horror as Blake brings a terrified stallion out and releases him. The horror is because Blake runs right back into the burning building.

Running towards the building I scream, "NO! Leave them!" Christian comes out with Fermeau and grabs me before I can get past him. I feel the heat of the fire from where we stand. Suddenly, Blake and Mac come out with Pegalea and Gray Lady. Several other hands are busily bringing terrified animals outside.

The hay must have combusted because there is a terrible explosion that knocks Blake and Mac flat into the dirt. Suddenly freed, both mares run terrified towards us. Christian shields me with his own body as we're knocked to the ground and run over. Blake is at our side immediately.

Christian is unconscious from a nasty bleeding head wound. Mac comes over to help Blake get him off me.

Handing me his cell phone, Blake says, "He's gonna need an ambulance." I call 911. The fire department arrives the same time as a multitude of neighbors. The stables are a total loss but they save the nearby barn and large garage. Christian regains consciousness and refuses to go to the hospital—whom does that sound like?

Blake tries to insist but Christian says, "Arson." Blake falls silent after glancing quickly my way.

Blake and I take Christian to the kitchen and an EMT treats the head wound as best as he can. He keeps insisting that Christian go to the hospital for stitches and x-rays. Christian firmly refuses and actually growls at the young man. Blake insists Christian go upstairs and to bed. It takes both of us to get him upstairs and settled into bed. I get him something for the pain.

I hear him tell Blake, "Watch her close." Blake's murmur is too low for my ears. Blake returns to the stables. Thank goodness the breeder books are kept in a fireproof safe with the other important documents. We lost all our tack, three mares, two foals and a yearling stallion. It takes us hours to get the horses settled down. Two area vets show up and pitch in to help. A lot of neighbors stay well into the wee hours of the morning to help with the excited and terrified horses. It's almost 3 a.m. when Devin spots me and makes me go to bed. I didn't even know he was here. I should have figured since he's a close neighbor.

I hear the Fire Chief tell the Sheriff, "It was definitely arson. The place reeks of gasoline and we found four timers." I pale and search the crowd for Blake. Mac is stuck to me like glue. It's almost 5 a.m. when Blake drops into bed beside me. He has showered but still smells of the smoke. He drops immediately to sleep and does not rise until after 2 p.m. I'm up at noon and making breakfast before I realize the time. Christian and Mac gladly eat my oatmeal and cinnamon toast. It's a very bleary eyed Blake who sits at the table while I give him tea, fresh oatmeal, fruit and wheat toast. I sit and he glances up.

I tell him, "We're comfortable right here. I know that stables are more urgently needed than the house. However, in the future, don't rush into burning buildings for animals—please?" He shakes his head.

Before cautiously sipping his tea, he says, "You'd have done the same if Christian hadn't stopped you. I know how much those horses mean to you." I shake my head.

I tell him, "No. The horses mean nothing without you. I can buy a million more horses—where can I buy another you?" He motions to come over. I slide into his lap and he lays his head on my breast.

He murmurs, "I feel the same way." We both jump when the front door chimes. Blake stands after I slide from his lap. He strides to the front door with me hot on his heels.

It's a very distraught Frank who immediately says, "Son! Are you OK? I pick up my morning paper and the headlines are of my son's stables exploding and burning." Blake pats his father's arm and motions for him to come in.

Blake says, "We're fine. We lost several fine animals but no one was hurt. The fire department saved the rest of the buildings. Sit down." We're in the living room.

Frank is still very upset, he says, "Katie girl. You look so pale. The papers said it was deliberate. Why won't people leave you two alone?" Frank looks directly at Blake who shrugs.

Then he says, "I don't know dad. This could be aimed at me, could be aimed at Katie. Its possible someone is just sick enough to start with our place for some sick or twisted reason. We'll just be extra careful. I'm beefing up security. Did you drive here?" Blake asks.

Shaking his head, Frank says, "Terry dropped me off on her way to town to shop. I figured someone here would take me home." He leans back in the chair and visibly relaxes. Blake has Mac run Frank home after almost an hours visit. Frank insists on seeing the damage at the stables.

Devin is gracious enough to take our horses back to his place. There go Blake and my early morning rides together. It's just not as much fun to ride in the Jeep to the stables to ride and then come back home. Christian must have a very hard head. He's a little sluggish for about 48 hours and then except for the bandage over the stitches, he's back to normal. The next two weeks are full of getting ready for Christmas. The stables are supposed to be under roof before Christmas. Blake is at the construction sight every spare minute of the day. Of course, there are still the usual fence mending problems and other problems and work associated with a ranch this size.

I almost have a heart attack when I get our grocery tab from town. We have a monthly tab for the cook at the bunkhouse to order supplies. Plus when I send Mac or Christian they don't have to worry with money. I start going through the slips and there are a multitude signed by Terry and Heather. I call the storeowner. He says Mr. Dailey OK'd the charges. I figure Blake has a deal with his dad about it. I casually mention it over dinner that night and get a totally blank look.

He asks, "What are talking about?" I bring in the receipts and show him. He shakes his head.

Blake says, "Something's going on with dad's money. I'm not sure I like it. I'm going to casually speak with him. Then I'm going to talk to the grocer. This is for lobster, steak and frivolous stuff. I'm not paying for his tootsie to eat high off the hog." Blake tosses the slips down and sits tapping his fork on the plate. Christian finally leans forward and lays his knife across the fork.

He softly says, "That's annoying buddy." Blake looks up like he was a million miles away. Blake smiles and then resumes eating. He helps with the dishes. Then we go for a nice long walk to his dads. Blake rings the bell. Heather answers the door.

She says, "Oh, it's you." then promptly shuts the door in our faces. Blake kicks the door with his foot and it flies open.

When he yells, "Dad!" Heather takes off down the hall like Satan himself is chasing her.

Franks voice comes from the back of the house, "Back here son. Come on in." Blake steps inside and I follow. The door mostly closes. He split the frame.

Taking my hand and pulling me back towards the family room, he says, "I'll replace it." Frank is sitting watching TV alone.

When Frank sees us, he says, "Oh, you brought Katie girl. Sit, we'll have a nice visit." He uses the remote and turns the TV off.

Leaning towards Frank, Blake says, "I owe you a new door. Heather shut the door in my face. I kicked it open."

Frank shrugs and says in a matter of fact voice, "She's a teenager. She's kinda mad at you for calling the cops. Terry sorta lets her run wild." Frank shrugs again and asks, "What can I do?" Blake rolls his eyes in silent agreement.

Blake softly asks, "Are you, ah, having money problems?" Frank glances quickly away.

Finally Frank says, "Yeah. I'm a little short right now." Then he turns back to face us to ask, "Why do you ask? Do you need something?"

Blake shakes his head saying, "No. Terry and Heather charged groceries on my tab. If you need money for supplies, let me know and I'll get them for you." Frank waves his hand at Blake.

Frank says, "No. I have another CD maturing first of next month. I just over extended myself some. Can you and me talk; man to man?" glancing in my direction. I nod and rise.

I tell him, "I'll just use your bathroom for a few minutes. OK?" Frank nods and smiles. It's quiet until I'm out of earshot. I wait in the bathroom until Blake comes looking for me.

Blake asks, "Did you fall in? Dad wants to know." I get a quick kiss before we rejoin Frank. When Terry comes home from shopping, Blake and I make our excuses. Christian is waiting in the Jeep. It takes him and Blake about 10 minutes to repair the door temporarily.

While he's climbing into the backseat Christian asks, "Temper tantrum?"

While starting the Jeep, Blake explains, "You could say that. I didn't care to have my father's door shut in my face by Heather."

Blake tells me, "Katie girl, that man is in one hell of a mess. He doesn't have enough money to pay his property taxes. I got the bill. It's double because it's six months past due." Blake falls silent until we get out at the house. Christian takes the Jeep on to the garage. Inside, Blake pulls me into the family room and onto his lap on the sofa. He sighs and sits silently for quite some time.

Blake finally says, "I think it's probably worse than he's letting on. I'm going to have Christian run his credit status tomorrow. If he's getting into debt on his limited income, he'll loose the ranch. I can't let that happen. That property has been in our family over 200 years. He had plenty of money from mom's parent's estate, insurance money and then Kyle's insurance money. He should have been able to live comfortably for the rest of his life. If he's cashing in CD's, he's spent several million dollars in ready cash." Blake stops and shakes his head. He drops his chin down onto my shoulder.

I immediately say, "If you need money, you know I have it."

He chuckles saying, "Thanks, princess, but no thanks. I have plenty. My honey isn't burning through my money." He seems to be searching for something under my tee shirt.

I warn him teasingly, "Don't play with those if you're not seriously thinking about some rather strenuous activity." The fingers get more persistent and tender in their touch. We wander back through to our bedroom for a nice long bout of lovemaking. In the morning, he's gone when I open my eyes. My computer is set up in the corner of the living room. I quickly dress and find Christian tapping away at the keys as Blake lounges in a nearby armchair.

Slipping onto Blake's lap I ask, "Good morning, gents. Did you eat?"

Blake says, "Nope." Christian is intently using the mouse now. The printer starts and after several sheets print, Blake leans forward and Christian hands them to him.

Hastily flipping through the sheets, Blake says "Hmmmm, not good."

"That was an expensive cruise. I wonder if Terry will sell some of the gold jewelry that's been purchased. There are also a lot of expensive dining tabs and of course, almost $8,000 in pizza and beer purchases." Blake remarks in a very somber tone.

Christian is scanning several pages and says, "You're gonna flip at the ATM usage and fees. Not to mention the phone and Internet usage bills. There are a multitude of clothing and electronics purchases. Here's the bill for Terry's new BMW which is tagged for 12/24 delivery." Blake just sighs and lays the pile of printed pages on the end table.

Blake says, "My dad only had one credit card for emergencies. Christian has found where over 30 new cards have been ordered over the past month and a half. His bank account shows he's still paying Terry for housekeeping and PT every week. Heather is getting $500 a week for an allowance. They are bleeding him dry at a fantastic rate. Well, he's a grown man. He gets the bills and writes the checks. He definitely would not appreciate my sticking my nose in. I'll just step back until it's time to pick up the pieces. I'm going over to the bank and make sure that they contact me before they put the place up for sale." He wraps his arms tightly around me. Laying back against him I watch as the printer spits out page after page of printout.

I'm finally put from his lap to get breakfast going. They eat and he heads to town. The rest of the week passes fairly quietly. The weather is cooperating and the stables are going up in record time. We get a nice Christmas tree. I spend several days shopping for gifts with Christian and then Mac. Christmas would have been nicer if Frank hadn't spent so much money on Terry and Heather. Blake has been monitoring his purchases and sadly shaking his head. The bank calls the minute Frank applies for a mortgage on the ranch. They don't want to give it to him because of his credit cards and recent spending sprees. Blake says he'll cosign and immediately pay off the loan to hold the lien on the property. We're invited over Christmas night to exchange gifts with Frank.

Christmas Eve is spent with Devin and Father. We arrive at 3 for an early dinner. Father gets tired easily and then becomes very confused. It's a formal affair. Blake and I dress appropriately. He's in a black tux. I'm in an icy white evening gown trimmed in ribbons of red. The material is satin and very clingy and flowing. I bought it in town several weeks earlier.

When he sees it, Blake's first comment is, "Oh, sweetheart, let's just stay home tonight." Then he comes over and slides his hands over the material before zipping me up. I get lots of little kisses on my shoulders and neck.

I softly tell him, "Well, Father will be heart broke." and he chuckles.

Blake teases, "You'll make it up to me later." I'll bet I could make it up right now—very easily.

Christian gives a low whistle as we come outside to get into the new Mercedes SL500 that Blake purchased for Christmas. He dashes to open my door and makes a sweeping bow as I approach. I give him a kiss and slide inside. At Devin's, the place is ablaze with lights and a nice Christmas tape is playing as we step into the foyer.

Devin greets us with, "You look beautiful, little sis. Blake—still handsome as ever. Father is back in the family room. He really enjoys the blinking lights on the tree. Doran and Rachel are here from Boston." Devin hands our coats to Truman who gives me a slow smile.

Cook appears and Truman softly says, "Doesn't our Miss Katherine look like an angel?" Cook nods and gives me a brief hug. Retirement is agreeing with Truman. He and Tom are fishing up a storm. I don't ever hear of them catching anything, just doing a lot of fishing. Blake hands Devin our gifts and we follow Devin back through to the family room.

Doran rises immediately and offers his hand to Blake saying, "Hello. You must be Blake. I've heard quite a few tales from Dustin." Blake grimaces at my brother's words but Doran laughs and continues, "I, however, will make my own judgments. This is Rachel VanDerGuilde, my fiancee'. Rachel, this is Blake and my sister, Katherine." Rachel stands and kisses Blake full on the mouth. That is something that causes him to rear his head up and away from her in shock. Doran laughs and sits beside Father.

Father leans forward and confides to Blake, "She did the same thing to me, son. It's just her way." Rachel is a tall willowy blonde with long heavy tresses of hair hanging straight down her back almost to her seat. It reminds me of when mine was that long and I glance across into the large oval mirror. My beautiful hair has grown about half way back to its usual length. Blake has suggested that I keep it at this length, he likes it. Rachel is wearing a Santa red and white trimmed dress with a short but extremely full skirt and matching red heels and red and white bracelets. She perches on the sofa next to Doran and periodically squeezes his knee. Blake and I take a seat in the nearby loveseat. Devin takes the other armchair near Father. Doran never changes his looks. His brown hair looks almost black in this light. His dark brown eyes are soft and friendly looking. He has a somewhat narrow mouth and upper lip but he usually smiles a lot. He appears thinner than when I last saw him.

When Father says, "My oldest son is not coming down for Christmas. He must be feeling guilty over selling my home. I was looking forward to seeing my grandson but I'll wait for Blake and Katie's child." Everyone looks at me. Blake coughs and I blush bright red.

Devin asks, "Well?" and I shake my head.

I tell him, "No. We have to wait several more months before trying again." I turn to face Doran to explain, "I had a miscarriage in June." As a doctor, he nods knowingly.

Doran quietly says, "You two are young. Enjoy yourselves first." I feel Blake begin to relax and warm up to him. Doran is extremely intelligent but very friendly and easy going. Dustin used to bully him the worst until Devin got big enough to beat up Dustin for Doran. I smile at those memories. Devin winks as though he's reading my thoughts.

Doran says, "So, Katherine, I hear you've had a very busy life since meeting up with Blake Dailey again. I'm happy that you're happily married.

How's old Fermeau?" There's his old teasing big brother tone. Doran's voice is mellower than Devin's.

I tell him, "He's behaving himself. Our stables burned, so he's here at Devin's." Doran looks over at Devin who nods.

Doran teasingly says, "Well, little brother didn't mention the fire or your miscarriage. I should have kept him up later last night." Devin rolls his eyes at Doran. Father gives a soft laugh.

Father says, "Katherine, your brothers sat up until at least 3 a.m. talking over all the old times and some of the more recent times. I'm sure Dustin's ears were ringing off and on." I notice that Father is looking a little weary today. His voice is steady and strong but he's not breathing real well. I get my asthma problems from him. I recall my mother telling me that he suffered miserably as a child.

Father brightly suggests, "Well, since we're all here, let's get these gifts opened."

Devin suggests, "What about having dinner first?" Father glances back towards the kitchen area.

He slowly says, "Well, dinner does smell rather inviting. Whatever you want." What a different man! I wonder if his medications are calming him. I remember how Franks changed his personality. Cook announces dinner. Doran and Devin get Father into his wheelchair and out to the table. Father is placed at the head of the table opposite Devin. Blake and I are on Devin's right with Doran and Rachel across from us. Cook has prepared a feast of roast duck, goose and pork. Father enjoys goose but I favor the duck. Doran keeps looking my way and smiling.

Over dinner we hear about Rachel's social activities and Doran's life at the hospital. He's chief surgeon now and very busy. They've moved their wedding three times. Rachel firmly says this June is D day or else. Doran smiles softly and kisses her hand. Once we have finished eating, Father is again ready to open gifts. I think he's beginning to tire and doesn't want to miss it. We retire to the Family room where Devin plays Santa. The gifts are mostly clothes but we still enjoy opening them. Doran and Devin then take Father back for bed. It's after 10 and Blake is visibly tired.

I tell him softly, "Let's go home." Rachel has been starring at him off and on all evening.

Finally she says, "Before you leave, Blake, you look very familiar to me. Have you ever been at any political or social gatherings in Boston?" leaning towards him.

He calmly says, "No. Not that I can recall." She nods and leans back, a soft smile on her face. When Doran and Devin return, Blake and I say our good-byes and get our coats. Blake is quiet in the Jeep on the drive home.

Once we're in bed, he turns to me and says, "I was in Boston on a job. I took out a very dirty politician. I remember her being at the campaign headquarters that night. I just wanted you to know that she wasn't an old flame or something." I chuckle.

Nestling up against him, I tell him, "Just as long as I'm your last and only flame." We lay quietly until sleep claims us.

Christmas morning arrives early. Blake is very busy getting my body awake. He says, "Princess, Santa Claus wants to visit you very intimately." I open my eyes and he certainly does. Santa has to wait while Mrs. Claus uses her a.m. seat first.

As I'm returning to the room, he remarks, "That's not very romantic." Removing my nightgown over my head seems to change his mind about what's romantic or not. We follow our noses to the kitchen after our gift exchange in the bed is over. Christian has breakfast all made.

He says, "Good morning and Merry Christmas." Blake pulls my chair out. We return the exchange and are all soon dining on steak and eggs. Mac is in a big hurry. He was in the Family room checking out the presents that mysteriously appeared over night. I put the Santa gifts out after everyone was in bed last night. The dishes are left soaking until the gifts are all open.

Blake thought maybe Mac would go home for Christmas. Mac said that if Blake didn't mind, this is his home and he'd rather stay here. Most of the hands don't have family either. I established a hat and everyone pulled a name out to purchase a gift. Blake and I dress and head to the bunkhouse for Blake to give our gifts to each hand. Mostly it's money or clothes but very appreciated.

I have prepared a massive meal and the hands have all been invited to the house for it. We have a full dining room and kitchen area. Blake is surprised at all the different dishes I have prepared. Our microwave does double duty today. Cook had gladly put my ham into their oven to leave room for the turkey for ours. There is not one scrap of leftovers in any of the serving dishes. I'm chased from the kitchen. When I hear nothing but silence, go out to find the kitchen and dining rooms both spotless and empty.

Blake is asleep on our bed. We have to be at Franks by 4, so I'm forced to wake him at 3:30. We dress and Christian helps load the few gifts into the Jeep. Blake is tight lipped. I know he dreads going over to his dad's only because of the multitude of bills Frank ran up going overboard on his purchases. The new BMW is sitting in front of the front porch. We're escorted back to the family room by Terry. She finally opens the door after Blake rings the bell several times.

She remarks, "Merry Christmas." Then she promptly turns and walks back through the foyer. The living room is full of opened gifts. Blake makes a strange sound as we pass the archways. Frank is seated in the one recliner and looks tired. Blake and I take a seat across from him after I kiss his cheek.

Frank says, "You look radiant, Katie girl. Blake, son, it's good to see you. This has been a long day. Did you have a nice Christmas?" Blake nods.

I smile and say, "Yes, and you?" Frank nods. Frank wants to open our gifts. I can tell that Terry is not pleased with hers but she smiles sweetly and thanks us. It's a very expensive dress from the shop she seems to frequent according to Franks credit card slips. The shopkeeper knew her very well and selected one that she thought would agree with the taste line of Terry's other purchases. Heather never even came down to open her gift. We got Frank some new clothes. Blake gave him a new CD for $100,000 that will mature in a year.

Frank opens the box and removes the certificate and tells Blake, "This is nice but you shouldn't have." Blake shrugs and smiles.

Blake softly says, "It's OK, dad, I can afford it. You took care of me while I was young. Now I'll return the favor." Frank nods and smiles. I got a nice new negligee and pair of earrings. Blake got new jeans and cologne. Terry serves eggnog and munchies. We don't stay very long. Blake tells Frank he looks tired and it's been a long day.

Blake says, "Work day tomorrow." gathering our gifts, coats and we take our leave. Back at the house, Blake flops into the one recliner and sighs.

He says, "It looks even worse in the living room than it did on paper. Come here, sweetheart and make your daddy feel better." He holds up his arms. I slide into his lap and warm embrace. We're busy enjoying each other when a cough sounds from the doorway. Blake looks beyond me and smiles.

He asks, "Yes?"

From the doorway Christian says, "Sorry to interrupt. Devin called earlier and wanted you to call as soon as you got home—no matter how late." before disappearing back upstairs. I stiffen in dread as Blake reaches for the portable and calls.

Blake says, "Yeah, we just got home. Oh, that's just great. Do you want us to come over? Are you sure?" Blake is rubbing my upper arm and smiling softly.

Before ending the call he says, "OK. First thing tomorrow morning."

He tells me, "Your brother had unexpected guests this afternoon. Dustin flew in with presents for your Father. I gather all hell broke loose. Doran ended up sedating your Father to keep him from having a stroke or worse. Your Father's medical coverage ran out while he was in the sanitarium. Dustin wants the three of you to split the cost of the medical bills. Doran wanted to know what happened to the money from the sale of the estate. He was informed that medical and legal fees used up all of your fathers money."

Blake chuckles and says, "I guess that means he didn't find where I hid the 20 million from Eleanor's life insurance policy. Unfortunately, your Father is upset. He thinks he's destitute now and he'll have to rely on charity of his children." I sigh against him.

Sighing against him, I say, "That is so like Dustin." I'm being carried into our bedroom. I soon forget all about other people's problems. The following morning finds us at Devin's for breakfast. Father is sitting at the table. It very obvious he's an emotional wreck.

Blake shakes his hand and sits across from him saying, "Good morning. Mr. Blackwood, please stop worrying." Father shakes his head and raises his hand to silence Blake.

Father says, "First, call me Father. Second, I have no choice but to worry. Surely you have heard about my oldest son robbing me blind."

Blake takes his hand firmly and says, "You have money. I previously hid 20 million dollars of your money. You are well set for the rest of your life." Father's face breaks into a large smile and relief flows from every pore.

He says, "Thank you, son. I'm changing my will. With my other two sons permission I would like to appoint Blake as my executor. I think that Dustin has showed his true colors." Doran slides into the table with his first cup of coffee.

Raising his cup towards Father, Doran says, "That's fine by me. That is a big job with a lot of hassles. Blake, sorry old man, you're welcome to it." Blake smiles.

Devin sits and nods in agreement saying, "The job is all yours, no contest." I'm not sure if this pleases Blake or not. Once Cook has filled the table with her wide assortment of pastries and breakfast foods, we dine and then make our excuses to leave. Father understands that Blake has work on his own spread. He again expresses a desire to come for a visit. I look at Blake and he nods.

Blake says, "Why don't you all come to our place for dinner tomorrow? Doran, how long will you be staying?" Father is all smiles at my invitation.

Doran smiles and says, "We're here until January 5th. I'll check with Rachel but I'm sure she'll agree to dinner at your place. What time?" He sets his coffee cup down and Cook immediately refills it.

I glance at Blake "About 5?" Blake nods. I don't want it too late because Father will be tired by the trip over and back and seeing the house. He seems so frail right now.

I ask, "Is beef roast agreeable to everyone?" I get nods and smiles all around.

"Any chance I can come early and spend some extra time with my baby girl?" We're all shocked at Fathers words. He has never referred to me that way.

Blake recovers first and says, "You are welcome at any time." Blake and I leave so he can get back to the ranch and start his workday. It's already after 7:30. Blake leaves me at the homestead and heads for the barns. I hear the pounding at the stables. The contractor says about two more weeks and we can move the horses back. Our new stables have an extensive water sprinkler system installed for safety. The Sheriff has seen Blake several times but they have not mentioned if they found the arsonist or if he struck anywhere else. I'm busy planning tomorrow's dinner and getting tonight's dinner underway and lunch started. Mac surprises me by suddenly appearing at the doorway.

I admonish him, "You are hanging around with Christian too much." He sheepishly grins.

Mac says, "I called my mom like you suggested. She was really glad to hear from me. Dad died and she's kind of alone." He pauses and looks down at his feet.

I quickly ask, "Do you need time to go see her?" He shyly nods.

I tell him, "I'm sure Blake won't mind. Did you ask him?" Mac shakes his head, suddenly very shy around me.

When he remains silent, I ask, "Do you want me to?" Mac nods and turns as Blake comes inside the back foyer.

Blake says, "Why is everyone so solemn in here? Who died?" shrugging from his jacket. Mac appears to be examining his feet again.

I answer, "Mac's father died. He was wondering if he could have some time to go visit his mom." Blake looks startled at my words and turns to Mac.

He says, "Of course you can have all the time you need. You're one of my best hands, but you only get one mom. Do you want to leave today or tomorrow?" Mac shrugs. Blake makes a motion with his head and Mac follows him upstairs to the sitting room. Over lunch, Blake tells Christian to run Mac to the bus station. Christian nods but keeps eating. Not much surprises him, I've noticed. Before I let Mac leave, I have a private word with him. He refuses the money I offer and gives me a shy hug before getting his bag from upstairs and going with Christian.

Blake says, "Man, he's so like Kyle. I'm starting to think of him as a younger sibling instead of a hired hand. It's hard to believe that he was one of the men who kidnapped you." sliding his arms around me as I watch the pickup head out the driveway.

"I know. I often remember how he watched out for me, even then." I remind him. He nods and chuckles.

Blake says, "Well, I'm watching out for you until Christian gets back." He swings me up into his arms and carries me into the bedroom for some wild and passionate lovemaking and one on one attention. I'm peeling potatoes for dinner. Blake is chopping carrots when Christian returns.

Christian teases, "He's safely loaded on the bus and headed for Idaho or Iowa or somewhere out there." grabbing raw potato slices and salting them before eating them.

I sternly tell him, "Stop that. I just yelled at Blake for doing the same thing. He must have eaten two whole potatoes. Honestly, you two eat faster than I cook." Both look sheepish, grin and head out to get some real work done. Well, I lost my helper. I guess it serves me right. Tonight's beef stew is a big hit. I made the usual amount of biscuits forgetting that Mac was gone. The biscuit plate still ends up empty. After dinner, Christian and Blake are back to their current chess game. I'm knitting booties and ruining Blake's concentration. Christian whips him royally tonight.

The next day is spent cleaning the house and cooking for Father's first visit. It's a good thing I started early. I'm just setting the bowl of chicken pot pie on the lunch table when the front bell rings. Blake rises and walks through the house to get the door.

Blake says, "Come on in. We're having a late lunch." I hear Devin's voice.

Blake says, "Chicken pot pie. No, you're welcome to join us." Now, I must have ESP because I made a double batch before I remembered Mac was gone. I have Christian get the large kettle from over the flames in the fireplace. Doran wheels Father right up to the table. Blake has already taken their coats.

Quickly grabbing the ladle Devin asks, "Rachel went to town to shop and she'll join us around 4 or so. Man, that looks and smells good. Did you make homemade biscuits?"

Father says in his stern voice, "Manners, boy." Devin jerks back and looks sheepish. Then we realize Father's joking. Father offers grace and before long, both large bowls are empty as well as the entire kettle. I popped the other two trays of biscuits into the oven when we started lunch. No more biscuits either.

Blake takes Doran and Father on a tour of the house while Devin helps me load the dishwasher.

As he starts the dishwasher, Devin says, "You are still one of the best cooks around. Man, I wish I could find a woman who looked like you and could cook." I just grin and shrug.

Christian says, "Blake knows he's a lucky guy." from in the family room as we join him. Father is seated in the one armchair admiring our tree.

"This is a nice place you have here." He tells Blake.

Blake says, "We can't wait for our new home to be finished. It's on hold while the new stables are being built."

Father nods and says, "Yes, the fire was a terrible thing. I always had that fear up home. Stable fires can cost you a lot of stock and money. Dangerous things—stable fires." He seems almost to be talking to himself. Doran finds my knitting and pulls out the booties I'm working on.

Doran teases, "Little Miss Katie, are you sure there isn't something we should know?" I shake my head and glance at Father. He's staring at the blinking lights on the tree.

I reply, "No, I'm just getting a head start for when I get the OK from my doctor to go off the pill." Blake stretches his feet out.

Father suddenly says, "A fire would be nice. It's a little cold in here." Blake starts a fire. I get an afghan for around Fathers shoulders. He really looks old today.

I leave to work on dinner. The conversation is man talk and sporadic. Doran asks about Blake's hopes for the future. I tune my ears for his answer.

He softly says, "A working ranch and a couple dozen children."

Doran laughs and Father says, "I'd like a lot of grandchildren. I'm going to stay with Devin, you know. I'll be just next door. Frank is planning on visiting me tomorrow before they leave." The entire room gets quiet as I return with a plate of Christmas cookies and take a seat in the empty recliner. I set the plate on the table and everyone is still rather quiet. Blake's face is full of shock. Father is staring at him unsure what he said to cause it.

I quickly say, "Well, that's nice. You two can hash over old times." to break the silence. Blake smiles at Father, rises and strides from the room. I'm trapped as the hostess. Christian materializes from practically thin air and follows him. Father looks over at me.

I explain, "He's going to check the stock before dinner."

In a few minutes, I rise and go out to finish the dinner. Blake returns an hour later.

I ask, "How is the stock dear?" and he tips his head.

As he hugs me, I whisper into his ear, "Father wondered where you went."

He says, "Thanks, sweetheart." Then he rejoins his guests.

Blake tells them, "Sorry to duck out. I trust my wife was a good hostess?" Devin found a horse race on TV and Father is intently watching. Rachel arrives in time to sit at the table and dine. She recounts her shopping experiences here compared to Boston. Father is tired. Doran insists they leave once dinner is completed.

From the safety of Blake's firm arms curled in his lap on the sofa, I remark, "How quiet the house seems now."

He says, "Yes. They're going to Europe." I don't need to ask whom. I just sigh.

Blake says, "He applied for one of those bill payer loans you see advertised on TV. They were only too glad to give him double the money he owes now against the title on the ranch. God damn, the man is cock stupid these days. Sorry honey." He falls silent. We're both starring into the fireplace flames. I have a feeling, the next two months are going to be long and hard ones.

CHAPTER EIGHT

A BULLET FOR ???

The month of January is actually one of the coldest on record. That just thrills me. I'm cold all the time. Blake contacts the loan people and buys off his father's loan. I'm slightly worried about Blake's money. I don't know how much he has put away or what his retirement income is. I only know he's been using a lot of his reserve to save his fathers place. The stables are finally complete and the horses are moved back at the end of January.

February 1st finds the crew back working on our dream home. Father comes over at least one day a week. It gives Cook and Devin a rest. Mac finally calls. He talks with Blake who keeps laughing and saying, of course. I find out 'of course what' when Mac returns with his mother. I'm expecting a gray haired woman. I'm not expecting the brown haired ball of fire that climbs from the Jeep when Christian returns from the train station. Mac drags her over to introduce her before she steps inside.

Smiling broadly, he excitedly says, "Mother, this is Katherine Dailey."

I motion to come inside saying, "Hello, please, come in." She nods and steps past me into the hall. I gesture towards the living room.

Christian comes in and says, "Go get the rest of her bags, boy." before heading up the stairs. I hand her coat to Mac who nods and leaves.

I tell her, "Have a seat."

She says, "I'm Juanita MacKensie. My son is so excited at my moving here, he's forgotten most of his manners. He does use them around here, right?" I nod and smile.

She continues, "Scott says you're the one who suggested he call me after Christmas. I'm certainly glad you did. My husband just died. I was so lonely for Scott. I hadn't heard a thing since he ran off over 8 years ago." She stops and leans forward to ask, "You look strange, what's wrong?"

I smile and tell her, "I didn't know Mac's name was Scott."

She says, "His acquaintances dubbed him Mac. He was eager to forget his old life so he dropped his own first name. He already explained about how he met you and your husband's daring rescue." I smile but I'm thinking he probably didn't tell her everything. I get a brief flash back of Jaycee in the hall and shudder.

She immediately asks, "Are you OK? You appear sickly. Mac says you took a bad fall and lost your baby last year. Have you recovered? . . . If you don't mind my asking." She has the nicest brown eyes and smile. Her face is round but her mouth is very sensual looking.

I tell her, "I'm fine. I'm being a poor hostess. Let me take you up to your room. You must be tired from your journey." She rises when I do, but shakes her head.

She says, "No. I enjoyed the trip. It gave me a chance to catch up on news with my son and then I met that handsome Mr. Soldyer. He's invited me to dinner tonight. I hope you don't mind?" I shake my head and lead her upstairs. My husband is in the process of setting up a double bed in the other front room. Christian smiles and waves when we enter.

"We should have your room ready in no time." Christian says to Juanita. From the looks of the room, someone has been busy already. There are two dressers, a vanity and chair and someone has unrolled the rug over the padding. I smile and go downstairs for drapes for the windows and towels for her use. By the time I return, the sheets are on the bed and she's hanging up her clothes. Both men have disappeared.

Juanita says, "I brought my own bedroom furniture. Mac said Blake offered the front room. I'm going to be doing the cooking and cleaning once you're in your new place." She and I work together well. We soon have the drapes up and the blankets on the bed. I show her where the bathroom and little sitting room are before I leave her to shower and dress for her dinner date. Mac is nowhere to be seen. Blake is in the family room. I start our dinner and walk in to talk with him.

While pulling me into his lap Blake says, "I hope you don't mind my offering her a place to live?"

I tell him, "No. This is your place. I think it will be nice having another woman around." He laughs and nods. Dinner is a quiet affair. Mac has decided to eat at the bunkhouse. Sam made his famous chili and Mac especially likes it. I sent a basket of my biscuits along. We dine in the breakfast area. Blake is watching me.

He remarks as he pushes his food around on his plate, "This is like being at the cottage tonight."

Laying down my fork I ask, "Did I make something you don't care for?".

Blake tells me, "No, I was thinking of dessert. I could really go for a little Irish lassie." He places his napkin on the table and comes around to scoop me from my seat. I giggle and struggle in his arms but not very hard. After our frolicking and love making, I go to sleep.

I stir slightly when I hear Christian remark, "This is odd. The dinner is untouched on the table. Let me check on them. You go on up, dear." From his tone of voice, they're not going to have separate rooms for very long. Christian appears in the bedroom doorway.

Blake says softly, "We're fine. We skipped dinner for dessert." Christian chuckles and disappears. He's probably going up for his dessert. Someone cleared and cleaned the kitchen.

I'm surprised in the morning at my clean kitchen. Juanita has already made a pot of coffee. Christian is enjoying a cup while she cooks breakfast.

I say, "Hello." placing the kettle on the stove.

Juanita says, "You look well rested this morning." flipping the cakes on the griddle.

I tell her, "I feel good." I get Blake's tea bag ready and do the toast detail. Actually, it is really nice having Juanita around. She pitches right in with the housework and is full of stories of her life with raising 7 children.

Most evenings, she and Christian disappear. Mac seems uncertain about his feelings about his mother and her new beau.

In March, Blake makes a large stock purchase and the hands are suddenly very busy again. Spring is in the air. The breeder book is full through next year. Frank and Terry are still in Europe. He sends an occasional post card.

Blake remarks, "He'll be back when his money runs out." Most of the time, it's a sore subject and left very much alone. The high point of our life is my last physical at the OBGYN who gives me the OK to get pregnant again. Now, if only Blake weren't too tired to work at the baby making process.

It's April before I even realize that March has even past. Juanita and I are very busy most days. Even with her extra two hands, we manage to find enough work to keep ourselves extremely busy. We take all the winter drapes down and wash them. I bought lighter summer drapes and we hang them after pressing them. Juanita likes to work in the yard so I have plenty of spring flowers in pretty little beds now. It's mid May already. Blake comes in early on Friday and he's obviously got baby on his mind. I'm on my knees scrubbing out the oven and suddenly he's right over me.

Lifting and pulling me from inside the oven, he says, "I thought of something much more interesting to do today." I get a nice shower and shampoo. Then I'm toweled dry until I can hardly stand it anymore. His lovemaking is long and slow and maddening. We lay curled together in the bed for quite awhile before his stomach growls.

He says, "Well, I guess the cook didn't make any supper." rolling over onto me again.

While he nibbles on my breasts and fingers, I huskily tell him, "She's not going to be able to make supper if you keep giving her your wonderful dessert." Since there are so many other people living with us, we dress before coming out into the kitchen area. You just never know whom you might find in the kitchen these days. Someone has left a nice casserole in the now clean oven with a note on the chalkboard to "ENJOY." Blake gets out plates and I set the table. Blake's standing at the refrigerator putting the water pitcher away. I'm standing at the sink rinsing dishes. There's a ping and the sound of a bee in the kitchen. I turn to discover Blake sprawled on the floor. I scream and run to his side as he's struggling to get up.

He says, "Get down, I'm hit." I slide on my knees across the floor. He has his left hand over a wound at his right shoulder. His right hand is hanging loose at his side. In spite of his protest, I run in a crouch to the bedroom to grab his pistol from the bedside. Back at his side, I engage the slide and hand it to him. I crawl and half drag Blake between the center island and the oven for shelter.

I whisper, "Let me get the phone to call for help." He violently shakes his head and then moans in pain.

He says, "No. You'd be in the open. Just stay here. We're safe. I don't think I'm hit that badly. Katie girl, how much am I bleeding in the back?" I slide behind him and his shirt is soaked.

I gasp out, "Pretty bad." The front door opens and I hear Juanita's laugh.

I scream, "Back here."

Christian gruffly says, "Stay here." before I hear the sound of his footfalls. He comes through the dining room and drops to his knees beside us. His gun is already drawn.

I tell him, "Blake's hit. He's bleeding badly." Blake sighs and leans back against me. I watch his eyes roll up into his head. Panicking I turn to Christian. Christian checks his pulse.

He says calmly, "He's just unconscious." He removes his belt and makes a tourniquet around Blake's shoulder.

He tells me, "Hold this as tight as you can. Juanita! Get in here and stay low." Juanita's pale face appears at my shoulder.

In horror, she says, "Oh my GOD!" Christian calls the bunk house and then 911. Within ten minutes there's all kind of activity in and around the house. Christian tells the EMT's he thinks a hunter's stray bullet came in through the window. Christian and Blake's guns are out of sight. I desperately want to go with Blake in the chopper.

Christian says, "I'll drive you. Mac, stay with your mother. Juanita, it's OK. I'll hurry back as soon as I can. My first job is to protect Katie and watch Blake's back. Mac, call Devin and tell him what's happened." Christian has me in the Jeep in record time. He has me change my clothes before we leave. By the time we arrive at the hospital, Blake is already in surgery. Christian dug the slug from the breakfast room wall, moved a picture over the hole and opened the nearby window.

I ask him, "Do you really think it was hunters?" riding along in the Jeep.

He asks, "Where were you standing?" his knuckles are white as he grips the wheel.

I tell him, "At the sink, rinsing the dishes. It sounded like a bee in the room."

Christian says, "It's from a high powered rifle. Between the slug and what you just described, Blake is the target. If you were at the window and he was at the fridge, he was definitely the target. Damn, someone's got a vendetta." The last is said under his breath. At the hospital we have to wait almost three hours while Blake's in surgery. The doctor finally comes and talks to us.

He says, "Mrs. Dailey?" I nod and he approaches closer to tell us, "Your husband is out of surgery. There was some arterial damage in his shoulder but the bullet passed through without hitting any bones or his spine. He'll probably be laid up for a month. He'll have to work at getting the full range of motion back in the shoulder, but I don't see any reason why he won't make a full recovery. He's in the recovery room now. I'll send a nurse as soon as you can see him. He'll be under sedation for at least the next 12 hours. I don't want him jerking around and tearing the stitches." The doctor shakes Christian's hand, nods and strides away. I didn't even catch his name. Christian takes my elbow and escorts me to the room where Blake is laying once the nurse comes. I'm allowed to sit beside him all night. He finally regains consciousness about 7 a.m. I'm resting my head on the railing on my hands when he touches my hair.

He rasps out, "Katie girl?" I lift my head and smile.

I ask, "How are you feeling?" And a nurse comes in response to a beeping noise on one of Blake's monitors.

He says, "Numb."

She resets the machine, checks his vitals and says, "We'll get him into a private room in a little while. Then you and the gentleman in the hall can go get some rest." She walks out. I realize Christian has been on guard all night. Blake's eyes drift shut. The doctor is in to check the wounds. Christian holds me in his arms in the hall.

He asks, "How are you holding up?"

I tell him, "Fine. Better now that he's awake." Christian nods at my words.

It's several more hours before Blake's settled in a private room. Mac comes to relieve Christian. Christian insists I go home with him. Devin is at the house. It seems the Sheriff is unable to locate the slug. It must have gone through the open window into the ground or whatever outside. While the Sheriff is explaining, Christian just smiles and nods. Devin lifts one corner of his mouth in acknowledgment of the secret code that seems to pass between them. Juanita insists I shower and go to bed. Christian asks Devin to watch as I sleep. Juanita takes an exhausted Christian upstairs. I sleep over six hours. Christian is already up and eating when I stumble out at 2 p.m.

He glances my way briefly and remarks, "You should get right back into bed. You don't look good." I drop into the chair opposite him.

I tell him, "I can't sleep anymore. I need to see Blake again. I'm so worried." Christian nods as Juanita sets a cup of hot tea in front of me. I manage to eat a little breakfast. Christian drives me into Dallas to see Blake.

Sheriff Ron is having a discussion with Blake when we arrive. "I don't know, Mr. Dailey. My gut feeling is that someone deliberately took a shot at you. I didn't find any evidence of casual hunters on your property. Have you riled anyone lately?" Blake looks past the Sheriff and smiles.

Blake says, "Sheriff, you don't want to upset my wife with your tales of people wanting to kill me—do you?" Sheriff Ron pivots and flushes at Blake's soft-spoken words.

Immediately, Sheriff Ron says, "No ma'am. I'm just making a supposition. Don't you get yourself all worried over my silly ponderings." He tips his hat and makes a very hasty escape. Christian checks the hall and then nods at Blake.

I sit beside him and take his hand. When I ask, "How are you feeling?" he smiles.

Blake tells me, "Much better with you to look at. Well?" This question he directs to Christian.

Christian says, "City job, definitely a city boy style. I made your contacts. We should hear back shortly. Can you travel?" Blake nods at Christian's words. I'm sitting looking from one to the other.

Placing his fingertips on my lips, Blake tells me, "Katie girl, we're going to the honeymoon cottage." I know to remain quiet.

Blake turns to Christian, "Take her home in an hour. How's Mac coming along?" He asks Christian softly.

Christian says, "Very well, the boy's a natural. You want him?" from his position at the doorway.

Blake softly says, "If you think he's good enough.".

Christian says "I do." and then clucks his tongue.

Blake turns his attention to me. He asks, "Did you get any rest at all, sweetheart?"

I raise my eyebrows and sweetly tell him. "You know I don't rest well without you beside me, darling." He gives me a lopsided grin and a wink. The doctor appears to check Blake's wound. We're removed from the room during the examination. An hour later, following Blake's wishes, I'm escorted home. Christian insists I get into bed and sleep. The third time I come out into the kitchen, Christian makes me a cup of tea. It knocks me out cold for over eight hours. I awaken at the cabin in Utah in bed beside Blake.

He says, "Good morning, sleepy head." I roll to face him and he grimaces as the bed jerks.

I quickly tell him, "Oh, I'm sorry." Then I move more slowly.

Blake says, "It's OK. I took a jostling during the flight and the drives. The wounds are a little tender right now. It's really not your fault. Could I trouble you for the urinal?" I slowly and carefully climb from the bed and get it from the bathroom. Once he's finished, I wash it and set it beside the bed on the table. Mac is sitting in the living room.

He quietly says, "Hi." I can't help noticing the rifle on the coffee table.

I ask, "Hi. When did you guys last eat?" He shrugs. I make myself busy in the kitchen. The refrigerator and pantry are well stocked.

In record time I have omelets stuffed with chopped vegetables, cheese and ham. I make Blake a cup of tea and a tray. Mac comes to the table. I sit with Blake. He seems weak. I realize it's probably from blood loss and all this extra strenuous moving. I gladly feed him. I'd chew for him if he'd let me. He eats about half and goes to sleep. I quietly leave the room and find Mac washing the dishes.

Pulling on his arm I tell him, "Let me get those." He nods and dries his hands before going outside to check the area. Once the dishes are done, I head upstairs for a pillow and blankets for Mac. I figure he'll probably sleep on the sofa.

For the next two days, Blake isn't good. He has a high fever and is very weak. I keep making homemade soup and pumping the broth into him with tea and lots of sugar. Finally on Wednesday, I watch his eyes come open and he smiles.

He softly says, "I think I'm gonna live." Now it's my turn to let out a big sigh. He asks, "Has Mac seen anything?" I shake my head. He waits while I get the urinal. After breakfast, when I check the wounds, they're not as inflamed looking. I clean and redress them. Blake sits up for awhile and then wants to speak with Mac. I call him in and disappear to take a nice shower.

Blake's busy on the laptop when I return. He looks up, smiles and keeps typing with his left hand. His right arm is in a sling to keep the movement down. He told me yesterday, he wasn't planning on moving it around a whole lot anyhow, just yet. Once he's through, he motions to take the laptop.

He tells me, "Christian says it's all quiet. He's called in some markers and has a couple of leads. Whoever's behind this hit is going to be very sorry. Christian says half a dozen of my friends are vying to get the guy and whoever's behind him. This is very frustrating. If I get testy, don't take it personal. I'm not happy about having to be babysat by another man." I nod and kiss his forehead.

He reaches up and cups a breast saying, "Nice. As always. Very nice." I remove a couple pillows and he takes an afternoon nap. Mac plays solitaire card games. I dig out a jigsaw puzzle from the attic.

Everything is quiet for a couple weeks. Like Blake warned, he begins to get short tempered and very frustrated. I'm not feeling very well. If I rest my eyes for even a moment, I'm asleep. I'm green in the mornings and thinking maybe I'm pregnant. Mac keeps looking, smiling and nodding. Blake gets a message from Christian that something's going on and to be extra careful. Blake is hardly able to get out of bed yet. He insists I begin putting a large Baretta in the back of my slacks under my shirt. Several times Blake yells at Mac for doing the same things at the same time. Poor Mac, he's trying so hard to please him and failing miserably.

Friday after breakfast, Blake is sitting on the sofa. Mac heads out to do a perimeter check. I'm in the kitchen washing dishes and a movement to my right causes me to freeze. There's a man all dressed in camouflage standing pointing a pistol at Blake. I realize he can't see me for the cabinets above the dishwasher. I slowly reach around with my right hand and pull the pistol from my back. The man steps into the room and a sideways glance left reveals Blake is sitting starring at him. The man has netting over his face that's leaf patterned. Blake isn't moving and the man steps closer.

In a low voice, the man says, "Your young friend is sleeping. It's just you and me, Tigerman."

Lips pursed, Blake nods his head and quietly says, "Are you afraid to show your face?"

The man reaches up and calmly removes the cap and netting asking, "Do you know me now? Maybe I don't resemble my father enough. Think Boston. Think about six years ago at a big political rally." Blake nods and smiles slowly. Blake says, "So—what took you so long?" his eyes constantly on the man.

The man says, "I been away getting schooling for this very day. I'm very patient—like you. How long did you sit before he crossed into your line of fire?"

Blake shrugs and says, "A day or so. It was a long time ago and not a very impressive hit." The man growls and his hand jerks slightly before he regains his composure and chuckles.

He says, "You're trying to rile me. Not today, a level head makes the hit—right?" Blake slowly nods again.

Blake suddenly asks, "Can you shoot?" He's starring at the man, but I sense speaking to me. I tighten my finger on the trigger. Then I realize I need to engage the slide mechanism on the barrel. I purse my lips and slowly reach for the slide. The slight noise causes the man to pivot and point his gun my way.

"Oh, the pretty lady from the window. You know I thought for a few minutes of putting one right between your lovely breasts or dark brown eyes. I've been watching you two for months. She's quite a piece of ass, Tigerman. Definitely the most beautiful body I've ever seen on a woman.

Has she ever killed a man? I'll bet not. Do you think I can shoot her and you without getting hit?" He pauses and chuckles. I watch as his finger tightens on the trigger.

Blake moves slightly and the man turns his gun back on him saying, "Well, I'll bet on her femininity, kill you and then take her back to camp. I've been watching you go at her and I'd like a turn." The Baretta jumps slightly in my hand. Almost simultaneously at the sound of the shot, the man jerks, pivots and brings up his gun. I catch a glimpse of Blake struggling to roll from the couch. I drop to the floor as several bullets bite into the wall behind me. Pulling myself around the end of the cabinets, I quickly pump three more bullets into the man as he struggles to rise from the floor. Blake is firing from his place on the living room floor. The man's body jerks as our bullets find targets. Finally silence settles over the room.

Blake softly says, "You lose." He glances my way and smiles. He can't get off the floor until he rolls onto his back into a sitting position. I quickly come over, keeping my pistol pointed at the man who's now in a spreading pool of dark blood. With my help, Blake gets to his feet. He checks the man's body and kicks his gun away.

Blake tells me, "He's dead. You did good, Katie girl." I'm unable to appreciate his praise. I'm busy vomiting into the sink over the pass through. I hear Blake's soft chuckle before his arms come around me.

He says, "Come on, he may not be alone. They would have heard the shots." We go quickly back into the bedroom. I get Blake's slender black case from the closet and open it on the bed. Blake uses the computer to call for help. Armed with two pistols each, we go to the front corner and sit nestled together. Blake's carefully watching the windows and doors.

Within several minutes, we hear slight sounds from the front room. Blake tenses and aims his pistol at the closed bedroom door. I'm holding my breath and trembling. Blake softly kisses my shoulder. I don't know how many hours we sat even after the house got silent.

Blake suddenly says, "Chopper." A few minutes later, I hear it. Within 20 minutes we hear a whistle. Blake counters with a different whistle. There are even footfalls.

Blake says, "Don't shoot Christian, sweetheart." I lower my gun and sigh back against him.

"It's me, old friend." Christian steps in the room after opening the door slowly. "We found Mac where they left him trussed up. Whose blood is in the other room?"

Blake says "The assassins." while Christian helps me onto the bed and then assists Blake getting up off the floor.

A deep voice says, "Hey, Tigerman, I heard someone was stupid enough to make you a target." And a massive bald black man steps into the room.

Blake softly chuckles saying, "Yeah, the guy bragged about watching me for weeks. Whitie, this is Katie girl, my wife."

The man walks around the end of the bed and leans close to say, "Pleased to meet you, little miss. She sure is pretty for a white woman." He straightens and glances around the room.

He tells Blake, "I was honored to get the White Knights call." He makes a motion slightly towards Christian who is picking up hardware from the floor. Blake takes a swig of water from the nearby water bottle. I lay on my side and pull the comforter around me. Suddenly, I'm very tired and trembling. Blake sits on the bed beside me and rubs my back until I go to sleep.

My rumbling stomach wakes me. I stumble from the bed into the bathroom and then out into the kitchen. Christian is cooking something that smells wonderful. Blake is sitting on the couch and the black man is at the table. He's just finishing eating a plateful of whatever Christian has going in the kettle.

I ask, "What's cooking?" walking towards the stove. My eye strays to the arched row of bullet holes. Christian catches me as I black out. Blake is sitting beside me on the bed. I have a cold cloth over my eyes.

He asks, "Are you OK?" leaning forward when I lift the cloth.

I tell him, "I think so." My stomach growls again.

Blake hollers, "Hey, Christian, bring her a tray before she bites me." and both men in the front room laugh.

I hear dish sounds and then Christian appears with a tray saying, "Here you go, little momma. You've had a rough day today. You just let me put a couple pillows behind you and then you try this stew." He quickly has me all set up.

After the first spoonful, I tell him, "This is delicious."

With a mischievous grin Blake says, "It needs your homemade biscuits."

Heading back to the kitchen, Christian teasingly mutters, "Complaints. All I even hear from the man is complaints."

Between spoonfuls I ask, "How's your shoulder?"

Blake answers, "Sore. Christian checked and nothing's torn. I'm proud of you, Katie. You saved my life today. I'm sorry to admit, but for a few moments I doubted you could shoot a man point blank." I nod and smile.

I softly tell him, "I had the perfect motivation—I'm in love and I'm pregnant."

His whole face lights up and he lets out this big whoop. Christian and the black man come running.

Together they both say, "What!"

Blake turns slowly towards them and says, "Katie girl's gonna have a baby."

The black man rolls his eyes and grins at Blake saying, "Shoot, that ain't no big deal, I've made a lot of ladies that way over the years. Congrats." Then he ducks back into the front room.

Christian comes around and says softly, "Are you sure?" I nod.

I say, "I found an old test and did it this morning. The stick is blue and laying on the sink in the bathroom. I was waiting for Blake to find it but he never got a chance to shave this morning." At my words, Blake dashes to the bathroom (as quickly as he's able) and returns with the stick.

"It's blue." He shows Christian who rolls his eyes and softly laughs.

He teases, "It looks more green to me." but then he pats Blake on the back somewhat firmly. Blake grimaces but smiles at me.

He asks, "Are you sure?" I shrug my shoulders.

I tell him, "Well, I've missed a few months but until I see the doctor . . ."

Blake says, "This is good enough for me." Blake lays the stick down and kisses my closest hand.

"When can we go home?" I ask both men together.

Christian says, "Tomorrow." I'm thinking that can't come soon enough.

There are a lot of men around the cabin most just nod and continue working. By afternoon, the bullet holes are history and all traces of blood are gone. As darkness falls, Whitie disappears outside briefly and when he returns he speaks quietly with Christian. Christian nods at Blake and they go outside.

Whitie says, "Man talk." He's a man of very few words. He must be almost 7 feet tall. His chest is very muscular and broad. He removes his jacket and underneath is a white tee shirt that reveals how fit he truly is. He flexes his muscles when he catches me looking. He laughs at my immediate blush and then shyly smiles. I'll just bet he has no trouble finding lady friends. Blake and Christian return. Blake motions for me to follow him.

In the bedroom, he closes the door and puts his arms around me. He says, "It's all over. You don't want the details—do you?" I shake my head and he continues, "Tomorrow we go home." He looks down into my upturned face and solemnly says, "I can't make you any guarantees, Katie girl. This could happen again or not. The windows at the homestead are all bullet proof. We have a new high tech security system. Christian says the hospital raised a ruckus when they discovered me gone. Your Father is fine. My dad is still in Europe." He stops and kisses my forehead. "Let's go to bed, we have a long tiring day tomorrow."

We're awakened at 5 a.m. and back at the homestead by 2. Blake is extremely tired. I'm miserably air sick the entire trip. Christian has two babies to tend until Juanita takes charge. For the next week, we're pretty much babied by everyone. Mac apologies several times to Blake.

Blake says, "You're young. You learned a lesson?" At Mac's nod, Blake shakes his hand. They've made peace. Mac even asks if I'm upset with him. I quickly say no. Dr. Whetzel confirms at my appointment the following week that I'm 8 weeks along.

Blake is all smiles and his only comment is, "No more stairs." The doctor laughs. Blake is quiet on the ride home. I have the distinct feeling he's thinking about the attempt on his life. He leaves the Mercedes at the front door for Christian to take to the garage. He rarely leaves the car in the same place. We walk inside. He takes my arm and pulls me back to the bedroom. I'm wondering what's on his mind until he turns me and softly smiles.

Blake says, "You're over dressed. I think you should disrobe and let me examine you. I want to confirm the doctor's diagnosis." I like the mischievous look on his face and quickly comply. I really like this doctor's thorough examination and diagnosis much better. We have a nice shower and redress to join the group in the family room.

Sitting on the love seat and pulling me into his lap Blake says, "It's confirmed." Christian winks and nods.

Mac smiles and says, "I thought so at the cabin."

Juanita grins broadly and says, "What?" No one mentioned anything to her.

I tell her, "I'm going to have a baby in seven months."

She gently admonishes me with much finger waging saying, "I'm glad to hear that. We'll just confine you to the first floor. Anyone who catches you doing stairs is going to severely punish you." Blake chuckles softly. I know what his punishment will be. Christian takes Blake to the front room to the computer. Juanita and I just sit quietly, each lost in our own thoughts. Blake hastily returns visibly upset.

Blake tells me, "Katie girl, I gotta go to town. Father's borrowing against the ranch again and the bankers want to see me right away." I get a quick kiss and he's gone. Mac goes with him to drive. I look at Christian as he settles in the nearby armchair.

I ask, "Is Frank going through Blake's money also?"

Christian shakes his head. "Not to worry. The man has plenty of money. He was a very hard worker." I nod.

Juanita and Christian are shaking their heads as I say softly, "Well, you know I consider my money available for his use.".

Christian tells me, "He'd never be able to live with himself. I know he'd let the ranch go before he'd ever touch a cent of your money, darling." Christian smiles but I realize it's the truth. As much as it would hurt him, his pride would never let him take my money for his father's foolishness. It's a very tense three hours until Blake returns.

"Well, that's it. I totally own the property now. He has borrowed 150% of what the property is currently assessed. The bank will tell him that they own the land the next time he tries to borrow against it." Blake sits heavily into the chair beside Christian. Juanita is in the kitchen working on dinner. I'm not allowed to help her this evening. Dinner is steak, potatoes and mixed vegetables and a very quiet solemn affair. Everyone seems lost in their own thoughts.

In mid June Heather graduates from high school. Blake thought her mother would return to attend. Blake reads about the graduation in the paper and goes over to find his fathers place totally deserted. He returns visibly upset but what can we do? She's 18 and her own mother left her alone. I offer the suggestion that perhaps she joined them in Europe. Blake just nods and grinds his teeth. July becomes unseasonably hot. We have to deal with a couple of brush fires. I'm minding the heat something fierce. Blake gets window units for the homestead. Most days I find myself parked in front of the coldest blowing unit.

Like summer is prone to do, this one slips past while we work. I'm over at our dream house almost every day. By mid September I'm bloated with Blake's child. I'm positive the child is male. He seems to be very active and always hungry. Blake has started touching the baby every time he gets anywhere near me. We have our first major fight over—you guessed it—finances. I guess it was the hormones from the baby. I want to purchase the furniture for the house with my money. Blake and I have serious words but finally, he gives in. That surprises me more than anything. We also reached an agreement to share his father's expenses. I pointed out the child is half Blackwood/Morgan. My poor Father couldn't seem to remember I'm pregnant until the baby begins to show.

Finally, the first week in October, we arrange our newly delivered furniture and settle into our dream home. It takes Juanita and I almost a week to get the baby's room the way I like it. Blake keeps checking the room for the daily changes until it stays the same for three days.

Then he teases. "Finally, you got everything right where I wanted it." I like the skylights in the sunroom, master bathroom and guest bathroom. The baby's room is the center smallest bedroom.

The first morning, I'm laying in bed trying to figure out where I am and Blake asks, "Do you need a map to the bathroom, my lady?" I turn to face him.

I say, "No. I just can't believe we're finally moved in and it's done. These last three weeks have dragged past." His hand slips over onto the baby and he gets kicked, as usual.

He says, "He doesn't like me to touch him."

"He's probably extremely jealous of anyone else putting their hands on me just like his father." I tease. Blake rolls up onto his side and pulls the covers down.

He asks, "So, you want to fool around a little here in paradise?" slowly sliding up my nightgown.

I ask him, "How can you possibly desire me all bloated like this?" I get these depressing feelings at the sight of the mound of baby belly now being revealed.

Blake says, "I don't know. The bigger you get with my child, the harder it is to keep my hands off you. I was never impressed or aroused by pregnant women . . . until now." He's sliding down his sweats and kicking them off. We start out kissing and end up back side-by-side in the bed only slightly breathless and very lethargic feeling.

We have a leisurely breakfast. Blake calls Devin to bring Father over. They have been very anxious to tour the place. Devin tells Blake maybe later, this is not a good day for Father. On bad days, he's totally lost and screams if they try and make him leave his room. I think his mind is shutting down. Devin finally had to get a nurse/companion for him. Cook was unable to get anything done and Truman couldn't spend every waking minute with Father. I'm sharing the cost and so is Doran. Dustin, of course, no longer returns our calls. I don't believe he really cares now that he thinks Fathers money is all gone.

Blake teases, "Well, what are we going to do for the rest of the day?" pulling on work boots. As if I don't know how anxious he is to get outside to work. I have laundry to do. Juanita will be here around 11. She comes over every day except Sunday about midday. She and Christian have set a wedding date for early January. They're honeymooning at the cabin. She's dying to go and has me tell her about it repeatedly. She got her diamond last week. Mac took the news with his usual silence. He likes Christian and already told him that he's glad his mom is in love again.

I'm bent over getting ready to pick up the laundry basket to take it outside and hang the sheets. Juanita teases, "Here, let me get that. You shouldn't be lifting in your condition. Honestly, can't you wait until I get here to do this?" She whisks the basket from in front and heads outside. I waddle out after her. Somewhere along the line we inherit a five year old Dalmation who's name tag read Patches. He immediately attachs himself to Mac. When Mac doesn't take him along in the truck he sticks to Juanita like glue. Today he's bounding all over the yard barking and generally feeling good. Blake says he's good around the horses. We were afraid he would chase them. Someone lost a good dog, I think. Blake doesn't want him in the house, so he lays on the back porch or patio and waits for Juanita to walk back to the homestead. Christian says he's good protection.

Once the laundry is completed, we start lunch in time to feed three hungry men. Devin calls and says Father is now teasing to see the house. I tell him we're having lunch and to bring him over. I have two more lunch guests. When Father sees Patches he says to Devin, "Where are my dogs?"

Devin sighs and says, "They're all dead."

Father nods knowingly and says, "From the tornado." We all raise our eyebrows at that one. He watched the movie Twister the other day and now he's lived through several tornadoes. There isn't any food left. Juanita insists on clearing while I give the grand tour. Father walks through the entire house slowly and examines every room very intently.

Finally when we return to the family room to sit, he remarks, "This home is very well built. You have used great taste in your decorating selections. I'm proud of you Katie." Devin gasps. Father has never called me anything but Katherine. Of course, everyone else now calls me Katie. I gesture for them to sit and take a seat.

Once Devin has the afghan settled over his legs he asks, "When is my grand child due?"

I tell him, "In about eight weeks." and he smiles. I'm suddenly struck by the thought that he may not be around in eight weeks. I must have paled because Juanita starts to get up. I shake my head. We move over to the sunroom area and enjoy the afternoon sunshine. Father gets cold very easily. Once he begins to tire, Devin suggests they leave so I can nap. Father nods agreeably and they're soon gone. Blake comes in very hungry for supper. Christian and Juanita join us because she didn't go back to the homestead to cook. After I paled, she was afraid to leave me even after my explanation. After the dishes are done, they leave. Blake and I sit in the formal living room and I recount father's visit. We retire to bed planning on the early church service in the morning.

I'm surprised at how rapidly Thanksgiving approaches. Doran calls and says that he and Rachel were married earlier in the week by the Justice of the Peace in Boston. They're going for a two-week honeymoon in Hawaii and will not be seeing us over Thanksgiving. I tell him about the house, Father and the baby. He promises to come and see the child around Christmas.

Blake says his father's credit is maxed out and they should be coming home before too long. His tone is hard. I realize this is beginning to put a strain on him. The phone rings the Monday before Thanksgiving. Blake takes it while I'm finishing supper preparation. He returns tight lipped and flops into the closest chair in the breakfast area.

He stiffly says, "Well, Katie girl, I just had to wire daddy and his honey enough money to get tickets to come home from Spain. They're money ran out. She even had to pawn several pieces of jewelry to pay their hotel bill. They'll need picked up at the airport on Wednesday. I'm sending Mac. I'm not in the mood to face him right now. He actually asked if I would have a cleaning service get the house livable. I said he married his housekeeper, put her to work." Blake falls silent and stares intently at the floor at his feet. I slide into his lap.

I tell him, "Honey, it's OK to have feelings like that towards him. He's not being very level headed. I guess he hasn't a clue that he's lost the ranch?" Blake shakes his head and puts his hands on the baby.

Looking up he remarks, "He's quiet."

I tell him, "He's sleeping. He's been sleeping all day so he can run marathons during the night." Blake chuckles and rises to help set the table and carry food over. This hasn't affected his appetite tonight. In fact, he's in the cookie tins while I'm doing the dishes.

He remarks, "These are really good." enjoying another large orange chocolate chipper. He loves my white colored chocolate chip cookies. I use cream cheese instead of brown sugar and grated orange rinds in the mix. It gives them a faintly orange taste. He's now got two more and struggling to get the lid back on the tin. Taking pity on the little boy look, I help. Wednesday morning, Blake is quiet and withdrawn. I know why and just give him plenty of space and keep silent.

At the breakfast table, he remarks somewhat casually, "I may have to go back to work." I raise my eyebrows and slowly shake my head.

I tell him, "No. Please don't go there. I have plenty of money and it would destroy me to lose you. Take my money, please." I'm pleading and tears run down my face. He slowly reaches over and wipes the tears away.

He says, "Not to worry. I have several large checks coming this week and plenty of reserve cash in Switzerland. But I do appreciate the offer. I'm sorry for causing the tears. You have such a golden heart and mine is so hard." He rises to kiss me before joining a waiting Christian. I pinch his butt before he walks away. I've half a mind to hide the mail until Monday but I remember he gets it from the post office box in Dallas by Courier. I have plenty of things to keep me busy.

I missed my last two ultrasounds so my doctor is not happy. I forgot to mark the calendar so then I also blew the rescheduled one. I got a stern phone lecture. Blake got a call from her about Monday's appointment. After which I got another long talking to and very stiff lecture.

Juanita is making their dinner here with me today. Mac and Christian both bragged about my stuffing and fancy breads. Juanita teases me about copying my dinner. Once the breads are mixed and in the oven, she and I work on chopping and assembling the stuffing. I won't put it into the bird until early tomorrow, but it's hard to climb out of bed because of the child. Therefore, I'm doing as much ahead of time as I can.

Mac returns about noon and flops down at the table. Juanita says, "Wash." He immediately sighs and then rises. Blake is now tight lipped and anxious to hear about the love birds return.

Mac seats himself again. Blake says, "So?" as Mac begins filling his plate. Mac shrugs and continues dipping things onto his plate as he speaks. "Well, like you said. He wanted to stop for supplies. Then he hadn't any money to pay so I signed your tab." Blake nods as Mac glances towards him for his approval.

Mac hesitantly says, "She's about five months pregnant—I think. I'm pretty good at spotting a baby as Miss Katherine will tell you." Mac grins and winks at me before beginning to eat.

Before he resumes eating Blake calmly states, "Well, I guess he's one proud old rooster then." The meal is fairly quiet and the serving dishes are soon empty. Juanita and I are left to clean up and even we're lost in our own thoughts. Blake wanted lasagna for dinner, which is easy enough to prepare. Christian invites himself after he hears Blake's request. Juanita watches and takes notes as I prepare the five-cheese mixture. We carefully layer and then she puts the four deep, square pans into the two ovens. I really love having a regular oven and the smaller chest high convection one.

Juanita prepares a large tossed salad while I make my biscuit dough. We have the dining room table set because Devin and Father are joining us. We're to come to Devin's about five tomorrow for a light dinner. We're all settled at the table. Father is offering grace and the front bell rings. Blake quickly rises closely followed by Christian. Juanita slowly shakes her head.

His voice is phony sounding when Blake says, "No. Come in. We're just setting down to supper. Have you eaten?" He's attempting to be cheerful.

Frank rushes into the room saying, "Katie girl, whatever you've made certainly smells delicious." He stops and gasps when he gets close enough to see my condition. "Well, congratulations boy! Like father, like son!" He pats my belly and looks across the table at Father. Father nods and smiles.

Frank says, "Dillon. You're looking good." Christian has retaken his seat after fetching an additional chair. Mac beat a hasty retreat to the kitchen to eat. There's another full pan cooling on the counter, he won't starve. Blake returns with two additional place settings.

After seating Terry, Frank sits in a chair near father saying, "Well, Dillon, old man, looks like we're going to be grand daddy's. Pretty soon, I'd guess or is Katie girl carrying twins?" She definitely looks pregnant. She has several dark pregnancy spots on her face.

Sitting beside me Blake says, "So far we've only seen one child." Devin resumes his seat once Terry is settled. To say the meal is tense would be an under statement. Terry had a little salad and asked for soda crackers. Juanita is intently studying both new arrivals. Once the food is gone, everyone retires to the living room. Frank is chatting with Father. Devin and Blake help empty the table.

Christian kisses Juanita and says, "We got work to do. Come on, woman. Let's go home. Miss Katie has plenty of help." I nod and Blake points at the door. Once the kitchen work is completed, we have no choice but to rejoin our guests. Terry asks when I'm due. I tell her about two weeks. Blake asks her where Heather is.

Terry calmly states, "We don't know. She joined us in Italy but didn't want to see Holland, so we left her." At Blake's sharp in drawn breath, Frank simply shrugs and looks away. I'm rather shocked. Even at 18, she's a bit young to abandon in a foreign country. Father is strangely quiet. I'm never sure how much he actually understands. Devin finally suggests they head home. Frank and Terry leave with them. Blake is silent for a while and then he suggests we go to bed.

Tugging me from the sofa he says, "We have an early full day tomorrow."

The next morning I get a helping hand from the bed and a nice back wash. I also have plenty of help stuffing the 3 birds. I'm making 2 birds for the hands. Buster, our new cook from the bunkhouse arrives for the bird that will go into their oven. I'll do their second bird in my smaller oven. Blake heads out to get the a.m. chores done. I have plenty to keep me busy. Father calls to wish me a Happy Thanksgiving and inquire about the child. Sometimes he just calls to chat.

Frank calls. Terry is too ill to cook. Can they join us? I hesitate and then say yes. After all, he's still Blake's dad. I tell Blake when he comes in for breakfast.

He smiles and says, "Don't look so worried. I still love him. It's just that some days I'd like to take him out back the wood pile—you know?" I smile. Blake goes to call Frank and officially invite him up after he's consumed his breakfast.

Bending to look into the oven he says, "Bird smells good already." I grab his butt. He pivots and says, "I just flashed back to dad's kitchen and my first view of your tight little end." He pulls me into his arms for a couple nice kisses and hugs.

He glances downward and remarks, "Your belly is lower." He's right.

I tell him, "I think the baby has turned and is almost in the birth canal. I felt the shift in the shower this morning." He's running his hands on the baby and softly smiling.

He says, "Soon, little guy. You'll be enjoying mommy's cooking first hand." Blake sets the table while I rest a little. My back has been having painful spasms off and on. I'm worried I might go early and ruin our holiday. The ringing doorbell signals Frank's arrival. Blake gets the door. I'm cutting and fixing a snack tray for the TV room.

Frank says, "Katie girl. It's just me. Terry is feeling really poorly and she begs your forgiveness. I'll eat enough for two." I get a crushing hug and quick kiss. Frank begins stealing goodies off the tray. Blake takes him and the tray to the TV room. I'm pretty tired by the time everything is ready to go onto the table. It's just the three of us and it seems strange at the large dining room table. Blake offers grace and we begin passing. I don't have any appetite. It doesn't take Blake long to notice something's not right.

Leaning towards me and taking my hand he says, "Katie, you're not eating. Your face is tense looking. Are you having contractions?" I shrug.

I tell him, "I'm having back spasms and this food is nauseating to me. I don't know. Maybe I'm just over tired." Blake stares intently into my face.

He asks, "Should I call the doctor?" I shake my head.

I tell him, "Don't ruin her holiday. I'm sure I'll recognize a contraction when I have one."

Frank smiles and says, "If memory serves me correct, you'll definitely know. Karen was in agony with every birth." He falls silent and looks very saddened by the memory.

I say, "Guys, eat. I put a lot of work into this meal. Don't let my tiredness spoil your appetites." I don't think Blake's really listening.

He takes my pulse and says. "It's a little rapid. Maybe you better lay down for awhile." He stands and gently tugs me from the table. Frank smiles and helps himself to more sweet potatoes. Since there's no Terry to frown, he's enjoying himself.

In the bedroom, when I first lay down, I do feel tired. Blake sits beside me. I point at the door saying, "Go have dinner with your father. I'll call if I need you." He frowns but rises and goes back to his father. After a while, I feel refreshed and then restless. I roll from the bed and rejoin the men at the table. I have a little appetite. Blake gets me a clean plate. Both men watch as I eat a small portion of everything. Blake and Frank clear the table and do the dishes. I discover a clean kitchen when I wander out from the TV room. Both men escort me back to the TV room. Frank leaves at 5 with a plate for Terry and plenty of containers of leftovers for him to enjoy.

Blake calls Devin and tells him the baby has dropped and we won't be joining them this evening. At 6, Father and Devin show up at the front door with goodies for us. Cook sent them over. Father is very concerned about me.

Father says, "Katie you look very tired. Devin says that the baby has dropped. Are you having any back spasms?" I raise my eyebrows and nod.

He continues, "Your mother used to have back labor instead of regular frontal contractions." while Devin gets him settled into the one recliner. Blake has a nice fire going. We sit watching the flames while snacking on Cooks goodies. Father insists they leave after only two hours. He tells Blake to get me comfortably settled into bed. I get a hug from both and Blake walks them to the door. Once the house is secure, Blake gives me a nice back and leg massage. I drift to sleep, secure in Blake's arms.

I'm dreaming that it's raining. I'm very wet and cold. I can't get my breath because I'm running from someone who's shooting. I feel the bullets rip across my abdomen and wake up screaming into Blake's concerned face.

He says, "Katie girl, wake up! You're having a bad dream. I think your water just broke." He continues softly crooning until I get my breathing under control and another contraction hits. He's right—the bed is a sodden mess. I hear the sirens coming up the drive as Blake struggles into dry jeans and a tee shirt. He opens the front door and brings the EMT's back to the bedroom. Once he's gotten me into a clean dry nightgown, I'm put onto the gurney. My doctor wants me at the nearby clinic for the birth due to my miscarriage. Blake must have called the minute my water broke.

The ride to the clinic is short and pain filled. Now that my contractions have started, I'm in total agony. Every ounce of my pain and agony are mirrored in Blake's face. I try and keep silent, but the pains are sharp and intense and long. At the clinic, Dr. Whetzel is waiting. Her assistants have me on the birth table in record time. A technician assists in hooking up the monitors and a nurse is bustling around. Blake is standing beside me holding onto my hand for dear life.

Dr. Whetzel checks and smiles saying, "Well, I see the crown. Greg, check that monitor I'm getting an echo on the fetal heartbeat." Greg must be the technician. He immediately begins checking the leads and monitor and turns to her to shrug.

The tech tells her, "It's not an echo. I'm putting on a second lead, here. There are two distinct heartbeats. I think we got a multiple here." Dr. Whetzel is bustling around between my legs.

She says, "Well, I got no indication of a second fetus. Of course, Mrs. Dailey did neglect to show for her last two ultrasounds. The other child must be smaller and hopefully not joined to the larger child." Blake goes pale. I'm getting a nice shot of something. I start to push at Dr. Whetzel's prompting. With a little effort, Blake's son makes his screaming entrance into the world. The second child needs a little repositioning before I'm allowed to push again. Blake watches in awe as the second child comes into Dr. Whetzel's competent hands.

She says, "Well, Miss Dailey, you look perfect. You have a daughter also Katherine. Greg, get this to the lab. I want to watch her closely for hemorrhaging around the weak spot from the miscarriage."

The nurse brings a diapered and bathed little guy over to my chest. Blake reaches out and tenderly touches him.

He asks, "Katie girl, can we call him Kyle?" I look up into his face. How can I refuse this man anything?

I tell him, "Kyle is a fine name. Do you think your father will be upset?" Blake shrugs.

He says, "He's my son. I think he'll carry Kyle's name on broad shoulders. How about Kyle Dillon Dailey?" I shake my head.

I say, "No. That's not fair to Frank. Let's give him a fresh middle name." At my suggestion, Blake thinks a minute. "How about Kyle Morgan Dailey." I smile. I see he's bound and determined to bring my family name into this.

I say, "OK. Now, what about our daughter?" We never even discussed girl's names. Blake's startled and he quickly looks over to where the nurse is weighing a quiet little girl.

He says, "Man, I'm drawing a blank. Let's talk about this after you're settled in your room. OK?" I nod. Kyle is moving around and making suckling noises. Dr. Whetzel chuckles as she stitches. They bring over Girl Dailey. She just sighs and lays against me.

Blake asks Dr. Whetzel, "She's so inactive. Is she OK?"

She lifts her to check her out and says, "Her pulse is good, color is good and her eyes appear fine. I think she's just tired from the birthing process. She had to wait her turn." Blake suddenly laughs and turns to me.

He says, "Hey, what a nice birthday present mother." I widen my eyes as I realize today is Blake's birthday.

I softly tell him, "Well, we won't forget this day each year."

I'm settled in my room. Kyle is returned and wants to nurse. Blake and I discuss girl's names while Blake rocks his daughter. Finally after much discussion, Blake suggests we combine our grandmother's names of Elizabeth and Anne.

Blake says, "We can call her Beth Anne for short." I smile and nod.

I tell her, "Hello, Elizabeth Anne Dailey. You're grandfathers are both going to fight over spoiling you." Blake takes a few minutes to call his father now that it's after 6 a.m. I hear Blake tell his father about the twins and ask him not to come in until after noon. All parties involved are rather tired. He explains.

Blake calls Devin to tell Father the good news. He suddenly jerks from the chair and strides into the hall. I feel terror and coldness in my heart. When Blake returns several minutes later, he's pale. Before he speaks I say, "It's Father—isn't it?" He nods and sits on the bed to pull me into his arms.

Blake says, "He died in his sleep. Devin discovered him at 5 when he went in to get him up. We will definitely remember this night for a long time." When I start weeping, both babies begin crying. Before long, Blake has me and both babies in his arms. A nurse comes in but Blake waves her out.

CHAPTER NINE

LIFE WITHOUT FATHER

Once I've calmed a little, I nurse a hungry Kyle while Blake rocks an upset Beth Anne. Dr. Whetzel comes in to check on me. The nurse probably reported the crying.

She asks, "Is there a problem?" after coming to stand next to the bed between the two babies.

Blake looks up and says, "Her Father died last night probably close to the time his grandchildren were being born." Dr. Whetzel turns and takes my hand.

She says, "I'm sorry to hear that Katherine. I knew, of course, that your father was ill. Dr. Black is a college of mine and had often discussed his puzzlement over your Father's condition with several neurologists. This will be a hard time for you. If you need to talk to someone, I'll be glad to listen or refer you to a specialist. I'm sure your Father was anxiously awaiting the birth." She nods at Blake and leaves. She is visibly upset. I think her father passed away several years ago and that they had been close. While he rocks Beth Anne, Blake calls his father to tell him of Dillon's death. He speaks softly and smiles at his daughter sleeping in his arms. Devin appears in the doorway about 11 a.m. I'm nursing Beth Anne and Blake is rocking Kyle.

Devin says softly, "Little sis, I'm sorry this happened. I'm also proud of you for having twins. So, can I hold one?" I offer him Beth Anne.

Devin says, "Hello, this must be Elizabeth Anne. What soft curls you have! I'm your Uncle Devin. I'm under your spell already. I called Dustin and left a message. I called Doran. He and Rachel are chartering a flight down. The funeral will probably be Tuesday. I asked the funeral director to hold it up so you'll be able to attend. Is that all right?" He turns to ask Blake.

"Yes. She'll probably go home Sunday. Is there anything I can do?" Blake asks as they swap babies.

Devin shakes his head saying, "No. We made the arrangements when Father changed his will. Doran says he'll do the estate if you're too busy with the new arrivals." Blake chuckles and suddenly quickly lifts his daughter.

He exclaims, "Hey, you're not supposed to wet that much!" standing to reveal a large wet spot on his jeans. I have to laugh; it looks like he wet his pants. Devin laughs because he could have been the recipient of that wet spot.

Smiling, he brags, "Hey, I've got good timing for an uncle.".

I tell him, "Give it time. You have a 50/50 chance of one of them getting you one way or the other." Blake is changing his daughter and turns to reply to Devin's last statement.

Blake says, "I can handle the estate in a couple of weeks. There's no hurry. Dustin went through most of the assets. The new will only covers the remaining insurance money which is to be split three ways after the funeral expenses are taken care of. It will probably boil down to about 5 million each. With Katie's approval ours will become college funds for his grandchildren." I look up and can't stop the tears from flowing down my face. Blake returns Beth Anne to her crib and comes to take me into his arms.

Between sniffles, I softly tell him, "I'm sorry. It's my hormones, I guess. I'm rather weepy today."

Devin says, "You're allowed little sis. Trust me, you're definitely allowed." Then he turns away, still holding Kyle. His voice sounds a little shaky. Frank picks that moment to arrive. He stops in front of Devin and looks down before softly speaking.

He says, "So, this is my little grandson. Blake—thank you for naming him Kyle. Can I hold him?" Devin nods and hands Kyle to his grandfather.

Frank remarks, "He's a little thing. As big as Katie was, I thought she'd deliver a football player. However," He pauses as he gazes down at a sleeping Beth Anne in her crib. "It appears she has delivered two precious babies to pamper and spoil. Grandpa is going to have a tough time deciding which to hold." Blake gets him settled in the chair and hands him Beth Anne. Frank sits silently with both children in his arms and smiles while looking from one to the other.

He looks up and says, "Katie girl, you and Blake have done me proud. Yes sir. Blake, I do appreciate all you've done the past few years. Especially, over this past year while I've been behaving like an old fool. Terry went through my mail while I was at your place yesterday. When she realized the ranch and my money were all gone, she packed up and left. I found out this morning when I called her doctor that she wasn't pregnant just getting fat. What a fool I've been! Son, I'm sorry to have to tell you this, but I've lost the ranch. The bank owns it, lock, stock and barrel." Frank falls silent and sits starring at his grandchildren.

Blake says, "Dad, I own the ranch. I bought the loans from the bank. You can live there as long as you're alive. Katie and I will make sure that you never want for anything. However, do me one small favor?" Blake pulls up a chair near his father and takes a fussing Beth Anne.

"Anything, son, anything." Frank chokes out.

Blake quietly says, "Next time you need sexual relief, let me take you to town and buy you a one night woman. Christian and I know of a couple of places that will give you good, clean relief—anyway you want it." Frank chuckles at Blake's straight forward and somewhat light hearted tone. I think this is the beginning of a new relationship between father and son—a more equal friendship based relationship. The men talk about Dillon and the funeral. I nurse a fussy Kyle and get a little nap in spite of their low murmuring in the background. I don't know when Devin left.

Christian, Juanita and Mac arrive to visit shortly after the dinner trays have been removed. They each have a gift and a kiss for me. Blake helps his twins open their gifts. Juanita takes Beth Anne and I'm surprised when Christian immediately picks up Kyle.

He softly says, "You're certainly a cute little dude." I watch Kyle smile a little at the sound of his voice. Eventually both babies have been held by everyone and come to mom for their supper. I'm surprised when Mac doesn't leave the room or appear the least bit embarrassed as I nurse.

He smiles at me and says, "I'd like to get married and have my wife nurse our children."

Juanita has a startled and slightly surprised expression on her face before Christian taps her nose and grins. Each gift contains a little outfit for each baby. My boxes contain lovely maternity nursing nightgowns. Mac's is a box of my favorite milk chocolate caramels. I open and begin enjoying them immediately. I have help—there are others who would like to keep me from putting on too much weight. Like, I'm not going to need extra energy to keep up with these two. Juanita shyly asks if she can come up and help with the babies.

I quickly say, "Please." Everyone laughs. I sleep very well after everyone has gone. I'm awakened by Blake when a little one needs nourishment. He chuckles.

He says, "I can't help with the feeding but I did handle the other end." planting a squirming Kyle at my breast. Kyle takes the nipple with a vengeance. He must have slept up an appetite. Beth Anne awakens shortly afterwards. Dad changes her before she comes to the breast. Kyle gets rocked gently by dad as Beth Anne calmly and slowly enjoys her nursing experience. There is a lot of Blake already in Beth Anne's movements and facial expressions. I wonder if either will have his gorgeous blue eyes.

We get several visitors over the next two days. Dr. Whetzel lets me go home on Sunday. All three of us are doing fine. As Blake is driving home I suddenly realize we only have one of each baby item.

I turn to him and he asks, "What? Obviously from the stricken look on your face, something just occurred to you." Then he turns his attention back to the highway.

I tell him, "We have twins." He raises his eyebrows and then quickly glances back at the road.

He calmly says, "I noticed that right off, dear." with a mischievous grin playing around his mouth.

I tell him, "We'll need additional everything."

He say, "All taken care of. Juanita and Christian have been very busy beavers. I think both babies should share a room for the next three or so months and then be separated. Don't you agree?" He turns skillfully into our driveway. Frank is standing at the split which runs over to his place. Blake stops long enough for grandpa to take a couple pictures. Then Frank climbs into his vehicle to follow us on back our driveway. Blake put in the connecting road about three weeks ago. It was annoying to drive out to the main road and then back Frank's driveway. Then we were making a rutted mess from cutting across this field. The gravel makes it much nicer. When we pull up out front for a minute I think Father is standing by the front door. When he steps from the shadows, I gasp because I realize that it's Doran. I remember that Father is dead.

Taking my hand Blake calmly says, "What's wrong? You do remember Doran was coming down for the funeral?"

I tell him, "Yes. But for a moment—he looked like Father standing there. Sort of super imposed over his features. I guess that it's post birth hallucinations or something." Then I fall silent and Blake kisses my hand.

He says, "Wishful thinking is more like it." Doran opens the door and reaches in to hug me.

He says, "Little sis, I'm sorry to come to visit under such depressing circumstances but thrilled at the opportunity to see my niece and nephew so soon after they've come into this world." Doran helps me out. Rachel is very happy to carry Beth Anne inside as Juanita grabs Kyle from his father's arms.

With a chuckle, she informs him, "I'm the nanny." There are plenty of things to carry inside and we don't lack for help.

I'm actually tired just from coming home. Kyle is very out of sorts and only wants Blake or I to hold him. Beth Anne is very laid back and basks in all the attention she is getting. Her Uncle Doran and Aunt Rachel are only too happy to take care of her every need—well, except one. Soon, Juanita is being physically dragged towards the front door by Christian.

He tells her, "We just live next door—not out of state. Let's go."

She looks at him and says, "OK, but I've just thought of something I want you to do." She gives me a wink and lets him tug her from the room.

She already made a casserole for dinner. For the rest of the day, I nurse and sleep. Blake does get me awake enough to eat.

I'm glad that the funeral is Tuesday. Monday I sleep and nurse and eat. At 6, we attend the viewing. Frank is over at our place for awhile in the afternoon to see his grandchildren. I vaguely remember getting a kiss on the cheek during one of my naps. I'm glad the viewing is at Devin's. It's pretty much a family affair. I wondered if Dustin would show up. Devin called and left a message with all the particulars. He did not get a return call or acknowledgment. We're there for two hours but it felt like two weeks. I keep crying and crying which gets the twins crying. Blake ends up comforting me while trying to bounce Kyle into some semblance of quiet. The result is Kyle vomits all over Blake and Devin's furniture. Cook just laughs as she helps with the cleanup. She promptly picks up Kyle who looked up and fell quiet.

The funeral service starts promptly at one and by three it is all over. Father's body is headed north for burial in the family plot next to mother. We sit around for awhile and sample all the dishes Cook made and several that some of the neighbors dropped off. Frank manages to divide himself between Beth Anne and Kyle. I don't think I saw him once that he didn't have one or the other in his arms. He even took them one at a time and standing next to the casket he talks with Father about his beautiful grandchildren. He assured Father that he would spoil them enough for both. I realized then that neither would have a grandmother and that both grandmothers would have adored them.

Back home, I take a long rest. Rachel and Doran are staying until Thursday. I have to smile because I think Juanita is glad they are leaving on Friday before the babies get too old. 'They grow up so fast.' She has told me several times. Once they have left, I have mixed emotions. Blake and I are sitting in the family room starring into the flames in the fireplace. Doran remarked several times about how beautiful our home is. Blake crosses his ankles and reaches over to take my hand in his.

He tells me, "Well, mother, it's quiet for the moment." I nod and smile. Both babies are sleeping in their nearby cradles. I'm sure Devin hardly has our brother and sister-in-law at the airport yet.

Squeezing my hand, Blake asks, "What are you thinking about so solemnly?"

I tell him, "About Doran's visit and Fathers death and the birth, I guess a lot of things. I haven't had much time for you lately." He chuckles at my soft words.

He says, "You have just given me two beautiful children. I'm sure there won't be any lack of baby-sitters available if we want time to ourselves once you've recovered from the birth. I was remembering your fall. In the delivery room, when the blood started flowing, I flashed back to that horrible day last year. Looking at my son crying in Dr. Whetzel's hands, well, I have had a lot of mixed emotions and thoughts. I was worried that you might hemorrhage during the birth." He falls quiet, resting chin on his chest. I squeeze his hand.

I tell him, "We Morgan's are tough." Then Kyle begins loudly sucking on his hand. That is his pre-meal action. Blake drops my hand to pick up his son.

With a quirky little smirk he says, "Well, mother, he's wet. Let me solve that problem and then you can solve the other." I'm soon solving the other problem with Blake leaning close and stroking his sons head as he nurses. Kyle makes little kneading motions with his hands as he suckles.

It's only two weeks to Christmas. This year the entire job falls on Blake. I'm busy with the twins in spite of Juanita and Christian practically living with us. Juanita mentions about pushing their wedding to March. Blake and I both sternly tell them no. Cook has already volunteered to fill in if necessary. She comes over and makes Sunday dinner and has Christmas dinner all planned. Buster, the bunkhouse cook has made his famous chili and stew several times. Juanita has learned to make my biscuits very well. Frank even came over Friday night with several large pizzas. Kyle seemed to really enjoy my milk the next day. Blake teased me that already pizza is his favorite flavor.

Christmas Day passes in a blur of activity. Of course, the twins are too young to appreciate more than the blinking lights. Kyle has already grown almost an inch longer than Beth Anne. Dr. Whetzel comes to the house to check them. Kyle weighs almost two full pounds more at birth. He has now pushed that to five pounds. Beth Anne is now two pounds heavier. Dr. Whetzel says she's a healthy baby. Both babies appear to have dad's blue eyes. Devin can't keep his hands off them on Christmas Day. He and Frank are holding one or the other until both babies are so cranky that Blake insists they leave them alone. Christian and Juanita leave two days after Christmas for Vegas and their wedding. This leaves more work for Blake on top of being kept extremely busy with ranch work. Mac appears at the house more often. I believe the homestead is quiet and lonely without his mother. Of course, Cook's good cooking may be the draw. In hardly any time at all, Christian and Juanita are back. While they are gone, Patches attaches himself to Mac and many times, he was stuck to Blake like glue.

Blake remarks one night, "He's a good dog." Patches is laying in the entry way. It's been too cold to make him wait outside. If he's wet or dirty, it's into the utility room. Usually, he's resting in the front foyer until Mac is ready to leave. From there he can see into the dining room, family room and living room without much effort. Blake got a nice rug for him. Someone is getting attached to the animal, I'm thinking.

Once the newly weds are back, Patches abandons his new friends for his old friends. Juanita is a glowing bride. Christian is quiet. He seems very relieved to see that everything is all right.

Blake tells him, "I told you to stay longer." but Christian shakes his head.

He quickly says, "We can go again. A month was long enough. She was talking about the twins and I could see she was worried about Miss Katherine." From the tone of his voice and facial expressions, I get the distinct impression that someone else was anxious to return.

Two days before Valentines Day, the phone rings. Juanita goes to get Blake immediately. I hate that. It raises the hair on the back of my neck and fills me with dread. Blake comes into the nursery where I'm changing a squirming Kyle.

He says, "That was Miss Heather. She's run out of money, been abandoned by her men friends and is sick. I'm sending Mac to England to bring her home. She's in a woman's hotel in London. Man, it ripped at my heart to hear her weeping. She called the house and asked for her mother. Frank said Terry was gone. I don't think he realized it was Heather. People have been calling there looking for Terry lately. He's thinking about changing his number." I'm getting my neck nuzzled and there are firm hands up under my top. Kyle grins and chortles at his father's face just over my shoulder. My eight weeks are up so I have a nice Valentine's Day planned for Blake. Suddenly I get a whiff of something which cannot possibly be coming from this sweet smiling baby now wearing a fresh diaper.

Blake exclaims with a frown on his face, "Oh, mother! Something stinks in here. I sincerely hope that it's just gas." Blake unclips the diaper and no—it is not gas and it's a runny mess. I sigh and wait for him to finish. He has been a little loose today. He's not running a temperature and I already called Dr. Whetzel. It takes Blake and I both to keep his feet out of the mess until I can get his bottom cleaned. He's grinning and thrilled at Blake being near him. He's definitely daddy's boy. Daddy removes his now clean and fresh smelling boy to the other room while mom eliminates the source of the odor. A quick check reveals Beth Anne is still sleeping. I'm not so sure that Kyle's belly isn't bothering him.

He's hungry and eagerly takes the nipple. He's not vomiting and his appetite is still good. We use bottled water. He goes to dad for some special water to prevent his getting dehydrated. He likes the water—hates the nipple on the bottle. Dad gets the usual frown and squirts a little into his mouth to get him going.

Blake croons, "It's a shame that mom doesn't have two different flavors. You should speak to God about that. God loves little children. Yes, He does. Kyle smiles and waves his fists.

Our preacher loves our twins. I missed a couple Sundays after the birth but caused quite a stir when we finally put in an appearance. I actually believe the sermon is shorter. Someone had a problem keeping his thoughts in order. Blake waits patiently while several neighbor women croon and fawn over the babies. Frank has even started attending with us 'to help with the babies' you understand. It's a very anxious three days until Mac returns from England with Heather. Blake wanted her taken to the homestead until she goes to the doctors. He doesn't want whatever sickness she contracted any where near the twins.

Mac comes over the following day and sits heavily at our table during lunch. Juanita is home taking care of a very sick Heather. Blake is very anxious to hear all about everything. He fills his plate and waits for Mac to get his portions on his plate and then purses his lips.

He softly asks, "Well?" Mac takes a big bite of his hoagie and then slowly chews.

Mac slowly says, "She's not contagious, although she did manage to catch something. It's something that she will pass in about four more months. She's pregnant. Imagine being that dumb. Man, her mom must have let her raise herself. She's now scared out of her wits. She has no idea who the father might be. She lived with a guy in Italy and then went to Belgium with a different guy and then over to Wales with a third man. I think they passed her around." Mac falls silent and eats for a few minutes.

He then looks up at Blake and says, "I'm marrying her. She's scared out of her wits and totally alone. I need a woman and want children. We talked a lot last night. She's agreeable." Mac continues eating. I sit in shock as my husbands eyebrows almost disappear into his hair.

Blake exclaims, "Are you out of your mind, boy?" Mac shakes his head and keeps eating.

He pauses long enough to tell us, "No. She's lost and alone. I've had strong feelings for her since way back when we were making love. I don't think I ever got over them. I'm willing to over look her past as long as she don't sleep around after we're married. I think she needs a stable life. I'll try and be a good husband and mom says she'll help her learn to be a good wife." Mac has finished his food and now waits for Blake's approval. Blake reaches across the table and takes his hand.

He solemnly says, "I'm glad Katie spoke for your life. You're a good man. I just hope that Heather grows into a good woman under your hands." Blake and Mac rise and leave me with a table of dirty dishes and fussy baby sounds from the sun room. Once the dishes are done and the babies are settled, I call Juanita.

She immediately says, "Hello. Katie I figure Mac laid his decisions on you and Blake?" I can almost picture her face.

I ask her, "Yes. How do you feel about all this?"

She chuckles saying, "Well, the poor girl really needs a mother. I intend to give her a guiding hand—against her backside—if necessary." Now it's my turn to laugh. I'll just bet she does.

Juanita says, "Well, looks like the preacher will be doing a marrying after the services on Sunday. Mac is getting the license tomorrow. Christian and he had a long talk. Secretly, my man is proud of my son. The spoiled little girl who went to Europe for a good time is no longer in evidence in the sick child that returned with Mac. She's lucky she didn't pick up a disease. The doctor ran all kinds of tests. We'll hear for sure on her blood work and stuff in two days." We chat about the babies. Juanita has to leave when Heather calls for her.

She says, "Probably vomiting again. The poor child has morning sickness all day long." I'm wondering about Frank when he finds out.

She must have lived under a lucky star. Heather's tests all come back good. She's just pregnant and severely under nourished. Sunday morning, we get to meet a very thin, very gaunt, very quiet Heather before the service begins. She's pale and almost lifeless. She has a death grip on Mac and jumps every time anyone talks to her. Frank plants his lips firmly together and remains silent. I'll bet Blake gets an earful later. She's wearing a cream colored suit which Juanita must have purchased. The jacket almost hides her condition.

After the services, she and Mac stand at the altar with Juanita and Christian. The service is brief and Christian pays the preacher. We all head to the homestead for a small reception. Frank declines with a slight head shake and heads for his home. I made Blake go into town and purchase several nice wedding gifts. Once we're at the homestead, Heather speaks with Blake softly and then comes over to say hello.

The first thing she says is, "I guess you don't think much of me." I shake my head.

I tell her, "I don't pass judgments on people. You make a good wife and life for Mac. He's a good man." She nods and smiles.

Looking down at her belly, she says, "He's the only guy who ever made love to me. The others, well, they, you know, just had me."

I tell her reassuringly, "Well, that's behind you. Now you have Mac and your baby to love and take care of." She looks up and smiles.

She says, "You're really a nice lady. You have two beautiful babies. I hope my baby isn't ugly." She sighs and drops into a nearby chair. I pat her shoulder.

I lightly tell her, "There aren't any ugly babies born in Texas." From my lips to God's ears . . . floats through my mind.

When the twins get fussy, we head for home. Once they're down for a nap, I pull Blake into our bedroom.

I huskily ask him, "Hey, lover man . . . feel like fooling around with this old mare?" I get a slow sexy smile as he sheds his jacket.

He says, "I thought you'd never ask. You know how we old stallions are . . . rough and ready." He grabs me teasingly and spins me around. We begin undressing and caressing each other. He's tender and I'm happy. After a while, Blake brings the twins over and we snuggle with them. Before long, Kyle wants his dinner. Beth Anne is content to stay on her fathers' chest and watch her brother nurse. I watch her pop a little thumb into her mouth and she closes her eyes.

Blake softly says, "I just love these two." It's written all over his face.

For the next two weeks, I've lost my helper. Juanita has her hands full with Heather. She keeps calling to check on me and then apologizing. I finally tell her that at three months, I'm feeling well enough to handle the two babies solo for most of the day. Besides, daddy seems to take long lunch hours and then come in early for dinner. He confides that Mac is doing more work. I believe someone gave Mac a raise in pay to help with his additional expenses. We have a medical plan which covers all our employees. I immediately added Heather to Mac's. I actually enjoy having the twins to myself. Kyle is the impatient one. Beth Anne is so good about letting me tend her squawky older brother.

Frank begins coming over in the afternoons. He must have met with Blake and talked out on the range somewhere. Blake simply states that Frank gave him a piece of his mind about Heather. He also said Frank's opinion is that Mac will be good for the girl. Frank likes to rock the twins and generally pretend that he's helping me. Actually, I enjoy the company. I get to hear quite a few tales about Blake as a child.

I especially like the one about when he was three and decided to pee in his dresser drawer instead of going out to the bathroom. It took Karen a while but she finally got it out of him that he was afraid of the long dark hall. She put a bucket in his room which he gladly emptied in the morning. I tease him about it and he chuckles as he remembers the red bucket. It was plastic and he was very careful not to spill a drop on his way to dump it.

It's not too hard to get Frank to stay for supper depending on what I'm making. He's still watching his weight. Since Dillon died, he's been extra careful. After all, he's the only grandpa these babies have left. He's been working with Blake and I think he's getting healthier and trimmer. Juanita has her hands full with Heather. I felt sorry for the girl. She must have suffered through every ailment you could have while being pregnant. Her ankles swell, she retains water and is constantly thirsty. By seven months, her back is bothering her. Her breasts are tender. She gets spots on her face which, totally freak her out. Mac has her in church every Sunday. She minds the heat fiercely. I can sympathize with her. Finally as she entered her ninth month, things leveled out but Mac told Blake she's extremely horny and all over him constantly. Blake laughs when he tells me and I chastise him. After all, a woman's hormones are nothing to make light of. Blake likes me to chastise him . . . it excites him. Heather goes a week past her due date. She's so anxious and terrified of the impending birth that she's driving Juanita crazy. Juanita says she feels really sorry because several times she caught Heather crying and wanting her mother.

Blake has a big Fourth of July picnic and barbecue. I'm surprised when Mac and Heather arrive. There are a lot of people there. Several of our neighbors are invited and Devin and Frank, of course. I thought for sure she'd have the baby during the festivities. Devin points out she's still carrying high. Blake says he thinks she'll go another week at least. He's right. July 11th, Heather finally goes into labor. By the third contraction she's ready to push. Juanita says she's hardly dilated. After 14 long hours of labor, Heather has severe hemorrhoids and a lovely baby daughter. They name her Emily Juanita MacKensie. Juanita is shocked but very pleased. Christian told Blake he thought Heather was bonding with Juanita.

A prouder papa I have not seen since November. Mac gives out cigars. I make Blake go outside with his. Of course, with the twins, I don't have to do more than point. He and Frank sit on my new porch swing and puff away. This is the first cigar Frank has had since before his stroke. Neither man finishes. I don't believe they enjoyed them as much as they thought they would. Frank even went into town on his own to get them a nice baby present. I know because he asked for suggestions. I was hoping that my birthday would slide past this year. Yeah, really.

Blake takes me out to dinner at a nearby rib place. When we return I know something's up, in spite of the lack of cars near the house. Sure enough, inside everyone yells SURPRISE! There are balloons and streamers, cake and ice cream and a pile of gifts. Doran and Rachel are even here. They stay for three days with us. Our first real guests in our newly finished guest room. Part of my present is the new addition of two more bedrooms. The center bedroom is going to be a playroom divided by the hall which leads to the two nice sized bedrooms which will share a full sized bathroom.

In August I have news for Blake. I'm pregnant again. I'm not sure what happened. We were taking precautions and somewhere along the line I miscounted or something. I'm not so sure it wasn't the Fourth of July party. Blake was extremely friendly after all his company left and the babies were asleep. He was very up and I got a full body treatment. I think he planted more than kisses on me. I immediately miss my period. When August rolls around and I miss another one, I got a little test. The stick turns blue and I leave it in the bathroom on the sink. Blake comes out with his face lathered and holding the stick.

He asks, "Is this one of those baby sticks?" I nod and continue making the bed.

He says, "It's blue. Is that good?" He's coming around the bed after me.

With a smile, I tell him, "That's very good, Mr. Stallion. You covered me nicely. I guess we may need a few more bedrooms at the rate we're going." I'm getting lathery kisses and since he's only wearing a towel from his shower, the stick seems to have excited him fiercely. I use the towel to wipe the soap from his face and he takes the opportunity to undress me.

He huskily says, "Well, I don't have to be careful now." Then he begins assuming his favorite position. I'm not about to complain. Breakfast is late and Blake gets a little behind in his chores today. The twins at nine months are getting to be quite a handful. Later today I'm wishing the stick had not turned blue but then I say a prayer so nothing bad will happen.

Heather is a good mother to her baby. Juanita says she truly loves Emily. She has heard Heather tell little Emily that she's never going to leave her alone and lost. Juanita says 'Honestly, the child says the darn-dest things.' I'll just bet that Juanita has a hard time not crying over those 'darn-dest' things. Mac told Blake that he can hardly wait to start working on his own child. Of course, most days it's hard to realize that Emily isn't Mac's child. He just loves her to pieces.

I visit Dr. Whetzel at the beginning of September. She confirms I'm going to have a baby about March. The twins have their first birthday right after Thanksgiving. This Christmas is more exciting but they end up cranky. My ultrasound in December reveals that Blake has again fathered twins. Dr. Whetzel thinks they are both boys this time. Blake rolls his eyes and apologizes. I know he doesn't mean it. He's very pleased and proves it when we arrive home. He's all over me like I'm sixteen and he's seventeen years old.

While trying to remove his busy hands, I tell him teasingly, "You are an octopus today."

He says, "Wrong animal." Juanita and Christian have the twins until we call for them. It's rather late and Juanita wants to know if anything went wrong when we arrive.

Blake proudly boasts, "No. We're having twins again." Christian rolls his eyes but grins while he shakes Blake's hand. Frank is shocked, pleased and almost beside himself when he hears the news.

Heather teasingly says, "Better you than me."

Mac tells her, "That can be arranged." I like their light bantering.

Heather and Mac go up to the cabin in Utah for a delayed honeymoon in February over Valentine's Day. Christian and Juanita keep Emily. I'm not surprised when Heather discovers she is pregnant several weeks after they return. Mac is definitely good for her and good to her. He is so in love with her. It brings a smile to my face to watch the two of them together. Juanita is thrilled that she's going to be a grandmother again.

On March 3rd, I was supposed to see Dr. Whetzel anyway. My water breaks in her waiting room. Four hours later, our second set of twins slide into the world, one right after the other. She was right. Two more beautiful boys I have never seen. Kyle and Beth Anne both have their father's beautiful blue eyes. Beth Anne resembles Karen more as she gets older. Kyle is definitely a Blackwood. I have pictures of my brothers as children and his face fits the mold.

Eric Blake Dailey is first and as we soon discover, he's the more impatient of the two. Jeffrey Franklin Dailey is larger but like his sister, a quieter baby. Dr. Whetzel suggests that we take a two year breather before I stop my birth control. I tell her Blake's the one with no control. He's holding Eric and he could care less what I'm saying. He's gazing down into his son's screaming face and smiling. Before long, Eric can come to nurse and Blake has Jeffrey.

Blake tells me, "This boy is solid. I think he has a lot of his grandpa Frank in him." I nod. From the looks of Jeffrey's face, I'd say Frank's genes definitely came through in his newest grandson. We're soon settled in our room and being visited by the older siblings, Grandpa and Uncle Devin. Frank has learned that he can usually use an uncle around when he has the twins to handle. Devin is only too glad to help.

* FIVE YEARS LATER *

I didn't think I would survive the terrible twos with two sets of twins. However, I managed. Blake is a good husband and father. At six, Beth Anne and Kyle are riding like pro's on their ponies. They love school. At almost four, Eric and Jeffrey never cease to try everyone's patience. Grandpa Frank loves them all to pieces. Its summer and I'm sitting on the swing nursing our daughter, Marisa Karen Dailey. She's almost a month old today. She's had a tough life already. She was premature and has fought for her life everyday. Blake and I prayed long and hard. She's finally strong enough to come home to stay. She is the only one with my dark brown eyes and red hair. Her father loves her completely already. He calls her Baby girl and she loves it. Blake swears she is a miniature me. Dr. Whetzel has said she will be our last. I had a very rough time and bleed through most of the pregnancy. I was off the pill almost two years before I got pregnant. Blake agrees to my tubes being tied. He is terrified of loosing me. Actually, I believe five children are plenty to love. I often think of Father and all the things I went through before the happy times started. Frank often reminisces about Karen, Kyle and my fall. He even remarks once about how old the baby would have been. I think that wound runs very deep, indeed. Heather and Mac have two sons. The oldest is Christopher Scott. He gives his Grandfather Christian a run for his money every day. The younger is named for Scott's father, William Blake MacKensie. Blake is surprised and very pleased. Frank has sort of adopted their three also. After all, playing Grandpa is his favorite past time.

Devin has been dating a girl from town for almost a year. I think it's getting pretty serious. Joy is a perky little blonde who has her own beauty shop in a nearby town. Devin went in one day because there were too many men already waiting at the barber shop. She cut his hair. He swears she did a Delilah on him. He got a good haircut and asked her for a Friday night date.

She says she washed his hair with a love potion. She asked me if I believed in love at first sight. I told her I fell hard for Blake at 14 years of age.

Blake and I are surprised when Frank invites Christian and Juanita to move to the cottage so they can get a break from the children. The old homestead is definitely full even since they moved out. Frank told us he heard from Terry. She called asking if he knew where Heather was. Frank said he told her to 'go to hell'. No way did he want her coming back and ruining Heathers life. Blake smiles softly and shakes his head. I wonder if Terry misses her daughter.

As I sit and gently swing my little girl, I can't imagine turning my back on any of my children. I wrap the blanket around her and she sighs in my arms. I watch her daddy ride up, dismount and swiftly come up to sit beside me and gently take his daughter.

He croons, "Hi, Baby girl. Is my Katie girl taking good care of you?" She smiles and briefly opens her eyes to try and focus on her daddy. Devin has the other four today. Joy is visiting and they're having a picnic. Joy • has been cutting the boys hair and teasing Beth Anne about removing her curls. Like her father would ever allow one curl to be removed from her pretty blonde head. Blake says having our children around for the day will either make them want to get married or run from each other. I know that depends on how the children act. Some days they are good—some days they are holy terrors. Blake pulls me against him and kisses my hair.

Between soft kisses Blake asks, "Are you happy, Katie girl?" I reach up to caress his face.

"When you're near, I'm always happy. Did you ever think your life would turn out this way?" I ask him.

He gazes out over the rolling green grass of our ranch and thinks a minute before answering. "No. All those years ago when I was teasing you until you lost your temper, I never pictured you beside me for eternity. When I came back and saw your cute tight butt sticking out of my father's oven, I wanted you. When I discovered you loved me, I was afraid of losing you. Some days, I still don't think I deserve all this happiness." He falls silent. I find myself remembering the young boy who captured my heart all those summers ago.

"No, you're wrong. It was just a matter of time. A long time ago, I put a contract on your heart. You're mine, Tigerman. Shot through the heart with cupid's arrow." I say as he smiles and turns slowly to gaze at me.

When he softly says, "And a better hit—I've never taken." I totally agree.

THE END